From the Hollow of a Sling

Between the Wars with Karl Popper & Gershom Scholem

Paul Simei-Barton

Cinnamon Press
:: small miracles from distinctive voices ::

Published by Leaf by Leaf
an imprint of Cinnamon Press,
Lytchett House, 13 Freeland Park, Wareham Road, Poole, Dorset, BH16 6FA
www.cinnamonpress.com

Print Edition ISBN 978-1-78864-870-7
British Library Cataloguing in Publication Data. A CIP record for this book can be obtained from the British Library.

In the EU, we are fully compliant with GPSR (General Product Safety Regulation). Our EU GPSR Authorised Representative, via Inpress Books, is LOGOS EUROPE, 9 rue Nicolas Poussin, 17000, LA ROCHELLE, France E-mail: Contact@logoseurope.eu

Designed and typeset in Adobe Caslon Pro by Cinnamon Press.
Cover Design by Adam Craig.
Cover elements: Dancers — suteishi/iStockPhoto; Eye — Ralf Geithe/iStockPhoto; Hebrew text — architectphd/iStockPhoto; Equations — andresr/iStockPhoto.
Cinnamon Press is represented by Inpress.

Paul Simei-Barton lives and works in Aotearoa New Zealand. His maternal grandmother Bida was born and raised in the pioneering Jewish settlement of Zichron Yaakov. With his partner Justine he founded Tala Pasifika Productions, a community based theatre company which produced several of his stage plays, short film scripts and TV drama. For 14 years he was theatre reviewer for the *NZ Herald.*

But the lives of your enemies

He will sling out as from the hollow of a sling.

1 Samuel 25:29

From the Hollow of a Sling

1

Picking the first of her runner beans Josephine spots clusters of wispy young pods emerging through layers of foliage, heartened to see the jerry-built trellis, for which she endured much teasing, proved sturdy enough to withstand the north-easterlies. In the kitchen her mood sours as the strings won't pull away cleanly and she must run a knife down the sides of each pod. Footsteps in the hallway and the thud of shoes landing heavily on the bedroom floor announce Karl's arrival. He shuffles into the living room, pouncing on the airmail edition of the *Times* as if it were an elixir. His voice flits through the crackling pages. 'Ivan has invited us to a picnic—he's looking to smooth things over; we had a disagreement.'

Josephine remains silent, eyes fixed on the attractive purple of the beans peeking through the sliced sides of their crisp green pods.

'I suggested we take on a tutor to free time for research and he took it the wrong way, said I was out of line, not following procedure.'

'Was it a suggestion or a demand?'

'Wouldn't have made a difference, he said if I don't like it I can lump it.'

Her capacity for sympathy exhausted by a recurring litany of complaints, Josephine responds bluntly. 'We've put up with worse.'

'I know, mustn't grumble, but there's a principle at stake—he needs to understand research must be properly funded, it's the whole purpose of having a university.'

'Did he say if we should bring anything on Sunday?'

'Your field glasses, apparently Nancy has developed a passion for bird-watching and he thinks you might have inspired it.'

'For the picnic.'

'I suppose some baking would be in order.'

With a smouldering memory of the 'too rich for my taste' judgement pronounced on the *sachertorte* she brought to a faculty high-tea, Josephine scours women's magazines for recipes, secure in the sensible choice of apple turnovers, until the moment she folds a tea-towel over the glazed pastries and realises the sprinkling of sesame seeds was a mistake. It will be seen as pretentious, an affectation marking her out as the kind of person who has no place among practical folk who don't make a fuss and don't mind mucking in.

Amused to think a sprinkling of sesame seeds could cause offence, Karl makes light of her apprehension. 'It will do you good to get out of the house.'

She bristles, exasperated by his failure to understand how New Zealanders see him, how they despise his air of intellectual superiority and are incensed by the way he insinuates everyone would be better off if they simply acknowledged the unassailable logic of his assertions.

On Sunday morning the toot of the Sutherland's horn throws Josephine into a whirl, anxiously checking her basket while Karl waves from the front step and strides up the driveway giving his best impression of bonhomie. Nancy vacates the front seat, greeting them warmly as she rearranges rugs and cushions to make room for herself and Josephine in the back.

'Gorgeous weather,' she remarks.

'Indeed, so kind of you to invite us.'

With one hand on the wheel, elbow resting on the open window, Ivan asks about news from Europe, listening sympathetically as Karl mentions the Sudetenland and holds forth on the abysmal failure to appreciate the gravity of the situation.

Nancy rolls down her window and catches Josephine's eye, a wry smile suggesting she has no interest in the men's talk. 'I can't wait to see the godwits, they arrived a few weeks ago but everyone has been so busy. I think they come from up your way don't they?'

'We see them occasionally in the summer months, though I think their breeding grounds are further north.'

Stealing a glance at Ivan's handsome profile as he eases into the sharp turns of the Port Hills, Josephine guesses Nancy is at least ten years younger than her husband. She worries Ivan's Essex Super Six with its spacious interior and smooth suspension, will arouse Karl's long held resentment over the discrepancy in their salaries. With Nancy chatting amiably about the godwits and their remarkable annual journey from one end of the earth to the other, Josephine is pricked by an awareness of her dour appearance, certain the invitation could only have come out of a sense of duty.

On reaching their destination Ivan drives off the metal road, parking in the shade of a solitary macrocarpa, gnarled and slanted by coastal winds. Taking in the sparse windswept vegetation Josephine appreciates the benefits of living in an uncrowded country; a few miles from the township, expansive marshland opens to a broad estuary, the ocean horizon in the distance, serene beneath clear blue sky. A profusion of seabirds occupy the shallow waters and Nancy quickly finds a spot to spread the picnic rugs before leading Josephine to a sandbank beyond which she spies the swirl and flutter of godwits feeding. Finding a hollow in the tawny sand, they train binoculars on the grazing birds, knee-deep in sparkling water, diligently probing and pecking with spear like beaks. With a preference for solitary birds Josephine finds the incessant jostling of the flock disconcerting, the darting and alighting causing a mess of blurred shapes to flicker across her lenses. Fixing on a single bird, she methodically notes the distinguishing features and in a whisper reports her conclusions to Nancy. 'We have a different species in Austria, no white wedge on the tail feathers, just black tips and lighter on the rump.'

Nancy is impressed, though she cares little for taxonomy, content to marvel at the delicate interplay of grey, black and beige in the dappled plumage, humming with pleasure as her binoculars magnify an intricate zigzag glimpsed beneath the wing of a bird taking flight. A cry of pure delight breaks from her lips when an unseen signal prompts the entire flock to rise, answering an obscure injunction to seek a new location. The twittering mass of birds swirl above the water, silhouetted against the cool blue sky before settling near by. Remaining in their sandy hollow Nancy and Josephine turn their attention to the elegant oystercatchers sporadically stabbing the water and stretching their sleek wings, unperturbed by the abrupt departure of their more industrious neighbours. Paradise shelducks glide into the space vacated by the godwits and Nancy suggests it is time to eat.

At the picnic spot they see Ivan and Karl strolling across a drift of dry cockle shells, heads bent in conversation, turning occasionally to glance at the birdlife. Karl's attention drifts to the ocean where the horizon, sharply delineated against the fading blue, lays just beyond the breakers, confounding any sense of distance. In a half-hearted attempt to maintain the deference Josephine has recommended, he murmurs assent to Ivan's insipid account of the university's budgetary concerns.

Noticing Karl's gaze fixed on the horizon, Ivan remarks, 'If you sail due east you'd be halfway round the globe before you hit the tip of South America.'

Nancy playfully catches their attention with an imitation bird call summoning them to the picnic. She unveils a magnificent fish pie, made with blue-cod, freshly smoked in Ivan's backyard smokehouse. Josephine's anxiety about the sesame seeds proves unfounded and though her apple turnovers draw lavish praise she feels Nancy's jam tarts are superior, with the rich sharp flavour of Doris plums in a light pastry. Ivan uses driftwood to fire up his picnic-billy. The device captures Karl's attention and peering into the soot darkened funnel, he admires the ingenuity of the design which has tongues of flame licking a suspended metal flask containing the rapidly boiling water.

Sipping their tea, conversation flags and Ivan forgets his wife's ban on talking shop. 'One of my doctoral students, not a bad bloke, has developed an enthusiasm for Wittgenstein. I thought I might send him to you for a chat.'

'By all means, though I don't imagine it will do much good. Wittgenstein inspires, or I should say demands, discipleship. What you call enthusiasm is usually more like zealotry, utterly impervious to criticism.'

Josephine winces as Karl unconsciously adopts the puffed-up tone she had warned him is so obnoxious to New Zealanders. Observing Nancy tossing a pie crust to the hovering gulls she knows whatever he may say, he has already struck the wrong note. She tries to catch his eye but Karl fails to notice.

'It's the ambiguity that makes him attractive, everything is so vague and suggestive the enthusiasts can load onto him whatever takes their fancy. *Tractatus* is exactly the kind of book you'd expect to come out of a Viennese café.'

Though she has no wish to prolong the conversation Josephine cannot let this pass. 'He wrote it during the war, in the trenches.'

'So they say, but Wittgenstein is the kind of man who wouldn't notice the difference—lives entirely inside his own head.'

'I imagine anyone who'd been in the trenches would notice the difference.'

Fearing her intervention will provoke further pomposity, Josephine fixes her husband with a solemn gaze. In the ensuing pause a twinge of conscience arrests the impulse to strike back and for a moment Karl senses Josephine's frustration, her silently endured embarrassment at his hectoring need to win every argument. With Josephine sharpening her gaze, Nancy and Ivan exchange glances and the stiffness of Karl's jaw gives way to a shrug. A muffled groan indicates he will let the matter drop, though Josephine expects objections and refutations will be raised later. Having witnessed the unbridled ferocity Popper brings to academic disputes Nancy is astounded to see him capitulate so cheaply. She looks at

Josephine with new-found admiration, recognising she misread her shyness as subservience. Flashing a smile in Josephine's direction, she recalls how one of her uncles returned from the war so shaken by the experience he has never spoken a word about it.

Ivan sees Karl's uncharacteristic passivity as a gesture of goodwill, a sign he is not nursing a grievance. He promises to send his student to chat with him and adroitly changes the subject.

'Perhaps a walk, there's a very pleasant bay beyond the spit.'

Needing no persuasion Nancy gathers a basket and towels. 'We must, the tides nearly in, it'll be perfect for swimming.'

Fearing he will be unable to suppress the elaborate arguments already taking shape in his whirring mind, Karl feigns tiredness, pulling a book from his jacket pocket. 'You go ahead, I might have over-indulged in your splendid pie.'

'Come Josephine, and bring your glasses, it's not unknown to see penguins at the bay.'

Ivan and Nancy set off with Josephine dutifully following a few paces behind.

'Will you swim?' Nancy asks.

'I didn't bring a bathing suit, though I might get my feet wet, a little paddle.'

The Sutherlands wear togs beneath their clothing and on reaching the bay Nancy wraps her skirt and blouse in a towel, plunging into the sea unhesitatingly. She dives beneath the breakers, driving into the broad swell, her powerful breaststroke creating a V-shaped wake as she heads into open water. Ivan enters gingerly, turning his back against the splash of the waves and floating in the lolling water between the breakers. Compelled to make an effort, Josephine removes her shoes, lifting her skirt to allow the waves to wash over her ankles. She finds the sucking motion beneath her toes unpleasant and, feeling she has discharged her obligation, retreats to a sandbank. Perched on a clump of marram grass she surveys the sweep of the bay, children gleefully outrunning the incoming waves, a gaggle of black-backed gulls scavenging among fishermen casting across the mouth of the estuary, a sailboat tacking beyond the breakers. By training her glasses on a pair of terns flitting along the shoreline she gains relief from a rising unease.

With the terns reeling towards the distant horizon she is captivated by the sight of Nancy returning from her swim, carried in on a wave she glides ashore like a goddess, foam at her feet, a halo of droplets catching the sunlight. Jogging lightly over the wet sand she joins Ivan who pensively turns to the ocean as she shakes water from her hair and runs a towel over her sleek limbs. Josephine notices a slight rounding of the belly hinting at a nascent pregnancy.

At the picnic spot they find Karl asleep, prone on the rug where they left him, an open book on his chest rising and falling with his breath. Ivan nods empathetically as Josephine explains he hardly sleeps at night. Repose lends an air of tranquillity to Karl's boyish face, plump and benign like a cherub, with nothing to suggest the lurking belligerence ready to flare like a blowtorch. They leave him undisturbed as Nancy uncovers the remaining jam tarts. She removes the towel wrapped around her waist and pulls a skirt over her damp bathing togs. Sitting awkwardly at the edge of the rug Josephine gratefully accepts the ginger-beer Ivan pours her, morose, isolated, weighed down by an awareness she has nothing to offer her hosts. All she can do is receive their kindness, expressing gratitude in her stilted, clipped manner. With a furtive glance she sees Ivan and Nancy basking in the effortless contentment proscribed to her, their bodies touching, not in an overt way, but naturally, his arm resting on her shoulder, her body sloping towards his. Karl's snorting breath draws her gaze to his shoes protruding over the edge of the rug. She sees his predicament as even more pitiful than hers; while she can withdraw into the anonymity of her solitary domain, he is forever compelled to join the conversation, demanding to be heard, unable to rest until he is accepted, acknowledged, given the recognition he deserves.

For a moment she feels it's not too much to ask. In sleep he has the vulnerability of an infant, utterly dependent on his mother's vigilance, with no inkling of the enmity surrounding him, the shaking heads, rolling eyes, clicking tongues and amused grins as he leaves the room. A single thought occupies her mind, pushing aside all objections, cancelling the embarrassment at his over-bearing manner; what if he is right? What if the restless churning of his overactive mind has conjured something that matters. It happened at Vienna university when the luminaries who used to mock him and laugh behind his back had to acknowledge his triumph. What if he *did* have something important to say, something which might tilt the balance, or at least give pause, not a solution but an opening? Something others don't see, something the clamouring voices warning of the inevitable showdown have missed, something more than grim pronouncements about the absurdity of mechanised warfare and morbid injunctions to prepare for the worst.

2

'Dora, Dora!'

Jolted awake by the sound of his sister's name, Karl blinks in darkness, perplexed by the lingering image of sagging canvas snapping into a neat rectangle. Commotion draws him to the hallway and, squinting into electric light, he sees Dora with a serge cape draped over her nurse's uniform. Mother clutches her and with nothing to suggest she will let go, he hovers in his night-shirt, scrutinising the face pressed awkwardly over his mother's shoulder.

He sees no emotion, perhaps disorientation as Father clears his throat and the embrace loosens. Mother steers Dora to the kitchen and as they press cheeks Karl catches a sharp whiff of camphor oil. With Hanya joining them he attends to the stove, reeling with wild conjectures on what could have brought his sister home at this hour. She settles on a stool, eyes fixed on the bench-top, ignoring the expectant stares. Mother rests a hand on her shoulder, setting her at ease while Karl coaxes flame from the lumps of coal cooling in the grate.

Speaking softly, Dora's gaze drops to the floor avoiding the straining faces. 'We were cut off; we'd run out of chloroform and there was no lint for bandages. Everyone was heading north and they told us to join the column. The men on stretchers went into a cart and we followed with the walking-wounded. In the morning a lorry took us to Budapest. We had a few nights in the barracks, then they put us on a train… said we'd been redeployed.'

Though bursting with questions, Karl holds his tongue and Father breaks the silence.

'Have they given you leave?'

'I'm to report to the hospital at 7am.'

'You must try to sleep.' Mother springs to her feet and bundles Dora out of the kitchen.

Exchanging worried glances, Father and Hanya follow. Karl is left fiddling with the damper, infuriated that mother's intervention prevented him from learning anything about the retreat. Unable to still the turmoil in his head, he drags a stool to the stove knowing sleep will be impossible. He wonders if he'd have lent a shoulder to the amputees hobbling from the advance and his pounding thoughts keep returning to his plan to resist conscription, frustration deepening as he recognises his assiduously rehearsed arguments will sound like childish whining when set against Dora's ordeal.

Hanya rises promptly with her alarm clock ringing. She went straight back to bed after mother took Dora in hand, determined her sister's arrival would not interfere with her routine. In the lamplight she runs a finger over a callous forming at the tip of her toe and tightens a ribbon around her ankle. Steeling her body against the cold she finds a point of balance, using the door handle as a barre. The exercises warm her limbs and with a trickle of light seeping through curtains she leans into a stretch, scarcely noticing the burning at the back of her knees.

In the dining room Mother pulls out hidden reserves of cheese, pickle and sauerkraut, urging Dora to have a decent breakfast. Helping herself to the unexpected abundance Hanya wolfs down her food, relieved to see a hint of a smile softening her sister's expression.

'How is your ballet?' Dora asks.

'I've stopped taking classes.' She'd like to say more, but decides it's improper to be chatting about dancing after all her sister has endured.

Sliding a gherkin onto Dora's plate, Mother chirpily explains. 'There was no need to stop, Magda asked her to keep coming but Hanya said she wasn't going to accept charity, which is nonsense. Frau Magda knows she'll be paid as soon as things get better.'

Hardly touching her breakfast Dora nods in response to Karl's offer to walk with her to the hospital.

Matching his sister's brisk pace through streets grey with mist, Karl thirsts for information.

'It must have been terrible out there, the retreat… I can't imagine.'

'It wasn't so bad. When the lorry picked us up the roads were clogged; we just had to sit tight.'

'Have you heard anything about men refusing to follow orders? We never get decent news anymore, they cut everything out of the papers. All we get is rumours.'

Dora replies as if chatting about the weather. 'In July there was an outbreak of dysentery and the latrines filled up. There weren't enough able-bodied men to dig a new ditch, so we borrowed the men's boots and dug it ourselves.'

Unable to decide whether she is being deliberately evasive or just misconstrued his question, Karl swallows his frustration and they walk in silence to Mohrengasse where another nurse greets Dora. Watching them enter the hospital by a side-door on Schmelzgasse, he sees women and children loitering on the pavement outside the main entrance. A boy holds a tin cup for collecting coins.

Crossing the canal at Schwedenbrücke uneasiness grips him, though everything appears normal with shop girls hurrying to work and streetcars filled with civil servants. At the Gymnasium he passes the throng milling in the cloisters and finds Max already at his desk. Slipping into the seat next to him Karl can't wait to share the scraps he has gleaned from his sister. His friend remains absorbed by jottings in a notebook crammed with a spiralling mess of equations, but his ears prick when Karl claims there's been a rout on the Southern Front. They speak in hushed voices, keeping an eye on the door. Professor Lassman will not tolerate rumours and the boys are adept at avoiding trouble. An air of apprehension has seeped into the schoolroom. Each morning Professor Lassman sets a lengthy translation then sits at his desk reading and rereading the morning papers. The exercises, dutifully handed in at the pause, are never corrected and though there are ample opportunities for slacking, most work diligently, clinging to their routines.

Karl has formed a dubious friendship with a group of pan-German enthusiasts gravitating around Heinrich Kirch, who projects an aura of brooding intensity with his deep-set eyes and high sloping forehead. He earned acceptance into Heinrich's circle due to his ability to discuss Fichte and Lessing, both well represented in his father's library. With Professor Lassman leaving the class to their own devices, Heinrich ignores the set exercises, scribbling notes in the margins of a well-thumbed volume of Schiller. When the Professor leaves the room he strolls to the blackboard and in elegant cursive lettering writes:

Thus gleams upon our barren life the poet's living world of shadows.

The class eagerly anticipate how Lassman will deal with this literary rebellion but he returns to his desk without noticing the quotation. At the end of the day as the boys are dismissed he glances at Heinrich and says, 'Schiller—very good—and it's true, only the poets can save us now.'

The spectre of conscription haunts Karl's dreams and occupies every waking moment. He's learnt to function with his mind in a riot—bold resolutions dissolving into crippling despair. He doubts he possesses the courage to resist conscription and his body quakes in loathing at the prospect of risking his life for a thing so utterly devoid of purpose and meaning.

The predicament is incessantly picked over by his scout troupe on their Sunday afternoon excursions in the Vienna Woods. Karl and Max belong to the *Jung-Wandervogel*, which broke from the national scouting association after it adopted the Aryan clause. Their troupe leader Rudolph Frank carries smuggled copies of Lenin's pamphlets in his rucksack and as they hike the beech forest Karl throws himself into fiery disputes about whether violence is compatible with the spirit of socialism.

Max keeps his opinions and when pressed tells Karl, 'If it comes to conscription or imprisonment, the choice should be obvious.'

3

On Tuesday and Saturday afternoons Max comes to Karl's house to use the Bösendorfer, which Mother makes available to families who sold their pianos to pay for fuel. She often sits in on practice sessions, making sure students are given food, though lately it is little more than corn-meal bread with lard. Since Alban Berg accepted Max as a pupil Mother takes a particular interest in his playing. She was at the Musikverein when the orchestra was booed off stage performing Berg's *Altenberg Lieder* and wants to understand what the fuss is about. Perching on the edge of the sofa, eyes closed in concentration, she searches for a structure to hold the sporadic fragments of harmony. Hanya stands close to the piano to turn the manuscript pages, drinking in the strange music and gazing at Max's hands as they hover over keys during extended silences. Untroubled by the absence of a tonic triad she imagines breathing the air from another planet.

In the upstairs library Karl sits in on conversations with Uncle Walter. The men speak in low voices dissecting reports from clients, reading between the lines of municipal orders, always arriving at the same grim prognosis. At mealtime Mother does her best to maintain normalcy, serving meagre portions of mashed turnips on the china plates with pink rose wreaths, her cheerfulness dented by long hours queuing for flour.

'I heard the most ridiculous rumour at the bakery this afternoon, a woman claimed a horde of Italian prisoners broke out of the internment camp and were about to attack the city.'

Father responds sternly, 'Mischief-makers spreading the usual nonsense—the mayor's office has issued a denial.'

Although it is clear things are unravelling, Father is taken aback when an official statement appears in the *Wiener Zeitung*. Placing the newspaper on the breakfast table he assumes an authoritative tone that heightens foreboding. 'You won't be going to the gymnasium this morning, municipal services are closed until further notice and we are advised to stay indoors.'

Karl spends the morning in the library where an ever-changing parade of Father's associates arrive for coffee and loiter in the hope of gleaning intelligence. It is generally agreed Kaiser Karl has left the city and is likely holed at the Eckartsau shooting lodge, which gives easy access to the Hungarian and Czech borders. Whether this constitutes an abdication provokes heated exchanges and as the conversation swirls, Karl's attention is drawn to the window with a clear view down Jasomirgottstraße all the way to St. Stefan's. The Cathedral Square is crowded and below in the Bauernmarkt, a steady swelling of workers and demobbed soldiers head towards the Ring. They appear drawn by an unseen force and Karl feels impelled to join them.

Slipping unnoticed from the house he follows on the heels of workers, unperturbed by drizzle carried on a chill wind. Entering Schauflergasse a distant clamour of voices sparks anticipation and their pace quickens. At the corner of Löwelstraße Karl slows to a halt. The thoroughfare overflows with a multitude funnelling into the Volksgarten. Bodies press past him and he hears eddies of laughter mixed with snatches of song from trade-unionists marching beneath embroidered banners. Watching the crowd swarming into the park, he worries it will be impossible to get close to parliament and decides he'll have a better chance of hearing any speeches by doubling back to the Burgtheater. Zigzagging through the tail of a procession blocking the Ring he dashes through the Rathausplatz, hoping the narrow streets behind parliament will provide access to the forecourt. Others have had the same thought and on both sides of the building the streets are clogged with an impenetrable mass of bodies.

It occurs to him his cousin Joseph might be inside parliament where he works as a stenographer. At the worker's entrance on Reichsratsstraße, he finds the door open and unattended. Most desks are empty and he cannot attract anyone's attention. When a clerk bolts past and races up the staircase, Karl cautiously follows. The second flight opens onto the Hall of Pillars, abuzz with coming and going, he feels certain no one will even notice his presence. Sidling into the vestibule he almost bumps into a parade of dignitaries filing out of the Parliamentary Chamber and heading towards the main entrance. Before he can ascertain what is happening he is swept along with a gaggle of clerks following the official party. They stride through the atrium and on the terrace are greeted by a thunderous uproar from a crowd stretching to the Hofburg.

Scuttling to the far end of the portico Karl makes himself inconspicuous, elated to be right at the heart of the action. He strains to make out the words of a Representative barking into a loudspeaker, unable to follow the harshly distorted sound or wildly vociferous outbursts from the crowd. Enthusiastic applause is punctuated with furious heckling, and he sees arguments breaking out amongst knots of onlookers. The explosive crack of rifle fire rings above the din and heads are turning in all directions. Urgently scanning the startled crowd, Karl cannot detect where the shot came from. With his heart racing he watches the official party making a shambolic withdrawal and the doors of the parliament are slammed. Below a brawl erupts as an enraged group of workers seem set on storming the building. When a bottle is lobbed onto the terrace he fears he could be in real danger but a solid contingent of police blocks both ends of the ramps and with the pressure of densely packed bodies absorbing turbulence, the surging energy subsides into sullen resignation.

As the crowd thins Karl tentatively makes his way down to the forecourt, lingering by the Athena fountain which strikes him as absurdly out of place—an ornate reminder of the self-satisfied pomposity of the old regime. With dusk falling he drifts home on streets littered with handbills, frustrated to have been so close to the action without gaining understanding. By remaining home, Father gathered a clearer picture and at the dinner table Karl's muddled account is interrupted by his father's succinct summary.

'The House has declared a Republic and our fate is in the hands of the French.

4

When school resumes details of the armistice remain sketchy and whispered conversation flickers around the room. Bold predictions on sweeping away the old order, mutterings about betrayal and fierce resolutions to resist occupation whatever the cost. As Lassman enters, the chatter is replaced by an expectant pause.

He starts well. 'Our enemies have triumphed but we are not defeated.' A cough makes him hesitate and he stares blankly at the faces in front of him before proceeding with a prepared speech. 'We are no longer masters of our own destiny, but we can still act with honour and dignity—think of Cicero, how he endured his fall from grace. We have a sacred duty boys—it falls on each and every one of you and even on your children's children: we must pledge ourselves to avenge this disgrace.'

Heinrich Kirch calls from the back of the room. 'Long live the Fatherland!'

There are a few muffled cheers and the room settles into grim silence. Karl has no intention of pledging to revenge or any other sacred duty. He wants to speak up and would have raised his hand if Max did not take hold of his elbow. Pleased with Heinrich's display of patriotism Lassman launches into a rambling account of how Cicero conducted himself when hunted down by the Second Triumvirate and concludes by setting an essay topic. 'Write about the Fatherland. What is the way forward? And what do we have to hold onto? I want your own thoughts, but if you don't know where to start look at Book Three of *Res Publica*.'

The class fill their pens, finding comfort in familiar routines. Watching Lassman sitting at his desk sanctimonious and complacent, his head buried in the morning paper, Karl can barely contain his fury. He's appalled Lassman had nothing to say about the lives lost, the boys fresh out of school killed or maimed, snuffed out for no purpose other than satisfying the pig-headed dreams of the imbeciles who thought war would be a grand adventure. He believes the enraged workers he saw outside parliament have a better grasp of the situation but recognises the schoolroom is not the place to speak his mind. He prefaces his essay with a quotation from a translation exercise set a few months earlier.

'O how tormented they were by feelings of shame and self-reproach, made worse when they remembered the splendour and pride of their setting out and saw how mean and abject was the conclusion'.

The passage, from Thucydides' account of the ill-fated Sicilian expedition, reminds him of his boyish enthusiasm watching the Austrian battalions parade on the Heldenplatz before setting out for France. Suppressing an urge to comment on the disastrous conduct of the war, he describes how the Athenians faced the humiliation of defeat, arguing their surrender was honourable because it was the only way to end the slaughter: *'Can we find the courage'*, he writes, *'to admit our reasons for entering the war cannot justify the loss of life? Like the Athenians of old, we must boldly declare the welfare of the people is more important than our ideals of honour and patriotism.'* With sentences rolling off his pen he feels exhilarated, though a small voice inside advises caution and he appeals to the authority of Scripture to conceal his pacifist sympathies. *'By forgiving your enemies you heap burning coals of shame on their heads.'*

Curiosity overcomes Professor Lassman and he prowls aisles reading over the shoulders of his students. Delighted by Heinrich's effort, he instructs him to read. In a strong clear voice, the aspiring poet delivers a wild pastiche of Fichte's *Address to the German Nation.*

'When our ancestors triumphed over the might of Rome, they were inspired by eternity and like a sacred flame their courage passes from generation to generation. Our forefathers refused to surrender, refused to accept the benefits of peace. Peace would have meant becoming half-Roman and a true German would rather die than become half-Roman…'

The oration draws enthusiastic support from Heinrich's circle but Lassman notices many students are unmoved. He asks if anyone else is prepared to read and when the class falls silent Karl cannot resist. Standing rigidly he improvises an introduction to diffuse Heinrich's efforts.

'The German tribes' heroic resistance against Roman imperialism is an inspiration to all who face military occupation, but our current predicament might more usefully be compared to the prolonged conflict of the Peloponnesian War…'

His skilfully reasoned arguments and cautious tone are well received and Lassman feels obliged to commend his effort. As an aside he adds. 'Of course the Jewish mind can never understand devotion to the Fatherland.'

There are murmurs of agreement and Lassman presses his triumph by calling on Klaus Bühler, a slow thick set boy who has learnt to expect chastisement whenever he hears his name. He rises looking confused and Lassman smiles reassuringly.

'The class would like to hear what you think of the Jew who would lead us out of our crisis.'

With whispers of support from his friends Bühler shrewdly ascertains what is required. 'I think he won't sound so clever when I knock his teeth out.'

The classroom erupts into laughter and Karl stares at his desktop, not daring to move his eyes. In an instant he understands he has crossed a line and nothing he can say will change that. When the students are released for the pause, he stays at his desk and turns to Max who remains seated alongside him.

'You should go.'

Max replies in a low voice. 'We'll be fine, though you should probably keep some of that stuff to yourself.'

Lost in a riot of regrets and justifications, Karl cannot formulate a response and retreats into an almost catatonic silence. As students return to their benches he locks his eyes on the desktop, deadening awareness of the threatening stares and concerned glances. At the end of the day he insists Max leave without him. Bracing against the churning in his stomach, he listens to the hubbub of departing students and when he's certain the gymnasium is empty takes a circuitous route home.

5

Sliding a razor over his chin, Karl erases the light stubble of two days spent in his bedroom feigning illness. He runs a comb through the tawny hair curving over his forehead, reassured by the solidity of his shoulders and the firmness of his jaw. Turning, his eyes shift sideways, catching the profile of a nose with just enough hook to disclose his heritage. In an instant the self-assured young man vanishes and a scared little boy looks back. Crushed. Muscles tightening against jagged memories of laughter filling the school room and Professor Lassman's smirking gaze granting an unspoken sanction to the careless brutality of his charges. Hours spent in fretful imagining have extinguished thought of facing his adversaries and he cleaves to an unshakeable resolution: he will not return to the gymnasium.

At the breakfast table Father barely pauses and with colleagues and clients arriving takes his coffee upstairs. Hanya chatters about a new dance troupe setting up shop in the basement of the Konzerthaus and Dora is an automaton, vacantly gulping coffee before heading into another twelve hour hospital shift. Mother coaxes her to eat a piece of cheese as if feeding an infant while Karl distractedly chomps on the black bread his sister won't eat.

'Good to see your appetite back.' Mother ruffles his hair as she clears Dora's plate.

'I'm not going back. I've decided to leave school.'

A sigh hums through Mother's tightly pursed lips as Karl supplies a pared-down summary of his confrontation with Professor Lassman. Her first impulse is sympathetic, prompted by memories of the dreadful bullying that forced them to pull him out of his drilling school. But with the Matura exam approaching she cannot countenance anything jeopardising entrance to university. She undertakes to talk to Father and Karl is pleased to have a respite before the inevitable showdown.

Retreating to the library he loses himself in Lasalle's *The Working Man's Program.* In the afternoon Max's distinctive piano playing penetrates his sanctuary and he makes his way to the music room eager to find out if his friend has been targeted in his absence. Hanya turns the manuscript pages and the moment Max finishes playing she is bursting to show her appreciation.

'So stormy and impulsive—I'd love to dance to it but I can't make head nor tail of the rhythm.'

'It's difficult,' Max replies. 'Schönberg refuses to use simple repetition—he applies mathematical patterns to the tonal arrangements and that's where you find the rhythm.'

Karl rolls his eyes, suspecting Hanya has no interest in understanding the complexity of the music. With rising frustration he notices Max listening intently to his sister prattling about a dance teacher from Paris and a new method that involves dancing in bare feet. When Max gathers his papers, Karl offers to accompany him on the walk home.

With an icy wind descending from the north the two boys stride vigorously down the Bauernmarkt. Max says things have settled at the Gymnasium and is surprised when Karl tells him he is leaving school. 'There's no need for that—just keep your head down.'

The suggestion he might have blown the incident out of proportion, raises a twinge of embarrassment. 'I can't stay there, it's like a mausoleum, nothing ever changes.'

'No one is listening to Lassman or Kirch. The demobbed soldiers will be taking charge and won't put up with any of that nonsense.'

As they cross the canal into Leopoldstadt, old men with unkempt beards gather outside their doors talking softly, glancing at the evening sky. Noticing Karl's quizzical expression Max explains the men are waiting for the third star marking the end of Sabbath and invites his friend to come inside. 'You're welcome to join us—it's nothing much, we light a few candles, have a sip of raisin-wine and Papa recites a psalm for the new week.'

Karl politely declines, alarmed at participating in something he knows nothing about. He's aware Herr Elstein is a religious scholar and always assumed Max went along with it out of deference to his father. It hadn't occurred to him someone with Max's intelligence could give credence to such primitive superstitions. Walking home in the fading light, a vague shame rises in the back of his mind. He supposes Lassman's nastiness should have stirred solidarity with his Jewish brethren but it would be a sham to profess allegiance to such a backward-looking religion. With Hebrew chanting, eerie and indistinct, seeping out of the apartments lining the street, he hurries towards Aspern Bridge.

Summoning Karl to discuss the schooling situation, Father conducts a detailed inquisition into the substance of the offending essay.

'What on earth did you hope to achieve?'

'He asked us to give our own views and that's what I did.'

'You can't be so naïve. You know perfectly well the Professor would not expect to be contradicted at a time like this. And what possessed you to read the thing to the class?'

Karl has already tormented himself with this question and knows the truth will disclose an inflated sense of his importance. 'Somebody must stand up to him, he wanted us to pledge ourselves to eternal vengeance.'

'But you're not standing up, are you? You're running away as you always do.'

'It's not a battle I can win.'

'Exactly—so why start it in the first place?'

Karl feels his face redden and is unable to control a squeak in his voice. 'I thought it was the right thing to do.'

'Making a spectacle of yourself—showing everyone how clever you are. And now we have to pick up the pieces.'

'All I want is to be able to say what I believe. That's never going to be possible at the Gymnasium.'

'It's not just the Gymnasium,' Father replies sharply. 'Surely you can see how dangerous it is.'

'What about the danger of keeping quiet? That's why the war went on for so long.'

Father exhales. 'Do you really believe you will persuade anyone with your clever little arguments? Nobody wants the truth. Right now all they want is someone to blame.'

Finding himself caught short, Karl absorbs the guilt of exposing his family to dangers he cannot face. 'Maybe I should have kept quiet—but if ever there was a time to speak it's now, we have to seize the moment.'

Recognising the phrase's significance, Father fixes him with a stare as if sizing up a disreputable client. 'I suppose the Party will let us know when the time is right?'

'It happened in Saint Petersburg.'

For a moment Karl fears he has said too much. A jittery energy races through his body. With chin jutting he matches his father's gaze, emboldened by the certainty everything will change and the hypocritical platitudes of his father's generation will be swept aside by the inexorable march of history.

Lacking the energy for a prolonged argument Father signals tacit approval for Karl's proposal to study for the Matura at the university and in the following weeks takes every opportunity to expound on the fallacies and hazards of communist ideology. Uncle Walter who studied economics under Carl Menger and is sympathetic to the socialist ideal, is wheeled in to add heft to the arguments.

'Marx's insights are often quite brilliant,' Uncle Walter intones with sonorous authority, 'he's opened lines of enquiry that are in a sense revolutionary, but the over-arching theory rest on a fundamental misapprehension of human nature.'

Irritated by the patronising tone Karl shows little deference for his learned Uncle. 'What you call human nature is a bourgeois fantasy that serves class interests—nature does not require exploitation of workers or mobilising our entire economy for the slaughter of our neighbours.'

Uncle Walter mutters about the insufferable arrogance of youth and persists, supremely confident in the superiority of his logic. Their arguments collapse into a sullen stalemate with Karl shrugging dismissively at intricately reasoned analysis of the errors in Marx's dialectical method.

'Exactly what you'd expect from those who reap the benefits of capitalist exploitation.'

6

Strolling leisurely through the Bauernmarkt, Karl enjoys seeing his old classmates scurrying to the Gymnasium in their uniforms. Having enrolled as an Auditor, his appointments with tutors usually finish mid-morning and his self-directed study for the Matura leaves time to take in the bracing scent of freedom. After the unvarying routines of the Gymnasium, university is wildly unpredictable. He learns to avoid the boisterous press of students spilling from the large lecture halls and in the library discovers a secluded bench behind seldom visited shelves holding the records of a geological survey. In this haven he studies or daydreams as the mood takes him. His gaze drifts through narrow windows to the vaulted arcade, which are cluttered with deck chairs for recuperating soldiers housed in the Ceremonial Hall. Seeing men with missing limbs and disfigured faces he realises how sheltered he'd been at the Gymnasium and is certain he is right to leave. Roaming the library he pulls a book from the shelves, reads a few pages and drifts to another section: a treatise on elementary particles; an ethnographic study of South Sea Islanders; a freshly printed volume on educating infants according to the tenets of psychology. It is as if the entire course of his life could be determined simply by lingering at a particular set of shelves.

From time to time he ventures on rambling excursions through the hallowed corridors and staircases of the university. The ornate atriums with their marble busts remind him of the phoney grandeur of the imperial regime and he prefers the arcades where political posters and handbills are plastered on every pillar. The layering and tearing of these dispatches track the shifting currents of the ideological warfare enflaming the student body. Idling in front of noticeboards or merging with students outside lecture halls, he catches alluring fragments of politically charged conversation and when factions mill in the courtyard there is a palpable undercurrent of violence. On one occasion he witnesses a pair of students retreating battered and bleeding into the *Hauptgebäude*. At the top of the steps they turn to face their tormentors shouting, 'All power to the Soviets! No surrender to barbarisim!' before disappearing into the sanctuary of the lecture hall.

Reluctant to return home after an aimless afternoon in the reading room Karl joins a small gathering at the base of the steps where the University opens onto the Ringstraße. A young man leans into the balustrade, hand cupped around his mouth as he harangues students departing afternoon lectures. His hoarse voice, punctuated by outbursts of bronchial coughing, accentuates the earnest sincerity of his delivery. Pressing forward Karl recognises the speaker as Paul Lazarfield. They attended the Freie Schule together and he'd visited his home in the Seilergasse, but lost contact when they entered different Gymnasiums. He feels a flicker of envy watching his old classmate speak with poise and energy. The late afternoon sunshine casts dark shadows on Lazarfield's boyish face and his voice rings with the conviction of a hardened campaigner.

'Today we stand at the edge of an abyss. The sons of the working-class lie slaughtered, our productive forces are annihilated. Capitalist warmongers amass fortunes amounting to billions while the men returning from the trenches are thrown to the scrapheap of unemployment. It's time to end the class-rule of the bourgeoisie. Only then will servitude and national hatred be uprooted. Only then can we say: This war was the last…'

The speech radiates through the knot of onlookers like a bonfire on a winter night. Karl notices female students almost swoon as they gaze at the young orator who finishes with a spine-tingling howl. 'No more exploiters and exploited!'

An old soldier raises his crutch setting off a barrage of applause. Karl accepts a pamphlet pressed into his hand by a fresh-faced young woman and joins a group attending a meeting in a back room of the Café Central.

He's given a warm welcome due to his acquaintance with Lazarfield and is thrilled to win acceptance. Scanning for a familiar face he sits alongside Jakob Weitig whom he knew from scouts. His friend, in a beleaguered minority defending the government's reforms, addresses a group of junior students in the tone of a well-meaning schoolmaster. 'I suppose there is no need for dialectical analysis when you could simply instruct us on what is to be done?'

Gottfried Wetzel responds with the twitchy confidence of a prize-fighter. 'It's perfectly obvious what is required—form workers' militia, confiscate dynastic property and take control of the means of production so the wealth of the capitalists can be used to guarantee the people's food supply.'

'Seize and appropriate whatever we can lay our hands on, that's your scientific analysis of what is required?'

'We'd only be taking back what has already been stolen.'

'Socialism cannot be built on bitterness and revenge—if you are serious about revolution it is going to require a much higher level of morality.'

The claim to moral superiority sets off an uproar and Gottfried's response is accompanied with indignant thumping of the marble tabletop. 'It doesn't matter whether it's democracy or monarchy, the capitalist state is always a machine for oppressing workers and however unpalatable that may be to your bourgeois morality, it is the very essence of socialism.'

Karl listens hungrily, eager to join the debate but fearful of saying the wrong thing. With a haze of tobacco smoke rising over the gathering he feels out of place, unsettled by the vivacious young women flitting from table to table, pausing to receive the groping embrace of older men. The discussion fragments into a buzz of one-on-one conversations that abruptly die as Paul Lazarfield crosses the room to greet a pair of late-comers. He orders three plates of food and Karl recognises the newcomers have the crucial advantage of belonging to the working class. One wears an infantry greatcoat and has the look of a man who has seen action. His companion is a stout woman with large expressive eyes. Plates of frankfurters in gravy are placed before them and in answer to Karl's whispered question, Jakob identifies the pair as Gebhart and Ruth Eisler—renowned revolutionaries allied to the Worker's Council controlling the military barracks at Grinzing.

As the Eisler's devour their meals, students jockey to be within earshot of Lazarfield's table. Karl remains seated alongside Jakob, surprised to be joined by Ruth Eisler who introduces herself as Gebhart's sister. Karl suspects she is unimpressed by the chattering students vying to display revolutionary zeal. Overcoming his shyness he mutters about how their group lacks experience of the conditions faced by the working-class.

Ruth chuckles loudly and leans in. 'If our proletarian brothers had half the enthusiasm of the sons of the bourgeoisie we could seize power tomorrow morning—before the shops open.'

Her laughter arouses Karl's curiosity. 'Surely the working class have the most to gain from revolution?'

'They are naturally cautious,' Ruth replies, 'which goes to show Marx was right about material conditions determining class consciousness. The bourgeoisie have no trouble imagining a world where everything is upside-down—it's not so easy when you don't know where your next meal is coming from. A few months ago we were ready for anything but now the men are just happy they're not going back to the trenches. There's never enough to eat—but we've gotten used to that and the soldiers are brilliant at foraging. Right now they're enjoying crates of schnapps liberated from the officer's quarters.'

Nodding appreciatively Karl awkwardly frames a question on how bourgeois students can most effectively contribute. Ruth responds bluntly, 'We don't need more pamphlets from day-dreamers and café idlers. We need disciplined intellectuals—people who can raise funds and submit to the authority of Workers Councils.' She invites Karl to visit their headquarters at the Grinzing barracks and listening to her account of the miseries endured by striking textile workers, he sees Lazarfield's group with their strident rhetoric and boyish bravado are a million miles from the worker's struggle.

7

A flush of embarrassment surges through Hanya's body as the instructor points to her feet. 'We don't use first position—it limits your natural impulses.'

Hastily adjusting her stance, she locks eyes on the girl in front, diligently following the unfamiliar warm-up which methodically works through every muscle, stretching and flexing fingers, toes, even eyebrows. Though the exercises are not difficult, she worries her movements lack the authenticity her teacher values above all.

Drawing the girls into a semicircle, Frau Gerty addresses them in a crisp voice. 'This morning I was looking at a political poster on a lamp-post. Moisture had dissolved the glue and a corner was flapping in the breeze, then all at once it shot into the air, as if the force of gravity had suddenly lost its power.'

The girls nod appreciatively before launching into exercises encompassing entrechat, soubresaut and grand jeté. Desperate to make a good impression, Hanya throws herself into the leaps and quickly learns nobody cares about the technical precision so rigorously enforced at her ballet classes. Spontaneity and boldness are all that matters and the only guidance comes from Frau Gerty's constant refrain: 'Follow the call of your bodies.'

When told the class will finish with an improvisation, her nerves jangle like a fire-bell. She drifts to the back, but Frau Gerty sets a task for each dancer and Hanya is told she is to be a messenger bringing hope to a city filled with despair. With the girls in front circling each other, eyes downcast, Hanya skips awkwardly through the group, muscles tightening. Aware of her diaphragm pushing against her stomach she feels the air beneath her feet and impelled by the momentum of her landing, leaps again and again as dancers turn towards her with arms outstretched.

Striding home she scarcely notices the bitter wind. A compliment from Frau Gerty left her glowing. It is as if she has opened a new book and can't wait to reach the final chapter. She knows she will have to shake off the fastidious habits of her ballet training and resolves to devote herself to whatever Frau Gerty requires. At the top of the Kohlmarkt a line stretches for a hundred yards as men wait for the tobacconist to open. Across the street, women who were standing outside the bakery when Hanya left home, shuffle forward hopefully while those at the tail of the queue look despondent.

At home she hears the dissonant sounds of Max's piano and gallops upstairs. Slipping quietly into the music room she takes a position close to the stool. He raises an eyebrow as she prepares to turn the manuscript pages. The piece is devilishly difficult and Hanya strains to follow the notes when a toss of his head prompts her to turn the page. His fingers release dense clusters of sound exploding into fragments devoid of structure or harmony. Gazing at Max through the side of her eyes she contemplates taking his head in her hands and kissing him on the mouth. A fit of coughing extinguishes her reverie and with Max hunched over the keyboard, her hand rests on his back, absorbing the convulsions wracking his body. He raises a handkerchief to his mouth and she strikes his back sharply, dislodging the phlegm. As the heaving subsides, Hanya presses a hand to his forehead.

'You should be in bed.'

'It's nothing, I've always had a slight weakness in the chest.'

He resumes playing, oblivious to the tumult welling inside the young woman standing inches from him. Alarmed by his pale complexion, Hanya scurries to the kitchen where mother fusses over a turnip stew that will not be ready for hours. She gravely describes Max's coughing fit and persuades Mother to give her money for broth.

Ignoring his reticence, Hanya leads Max across the street to the Bauernmarkt Café where they take a table next to a sullen group of card players. She orders soup with rolls and though the thin liquid is muddy-brown, it is steaming with a thick layer of barley at the bottom. She chatters excitedly about her dance class and enquires after his music lessons.

Max keeps his eyes on the tabletop as he speaks. 'We have a recital next week, you could attend if you're interested.'

'I'd love to!' she exclaims, instantly regretting the intensity of her response. In a more measured tone she enquires about acquiring a ticket.

With a blush warming his sallow cheeks Max replies, 'It's at the Schwarzwald School, but it's only for invited guests.'

'I'd be honoured.'

'There are some unusual rules for the audience—Schönberg is very particular about such things.'

Hanya peppers him with questions which he answers matter-of-factly. Glancing through a frosted window at the darkening street he politely thanks her for the soup and says he must get home. Outside she impulsively places a hand on his shoulder and pulls him into an embrace. They share a fleeting intimacy, disengaging with nervous giggles. Watching him walk away Hanya feels like she has passed a test and won entry into the exalted company of those who live for their art. She recalls what Frau Gerty said about finding the audacity to throw yourself into a leap without thought of how you handle the landing.

At the dinner table with her mind racing, Hanya listens as Karl and Father rekindle a stale political argument. She needs to talk but Mother looks exhausted and Dora appears satisfied in her self-imposed isolation. When mother serves coffee Dora excuses herself and Hanya decides to chance her arm. Following her sister to her room she finds her snuggled beneath a thick eiderdown. Perching on the edge of the bed Hanya hopes to recover the intimacy they enjoyed before the war when they'd spend hours doing each other's hair to match the styles of the chic young ladies seen sitting at the tables in Demel's. Dora props herself on the pillow and Hanya tells her about Max's cough.

'Do you think you could bring some medicine from the hospital?'

'And who is Max?' Dora asks.

'He comes to use the piano—one of Karl's friends from the Gymnasium.'

'Is he coughing blood?'

Hanya's pretty forehead creases and Dora gazes at her sister open eyed with a hint of a smile. 'Is he good looking?'

'He's an artist—terribly serious about his music. He's invited me to a recital next week… but I can't tell if he has feelings or if he just thinks I'm interested in the music. We talk about art and music and dance all the time and he knows all about the latest—' Aware she is gushing, Hanya stops.

A wistful expression flickers across Dora's face. 'I'm sure he likes you. Why wouldn't he? Just enjoy yourself, and don't hold back.'

Gazing at the pattern of the Persian rug Hanya imagines what Dora must be thinking about her silly girlish crush, 'Did you meet anyone while you were away?'

'No.'

'You haven't told us anything. If you'd try to tell us what happened we might be able to help.'

'I don't need help.'

'I didn't mean that... but was there anyone you met, anyone special?'

Dora sags into the pillow, her eyes fixed on the ceiling. 'They all fell in love with us. They'd grab hold of you and tell you how beautiful you are while you're clearing a bedpan or draining puss. Some of the typhoid patients got gangrene and if amputations didn't stop it spreading we'd put them in a tent away from the main ward. They'd lie there with their flesh rotting, eventually it would reach their heart or brains and they'd die in terrible agony. There were boys no older than Karly begging me to kill them.'

Hanya's eyes fill with tears. She takes her sister's hand and squeezes it softly. Dora pulls away. 'I shouldn't have told you that.'

'I'm glad you did.'

'I need to sleep. And don't tell anyone what I said.'

With no idea how to respond, Hanya rises from the bed. She pauses at the door halted by a voice from another world. 'Don't make yourself miserable about things that don't concern you.'

8

With the twin spires of the Votivkirche sliding across the grimy windows of the tram, Karl loses his train of thought, distracted by a persistent high-pitched vibration coming from a sheet of brown paper taped over a broken windowpane. He's aggrieved Max declined to join him, annoyed his friend is so bespotted with Hanya he's lost all interest in the workers' struggle. As the trolley passes beyond the familiar buildings of the central district he frets over how he will introduce himself, unable to decide if it would be presumptuous to address them as comrades and certain that whatever he says will sound ridiculous. At the terminus litter blows through the street and garbage is piled around the statue at the bottom of Grinzinger Allee. Shuffling towards the park he notices two lads scooping armfuls of dead leaves, stuffing them into a sack. The trees have had branches hacked at for firewood and Karl feels guilty knowing his father would have used connections at the mayor's office to secure their last coal delivery. He considers catching the next tram home but tells himself fussing about personal embarrassment is a trivial indulgence compared with the hardships workers endure.

His first view of the barracks complex is unnerving, rows of identical buildings with low pitched roofs receding like a maze. He asks directions from an old soldier idling at the main gate who vaguely points to a parade ground and tries to cadge a cigarette. Unable to oblige, Karl apologetically takes his leave. After searching for the best part of an hour he locates Barrack 43 and steels himself to knock. A young man looks him up and down and with assumed gruffness Karl says, 'I'm looking for Ruth Eisler.'

A gesture of the head ushers him inside where a meeting is in progress. Scanning the room he catches sight of Ruth sitting with her back to him, talking to a group of students about apportioning supplies. The business concludes with a call for volunteers and looking around the room Ruth notices Karl hovering by the door. She greets him warmly, introducing him to the crew assigned distribution duties. Karl eagerly offers to help. Their first stop is an enormous warehouse where a scribbled note with Ruth's signature secures the release of several dozen field blankets. Karl's outstretched arms are piled with heavy blankets and he follows Ludwig who knows his way around. Each of the barracks they visit has its own character. In one the only language spoken is Hungarian, another houses families of Jewish refugees and another has been converted into an artist's studio. The supplies are received with good-humoured expressions of solidarity and, as they complete their rounds, Ludwig casts his eye over Karl's grey woollen suit. 'You better come with me.'

Returning to the warehouse, Ludwig leads him to a palette stacked with infantry greatcoats.

'Find something that fits—can't have you dressing like the bourgeoisie.'

Karl hesitates. 'I don't know if I should, I'd intended to resist conscription.'

With a dismissive grunt Ludwig drapes a coat over Karl's shoulders. 'The army belongs to the people now and there's nothing better to keep you warm.'

With the coat hanging heavily on his shoulders, Karl feels the coarse grey serge imparting a sense of belonging. Everyone in the barracks wears bits of military uniforms though he discovers few of the students in 43 served. The atmosphere reminds him of scout camps where everyone is keen to busy themselves with mundane tasks and there is a constant hubbub of unstructured conversation. He heads home pleased with himself and promising to return.

With the contents of her wardrobe strewn over her bed Hanya settles on a wine-coloured chiffon dress. By adding a beret and an incongruous sable scarf from Mother's wardrobe she convinces herself the outfit has a bohemian flavour. Mother does a poor job concealing her amusement at Hanya's uncharacteristic fretting and insists her brother attend the concert as a chaperone. Glancing at Karl's newly acquired army greatcoat Hanya begs him to make an effort to dress for the occasion but her pleas are ignored.

The auditorium at the Schwarzwald School is built in the modern style with a spiderweb of metal rods supporting light bulbs in glass globes. A few dozen guests wrapped in overcoats are scattered among the benches of the unheated hall and Hanya waves enthusiastically when she spots Max seated at the side of the stage. He responds with a barely perceptible nod. Before taking their turn at the piano each musician announces the title of the piece and the name of the composer. When they have finished, they remain still for a few moments before returning to their seats. Only the clicking of their footsteps across the stage breaks the icy silence. Hanya is awed by the gravity of the occasion, but cannot come to terms with the prohibition on applause. When Max finishes a four-handed duet with an older student she has to sit on her hands to prevent herself from clapping. To convey her excitement she smiles and vigorously nods her head, but Max returns to his seat without looking her way and the expressions of the other musicians are frozen in utmost seriousness.

Afterwards at the Café American, Max explains, 'As soon as you have applause there's an element of competition and Schönberg believes any sort of public appreciation or criticism will compromise the purity of the music.'

Karl snorts. 'Why bother with an audience at all. If you want to preserve your purity you might as well play to an empty hall?'

Mortified by her brother's outburst Hanya nods appreciatively as Max replies, 'Well why not? Schönberg puts up with all kinds of nastiness from people who haven't the faintest idea what he is trying to achieve, but he still insists anyone who is interested should be allowed to listen.'

Before Hanya can chime in Karl is back on the attack. 'So only those who are sufficiently enlightened can express an opinion—which means your supposedly progressive music is strictly for the bourgeoisie.'

If it's strictly for the bourgeoisie, Max wonders how he got a look in. He thinks of his father, working himself to the bone at his tailor's bench in the forlorn hope of one day winning admission to the class Karl is so eager to disparage.

Karl's comments attract the attention of Alban Berg, who plonks himself at the table and rests a hand on Max's shoulder. 'You should listen to the comrade—when the revolution comes we can't be playing music the workers don't understand.'

Unsettled by the ironic tone, Karl lowers his eyes as Alban continues, 'My question is, after centuries of oppression and neglect, can the proletariat create something that will transform human consciousness—or will the art of the new man have the flavour of boiled cabbage?'

As it becomes clear no one will answer, Karl feels compelled to take up the challenge. 'Under present conditions art and music are luxuries the proletariat can't afford, but that doesn't mean art belongs to the bourgeoisie. Without the labour of the working class you wouldn't have the conditions to sustain any sort of artistic production.'

The youthful figure in the infantry coat speaking with such conviction has heads turning and Hanya is infuriated to see Karl's half-baked ideas commanding so much attention. As she studies the faces around the table she realises the army greatcoat has won them. Of course they would sympathise with a young boy fresh out of the trenches. She would like nothing better than to expose his fraud but fears he will create a scene. In silence she gazes at Max's liquid eyes, an oasis of calm amid the vehemence of the debate. Her foot extends towards him, cautiously probing the space beneath the tabletop. When she finds her mark she pulls back as if the contact was accidental. Max registers the touch and is puzzled when the shoe returns, hooking itself around his calf, rising and falling in a persistent caress. His darting eyes catch Hanya's mischievous smile and he scans the faces of the debaters before turning to Hanya with a shy grin. His foot is nudged towards a leg waiting to receive his touch and as conversation ricochets around the table they surreptitiously delight in their private communion.

Walking home in the bracing night air Karl relives the debate blow-by-blow, pouring scorn on his opponents' faulty logic, bombarding Max with precise refutations of comments made in jest. He fails to notice Hanya has taken hold of Max's hand. She leans into his shoulder, rolling her eyes at Karl's unceasing monologue. In the following days Hanya carries the memory of their intimacy like a hidden jewel. In a blaze of wild imagining she pictures herself with Max in the private compartment of a train racing to engagements in Berlin and Paris. He will perform at a magnificent concert hall and she will be in Frau Gerty's latest dance piece, the talk of the town. They'll stay in a small chic hotel and spend evenings at cafés in the company of artists and composers.

Max's piano practice becomes the centre of Hanya's existence and awaiting his arrival she loses equilibrium. Anxiety bordering on panic alternates with sombre moods suffused with longing. On an afternoon when Mother is called away by her charity work she stands nervously at the piano waiting to turn the manuscript pages. Leaning into Max's thigh she cautiously allows her fingers to slide through his hair. He offers no resistance and when the piece finishes, she lowers herself onto the piano stool. Her hand rests on his shoulder and gentle pressure draws his face to hers. As their lips touch Max's racing thoughts are obliterated by a rush of unfamiliar sensations. Upstairs in the library Karl has stumbled across Kierkegaard's *Either / Or*, intrigued by a title that strikes him like a message from on high. The provocative writing matches his unspecified discontent and when he notices the piano playing has stopped, he decides to try once more to interest Max in what is happening at the Grinzing barracks. Tripping lightly downstairs he enters the music room. Max abruptly disentangles from Hanya's embrace and registers the shock and disbelief on Karl's face. For a moment he stands immobilised—even if he knew what to say, he would be incapable of uttering the words. Compelled by an impulse to be elsewhere, he snatches his manuscript papers and bolts for the door.

'You might have knocked,' Hanya pronounces with forced coolness.

Karl glares fiercely at his sister who faces him with an unbearably smug expression.

'If you are using physical intimacy to secure his friendship you are no better than the harlots on the Vorstadt.'

Pulling aside the curtains, Hanya watches Max scurrying home, her eyes fixed on the street as she addresses her brother. 'Don't stick your nose into things you don't understand.'

9

With muffled chanting rising through the floorboards from the apartments below, Max helps his father spread a linen cover over the work bench. Mama tosses a fragment of dough into the stove and lights candles. In the evening light trousers hanging over the window frame casts a peculiar shadow on the table where Max's sisters take their places. Observing the actions that have never varied since as far back as he can remember, Max is struck by how sordid it all looks. The velvet cloth covering the challah loaf is frayed and the soup has an unpleasant greyish hue. Four fried herrings, which will be cut to provide a portion for each family member, look ridiculously meagre on the large blue serving plate with chipped edges. Max hears the joy in his father's voice as he recites the Kiddush.

'Thou has chosen and sanctified us above all peoples and love and favour has made us to inherit Thy Holy Sabbath.'

Noticing the wide-eyed anticipation of his youngest sister waiting to moisten her lips with the shared cup, he feels out of place and understands he is seeing everything through Hanya's eyes. He imagines her standing at the table alongside his sisters, curious and sympathetic, naively reassured by Mama's kindly smile, never suspecting that behind those dark eyes a spirit of malevolence would be formulating elaborate curses and silently drawing all the plagues of Pharaoh upon the strange girl who would lure her first-born into the stinking pit of apostasy. He sees himself at the pivot of an insolvable equation. On one side his family obligations laid out in an orderly progression and on the other, the memory of Hanya's breath inside his mouth, erratic and beguiling like a sequence of prime numbers.

At Torah study Max sits listlessly among young men listening to the elders raking over commentaries on the marriage of Isaac and Rebekah. A lengthy dispute over Rabbi Akiba's calculations on Rebekah's age at the time of her betrothal peters out and the senior Rabbi closes the session with a homily comparing the marriages of Isaac, Jacob and Moses.

'In each case,' he intones, 'the Patriarchs travel to a foreign land and meet their beloved in the evening, when the animals are being watered. But in Rebekah's case the Mishnah tells us the water rose up miraculously, as when Moses gathered the people before the well at Beer, and Israel sang, *Spring up, O well.*'

Walking home Max composes his own romantic *aggadah* in which the foreign land is the music room on the Bauernmarkt, the well is the piano Frau Popper has made available to the children of the poor and the water rising from the earth is the sublime music of Schönberg. After the family meal he can attend piano practice. Though many in the community believe students should refrain from practice during Shabbat, Reb Elstein argues all music is a song of praise and the Sabbath is not violated unless a man earns his livelihood as a musician. Max returns to the Popper residence with trepidation but a feeling of invulnerability lightens his step as he climbs the stairs. He can look Karl in the eye even though his friend turns away without a word. Frau Popper sits in on the practice and Max is gripped by a slowly rising conviction that all obstacles can be worn down so long as he is shrewd and persistent like Jacob at Haran. As he leaves, Hanya slips a note into his manuscript papers suggesting they meet at the skating rink outside Stadtpark after her dance class on Wednesday evening.

Arriving early for the rendezvous Max paces the rink, his muscles tightening at the back of his neck. He catches sight of her on Lothringerstraße, striding towards him with her face glistening from the exertion of the dance class. She leans into his frozen body pressing her cheek against his. A gloved hand finds his and their fingers interlock as she nudges him towards the Stadtpark. They take the broad path following the Wienfluss. A layer of decaying leaves muffles their footsteps and sporadic gusts dislodge droplets from the bare branches above. Hanya chatters excitedly about the new work Frau Gerty is creating.

'It's terribly avant-garde—sure to cause a scandal. She's based it on the Ford System, so it's all very mechanical. We've been springing up and down like pistons.'

'Sounds marvellous.'

In his nervousness Max cannot convey his usual enthusiasm. Hanya leads him across the lawn and in the shelter of the band rotunda they stand, watching an old man fossicking for cigarette butts around the benches on the perimeter.

'Has Karl said anything?' Max asks timidly.

'He tried to lecture me but I told him not to speak of things he doesn't understand.'

'What do you think your parents would say?'

'Mother likes you.' Hanya adopts a flippant tone to dispel the anxiety. 'She believes you are destined for great things—she's certain we shall be watching you perform at the *Musikverein* one day.'

'I only wish things were as easy with my parents.'

'What do you mean?'

Hanya realises how little she knows of Max's family. All their conversation has been on music and art. Glancing at his face she sees he is struggling to speak.

'Have you told them about me?' she asks shyly.

'I can't.'

'Why ever not?'

Max picks up the hurt in Hanya's voice and regrets he raised the issue. 'It's hard to explain.'

'You mean they wouldn't approve of me.'

'They expect me to find a daughter of the Covenant—a Jewish girl.'

This time it is Hanya who is unable to speak and a ghastly silence falls between them. Max stares into the darkening shadows beneath a clump of linden trees.

Hanya takes in his anguished expression and speaks in a pained voice. 'Have they chosen someone for you?'

'Not yet… but mother is always looking.'

Hanya bites her lip. She cannot believe Max would consent to something so primitive. Observing his hands locked in his jacket pockets, a trembling in his chin, his dark eyes fixed on the distance, she recognises she must take the lead. 'Will you let them choose for you?'

'No of course not—but it's difficult.'

'Let's walk.' She slips her arm into the gap between his elbow and torso and guides him towards a narrow pathway lined with birch trees.

'So what are we to do?'

'I wish I knew.'

'We could always elope—run away to Berlin.'

Max contemplates the impossibility of explaining why he cannot leave his family but before he can voice his thoughts Hanya changes tack. 'You do realise most of my family are still Jewish.'

'Yes I know—one of your uncles arranged for me to use the music room. He's an elder at our synagogue. But my parents are very old fashioned.'

'And they want nothing less than a true daughter of the covenant. It seems terribly unfair. I didn't choose to be baptised. I could easily convert.'

Max is amazed Hanya can treat the matter so lightly. 'What would your parents think?'

'They shouldn't be too concerned. We're not religious. Daddy does a lot of work for the Municipal Council and we have to keep up appearances.'

'They would allow you to convert?'

'I can't see why not. Father probably will not approve but he would never forbid it. His family cut him off when he was baptised and he doesn't talk about it, but we keep in touch with Mother's relations. We all attended my cousin Myra's wedding—it was rather lovely, under the canopy with flowers and candles.'

The idea such an intractable problem could dissolve like a puff of smoke is beyond comprehension for Max. He tries to explain conversion would not be easy, but Hanya skips breezily over whatever obstacles he presents.

'It's been such a long time since we've been able to find a pork chop,' she laughs, 'I do not believe I would miss it.'

'You realise there are 613 mitzvah,' Max replies with mock solemnity.

'Well I could never remember them but as long as you keep reminding me I would do my best.'

Hanya giggles and Max cannot help joining in, captivated by the lilting rhythm of her laughter. For a moment he allows himself to believe love could conquer all. He knows his mother's opposition will be implacable, cunning and relentless, but banishes her image and surrenders to the joy of holding hands with the gorgeous, unpredictable creature who is so improbably attracted to him. The Stadtpark, even in its dilapidated state, with litter scattered across the untended lawns and drifts of leaves clogging the gutters, retains an enchantment. The broad pathways and spacious planting whisper of a more gracious era. Hand-in-hand they gravitate towards a stand of mature spruce trees. A gentle rain seeps out of an asphalt sky and in the seclusion of the thick foliage her arms encircle his waist and her face lunges towards his mouth.

Returning to Leopoldstadt Max feels the heaviness of the neighbourhood press on him like a damp blanket. Knots of old men with untrimmed beards and phylacteries gather around doorways. He keeps his eyes downcast, avoiding the faces accusing him with words from the Book of Proverbs: *'Why should you be intoxicated, my son, by another woman and embrace the bosom of an adulteress?'*

At the synagogue the disgrace of apostasy is often discussed and while many are quick to condemn, the Rabbi has declared the offspring of those who marry the goyim, should not be held responsible for their parent's transgression, for Jeremiah spoke to the time of exile when he said: *'In those days they shall no longer say the parents have eaten sour grapes and the children's teeth are set on edge.'*

At night with the rest of the household sleeping, Max sees his father reading in the glow of a kerosene lamp. Reb Elstein looks towards his son noticing the furrows creasing his forehead. He carefully sets aside the heavy volume from the synagogue's library and Max asks how he should treat his Jewish school friends who have accepted baptism. His father answers with vehemence as if he had been waiting for this very question.

'A Jew can never stop being a Jew. Our unborn souls were present at Mount Sinai when we accepted the yoke of the Torah.'

Max nods in deference and before he can frame another question his father continues in a gentler tone. 'Some choose apostasy to fill their purses and some to avoid persecution. In Spain the Marranos were baptised and lived as Christians for centuries and yet they secretly passed on their observances from generation to generation. "*A man may wet himself in the water of baptism but he will wipe himself clean with a talith.*" In spite of our transgressions, a Jew is still a Jew, for the Almighty-Blessed-Be-He dwelt among us in the midst of our defilements.'

Although mother will not be swayed by the learned references Max is pleased to know a true understanding of the Torah rises above mean-spirited prejudice. He discerns a shrewd wisdom in Hanya's flippant offer to convert and resolves to keep their relationship secret. Laying alongside his brother he feels no need for sleep and contentedly gazes at the ceiling recalling the soft grey of the evening sky, the chattering of starlings and the sharpness of the spruce needles rubbing against his back as she pressed her lips against his. When sleep comes a surging sensation propels him through spacious corridors and lavishly appointed mansions.

10

Crossing the parade ground in the fading light, Karl strains to recover the bracing invulnerability that carried him from the Bauernmarkt, scoffing at his father's prediction he'd soon be home with his tail between his legs. Lingering outside the barracks he wishes he'd been a little less strident declaring he could no longer take advantage of the comforts that come from appropriating the labour of the working class. What if the working class doesn't want him? A muffled groan rises at the back of his throat as he imagines the humiliation of crawling home to face father's condescending smile. In a fatalistic mood he steps up to the door and his overly assertive knock is answered by a nonchalant call to enter. Clutching his suitcase, he stands awkwardly in the aisle between two rows of bunks, his chest tightening as he attracts glances from young men playing cards.

He wants to announce himself boldly but his voice slips to a nervous squeak. 'I'm hoping I can join you.'

A low voice replies, 'Both those bunks are free.'

He turns to see Ludwig propped on his elbow with an open book. A toss of the head directs him to the unoccupied bunks. Karl senses no response is required. Placing his suitcase on the top bunk he hangs his greatcoat on the bedframe and sits on the lower mattress, his head whirling. The card players carry on playing and Ludwig remains studiously absorbed in a heavy volume, which Karl assumes must be Marx. Afraid he might do something wrong, he waits, eyes on the floorboards until Ludwig sets aside his book and offers to show him around. At the far end of the room a makeshift kitchen has a kerosene stove set on a trestle table and the annex housing the latrines is equipped with a row of wash bowls with pitchers and slop jars beside them.

Following Ludwig's lead he joins a line for a bowl of soup and takes a seat at the dining table. It is not difficult to strike conversation and Karl quickly acquires a working knowledge of the unwritten protocols governing residency in the liberated barracks. As soon as the meal is cleared, card games resume and Karl volunteers to help wash dishes. He takes to bed early and despite the discomfort of a musty kapok mattress, drifts into a fitful slumber before awakening to a chorus of snoring and coughing. With his head propped on the iron bed frame, he stares at the dark rectangles of the barracks windows, taking in the cool air filled with the odours of stale tobacco, damp clothes and leather boots. Surprised how easily he won acceptance, he understands just being young is enough. Whatever their background or beliefs, his generation are united in contempt for their elders. They remember how proud and certain their fathers were before the war and see them now—feeble, deluded, inarticulate, clinging to things they no longer believe, obstinately refusing to imagine a better way.

Rising in an optimistic frame of mind he joins the morning routine—a cold-water wash and a shared basin of warm water for shaving. The spartan conditions remind him of scout camps, though the atmosphere is less regimented. He takes a tram to the university, accompanied by Ludwig and students studying at the Polytechnic. In the cramped intimacy of the trolley Karl feels he is being sized-up and when he raises his eyes Ludwig is staring at him as if deliberating on what to do with an irksome child.

'I suppose you're one of Lazarfield's mob.'

'I've been to a few of his meetings,' Karl replies apologetically, 'though I'd have to say there's a lot of talk and not much action, that's why I came to the barracks.'

'Café socialists,' Ludwig snorts. 'If you want to make yourself useful, meet me at the central Bahnhof, Platform 2 at 1400.'

The intriguing invitation plays on his mind during morning tutorials and Karl feels inordinately proud when he overcomes an ingrained habit of obedience and skips his afternoon lecture. Ludwig arrives promptly at the platform and traveling out of the city on the northern line remains infuriatingly mysterious about their destination. Gazing at the factories of the Ninth District, Karl listens attentively as Ludwig addresses him in the mildly irritated tone of a man with more important matters on his mind.

'The trouble with bourgeois intellectuals is they're infatuated by their own ideas. They can't see that opinions have no objective value—what you think doesn't change the way things are.'

As the train approaches the Stubenring terminus, Ludwig leans towards him until their heads almost touch. 'When we get there don't ask questions. There are informers working for the government and our people won't know if you can be trusted.'

'Will we be doing anything illegal?'

Ludwig responds with a rare chuckle. 'That depends on the outcome.'

Embarrassed by the stupidity of his question Karl recognises, with trepidation, he's joined a band of real revolutionaries deadly serious about overthrowing the government. History will decide whether they're denounced as criminals or lauded as the heroic vanguard of a new dawn.

Entering Party headquarters, on the second floor above a tailor's shop, they are greeted by an old soldier, striking typewriter keys with two fingers. He tells the boys to help themselves to the coffee simmering on an alcohol stove. Stacks of pamphlets are laid out on a long table and Karl hears voices from a meeting taking place in an adjoining room. They set to work counting out and wrapping bundles of pamphlets. It's a mundane task, but Karl feels he is doing something useful and looks back with scorn at the self-indulgent chatter of the student meetings at the Café Central. Ludwig takes him on a delivery run to the outer districts, beyond the Gürtel, where the munitions factories have all closed. The scenes of desolation bring him close to tears. Bleak tenements with children squatting in stairways that stink of cooking fat and boiled cabbage. Women in stained overalls gossip in the passageways, their gaunt faces stamped with resignation. Having grown up in Favoriten, Ludwig is accustomed to poverty and seems oblivious to the desperation. His only show of emotion comes as they pass an alcohol counter selling an acrid smelling tea laced with schnapps. The grog-peddler is lording it over a man begging for credit and as soon as they are out of earshot Ludwig spits out his anger.

'Parasites—the Worker's Militias should eliminate them. You'll never get class-consciousness as long as there's money to be made inebriating the proletariat.'

Karl walks stiffly, feeling out of place among the rows of concrete buildings stained with soot. Ludwig tells him not to stare and warns there are gangs of unemployed youth who relieve their boredom by beating-up Communists.

As he learns the ropes Karl is surprised by the generous hospitality extended by Party members. He is ashamed to accept food from impoverished families crammed into single room apartments that also serve as workshops for shoemaking or tailoring. Lingering in a tenement courtyard while Ludwig meets privately with the chairman of a Worker's Council, Karl approaches a sad-eyed waif sitting alone on a concrete stairway, legs dangling through rusty cast-iron railings. His name is Otto and he cannot say for sure how old he is. He seems unaware the war has ended, knowing only that his father has gone to fight the French. As he pieces together the boy's casually inscrutable pronouncements Karl's eyes cloud. He guesses his age at seven or eight. As far as he can tell his mother is sick or has died and Otto spends his nights on the third-floor landing relying on neighbours for food and visiting the soup kitchen at the church hall on Sunday evenings. Karl presses the money he's carrying for his trolley fare into the boy's grubby hand and Otto gazes at him as if he'd stumbled across a creature from another planet.

When Ludwig emerges from his meeting Karl tells him what he's learnt of Otto's circumstances and suggests they try to find a place for him in an orphanage.

'He's better off with his own people,' Ludwig growls.

'I'd say he hasn't eaten for a good while—I gave him my tram fare but it's hardly enough for a decent meal—'

Karl's appeal is cut short by a snarling tirade. 'If you care about the boy try analysing his objective situation. He's hungry because someone appropriated the value of the labour that should be sustaining him. Prancing around like Lady Bountiful might make you feel better but it's worse than useless—you're propping up the lie that capitalism will take care of him.'

Ludwig strikes out for the trolley terminus and Karl follows a few paces behind, not daring to respond. When he is unable to pay his fare Ludwig tells him to walk home and use the time to analyse the impact of his actions. Two hours later, doggedly following the tram lines with his head bent against biting sleet, he cannot refute the logic of Ludwig's position. There are thousands of boys like Otto and many must be even worse off. Singling him out for special treatment perpetuates the illusion of capitalist benevolence. The only realistic remedy is to overthrow the system that thrives on the misery of the working class. At the barracks Karl swallows his pride and declares he can see why charity is wasteful and counter-productive. He's surprised to find there is kudos in admitting error. Ludwig commends him with an uncharacteristic recourse to metaphor.

'Caterpillars are perfectly happy chomping at leaves when that's all they know—when you understand class struggle you step out of the cocoon of bourgeois consciousness and you're ready to fly.'

On Friday evenings raucous meetings in the drill hall attract a motley bunch of workers, students and artists, mingling with the throng of de-mobbed soldiers in their grey field uniforms. Sitting at a long table at the front of the hall with a committee of NCOs, Ruth Eisler has the unenviable job of maintaining order and introducing speakers. Representatives from Worker's Councils report on progress in their districts and when Ruth calls for speeches from the floor, soldiers emboldened by hasty consumption of alcohol fume about unpaid wages, mocking the fat-bellied generals and cowardly politicians who sent men to be butchered without ever leaving their feather beds. Ruth endorses these raw expressions of proletarian resentment while gently nudging discussion towards a deeper understanding of class struggle. In the volatile atmosphere shouting matches can erupt at any moment. Earnest speeches about capitalist warmongers manipulating workers into slaughtering comrades from foreign lands are heckled by battle-hardened soldiers who swear they'd rather die with honour than kiss the arses of gutless French bastards.

Fascinated by the unpredictable twists and turns Karl longs to join the debate but cannot steel himself to face the unruly crowd. When the meetings close and soldiers drift away in search of alcohol and women, he joins a select group who gather to evaluate proceedings. There is meticulous analysis of the popular speeches and impassioned debate about the way forward. Karl recognises his opinions count for little, but Ruth encourages him to speak, and he's flattered to get a hearing.

'We can't fault soldiers who've been taught to hate the French, but we need to make them see French workers didn't choose to fight and none of them are benefitting from their victory.'

Ruth's brother Gebhart responds gruffly. 'A mass meeting is no place for lectures on international solidarity but we can't be stirring up resentment against the French—England and France will seize any opportunity to invade, they're scared to death by what the Bolsheviks achieved.' He speaks with the authority of a man who has seen comrades slaughtered, silencing opponents with the harsh wisdom of a soldier. 'Provoking a battle you have no chance of winning is not just stupid, it's a crime.'

Much as he admires Gebhart's principled commitment to pacifism, Karl feels closer to Ruth, an unlikely revolutionary who radiates matronly concern for the ragtag mob of rebellious youngsters who've made the barracks their home. Although not much older than Karl she gave birth to a son during the war and pins her hopes on the upcoming generation. 'You're the ones who will inherit the sacred task of building a socialist future, the men who served in the trenches are scarred by the brutality they experienced and the older generation are crippled by their pessimism.'

Though his bourgeois status counts against him, Karl wins the trust of the Party leadership and his work as a message boy often takes him to Ruth's home in Leopoldstadt. He is surprised to find her father is a renowned intellectual and Ruth and Gebhart have to claim their proletarian credentials from their mother's side. Their father was disowned by his aristocratic family when he took a domestic servant as his wife and it is clear he has fallen on hard times. Their single room apartment is dominated by a heavy Biedermeier writing table with piles of books and sheaves of manuscript scattered over all available surfaces. The old man is cheerfully oblivious to his dilapidated surroundings and always hungry for conversation. Recognising a kindred spirit he takes Karl under his wing, assuring him the revolution needs intellectuals just as it requires the energy of the working man. After the scornful disapproval dished out by his own father, Karl admires Herr Eisler's enthusiastic support for his daughter's political commitments. Delighted to have an attentive listener the old man gives a vivid account of Ruth's attempt to establish a Socialist Republic on the day the armistice was announced.

'She was right in the thick of it, with Egon Kisch's Red Guards. They commandeered the offices of the *Neue Freie Presse*, made it the headquarters of Vienna's first Soviet. Ruth got herself installed as editor and they put out editions announcing the worker's rule.'

Ignoring Ruth's call to shush, he fossicks among piles of pamphlets and holds up one of the papers she edited, with a hammer and sickle prominently displayed.

'Of course it didn't last, the militias stayed loyal to Adler and Ruth landed up in jail. Luckily I still had a few friends who'd stuck with the Social Democrats and got positions in the Cabinet. She was in the lock-up for six weeks before I convinced them to grant an amnesty.'

Ruth seems embarrassed and sees the failed putsch as an object lesson on the folly of romantic adventurism. She speaks lightly about a comrade catching a bullet in the belly and as she recalls her time in prison Karl notices her hazel-flecked eyes are sheeted with moisture.

'The warders treated us differently from the other prisoners, I think they were scared of us—everything was so topsyturvy they worried they'd come to work one morning and find all the important people in the cells and the crazy communist troublemakers running the country.'

This draws a guffaw from Gebhart and Karl asks if the other prisoners were receptive to socialist ideas.

Ruth responds as if addressing a wider audience. 'The prostitutes who showed me the ropes don't need anyone to tell them their bodies are commodities exchanged for profits they will never enjoy. Every day they see the naked truth of bourgeois morality and face the brutality of a class that has lost all capacity for human decency.'

Rattling towards the university on a crowded trolley, Karl thinks of the prostitutes on the Vorstadt and his disgust at their cackling. Jumbled memories flash through his mind; emaciated women peddling their bodies on the street, unemployed youth idling outside tenements in Favoriten, and little Otto huddling half-starved in his stairwell. Driving it all he sees the vast machinery of the capitalist state, coldly supervising the appropriation of wealth that comes from the sweat of working men. These thoughts arrive with arresting clarity like when he first peered through a pair of reading glasses and the soft lines of type floating on white became hard-edged letters embedded in the texture of the paper. In an instant he knows he's achieved what Ruth calls revolutionary consciousness. Catching his reflection in the window he notices he is smiling idiotically and glances to the grim faces bracing against the jolting of the trolley. Buoyed by exhilarating certainty he feels part of an unstoppable force casting aside the ignorance and timidity of his father's generation, with every action, no matter how small or insignificant amplified by the solidarity of likeminded comrades bound by the hard truth of scientific analysis.

11

With clumps of snow sliding from the roof-tops, Karl sees new growth appearing on trees hacked at for firewood and a thawing in relations at home allows him to attend family meals on Sundays. Mother enforces a strict ban on discussing politics, so much of the meal passes in silence. Father politely enquires about Karl's progress at university and Hanya prattles about her dance classes. Although they hardly exchange a word Karl feels drawn towards Dora. He senses she understands the bankruptcy of the old order, but has seen too much to hold out hope. He wants to reassure her a new dawn is coming.

In the barracks a more sombre mood prevails. Pan-German fanatics are winning over unemployed workers with rowdy street marches stirring up primitive resentments and a lust for vengeance. Elsewhere reactionary forces are on the rise; in Hungary a French blockade is strangling Bela Kuhn's Soviet Republic and Ruth is devastated by news of counter-revolutionary forces smashing the Workers' Soviet in Munich. The unexpected triumph of this ragtag coalition of workers and anarchist intellectuals kindled wild optimism, making it possible to imagine a crescent of Soviets stretching from Russia through Hungary, Austria, Bavaria and even to Berlin. The brutal suppression of the Munich uprising delivered a clear message: Workers who act in isolation will be ruthlessly destroyed.

Fearing the opportunity may be slipping, Ruth speaks of the need for boldness, a spirit of recklessness balanced with precise analysis and meticulous planning. Like launching a kite in fickle winds, a split-second judgement will determine whether the revolution soars into a bright future or is driven into the ground. Ludwig includes Karl in a group of his most trusted supporters and at a clandestine meeting reveals the Party has settled on the 15th of July for a general uprising. The St. Germaine Treaty requires all militia be disbanded on this day and Ludwig explains this will be a catalyst to spark the revolution. He addresses his comrades with the gravity of an officer outlining a battle plan.

'The Volkswehr will never agree to give up their arms and we'll support their resistance with a mass demonstration. If everyone plays their part we'll get rid of the bourgeois back-sliders and install a workers government.'

Galvanised by the urgency of the moment Karl is gripped by the apocalyptic optimism sweeping through the barracks like a virus. At night he joins paste patrols dodging the police and Nationalist gangs to plaster hand-bills on lampposts and advertising kiosks. Days are spent criss-crossing the city distributing pamphlets, placards and flags. By word of mouth the call to assemble with weapons in hand spreads through Party networks and stocks of ammunition are stashed in basements and café kitchens. There are rumours of secret negotiations at the Hungarian embassy and Gebhart hints that if the uprising is successful Bela Kuhn's troops will cross the border to support the establishment of a Worker's Soviet in union with Hungary. With the day of reckoning drawing closer, Party leaders go into hiding, fearing the police may launch a pre-emptive raid on the Grinzing barracks. As a precaution Karl returns home at night to sleep in his old bedroom. He is surprised to find his Father remarkably well-informed about the planned action. On the evening of the fourteenth, he pokes his head into Karl's bedroom. 'You'd be well advised to stay home tomorrow; I understand there is to be some sort of demonstration and if it gets out of hand the army will be maintaining order.'

Supressing the urge to argue Karl remains silent and the door clicks shut. Though exhausted by the whirlwind of preparations he cannot sleep. Eyes wide open he gazes at the ceiling adrift on a sea of possibility. In the morning he slips out of the house while Father attends to his appointments. The streets appear disturbingly normal with bright sunshine casting dark shadows across shop fronts. Outside the Burgtheater a blue banner with gold lettering announces a production of *Antigone*. Anxiously scanning the Ringstraße for activity he stumbles against a pair of boys playing marbles on the pavement. At the Volksgarten he is relieved to see a crowd in front of the Theseus Temple, the red flags he helped distribute stirring proudly in the breeze. Workers and students arrive from all directions and Karl greets comrades from the barracks. Ludwig, wearing a marshal's red arm-band, brusquely informs him the Police struck hard during the night.

'They've blockaded the barracks in Rudolfsheim—our best battalion, the forty-first, is trapped inside.'

On the steps of the Theseus, Gebhart bellows into a megaphone. His speech is frequently drowned by angry shouts of support and Karl detects a hint of desperation in his voice. 'They have no right to detain the democratically elected representatives of the proletariat,' he howls. 'Our leaders have been illegally detained; it's our job to set them free.'

The proposal is greeted with enthusiastic cheers and the crowd coalesces into a densely packed column, lurching towards the law courts. Karl joins the tail of the beast, his footsteps falling into the rhythm of the march. High pitched female voices shouting in unison rise above the dull rumble of thousands of boots. When his section runs into the mass of bodies pressing against the courtrooms, a delegation has already gained entry. The crowd wait restlessly, some breaking into song while others chant slogans. Within minutes an announcement from the courtroom steps filters to the back and Karl learns the prisoners are held at the police station in Hörlgasse. Like a swarm of finches abruptly changing direction the marchers turn and the column heads back down Schmerlingplatz. Karl finds himself near the front as they pass the heavily guarded Rathaus and on entering the Hörlgasse he pauses.

Ahead where the road rises, wooden barriers block the street and the Police Station is guarded by a formation of troops with rifles. He slows as working men surge past, undaunted. Peering up at the apartments lining the street he can make out the faces of the bourgeoisie peering from behind their curtains. He recognises Professor Hofer, the Latin master from his drilling school looking down on him. With a shudder he recalls being summoned to the front of the class along with Max and two other Jewish boys. Hofer would test them on declensions they had not yet studied and at each mistake his cane would cut into the back of their legs. The stinging blows landed on the tender flesh at the back of his knees and, while the other boys could stoically absorb the punishment, he would cry out and earn additional swipes, to the delight of onlooking classmates. He stands paralysed, certain Hofer is staring directly at him. Bodies brushing past jolt him out of his reverie. He glares back at his tormentor, raises his fist and with a yell shoots forward surrendering to the crowd's momentum.

Through the surging mass of bodies he catches fractured glimpses of soldiers lined in formation. The rifles raised to their shoulders tilt upwards and an explosive volley fills the air. The men in front of him instinctively hug the ground or scuttle to the sidewalk, searching for cover. Karl crouches behind a lamppost, surprised at how calm he feels surveying the chaos. From the back of the march men and women race forward ignoring the warnings barked at the crowd. A barrage of missiles is hurled at the troops and when a soldier stumbles forward, barrels are lowered and rifle-fire fills the air. It takes moments before anyone registers that many of the bodies lying in the street have been hit. In the turmoil Karl is jostled into a group retreating into the portico of an apartment building. Looking past an array of letter boxes he gasps at a young man spread-eagled on the asphalt, limbs bent, eyes gazing skyward and a dark pool of blood spreading from beneath his back. An unearthly screech pierces the din and he sees a young woman throwing herself at the body. She clutches the lolling head, frantically appealing for help. A man crawling on all fours pulls her towards the sidewalk but she wrenches herself free and clings to the motionless body, sobbing uncontrollably. Before he can take in what he has seen Karl is bustled into the forecourt of the apartment building. Confused faces question each other until a marshal assesses the situation and directs them to a corridor leading to the stables. In the courtyard the men spread out without a word and find a gate opening into a narrow alleyway.

Karl follows quickly and finds his bearings when he catches sight of the spires of the Votivkirche. Making his way into Türkenstraßehe can still hear sporadic gunfire. He contemplates rejoining the march but on reaching Maximilian Platz sees a crowd spilling out of the Hörlgasse. Flags and placards are jettisoned in the gutters and people cram onto the trams heading out of the city. Crossing the Schottenring, Karl ducks into the University, knowing he can return home by keeping to the back streets. He becomes aware he is trembling and hurries forward with his head bowed. Reaching his bedroom he closes the door and flops onto the bed still wearing his greatcoat. With barely enough energy to kick off his shoes his body shrinks into the mattress and every thought leads him back to the memory of the young woman clutching the head of a lifeless body. Hours later Mother appears at his bedroom door to summon him to the dining room. He can do little more than shake his head and grunt when asked if he is unwell. He registers Mother's hand pressing against his forehead and as if in a trance hears his Father's coldly authoritative voice, 'You should have stayed at home as I told you.'

By remaining stubbornly silent Karl is left alone. Any possibility of sleep is demolished by frenetic attempts to analyse the situation and once morning comes he is immersed in a clamour of self-recrimination and guilt. Mother places a breakfast tray at the side of the bed and his humiliation is driven home by a newspaper folded to display a headline serenely announcing, *Order Is Restored*.

12

In July's bright afternoons Hanya and Max have taken to walking aimlessly through the city. In the Prater, nestled on a secluded bench, fingers entwined, they watch sunshine flicker on the surface of the grey Danube and talk about the latest developments in music and dance. When Hanya runs out of things to say Max shares his enthusiasm for Einstein's theories. His admiration for the man borders on idolatry and though Hanya has little interest in the peaks and troughs of electromagnetic energy, she's happy to listen, impressed by his understanding of things everyone else regards as incomprehensible. To prevent the conversation becoming one-sided she mentions something she heard from her dance teacher.

'Frau Gerty told us the energy that makes the planets rotate around the sun is the same as the energy which draws lovers together.'

Max considers the proposition. 'That might have been possible under Newton, but Einstein has shown gravity is not really a force at all. The planets are not drawn towards the sun they are just responding to the conditions of space and time.'

'In that case I'll stick with Newton.'

Max is unsure whether she is in earnest. 'It's like water flowing down to the ocean, there is no mysterious force drawing the water to the sea—it just follows the contours of the terrain.'

'What absolute nonsense, of course water is drawn to the sea. It will overcome every obstacle to get there and it will never be satisfied until it reaches the ocean.'

Resting her head on his shoulder she laughs. Their kisses, languorous and arousing in anticipation of unknown pleasure.

In spite of the ruinous inflation the amusement stalls in the Prater find eager customers among working folk determined to learn how to smile again. The winter months were so grim that warmth and sunshine are themselves sufficient to fulfil diminished expectations. At the tobacconists men happily queue for hours to obtain a packet of dried beech leaves and café menu boards make a sport of applying preposterous French titles to meat substitutes cobbled together by their beleaguered chefs. By walking instead of catching the tram and skimping on café lunches Hanya has put aside money from her allowance so they can sample amusements offered by cheaper vendors. A fortune teller with a harsh Slavic accent, triggers a bout of giggling when she assures them they will have many children. Max is intrigued by the flea circus and hours later cannot decide whether the fleas are trained or the filigree attachments merely create the illusion they are following the circus master's command. Hanya longs to ride the big wheel but Max refuses to countenance such extravagance. Father, normally cautious in financial matters, has advised her to spend her allowance as quickly as possible for however worthless it may seem today she can be certain it will be worth even less by the end of the week. Max has never seen the 10,000 kronen notes Hanya has crammed into her purse and she has to lie about the ticket price to persuade him to ride Potzloch's Grand Carrousel. Dodging stags and the outstretched wings of swans, they make for the inner circle where they can ride together in a gondola harnessed to a whale. Resting on silk cushions, the accelerating motion gently presses them together. Max drapes his arm around Hanya's shoulder and in the swirling parade of antlers, elephants and prancing horses, he laughs out loud. Hanya squeals with delight and like children they fall into the timeless world of sensation.

To avoid thinking about the charge down the Hörlgasse Karl focusses on his university studies, pained by memories of lives lost for a venture that was never likely to succeed. Though reluctant to return to the barracks he cannot suppress the urge to talk with Ruth. Catching the trolley to Grinzing he wonders if he'll find she's in prison or even among the dead. The old barracks room is nearly empty. Ludwig sits at the mess table with his nose in a book and a couple of younger boys eat mashed turnips flavoured with horse bones. Taking a seat, Karl declines the offer to help himself to the food and in response to Ludwig's gruff questions describes how he saw one of the marchers shot dead a few meters in front of him.

Ludwig shrugs. 'By our count twenty-three comrades were martyred. The mistake came when we left the Law Courts—the march reversed instead of wheeling around and the leadership were stuck at the back. We had men who were ready to deal with the troops, but by the time they got to the front panic had set in.'

Karl imagines how much worse the carnage could have been if the marchers had returned fire. He asks about Ruth and is relieved to hear she is unharmed.

'She may be sent to Berlin—we have to deploy our best cadres where there is the greatest chance of success.'

'Do you think I could talk with her?'

'I don't see why not, she's always had a soft spot for intellectuals. We have to consolidate the organisation in case she's ordered to leave—if you're up for it she may have a job for you.'

At the Eisler apartment in Leopoldstadt, Karl is warmly welcomed and Ruth draws him into a tight embrace. If demoralised by the failure of the uprising she does a good job concealing it. In her business-like fashion she asks for his assessment of the action, listening attentively as he searches for words to describe the young man felled. 'There was a girl clinging to the body, screaming… they both looked so young.'

Sensing his disillusionment Ruth responds without a hint of condescension, 'We were completely outmanoeuvred and we have only ourselves to blame. We learn through action and every action brings us closer to our goal.'

Karl bristles at the suggestion of inevitable triumph. It reminds him of the war-time editorials insisting every setback was a step forward on the long march to victory.

Ruth peers into his eyes, addressing him with disarming sincerity. 'This won't be our last defeat Karl. Our class-enemies are ruthless but the men who produce the wealth will take back what is theirs.'

Avoiding her gaze he poses the question tormenting him. 'Do you think there was ever any chance of success?'

'It's impossible to say, revolutionaries can't indulge in prophesy. If we only took action when we were certain of success we'd never get out of bed. The Paris Commune ended in terrible defeat and in Munich workers were butchered in the streets, not just a handful but in their hundreds.'

Her confidence is infectious and Karl departs with mumbled promises to stay the course. Drifting aimlessly through inner city streets, he glances enviously at untroubled souls enjoying the conviviality of cafés and his doubts come surging back. With the evening sun piercing a band of cloud he paces restlessly around St. Stefan's Square, teasing out fragments of Ruth's speech. He cannot fault her reasoning. There are times you must throw caution to the wind and the communist can hardly be blamed for the brutality of the soldiers. He knows there will always be setbacks, what troubles him is the possibility the action could have succeeded. If the trench-hardened veterans at the back of the march had returned fire, the government soldiers might have panicked and with Bela Kuhn's troops waiting at the border it's possible they could have seized power. You don't need a prophet to know what would follow. At best they'd have been isolated and disarmed, but if they won over the mass of de-mobbed soldiers they'd be in breach of the Treaty, the French would have cause to invade, and the slaughter would start all over. The idea that this time they would be fighting for something worthwhile only makes him laugh.

He knows what he's supposed to believe: workers conditioned by centuries of exploitation can only develop class-consciousness when there's a change in material conditions. It all made sense when he was in the Grinzing barracks studiously analysing what needs to be done. Now the whole idea of *false consciousness* strikes him as nothing more than a polite way of saying workers are too stupid to understand their own suffering. He knows Ludwig would scoff at his bourgeois squeamishness, but he cannot shake the memory of the young man bleeding to death in the Hörlgasse and he's happy to admit he doesn't have the stomach for it. Violence has its own logic—it provokes further violence and instead of the liberation of mankind you get the ancient cycle of bitterness and revenge. It only makes sense if you believe the proletariat is nobler and less selfish than everyone else. The workers he's met can't begin to measure to that expectation—they're hungry and frustrated, ready to try anything to ease the misery of their daily lives.

With the scuffing of his boots dispersing into the night, the zigzag patterns on the roof of Saint Stefan's look immutable. He wants to talk to somebody but the thought of telling Mother how he feels shames him. He climbs stairs and knocks softly on Dora's bedroom door. She wakes at the sound and lights a bedside candle. Karl sits on the edge of the bed gazing at his sister's pale complexion illuminated by a flickering light.

'I saw a man die,' he says, 'shot dead in the street… just days ago… in the Hörlgasse.'

Unperturbed, Dora listens calmly to her brother's confession and responds matter-of-factly. 'A lot of people have died, at the field hospital there were packs of wild dogs that came at night to dig up the fresh graves behind our tent. We'd hear them fighting off the swarms of rats.'

Karl feels like a child pretending to be a man. He apologises for disturbing her sleep and in a stupor retreats to his bedroom.

At the breakfast table he feels like a tourist observing the strange habits of people in a foreign land. Father mutters dire predictions about the government's reckless policy of printing money while Mother's unwavering cheerfulness is a grotesque mask that cannot conceal her frayed nerves. Hanya's dance classes give her an obscene vitality at odds with the rest of the family. She wolfs her food and bolts for the door nattering about rehearsals. Watching Dora chewing slowly, without drawing nourishment from her food, Karl is drawn to her sadness. In their late-night conversation he glimpsed the abyss, the unfathomable cruelty that mocks his naïve belief in a socialist utopia. Her silence testifies to the ugliness lurking beneath the facade of everyday existence and he longs to enter her solitary world, to grasp the self-sufficiency that sets her apart from the deluded masses. When Dora leaves for the hospital he ignores Mother's enquiry about his studies and returns to his bedroom.

13

Hanya likes to imagine the basement studio beneath the Konzerthaus is a sacred cave and the dance troupe are Nibelung forging a strange new device without fully understanding its purpose. With opening night closing in, free-spirited improvisation has given way to a more demanding regime. The syncopated piano piece accompanying the dance is overlaid with harsh percussion made by striking sheet metal with a mallet and as the music is played over and over, Frau Gerty urges the girls to let the rhythm enter their subconscious so they will respond without thought or hesitation.

The rehearsal regime makes it difficult to spend time with Max, but she is certain they are moving towards a union of souls regardless of their parents views. On Friday evening's when Max must attend his Sabbath duties, Hanya has taken to visiting Mother's sister Zipporah who is intrigued and more than a little suspicious about her niece's sudden interest in the customs of her ancestors. She shrewdly suspects a boy is involved and with discreet inquiries learns Hanya is smitten with the highly regarded eldest son of Reb Elstein. Zipporah views the budding romance as a blessing and warmly welcomes her niece into the intimacy of their crowded third floor apartment in Leopoldstadt. Her younger cousins look up to their sophisticated visitor as if she were a fairytale princess and no matter how many times Hanya offers, her aunt will not allow her to help with housework. Finding a perch amid the chaotic activity, she observes the business of preparing and clearing meals, accompanied by lively conversation and shrieks of laughter. Tasks are assigned by an unseen authority and no one crosses the boundaries of their delegated roles. She has given up trying to keep track of her cousins, realising with trepidation her Aunt must have given birth every year from a young age. On warm evenings the bustling vitality spills onto the street where children spin tops and whirl skipping ropes while knots of men engage in lively debate in harsh accents.

With a fondness for salacious gossip, Zipporah eagerly informs Hanya about the numerous transgressions of unknown relatives. Though she exercises discretion when speaking of Hanya's parents it is obvious Mother's marriage has caused dismay. Her Father's position with the Municipal Council commands the greatest respect, but it is clear Zipporah holds him responsible for her sister's disgraceful neglect of family obligations. She never misses an opportunity to express bewilderment as to why anyone would knowingly choose to turn from the beauty of the Torah. Such madness can only be the work of the Evil One, as was most certainly the case with her neighbour's daughter, an intelligent well-schooled young woman, who only the other day was caught washing butter plates and meat plates in the same bowl.

Taking her place on a bench with elbows and knees rubbing against her cousins' coarse dresses Hanya absorbs the solemnity of a Sabbath meal. At the head of the table Uncle Martin shakes off the weary, obsequious demeanour of a street peddler and assumes the gracious authority of an aristocrat. Around the table silence reigns as he intones a blessing in a language Hanya cannot understand. As twilight closes in, her cousins, fluent in German, Hebrew and Yiddish, join the plaintive melody of a psalm that might have been heard in the court of King David. The simple fare is served with the clattering of cutlery and the warmth of light-hearted conversation. Soup, potatoes, black bread and fried fish served cold, its flesh firm and moist beneath crisply browned skin. Uncle Martin hints at his knowledge of Hanya's secret liaison and confidently proclaims, 'The light of a Jewish home will guide you back to your people as surely as the exile of the *Shekinah* will end when we live in obedience to the Torah.'

The plates are cleared and the cousins giggle at Hanya's confusion when she is presented with a bowl of water to wash her hands. A pair of cushions are delivered to Uncle Martin and placed behind his shoulders. He tilts back his head and slumps in his chair, his worry-creased face rejuvenated by a foretaste of the leisure he will enjoy in the golden chairs of paradise. Hanya is attracted and repelled by this alien world, as if a centrifugal force draws her in and flings her away.

At home she is mortified to learn Zipporah has met with Mother and discussed every detail of the impending marriage from the appropriate length of the courtship to the correct method of kneading pastries for the wedding banquet. In her embarrassment Hanya insists they are just good friends and silently resolves to persuade Max to flee with her to Berlin. Mother interprets her response as a sign the affair is a passing trifle, confident her talented daughter will find happiness in a more appropriate match. When she raises the matter with Father he groans.

'We're ill-placed to deal with the expense of a marriage.'

'I'm sure it won't come to that, Hanya is a sensible girl. I'm far more worried about Karl—he's terribly gloomy these days.'

'Letting go of illusions is always painful,' Father observes. 'He spends far too long dreaming about what ought to be—it's time he learnt to deal with the way the world is.'

Entering the music room to sit in on Max's piano practice, Mother smiles warmly and asks if they might have a word after he finishes playing. With his thoughts racing Max makes a hash of familiar pieces and finds a mirror for his anxiety in one of Berg's experimental compositions that pushes towards the extreme limits of dissonance.

Observing his nervousness as he collects the manuscript papers, Mother does her best to put him at ease. 'I'm afraid the music is quite beyond me, but your playing is marvellous—the fingering looks so difficult and you handle it effortlessly.'

Gazing at the carpet Max squeaks out his appreciation for the compliment.

'I've noticed,' Mother continues in her most reassuring voice. 'Hanya seems to have developed certain feelings towards you, and I want you to know if the feelings are reciprocated, we have absolutely no objection to seeing the relationship develop.'

In the ensuing silence Mother worries she might have struck the wrong tone. 'Of course it's none of my business and please don't tell Hanya I mentioned it—she'll be furious if she thinks I'm interfering.'

Max nods vigorously to compensate for his inability to speak.

Unaccustomed to such a one-sided conversation Frau Popper proceeds cautiously. 'I was hoping we could talk about Karl.'

Max anxiously recalls the moment Karl interrupted him smooching with Hanya on the piano stool and several fretful moments pass before it dawns on him that Frau Popper has no knowledge of the incident.

'He's fallen into a terrible bout of melancholy. Scarcely leaves his room and I'm afraid he's neglecting his studies. I thought it might help if you were able to speak with him.'

Though he doubts he will have anything useful to offer, Max readily agrees.

Sidling gingerly into the bedroom he finds Karl reading in the soft light from a window overlooking the courtyard. Books are scattered on a writing table, some open and others in stacks five or six high. The titles are unfamiliar and it's not difficult to surmise his reading bears little relation to the University curriculum. Their longstanding friendship allows them to brush aside the lingering awkwardness and they quickly fall into the relaxed small-talk of their school days. When Max enquires about the upcoming examinations Karl adopts a more belligerent tone.

'Can't see the point of it. When I was at the Grinzing barracks I started a carpentry apprenticeship, making toys for a nursery school and I'd have to say it was a lot more satisfying than the meaningless drivel you get at university.'

Max thinks of the tedious hours assisting his father's tailoring and cannot imagine Karl's overactive mind would find satisfaction in manual labour. Scanning the books on the desktop he spots a copy of *Die Presse* folded open at an article headlined, *'Photograph Proves Light from the Heavens is All Askew.'* Max has been reading everything he can lay his hands on about Eddington's expedition and casting his eye over the article he sees sentences underlined and comments scribbled in Karl's handwriting.

'What do you make of this?' he asks.

'I can't see the point of trying to prove a theory no one understands.'

'Einstein is not so difficult if you stick to the mathematics.'

Though he envies Max's ability to breeze through the thorniest calculations Karl doubts his friend actually understands the theory that has left him flummoxed.

'So you are saying you could explain it to me?'

'It would take time.'

'If time is relative that shouldn't be a problem.'

Max laughs. He's missed Karl's pugnacious spirit and secretly longed for someone prepared to listen to his hard-won understanding of the mathematical truths he regards as something akin to the revelation at Mount Sinai.

Uncertain where to start he reminds Karl of what they learnt about electromagnetism at the gymnasium—how Maxwell's Equations and Faraday's experiments led to the invention of wireless telegraphs.

Karl cuts him off. 'That sort of science has actually proved useful to society, as far as I can tell the only benefits from Einstein's theories are minor corrections to the positioning of distant stars.'

'That's a small part; he's trying to explain recent experiments which are quite puzzling—it seems the electromagnetic waves generated by Hertz's devices don't slow down as they move through the ether and it's also been shown that particles in very rapid motion somehow increase their mass.'

Karl folds his arms as Max attempts to show how Lorentz Transformations account for the increase in mass for bodies in motion. Scribbling an equation on a scrap of paper he demonstrates how measurements of identical lengths on moving bodies will vary if two bodies move in relation to each other.

'So you get these discrepancies if you are dealing with measurements made simultaneously on bodies in motion, but everything falls into place if you stop treating space and time as if they were separate entities.'

At this point Karl's simmering frustration boils over. 'This is why I can't take theoretical physics seriously. You're talking about abstract concepts that have nothing to do with the way we actually experience the world. Space and time are two different things and they are certainly not dependent on the observer. It doesn't matter whether you are a South Seas Islander or a student of physics at Vienna University—the sun still sets when it's supposed to and a solid object is always going to be different from a line.'

Max listens patiently as Karl holds forth on how the whole basis of scientific enquiry is threatened by Einstein undermining the validity of objective observation. Unable to match his friend's prowess as a debater Max realises analogies he's gleaned from Eddington about travel in imaginary spacecraft are not going to cut the mustard for such a skeptical antagonist. He suggests they should meet on Sunday afternoon.

'We could take one of the trails at Nussdorf and I'll bring a copy of what Eddington wrote about his expedition.'

Invigorated by the argument Karl feels certain he will be able to point out the absurdities of the fashionable theory as soon as he has a better grasp of the mathematics.

14

Arriving at Burggaße Bahnhof, Karl finds Max studying the schedules and though their train is not due for fifteen minutes, he shepherds Karl to the far end of the platform. With the express train to Linz approaching Max tells him to listen carefully to the whistle. As the train approaches they hear a high-pitched blast of the horn abruptly dropping in tone as the express rumbles past. Max claims the express train passengers would not have heard any change in the tone of the whistle and later, when they are riding their train, he lowers the window as they cross a street in Döbling. As predicted they hear the whistle as a continuous note without variation in tone or pitch.

'So the whistle is an unchanging sound for the passengers on the train but everyone standing in the street hears a shift in tone as the train races past—and this would be confirmed if you had two mechanical recording devices, one on the train and one on the street.'

Karl remains skeptical. 'That's hardly a reason for dismissing the possibility of objective observations.'

'But that's not what Einstein is saying—he is trying to show that if you want to make accurate observations and measurements you have to account for the circumstances of observers moving in relation to the events they are observing—for astronomical observations this is crucial because what we see and when we see it is always effected by the motion of our planet.'

As Karl sinks into silent reflection Max tells him they will pass the next station without stopping.

'So let's imagine at the exact moment we pass the station, somewhere in the distance behind us two clouds collide creating a burst of thunder and lightning. We'll know when this occurs either when we see the lightening or hear the thunder but both ways of knowing will occur at different times for the people standing at the station and for the people on the moving train. When we see the lightening, it will already have been seen by the people at the station and from their point of view, the people on the train will experience the lightening at some time in the future. If the clock at the train station and the watch in your pocket were synchronised to tell exactly the same time, each time-piece would show the lightening burst occurring at a different time—and you cannot say one is correct and the other incorrect.'

With Karl raising his eyebrows, Max concedes the time differences will be miniscule due to the slow speed of the train and the small distances involved, but the differences are enormous when you consider how earth and all the other planets are constantly hurtling through space and time.

'We have to stop thinking that events occur simultaneously for observers in different locations. What is past for one will be future for the other and vice versa. Understanding this phenomenon made it possible to calculate the speed of light: Astronomers studying Jupiter's moons could accurately predict when the moons would be eclipsed by their planet. But when they made actual observations, the eclipses were always a few minutes earlier or later than predicted. They quickly realised the time it takes for light to travel from Jupiter to Earth would vary as Jupiter's orbit took it closer or further away from earth, and by assigning a value to the speed of light they could precisely predict when the eclipses of Jupiter's moons would become visible on Earth.'

Sensing Karl's defences are down Max asks him to engage in another thought experiment. 'If I were to drop a marble from the ceiling of this carriage, at the exact centre point between the front and the back—will it land at the centre point of the floor?'

Karl is unprepared to risk answering and Max assures him that as long as the train is moving at a constant speed the marble will behave as if the train was stationary and fall directly onto the centre-point of the floor. This means the marble would fall in a perfectly perpendicular line for observers within the carriage but observers standing outside the train will also see the movement of the carriage, so for them the marble would curve slightly away from the perpendicular. A similar effect would occur for observers on the train if the brakes were applied at the exact moment the marble dropped. The change in the speed of the carriage would cause the marble to deviate from the perpendicular and this curve would be proportional to the change in the velocity of the train.

Alighting at Kahlenberg Bahnhof, Karl feels relieved to have his feet back on firm ground. Standing on the platform, he looks back to the city, relieved to find everything in its proper place. On the train with his mind racing, a flight of fancy had him imagining a railway line following the circumference of the earth. By Max's logic if a train ran in a westerly direction at the same speed as the earth's rotation, the sun would never set and the passengers would live in a world of perpetual sunlight. Rummaging in his rucksack Karl finds a cheese he slices with his pen-knife. While Max presses on with his exposition, his instinctive skepticism is overcome by excitement at seeing the scattered pieces of a puzzle coalesce into a logical pattern. He thinks of Meno's slave and imagines he can follow the explanation because Max is pointing towards a truth he has always known. Circling above Nussdorf the boys gaze at the bright green vine leaves soaking up the sun's rays. Along the hiking path trees have been felled for fuel but the new growth is abundant and as they move to higher ground the slender grandeur of the beech asserts itself. Karl begins to feel a working understanding of the theory is within his grasp. One thing is clear: The editorials lambasting Einstein for giving the observer sovereignty over what is observed are missing the point. With embarrassment he realises those who denounce Einstein have failed to comprehend what he is saying. Exhilarated by the prospect of understanding something so widely misunderstood he nourishes his ambition with an image of a mountaineer doggedly ascending to an elevated realm where a fortunate few are rewarded with a clearer view of the world.

Buoyed by anticipation, Karl strains to hold the rapidly accumulating information and as Max turns to Einstein's way of explaining gravity he fears a moments inattention will make everything fall apart.

'Newton's breakthrough in understanding gravity came from Galileo's discovery that in a perfect vacuum a feather would fall just as fast as a cannon-ball. By applying this principle to astronomy Newton realised a small comet approaching the sun would accelerate towards the sun at the same rate as a large planet in the same vicinity and he showed the gravitational attraction between two bodies is proportional to the product of their masses. His calculations gave us very accurate descriptions of the way planets move but his method assumes it's possible to know the distances between moving bodies at a particular point in time. Einstein showed you can't actually do this if you account for the movement of the observer. Under his system, we no longer think of gravity as an attractive force—it's just how a moving body responds to the conditions at a point in space and time. When astronomers compared the two systems they found Einstein's calculations slightly more accurate in predicting the point at which Mercury's orbit reaches its perihelion. But the variations are so small they could not be regarded as proof and this is why Eddington's photographs are so important.'

Karl pauses, gazing pensively at the sky as Max brings his exposition to a triumphal conclusion. 'On the 29th of May 1919 the matter was put to rest because the shadow of a solar eclipse passing over an island off the coast of Africa made it possible to see the light from a distant constellation that can normally only be seen at night. When you compare the photographs taken at night with those taken during the eclipse, you can see the light rays are slightly bent as they travel past the sun.'

'So if the photographs hadn't shown the bending of the light, Einstein's theory would have been kaput?'

'Exactly.' Max can scarcely conceal his excitement. 'The variation in the photographs matched Einstein's prediction and now we know for certain the light from the stars is gently turned by the curvature of space and time.'

As they travel back to the Bauernmarkt, Karl takes on the wild-eyed fervour of an evangelist. He is no longer asking questions but looks to Max to affirm feverish speculations on how the logic of cause and effect must be reconstituted to account for the impossibility of events occurring simultaneously. Max smiles and tries to direct him back to the mathematics. He points out that numbers are better than words if you want to understand how the universe works. His only philosophical speculation is to observe how strange it is that the days of creation are numbered—even stranger that there are four prime numbers within the seven days.

Mother greets them on the stairs and insists Max must stay for dinner. She was so pleased to hear they were hiking she spent the morning scouring markets and somehow obtained a whole chicken. Rubbing paprika into the flesh she simmered it with onions until the meat falls off the bones. There is a generous helping of spätzle to soak the fragrant yellow sauce and while Max enjoys the feast Karl enthusiastically takes up the cause of answering Einstein's critics. Mother is delighted to see he has regained his familiar belligerence, but Hanya is infuriated at the way he monopolises the conversation. She cannot get a word out of Max and when she stretches out her foot to gently rub his calf he does not respond. As soon as the meal is finished he apologises he must return home. Hanya follows him downstairs and presents him with a ticket to the opening night of Frau Gerty's season, now just over a week away.

With night closing in, Karl makes himself comfortable beside the reading lamp in father's library. Max left him a lengthy journal article in which Eddington explains the significance of Einstein's theories and he works through the dense text line by line, jotting notes in an old exercise book. He senses his mind expanding to accommodate the network of interlocking concepts and on closing the journal is filled with pride at his accomplishment. He imagines the carpenters at the workshop in Grinzing barracks might feel the same way when the carefully shaped pieces of a joint slot together in a perfect fit. Unable to sleep he takes to the streets, striding buoyantly past rows of silent apartments. There is a faint grey softening the sky in the east and the patterns of the constellations look sublime. He thinks of the masses laying in their beds, snoring and farting behind the brick walls of their apartments and recalls Ruth's certainty that the inevitable triumph of the proletariat has been proven by scientific method. Against the rigour of Einstein's theory and the physical proof of Eddington's photographs, her belief in the iron laws of history seems as childish as wishing upon a star.

15

The dancers emerging from the studio beneath the Konzerthaus adhere to each other like strands of knotted fibre as they traipse through the Stadtpark, radiating good health and attracting envious stares from grim-faced workers. On fine days they lunch on the lawn in front of the band rotunda, luxuriating in the sunshine before returning to the gloom of the basement studio. In the evenings they converge on the Café Herrenhof where Frau Gerty and her associates occupy a large marble table set against the bay window. Anxiety about inflation has given way to recklessness and Hanya thinks nothing of handing over bundles of freshly printed notes in exchange for a gritty coffee substitute. Publishers, poets and writers vie for places within Frau Gerty's circle and their scintillating conversation captivates the room. Listening to the impassioned disputes, Hanya favours the publisher Basil Schoff whose heartfelt declarations about artists restoring the damaged soul of the nation are mocked by Dr. Jorg, an elegant nihilist who views the arts as nothing more than a gaudy parade of petit-bourgeois illusions.

From time to time the combatants visit the dancers' table like knights seeking a benediction from their ladies. The older girls, adept at the art of flirtation, welcome these visitations, but when Dr. Jorg approaches and casts his piercing gaze over Hanya's blushing face, she turns her eyes to the tabletop.

'Such eyes should never be downcast,' he utters in a mellifluous voice, drawing hoots and whistles from the other dancers. Tongue-tied and frozen, Hanya fears she will be exposed as a charlatan who has no place among such charmed company. With shrieks of laughter and lewd whispers rising around her, she abruptly pushes back her chair, knocking over a coffee cup as she bolts for the door. Therese rolls her eyes and follows. Laying a firm hand on Hanya's shoulder she offers a reassuring smile.

'I need some fresh air,' Hanya squeaks as she lurches into the vortex of revolving glass. Therese follows, a tilt of her head arresting Hanya's flight. Lingering at an advertising kiosk Therese lights cigarettes, her insouciance setting Hanya at ease.

'Don't worry about Jorg, he can be a terrible bully when he has an audience but away from the crowd he's the perfect gentleman.'

Inhaling softly Hanya regains composure and Therese guides her back to the table, whispering about how Jorg has rebuffed advances from most of the girls in the troupe. Hanya stiffens as the Doctor's dark eyes bore into the side of her face. Noticing her discomfort, Therese extends the protective wing of an elder sister and invites Hanya to accompany her home. Rising languidly she leads her out of the café, matching Jorg's glare and swaying her hips as she sashays past his table.

Pressed in a crowded tram Hanya searches for a way to express her gratitude to the girl she had secretly looked down on due to the sloppiness of her dance technique. Desperate to learn the secret of Therese's easygoing confidence, she clings to her as they alight in the Vorstadt. The coarseness of the neighbourhood makes her uncomfortable and her anxiety rises as they step into the narrow corridor of an apartment block where children toss knuckle-bones on a bare wooden floor. Climbing stairs they enter a cramped, dishevelled apartment and glancing around the dimly lit room Hanya catches the expressionless eyes of an emaciated woman hunched on the edge of an unmade bed. Two young girls work at a seamstress' bench, one bent over a sewing machine while the other guides a bulky mass of linen to the whirring needle. Therese brusquely introduces her family and guides Hanya into an adjoining room. The private chamber is like another world and Hanya suppresses a gasp as she takes in the velvet bed-covering and a dressing table with gaudy perfume bottles stacked in front of the mirror; it dawns on her, Therese is a *süsse mädel.*

With Hanya hovering awkwardly by the dressing table, Therese plonks herself on the bed, reclining on the satin cushions.

'You can bring him here,' she murmurs, lips curling into a mischievous smile.

Determined not to show her naivety, Hanya swallows the shock and assumes a nonchalant air. 'You mean Jorg?'

'He's obviously obsessed with you.'

Despite her efforts, a nervous giggling reveals Hanya's inner turmoil. 'I'm afraid he's going to be disappointed—my heart is taken.'

'Follow your heart.' Therese chuckles. 'Max is a sweet boy and he will never hurt you. But Doctor Jorg, oh-la-la, you'd be the envy of every girl in the troupe.'

Aware she's out of her depth, Hanya is surprised how easy it is to play along. 'I don't know what they see in him.'

'You're right—he would only break your heart.'

Therese directs Hanya to sit at the dressing table and peers critically into the lacquer framed mirror. She playfully holds one of Hanya's plaits. 'It's time we did something about this.'

Hanya needs little persuasion. Apart from little Hilde with her gorgeous blonde curls, she is the only member of the troupe whose hair is not cut in a stylish bob. Therese works with nimble expertise and says she can get a good price for the hair from a wig-maker who lives in the building. She models the cut on a newspaper photograph of a cabaret singer from Berlin and the girls slip into the relaxed intimacy Hanya once enjoyed with her own sister.

She strides home and Mother smiles indulgently at the new hairstyle, quietly delighted at least one of her children appears happy. In the privacy of her bedroom Hanya supposes she should be flattered by Jorg's advances but feels certain he sees her as nothing more than an amusing trifle. Haunted by the memory of his glaring eyes she's gripped by a strange foreboding, imagining an obscure force might rise up and compel her to succumb. To banish the thought, she decides to take up Aunt Zipporah's invitation to attend the synagogue.

Walking to Leopoldstadt she slyly catches her reflection in the shop windows. A modern young woman looks back—stylish and self-assured, no hint of the emotions swirling beneath the gleaming rayon of her sleek blue tunic. Across the canal she notices Hebrew lettering above shop doors and in Tempelgasse knots of men with unkempt beards and wide-brimmed black hats scowl at her. She is relieved to hear excited shrieks from her young cousins, grooming one another as they assemble haphazardly outside their apartment block. Zipporah makes no attempt to hide her disapproval of her niece's appearance and Hanya declines the offer of a wig, bristling as her Aunt pulls her cloche low over her forehead to hide her short hair. If she is to find a place within the world of her ancestors, she is determined it will be on her own terms. Walking hand-in-hand with her cousins, she has no desire to blend with the dark throng filing into the ornate temple.

From a wooden bench in the women's balcony she surveys the heavy shawls and dark headscarves of women who look like they have recently arrived from the East. Some have babies slung on their backs like peasants and the children wear a hodgepodge of threadbare hand-me-downs. She's pleased to spot a few smartly dressed women with silk scarves and fashionable cloches dotted among the congregation. Turning to the lower floor she searches for Max, but the men's faces are obscured by a sea of wide-brimmed hats and felt caps. Zipporah discreetly points out Max's father sitting with the elders alongside the ark.

'If everyone knew as much Torah as him,' she whispers, 'the Messiah would soon be here.'

Her gaze drifts to the Oriental crenelations on the eastern wall, thrown into sharp relief by flickering candle-light. In response to the cantor's call, a low rumble of Hebrew verses echoes off the high vaulted ceiling. Detached and curious Hanya lets the melancholy sound wash over her, attracted by the harmony of untutored voices rising and falling in unison. The Torah scroll is drawn from the ark and unfurled on a heavy wooden table. Monotonous reading in an unknown tongue lulls her into a trance and she contemplates the quivering pattern of intersecting triangles woven into the silk of the ark curtain. When a scholarly looking gentleman peers through the heavy lenses of his spectacles and addresses the assembly in German she perks up. He paints a vivid picture of the oxen from the Book of Samuel, who though unguided and free to roam, returned the Ark to the scattered people of the Covenant. He claims the beasts' instinctive obedience speaks of a wisdom deeper than human reason.

As the sermon concludes Zipporah's eldest daughter leans towards Hanya and whispers in her ear, 'Don't be alarmed if there is some wailing, it's the Ninth of Av and we're supposed to remember the destruction of Jerusalem. It will be much better next week, it's a feast day and there'll be dancing and special cakes.'

Nodding, Hanya hears the congregation responding to the rabbi's exhortations with murmurs and occasional cries of anguish. As the cantor leads a forlorn chant everyone rises and Hanya is surrounded by bodies rhythmically rocking. She recognises the women are unconsciously responding to the internal rhythm Frau Gerty has been trying to draw out of her dancers. Attuning her body to the tempo of the chant, she joins the women, no longer an observer, swaying in unison with the mass of bodies, sharing the burden of sorrow her people have endured. Her communion is short lived. High pitched wailing assails her ears and the peasant women in front of her shake, raising arms in supplication and pounding their breasts. Hanya watches aghast as the frenzy builds to a crescendo before subsiding into a low rumble of moaning. All around heads are bowed in resignation, lips trembling with gabbled whispers. The air is thick with perspiration mingling with the musty smells carried by unwashed clothing.

In her isolation Hanya sees a broken people stubbornly clinging to primitive rituals, blindly following the path they were born into.

The women spill out of the synagogue, heads bent in silence as the late morning sunshine casts dark shadows across their faces. A hubbub rises as the women exchange gossip. Hanya stands within a cluster of her cousins watching her Aunt move purposefully through the crowd, pausing every two or three steps to press cheeks. Her position in front of the huge doors offers a clear view of the men filing out of the synagogue and gathering on the crowded pavement. She catches sight of Max who throws an embarrassed smile in her direction before turning towards his companions. There is no contact between the sexes and while the women enjoy idle conversation the young men have a few minutes of unsupervised time before they are summoned into a side room for Torah study. Max shyly steals a glance at Hanya as he disappears back into the synagogue. He has learnt Zipporah is working on his behalf in a carefully strategised campaign to bring about their union. Beginning with his most distant relatives she is singing Hanya's praises while methodically moving closer and closer to his immediate family. She earnestly describes the devotion awoken in her niece's heart even though her parents shamefully neglected to instruct her in the Law. The sermon about the oxen returning the Ark to Israel struck Zipporah as prophetic, confirming the righteousness of her cause. With boundless optimism she believes Hanya's marriage, if properly managed, will lead her family back to their rightful place within the community. Her brother-in-law's disgraceful apostasy still arouses hostility but after the suffering of the war years she senses a willingness to forgive.

Hanya remains oblivious. Everything about the community strikes her as restrictive and depressing when set against the thrilling new world of Frau Gerty's dance troupe. She sets her mind on elopement to Berlin where she is certain Max's talent will be recognised in the grandest concert halls. Politely declining her aunt's injunction to join the family meal, Hanya explains she must hurry away to her dance rehearsal.

Zipporah bustles her niece from the synagogue and as soon as they are out of ear-shot launches a furious interrogation. 'You must end this nonsense immediately, Max's father is an elder, a holy man, we cannot possibly expose him to such a scandal.'

'It's a perfectly respectable dance troupe, it's artistic—but in the modern style.'

'Modern style! Out of the question—your father's apostasy makes the marriage hard enough, but dancing!'

'I've never said anything about marriage,' Hanya interrupts.

It dawns on Zipporah that she is face-to-face with the modern woman the Rabbi has warned against in so many impassioned sermons. Breathing through her nose she suppresses the urge to slap the face so brazenly staring back at her.

'You can't be blamed for your upbringing.' She sighs, silently cursing her sister for teaching the girl to accept the blasphemous debauchery of this pig-eating nation.

'It's all right Aunty, I can look after my own affairs.'

Zipporah secures a promise that there will be no mention of dancing and sends Hanya on her way, fervently praying the silly girl will come to her senses once the marriage is solemnised and she is blessed with the yoke of motherhood. Hanya worries she might have disclosed too much to her interfering Aunt and resolves to carry out her plans in secrecy. She knows she can never belong in such a backward world and in a moment of lucidity understands her task is to free Max from the bleak prison of family obligations.

16

Stepping onto the bare stage of the Konzerthaus, Hanya gazes at the empty auditorium, the thrill of anticipation subsumed by a punishing schedule of rehearsals, costume fittings and interminable sessions with dancers holding their formations while theatre technicians scale ladders and position the arc lights. Frau Gerty frets about the smallest details, ruthlessly expunging anything artificial or dainty. The whirlwind of preparations races past and Hanya finds herself striving to calm her nerves as she waits behind the velvet curtain of the Konzerthaus' French Hall. She fears her body looks gangly alongside the athletic physiques of the older girls, looking composed and self-assured in short silk pants and brightly patterned blouses. The house-lights dim and the chattering voices in the auditorium subside. As the curtain parts, metallic percussion triggers erratic gestures flowing in a chain-reaction from one dancer to another, until the diagonal line of bodies jerk and quake with the restless energy of an industrial machine. Frau Gerty enters as a factory worker with movements both graceful and clumsy. Her jaunty gait recalls Charlie Chaplain and chuckles of recognition resound out of the darkness of the auditorium. With limbs interwoven dancers shudder in unison as if a giant machine is shifting its gears. Aware of nothing other than the motion of her body, Hanya exhales smoothly, muscles taut, limbs attuned to the pounding percussion.

In his apartment in Leopoldstadt, Max sits at the table squirming. A hand in his trouser pocket fingers a paper ticket promising admittance to the Konzerthaus Hall for a performance by the *Bodenwieser Tanzgruppe*. Every impulse urges him to run out of the dismal candle-lit room, but the Sabbath meal that should have finished an hour ago has been prolonged by the presence of a Sabbath guest—a schnorrer who lives alone in an attic room atop the building. Father met him on the stairs and brought him to the table to fulfil the duty of hospitality on the blessed night when servant and master sit as equals. The old man is intimately familiar with *The Book of Splendor* and relishes the opportunity to dispute with Reb Elstein on matters close to his heart. While Max racks his brains for an acceptable way of excusing himself, the age-ravaged schnorrer holds forth on the terrible power of the fifth *sefirot*, spewing arcane references to explain why a time of stern judgment must be endured before the right hand of the Holy-One-Blessed-Be-He will be raised in mercy.

A shrill steam-whistle blasts through the auditorium and the dancers shunt into a grotesque tableau, jutting elbows and knees silhouetted against the searing illumination of the footlights. Holding her position in the frieze, Hanya becomes aware of the audience beyond the line of darkness at the edge of the stage. She hears gasps as Frau Gerty performs a lavishly sensual solo; with a voluptuously elongated yawn she shakes off the influence of the machine and takes on the spontaneity of a child, throwing herself into the joyful pursuit of leisure. Her reverie is arrested as a second blast from the whistle awakens the line of dancers, drawing her back to the regimented world of mechanised labour. The transition is handled with exquisite subtlety as defiant remnants from her fleeting freedom are inexorably crushed by the relentless rhythm of the machine.

In the musty dampness of the upper-story landing Max holds a lamp for the schnorrer who searches the recesses of his overcoat for the key to his attic room. In his impatience Max wonders why anyone would bother to lock such a mean abode. The old man had nodded off, head tilting perilously forward as a longwinded speech surrendered to the need for sleep and Father instructed Max to accompany their guest to his room. As soon as he receives the old man's croaking benediction Max flies downstairs, his heart set on the Konzerthaus. Hoping he might slip into the back of the auditorium before the performance finishes, he bursts into the wide promenade of the Stadtpark. The moment the Konzerthaus comes into sight his heart sinks. Smartly dressed couples emerge leisurely from the French Hall, congregating on the steps. Max lurks in the shadows ashamed of how shabbily he is dressed. His threadbare jacket and scuff-marked boots would stick out in such refined company. The splendidly attired theatre patrons remind him how gay the city was before the war and he convinces himself there was a benign providence at work in the schnorrer's interminable orations. Wincing at his foolish hopes of entering her world, he wants to flee but recalling the sweetness of Hanya's face as she pressed the ticket into his hand he feels obliged to at least offer an apology.

In the cramped intimacy of the dressing room the memory of thunderous applause filling the auditorium flows through Hanya's body like a narcotic. Peals of laughter accompany every fragment of conversation and the bubbling exuberance surges to a crescendo when a gaggle of Frau Gerty's admirers burst into the room carrying flowers and champagne. Corks bounce off the low ceiling setting off high-pitched shrieks as girls rummage for glasses and coffee cups to catch the foaming liquid.

Basil raises his glass and shouts above the hubbub. 'To the eternal slenderness of youth!'

Joining the raucous cheering and clinking of glasses Hanya turns to find Jorg's face inches from hers. He tilts his glass, uttering a single word, 'Glorious.'

Before she can respond he withdraws with an elegant bow and Therese winks suggestively. Basil announces all must repair to Universitätsstraße for a reception at Frau Gerty's apartment. Hanya is shocked to see girls pulling off their costumes and changing into evening dresses without regard for the gentlemen slouching at the door and perching on the dressing tables. She grabs her bag and pulls Therese to the adjacent toilet. While teasing Hanya for her modesty, Therese pays careful attention to their grooming, expertly applying bright lip-colour and a dusting of powder to enhance Hanya's glowing complexion. Looking poised and elegant they merge into the vivacious crowd in the foyer. Mother is overjoyed to see how Hanya has grown into such a sophisticated young woman and even Father seems quietly chuffed. After securing assurances Therese will accompany their daughter home, Hanya's parents depart. Frau Gerty and her retinue sweep through the foyer with Hanya and Therese excitedly following. As they approach the heavy glass doors Jorg stealthily insinuates himself between the two girls and wraps an arm around each of them.

'There is an unlawful spirit abroad.' He chuckles.

Breaking noisily onto the portico, Hanya catches sight of a forlorn figure hovering awkwardly on the street below. She shakes off Jorg's embrace and scuttles down the steps only to find Max will not look her in the face.

'I'm terribly sorry, he mutters, grimly staring at the pavement. 'I couldn't get away from our Sabbath meal.'

'What a pity.' In the ensuing silence Hanya is gripped by the urgency of taking Max from the stifling influence of his family. 'You must join us for the reception,' she declares with an intensity that only heightens Max's inadequacy.

'I'm sorry but I can't.'

'You must, just for a little while—it will be lovely.'

Shuffling away Max glances over his shoulder. 'I'm sorry, I can't, I just can't.'

There is no response to her plaintive attempt to call him back and Hanya does her best to conceal her embarrassment. Therese turns her in the direction of Frau Gerty's party, happily cavorting ahead in the half-deserted street. Silently observing, Jorg lights a cigar and follows a few paces behind. Therese's cheerful banter revives some of Hanya's wilted enthusiasm and once they reach the apartment the effect of the hastily gulped champagne has pushed the image of Max's woeful grimace to a remote corner of her mind.

Delighting in the heightened perception that comes in the earliest stages of intoxication, Hanya is over-awed by the tastefulness of the entrance hall. On a gracefully proportioned commode, a rotund porcelain Buddha sits alongside a crystal vase holding trumpet lilies and a delicate spray of honey-suckle buds. The girls instinctively gravitate to the edge of the room, hovering in front of a painting in the modern style showing a strikingly beautiful woman dissolving into a sumptuous cascade of oriental motifs. An attentive waiter delivers champagne flutes and though the room is filled with distinguished guests, Frau Gerty leaves her circle and crosses to greet them. With disarming sincerity she compliments their performances and thanks them for their dedication during rehearsals. Unaccustomed to hearing their taskmaster speaking so kindly Hanya does not notice Jorg has deftly inveigled himself into the conversation.

'You do realise this gazelle has subverted your intention. You wish to express the dehumanising effect of the machine but in these girls the energy of youth is irrepressible and by constraining their movements you only enhance the impression of vitality.'

Frau Gerty smiles reassuringly at the girls, calmly turning to face Jorg's impudently staring eyes. 'Your interpretation is coloured by your own preconceptions, the machine can only reflect the *daemon* of its creator.'

'I'm glad you've not succumbed to the sentimentality of the Parisian school with their ridiculous deification of guitar players.' Jorg inclines his head towards Hanya, 'The women of today care nothing for folk music or pastoral reveries—their natural habitat is the street-car and the skyscraper. Would you not agree?'

Emboldened by the champagne Hanya blurts what she can remember from Frau Gerty's talks about the spirit of the times. To her surprise Jorg responds without the slightest condescension.

Hanya notices Therese is not intimidated by the intellectual tone of the conversation and makes no attempt to conceal her lowly origins. She disarms any attempt at seriousness with peals of throaty laughter and allows her body to respond freely to the jerky rhythms emanating from the gramophone. Leading Hanya through elegantly appointed rooms she hungrily helps herself to the supper and samples the perfume she finds on a dressing table in the bathroom. Jorg refrains from monopolising Hanya's attention, dispensing flattery and provocation in equal measure. Moments of dangerous proximity are followed by alluring withdrawals and his touch, alighting on her shoulder or sliding tenderly over her hips, light and fleeting as a butterfly. Hanya responds with cool nonchalance, learnt from observing how Therese fields advances from her bevy of admirers. Jaunty ragtime tunes from the gramophone seep into Hanya's muscles making it impossible to stand still. Sharp clear notes tumble over each other as if the melody was racing to catch up with the rhythm and incomprehensible Negro vocals hover over the piano like fire from heaven. Joyous laughter, childlike and spontaneous, spills out of her like champagne surging from a freshly opened bottle. Maintaining a studied indifference to Jorg's advances she is flattered by his persistence and as if filling a scrapbook, accumulates vivid impressions: the rich silk of his oyster-neck-tie, the firmness of his jaw above a starched collar, a strong scent of tobacco mingling with something more refined and his gravelly voice flowing smoothly like water in a canal.

With the moon rising a languid yearning infects the gathering and Therese becomes more responsive to the pawing attention from a well-known publisher. She drags Hanya into the sanctuary of the toilet and bluntly asks if she intends to leave with Jorg. The question jolts Hanya out of her hazy intoxication, abruptly ending the euphoria she'd hoped would last forever.

'You don't have to,' Therese continues cheerfully. 'I can easily take you home—if that's what you want.'

Unable to face Therese's quizzical stare she glances at the mirror scarcely recognising her startled reflection, immobilised by indecision. The allure of the unknown draws her towards a threshold she feels compelled to cross and she answers firmly. 'I'll go with him.'

'Are you sure?'

Muscles in her stomach tighten as Max's mournful grimace flashes through her mind and an exhilarating wave of certainty extinguishes any thought of turning back.

'I'm sure—but you must promise never to say a word to Max.'

'Of course.'

Descending the marble staircase, Jorg offers Hanya his arm and addresses her with exaggerated courtesy, tinged with irony.

'May I have the honour of escorting you home and as the night is warm and the moon has risen perhaps we might take a stroll through the Prater?'

Hanya threads her arm into the space formed by his jutting elbow and glances at Therese who flashes a mischievous smile as she is whisked away in her publisher's cab. They walk in silence. The sharp clicking of heels mixed with the measured thud of leather shoes resonate in Hanya's mind. The swell of intoxication carries her forward, untroubled by her wickedness and amused by her daring, as if embarking on a carefully planned adventure.

Confident of his prize, Jorg walks unhurriedly. The amusement stalls are closed though lights still shine from some restaurants overlooking the Danube and they pass several other couples on the tree lined pathways. Fragmented clouds drift across the sky making the moon appear and disappear above them. When they find a clear view of the river Jorg pauses and Hanya leans into his elbow. She awaits his kiss but he merely drapes an arm over her shoulder and asks if she is cold.

'Not at all,' she replies, doing her best to conceal a nervous squeak.

Jorg opens a silver case and offers a cigarette. Afraid she might embarrass herself she inhales gently, taking care not to draw the smoke into her lungs. The aroma of strong Turkish tobacco calms her and for a moment she is content to gaze at the dimly reflected moonlight rippling on the placid surface of the river. His stillness attracts her. She knows she will never love him as she loves Max and feels certain her experiment in recklessness cannot change what is in her heart. More than anything she wants to enter the world of adults and take hold of the power that allows Therese to move among men with such self-assurance. Max would never think of such a thing before marriage, but she can see no reason to wait any longer for the experience all her friends have enjoyed.

She hops restlessly from foot to foot and as if reading her thoughts, Jorg breaks the silence, speaking in a mellow baritone. 'I won't offer the cheap poetry men like to use at times like this… I cannot promise you anything beyond what we have right now. Your beauty attracts me and I believe I could make you happy.'

Hanya wouldn't have minded a bit of poetry, but she turns towards him and simply says, 'I would like that.'

He kisses her boldly, the firm pressure of his lips opening her mouth so they taste each other's breath. Clasping her hand, he guides her towards the Great Wheel that stands in silhouette against a sky peppered with faint pin-pricks of starlight. Striding briskly down an avenue lined with the empty shells of entertainment booths, Jorg leads her off the pavement to the curved bulk of a carrousel enclosed by a heavy green tarpaulin. He unthreads a twine cord and raises a corner of the covering. Entering the dark drum they feel their way past wooden horses and the rounded form of a tin elephant. As her eyes adjust Hanya can make out the shapes of animals poised on their metal poles. Squeezing the reassuring firmness of Jorg's hand she laughs nervously, like a child creeping into a forbidden room. He pauses against a white swan and leans into her body. Their open mouths join and Hanya receives the harsh scent of tobacco from his tongue. His hands grip her hips, lifting her upwards and placing her on an upholstered seat affixed to the swan's back. She kicks off her shoes and jostles awkwardly into position, unable to suppress a giggle as she finds herself sitting astride the swan with her knees raised, feet searching for somewhere to rest. His chin presses against the back of her neck and his hands are under her dress running over the bare flesh of her thighs. She raises her arms as the hem of her chemise is lifted and smooth fabric slides over her face. With a shiver she glances down and sees her clothes falling into a bright pool of satin on the dark floor of the carrousel. She tries to turn to face him but his lips slide over her back placing delicate kisses against the ridges of her spine. His hand slips beneath the waistband of her silk drawers and she feels probing fingers inside her. Instinctively arching her back she releases a startled gasp and feels moisture between her thighs. The hand withdraws, tearing at the undergarment, the only impediment to their union. Lurching forward under the weight of his body she grasps the neck of the swan. Her thighs latch onto his hips and with ankles locking behind his back she braces against the unexpected force with which he enters her. His thrusting draws forth strange animalistic sounds and she falls into a haze of unfamiliar sensations.

In the stillness she senses a softening between her thighs. Her hands slide over the cold surface of the swan and she longs to hold him. Pushing upwards she twists her body, wrapping her legs around his waist. With her breasts pressing against the fabric of his jacket she wants to touch his flesh. Buttons pop as her hands scramble beneath his shirt, clasping his shoulders. She clings to him for as long as she dares before sensing his discomfort as he discretely adjusts his body. Easing out of her embrace he hands her a handkerchief. While she wipes herself and fumbles with her chemise he straightens his jacket and lights a cigarette. Little is said as they walk arm-in-arm towards the Bauernmarkt. Hanya feels detached with a jumble of thoughts racing inside her head. Jorg bestows a parting kiss and whispers an assurance he will contact her next week. Removing her shoes and treading lightly on the stairs she finds her bedroom without disturbing the sleeping household. Although she can hardly see anything in the darkness the familiar contours of the ornaments on her dressing table strike her as girlish and she feels a tinge of melancholy as the room she had always regarded as a sanctuary no longer feels like home.

17

Abandoning any expectation of sleep, Max gazes into the darkness, ready to try anything to end the tedium of endlessly reliving the moment he turned and walked away. He searches for mathematical patterns in the musical scores he has committed to memory, but even with his eyes wide open, an image of Hanya's face barges into his consciousness, lips parted, eyes eagerly inviting—and his ridiculous, cowardly, inexplicable retreat. Unable to stop his teeth grinding, he rises abruptly and bumps into Papa's reading table. With heavy snoring and the rasping of little Greta's congested breath penetrating the threadbare curtain around their bed, he lights the kerosene lamp, trimming the wick until a pool of light illuminates the densely packed letters of the Tanakh. The injunctions against the strange woman are playing on his mind and he cannot recall whether it is her mouth or eyes that are likened to a pit. Flicking restlessly through the pages of *Tehillim* the proverb eludes him, and he stumbles across a psalm that provides a measure of solace.

O Lord, my heart is not lifted up,
my eyes are not raised too high;
I do not occupy myself with things
too great and too marvellous for me.
But I have calmed and quieted my soul,
like a weaned child in its mother's arms;

A pre-dawn chill sends him back to bed where he soaks up the warmth from his brother's motionless body, soothingly cocooned in the blanket as it traps their heat. Sleepless hours have dissipated the whirlwind of emotion and his mind settles into a strangely gratifying emptiness. He lies on his side impassively observing the daylight trickling through the curtains, spreading a wash of muted colour over the sparsely furnished room. Mother is first to rise, tending to the stove and busying in the kitchen while father recites a hymn of praise and the little ones enjoy moments of aimless meandering before falling into the noisy business of preparing for school. Max joins the routine, emptying the piss-pot and packing his satchel. He lines up with his siblings to receive father's blessing and together they troupe downstairs to enter a new day.

In the schoolroom Hanya's memory floats before him like a pillar of cloud, mysterious, alluring and vaguely intimidating. Losing his nerve outside the Konzerthaus was humiliating but in recognising his limits he believes he has a clearer understanding of who he is. It will be a relief to turn his attention to schoolwork and though ashamed to admit it, he is better suited to mathematics than romance. Best to end it before he makes himself pathetic. He feels certain Hanya will be pleased to pursue her career without the encumbrance of a doomed affair. The prospect of returning to the music room fills him with dread but he feels obliged to make his intentions clear.

Hanya has been anticipating Max's arrival with growing anxiety and on hearing discordant tones from the piano punching through the walls, her impulse is to run to greet him. Descending the stairs she hesitates, as if waiting on the counsel of an inner voice. She wants to tell him about the Negro music she heard at Frau Gerty's party and they must talk about Berlin, where all their problems will be answered. Her indiscretion with Jorg has stirred up guilt, lightened by the hope there will be a time when she can honestly tell Max of her lapse. For now she must focus on helping him escape the crippling influence of his family.

She enters the music room impelled by her own momentum like a skater gliding into a hard turn. Max raises his eyes in acknowledgement. Standing by his side she loses track of the notation and responds urgently when a tilt of his head prompts her to turn the page. His fingers dancing nimbly over the keys awakens a sharp memory of Jorg's caresses. She refuses to see the incident as a betrayal, telling herself she has simply prepared for the time when she will give herself to him without reticence or anxiety. Though reluctant to talk Max knows certain things must be said if he is to regain any semblance of peace. When he breaks off playing Hanya nestles onto the stool, the weight of her body pressing against his shoulder.

Squirming to the edge of the seat with eyes fixed on the piano keys he addresses her in a formal tone. 'I'm so sorry I missed your performance, we had an unexpected visitor and it was impossible to get away.'

'That's quite alright. It was such a wonderful night—it would have been perfect if you were there.'

Silence falls between them as Max struggles to formulate a response out of the prepared phrases jostling to be spoken.

'It's alright,' she says.

'I've been wanting to tell you… I'm starting university next month and I won't be able to keep meeting with you.'

'Don't be ridiculous.'

'I've been thinking about it a lot and I'm sure it will be for the best.'

'What nonsense. You must come to Berlin with me. I can find work and you could—'

'It's not possible. I've enrolled at the university.'

There is something in his voice she has never heard before, a coldness that shatters her composure. 'It's your family, isn't it—'

'No it has nothing to do with them… you mustn't let me hold you back.'

With her chest convulsing Hanya buries her head in his shoulder, her cheeks wet with tears. Max knows he should put his arm around her but is struck by an overwhelming fear that if he does so he will be trapped forever. He rises abruptly.

'I'm sorry, I should have said something sooner. You have been so kind to me and I will always treasure your friendship but it can never be anything more than that—you must see it's for the best.'

As she takes in his words thoughts vanish and she strikes at the thing hurting her. 'Go then, go back to your Mummy and Daddy—if that's what makes you happy.'

Grabbing his manuscript papers Max lurches for the door. Even before he reaches the stairs he regrets it, but nothing could make him return. Panting toward Leopoldstadt he feels only regret. His meticulously constructed certainty vanishes and with a sigh enveloping his body, he knows he is running from the only thing in his life that is right.

Hanya contemplates flinging herself onto her bed and melting into the warmth of her eiderdown, but a more powerful impulse compels her to get out of the house. The red coat. A cloche pulled to conceal her eyes and a dab of powder to cover the traces of her tears. When she reaches the Herrenhof it would be impossible to discern her turmoil. Pausing before the revolving doors she peers through a mess of reflections glimpsing the familiar contours of the dance troupe gathered at their usual table. Although classes have ended, the girls hold onto the memory of their moment beneath the floodlights. There were tears when Frau Gerty announced she was taking up a position at the Burg and would have to disband the troupe. Each girl was given a small payment from the ticket receipts and though Frau Gerty apologised it was a mere token, Therese was thrilled as she calculated it would be sufficient for her fare to Berlin. She no longer talks about Berlin as if it were a glittering prize in a fairytale.

She's planned every detail and seems set on recruiting Hanya to join the adventure.

Flattered by the attention, Hanya responds excitedly. 'I used to dream of Berlin, I remember one night when I was very young, we were in the Prater and I saw a strange glow just above the horizon—I thought it was coming from the electric lights in Berlin.'

She confides the only thing holding her back is Max—she cannot abandon the forlorn hope of somehow luring him away from his family.

'Send him a postcard from the Kurfürstendamm.' Therese smiles. 'If he truly loves you he will come and if he doesn't there will be plenty to take your mind off him.'

Unable to fault her friend's logic Hanya adopts a flippant tone as Therese knowingly teases out the details of her late night liaison in the Prater. She did not expect to hear from Jorg again and is taken aback when he strides into the Herrenhof, briskly arranging for Hanya to join him for a meal. After he leaves Therese regales her with a salacious account of what she should expect. She notices a jitteriness in Hanya's laughter and shrewdly ascertains the cause of her anxiety. They take a tram to Therese's apartment in the Vorstadt where Hanya gratefully receives instruction in the arcane science of avoiding pregnancy.

At the Rebhuhn a waiter in a striped apron greets Hanya with a deferential bow, ushering her into a private room where Jorg reads the latest issue of *Die Fackel.* It's an old-fashioned place, worse for wear. Hanya notices a frayed hem on the red table-cloth and cigarette burns on the upholstery. An electric candelabra is voluptuously multiplied in the cubicle's mirror panels and a chaise longue bedecked with velvet cushions makes it impossible to mistake the room's function. Jorg points to the menu-card.

'I'm afraid most dishes are unavailable but the Norwegian sardines are quite tolerable.'

He orders a litre of dry Riesling poured icy cold from a carafe as sardines are served on crisp white bread with caper berries. After a few bracing gulps of the potent liquid Hanya overcomes her nervousness and returns his scrutinising gaze with unblinking eyes. Far from being intimidated by their impending intimacy the prospect engenders a carelessness and she is nonchalantly evasive as he peppers her with questions about her ambitions. When she mentions Berlin he raises an eyebrow.

'If you're going, go as soon as possible; the city has given itself over to a

Witches' Sabbath that cannot last. The Germans are so diligent in their debauchery they'll soon run out of steam. Hanya listens attentively as he presents his analysis of the forces giving rise to a new Babylon on the banks of the Spree. 'The sons are taking revenge on their fathers. They were brought-up believing authority infallible and their disillusionment has infected the city like a virus. You'll find grocers and bespectacled stock-brokers learning Cuban dances and gyrating to Negro music. The collapse of money did the real damage—far more effective than artillery shells. They've reverted to trade and barter like a medieval village.'

As he speaks Hanya notices his eyes, normally tinged with sadness, brighten and take on a dreamy aspect. Therese told her he served in a military hospital and she regrets she has not taken the time to read any of his articles. He questions her on her tastes and Hanya is eager to show her familiarity with the avant-garde.

'I've developed a fondness for Schönberg and Alban Berg.'

'I suppose they're onto something, but so serious, their concerts make you feel you're taking on holy orders.'

Recalling the sombre recital at the Schwarzwald School Hanya releases a peel of laughter. 'I've never understood the prohibition on applause.'

'The avant-garde can no longer match what is happening in the streets—the other day I saw a marvellous display of women's hats in the Kohlmarkt, far more engaging than any of the dismal paintings I'd viewed at the Künstlerhaus.'

Hanya feels she should be taking notes and studies the off-hand manner he handles his food. The dishes are plain but prepared with care. His sausages served in a red-wine sauce have marjoram leaves floating among mushrooms and her frankfurters are daintily dressed with French mustard and freshly grated horse-radish. She smiles at the waiter hovering briefly as if expecting a compliment. Jorg has none to offer and launches into an exposition of his theories on millinery.

'There can be no doubt the cloche is an improvement on the board-rimmed monstrosities that were all the rage before the war, but I feel ambivalent about the bob—long flowing hair is a truer expression of feminine energy.'

'It's a lot easier to manage.' Hanya tosses her head and touches the edge of the sharply scissored hair swinging just below her ears.

Jorg appears suitably entranced. 'In Berlin women wear trousers and the men are all powdered and rouged—testimony to the abject failure of the military ideal. But there's no escaping the laws of biology, with so many men slaughtered or mutilated the women have to fight over a greatly diminished supply of men—most of whom have been coarsened by the war and made feeble by defeat.'

Hanya wonders if the remark is intended as a reminder she should be grateful to receive his advances. She finds his cynicism distasteful and there is a freedom in knowing he will never win her heart. The waiter brings Turkish coffee with a bottle of apricot brandy. As he adds a drop of ice-water to settle the coffee-grounds, a momentary exchange of glances signifies they will no longer be disturbed. The transition from the table to the chaise-lounge is handled with the same easy grace that pervaded the meal and Jorg makes it clear he has no inclination to ask for anything not freely given. Hanya has enjoyed the meal and doesn't want to appear ungrateful. Her arms encircle his neck like a ribbon and she draws his face to hers. In the silence of a kiss her thoughts dissolve until there is nothing more than a feeling of belonging, not to the person with whom she is entwined, but to the secret inarticulate realm of sensation. His touch becomes firm and purposeful and with her pulse quickening she is alert and decisive, removing just enough clothing to accommodate the logic of their passion. In the convulsive moment of their union she is struck by an image of the portly waiter in his striped apron listening outside the door. She gasps, fists clutching the soft flannel of Jorg's jacket and inhales erratically through her nose, keeping her mouth firmly shut. The only sound is the rustling fabric, joined by a low groaning and sharp intakes of breath.

18

Ensconced in his favourite armchair Karl spends days without leaving Father's library. The restless energy he'd channelled into political activities is now almost entirely directed to his university studies. Having passed the Matura with distinction, he's moved ahead of friends who graduated through the Gymnasium and enjoys playing the old hand as he guides Max through rituals of university life. They avoid the student cafés and have joined a small group of undergraduates who scorn the regimentation of the hiking clubs but eagerly take to the woods whenever the weather is favourable. For weekend outings Max must secure permission to miss Sabbath school, but his father recognises the value of establishing friendships within the academic community and gives his blessing.

The group favour the steeper, more rugged trails and in place of song engage in intellectual disputes which often erupt into impassioned argument. Karl vehemently opposes intensifying class struggle and sees educational reform as the key to a much needed realignment between capital and labour. With a number of aspiring school-teachers in the group there is always robust discussion on the latest educational theory and Karl debates with relentless ferocity, even on the most minor points. One of his adversaries, studying psychology, bluntly tells him the need to dominate every argument is evidence of a repressed infantile neurosis. The mountains have a way of dissipating animosity and such jibes are taken in good humour. There is one member of the party with a unique ability to disarm Karl's fusillades. Josephine's melancholy demeanour gives the impression of shyness, but when pressed she offers succinct comments revealing her long interludes of silence are not spent daydreaming, but are given over to razor-sharp analysis of competing positions. Karl is entranced by her humble, apologetic manner, at odds with her ability to get straight to the heart of an argument. Equally impressive is her encyclopaedic knowledge of local fauna and an uncanny ability to identify species from the tiniest fragments of bird-song. When conversation is fractious she will draw attention to the unnoticed colouration of an elm tree in bloom or describe how the call of a young crested-lark differs from the sharper sound of the adult birds.

Following a suggestion from his tutor, Karl volunteers for a municipal programme providing after-school assistance to working-class students. The surly belligerence of proletarian youth is a sharp testing-ground for academic theories about awakening wonder in a child. The homework sessions are dismally unproductive and frustration at his failure to inspire interest prompts Karl to try a different approach. He tells the boys to put aside their homework and asks what they most enjoy. Persistence overcomes their reticence and one boy becomes uncharacteristically animated, boasting of his prowess in bare-knuckle fighting contests that are a popular pastime in the tenements where he lives. Karl brings boxing gloves to their next appointment. Though pugilism was the only physical training at the gymnasium for which he'd shown aptitude, Karl cannot match his pupils' vigour and feels the shuddering jolt of leather gloves stinging his face. He acquits himself well enough to earn the boys' respect and is deemed to have lost his bout by concession. In the aftermath he draws the students into a rough Socratic dialogue.

'Would you agree, that when a boxer commits to a punch or a block there is no time for deliberation or conscious decision-making?'

The premise is met with quizzical looks, but there are enough mutterings of assent for Karl to extend the enquiry. 'Can we also agree, a prize-fighter will train for a contest with a carefully thought-out regime of exercises so his body will respond without hesitation in the heat of battle?'

By applying the same logic to education he persuades them to agree to an hour of concentrated study before concluding their sessions with a supervised bout of sparring. The experiment has him arriving home with a swollen lip and bruised eye. Mother is thrown into a mild panic, listening aghast as he explains the injuries are a small price for the breakthrough with his students. She is astonished anyone would go to such lengths in the slim hope of awakening educational ambition in the city's wayward youth.

At the dinner table Father's irascible energy has given way to enervating pessimism as he watches a lifetime of toil melt under the ruinous inflation that shows no sign of abating. He finds no consolation in knowing most of his colleagues are in a worse predicament and having considered the futility of every available course seems content to work tirelessly without expectation of reward. In deference to her husband's melancholy, Mother conceals any suggestion of happiness. She detects a hint of cheerfulness in Karl's eyes when he adopts a nonchalant tone, announcing he plans to meet the family of one of his hiking companions. Mother lures him into revealing the girl is Catholic and lives with her family in Döbling, but he clams up as soon as she attempts to learn more.

Hanya spends as little time as possible at home. Most mornings she meets Therese at the Herrenhof where they chatter incessantly about Berlin. Jorg has supplied them with an address where they will find lodgings and he promises to visit once he has taken care of publishing business in Zurich. In raising the matter with her parents Hanya makes it clear she intends to carry out her plans with or without their support. Father is too weary to offer serious objection.

Though sympathetic Mother is forthright in airing her concerns. 'Couldn't you continue with your classes here? Berlin has such a terrible reputation for depravity.'

'We won't have time for any of that.' Hanya chuckles. 'Frau Gerty has stopped giving classes now she's at the Burg. She recommended the Eurythmics academy in Berlin, says it's the best school in Europe.'

Mother suppresses her suspicion about Therese's moral character and Father sardonically comments, 'The way the mark has fallen, Berlin is the only place on earth where the krone still holds some value.'

Dora shows no sign of interest in the conversation and Hanya is surprised when Karl encourages her to pursue her ambitions. She suspects it is an underhand way of saying he'll be pleased to be rid of her, but cannot doubt his sincerity as he commends her daring.

'It takes courage to give up the security of home. At the homework centre my students cling to what they know—they'd rather follow their parents into unemployment than risk doing something new.'

Overlooking the paternalistic tone, Hanya is touched he recognises the difficulty of coping without the support she used to get from Max. After their last encounter he sent Mother a note explaining his University studies left him with no time for music and she's not heard a word since. Visiting his home is out of the question and she fears if she posts a letter it would be intercepted by his parents. Karl agrees to personally deliver a farewell note and she feels confident prudishness will prevent him from opening the sealed envelope.

Little is said as she prepares to leave and Hanya offers a brusque assurance she will return before the end of the year. Her vagueness creates a foreboding and Mother chokes tears as she makes her promise to write regularly. At the station Hanya cannot find Therese and takes her seat in an empty compartment. Resting her elbow on the frame of the open window she chats to Mother, eyes darting around the platform as she frets about what she will do if Therese does not arrive. The idea of leaving without her is terrifying, but after all the preparations it would be impossible to return home. The sight of Therese tripping buoyantly down the platform accompanied by her younger sisters brings huge relief. As soon as she joins her in their compartment the whistle sounds and the girls lean out the window fizzing with excitement as they watch their loved ones diminish into the crowd milling on the platform.

Karl notices his mother clinging to Father's elbow after the train has disappeared. The image of the two of them gazing at the empty railway tracks strikes him as poignant. They look like any other bourgeois couple, neatly dressed, dignified, anonymous, but their bearing projects an impression of overwhelming sadness. Following behind as they walk home he is ashamed he never appreciated their uncomplaining endurance in the face of so many disappointments. It's so easy to scoff at the bourgeoisie, it has almost become a reflex, but their pain is as real as anybody's.

19

Max's decision to terminate practice sessions at the Popper residence was not entirely driven by embarrassment at the breakdown of his relationship with Hanya. His mathematical abilities, often mentioned in school reports, had been noted by the *Kultusgemeinde* and when the Matura exam confirmed his talents, Dr. Joseph Fleischl offered to pay his tuition expenses through the *B'nai Brith* fraternal society. A summons to meet his benefactor triggers intense nervousness, scarcely allayed by father's confident assertion. 'By accepting alms we ensure the Doctor will receive blessings greatly exceeding the value of his gift.'

Max finds Dr. Fleischl's book-lined study intimidating and wriggles in his seat while his father engages in friendly banter. He remains tongue-tied when questioned about course preferences and Dr Fleischl addresses his remarks to Reb Elstein.

'Choose subjects that will engage the boy's capabilities, one should avoid conjecture on the potential profitability of different courses. Some liberal arts papers would not go amiss. I know he has musical talent—but the commitment required to attain virtuosity could easily hamper his academic progress.'

The interview concludes with the gift of a slide-rule in a leather case and Max enters university burdened with anxiety about living up to expectations.

Though he throws himself into a demanding regime of study his concentration is frequently disrupted by a piecing awareness of his cowardly response to Hanya's advances. Tender memories are enflamed when he learns of her departure for Berlin and he winces as Karl hands him an envelope addressed in Hanya's handwriting. The letter remains unopened in his jacket pocket until late afternoon when he finds a secluded bench in the university library. Her overwrought phrases stir feelings he'd worked hard to supress and her open declaration of love makes him squirm. He wonders whether it is possible to be in love and not to act on it—surely if his love were real there would be no hesitation, just an unstoppable will to action. Her letter methodically demolishes his objections to joining her in Berlin. He could truthfully tell his parents he wishes to transfer to the University in Berlin where the mathematics faculty is regarded as the best in Europe and she earnestly assures him she will return to Judaism and do whatever it takes to win over his family. The only obstacle holding validity is his obligation to Dr. Fleischl and he clings to this even as he knows the real stumbling-block is his timidity.

Walking home the rhythm of his footsteps settles his mind and as if it were somehow implanted in his brain, he hears solemnly intoned words from the Torah scroll.

Yitz'chak took Rivkah, and she became his wife, and he loved her.

Marvelling at the simplicity of the verse his imagination loosens a feeling of weightlessness, like a paper boat flowing with the current of a canal. *He took her, she became his wife, he loved her.* He sees himself seated on a train with the city flashing by and in an instant a flood of anxiety washes over him. He is ashamed to admit he has never made a decision by himself. His life has been a single continuous act of obedience. More than anything he wants to avoid another sleepless night weighing the pros and cons of a matter that cannot be settled by rational deliberation. Before handing him the letter, Karl asked him to join a weekend excursion to Mount Schöpfl. He'd apologetically declined, claiming he must attend to his studies, but decides a vigorous hike in clear mountain air might be exactly what is required to dispel the malaise of chronic indecision.

The hiking party trudging up the Reichenbach valley from Schöpflgitter presents an odd spectacle. Karl wears his old army field-coat while Josephine and her friend Emilia are well equipped for the mountains with knapsacks, water bottles strapped to hips and woollen stockings rolled over trousers. Max has a blanket slung beneath his satchel and Lukas, who attended the same gymnasium as the boys, is in a flannel suit, looking like he just stepped out of a café in Herrengasse. Rising towards the mountains they stride briskly past agricultural labourers working in the fields. On entering the woods Max feels invigorated. Autumn has not reached the higher slopes and the golden leaves, thick underfoot in the river valley, cling to the mature beech trees rising around them. Dismay about Hanya stays with him like a dull ache from a strained muscle and to empty his mind he attunes his ears to the chattering of larks who appear to be following them. On reaching the crest of a ridge the air fills with brown and yellow butterflies and the noisy demands of Leopoldstadt and the university fade. From time-to-time Lukas sings fragments from Silcher's setting of *Lorelei* and the group avoid the fractious debates that usually accompany their excursions. Karl takes an occasional pot-shot at Lukas's romanticism, but these are parried with humour and most of the conversation revolves around Josephine's commentary on the abundant birdlife.

Maintaining their pace, they are weary but in good spirits, approaching the hut where they will spend the night before attempting the summit. A thin column of smoke rises through the treetops bringing anticipation of a hot meal, but as the hut comes into view harsh male voices bark out *Lützow's Wild Hunt* and a wave of apprehension passes through the party. A young man carrying a bundle of firewood casts a suspicious eye over the group and calls out an ambivalent greeting.

'Plenty of room—but if you're Jewish you sleep in the shithouse.'

A silent exchange of glances confirms the grim calculus. Josephine and Emilia would earn a pass, though elements within the *Wandervogel* believe women have no place in the mountains. Karl might get by if he kept his mouth shut, but with their dark eyes and black hair, Max and Lukas are gripped by an icy fear as they imagine how their proximity to two flaxen haired maidens will be interpreted. With more of the scout troupe spilling out of the hut they scramble off the track and Josephine leads them through a steep grove of pine trees. Their retreat is accompanied by a barrage of crude insults and a fusillade of stones pinging against the tree trunks. Josephine knows the topography and assures them it will be easy to find shelter in the farmland on the western side of the hill. They slump on with each member of the party silently nursing their own thoughts. The trees give out a thick scent of resin and the ground is carpeted with pine needles overlaid with flakes of bark and a scattering of pine-cones.

Withdrawal of hospitality could be counted as a minor offence, but the incident has a bitter aftertaste, like bile rising in the oesophagus. With the evening sun scraping the bark of ancient conifers they descend into a gently sloping valley, their thoughts unspoken until Lukas skirts the subject.

'It's a crude type of nature worship—there's a void in their lives where God used to be but there's no real reverence for nature, just a kitsch fantasy: The holy mountain, last sanctuary for the ancient solidarity of the tribe—and of course it must be kept free from impurity.'

Despite his aversion to anything that smacks of mysticism, Karl nods in agreement. 'I suppose on a subconscious level they see us as intruders violating their sacred space... you'd probably get a similar reaction if a scout troupe dressed in lederhosen wandered into a synagogue.'

Though Max holds his tongue, Karl's comment strikes him as particularly stupid. He conjures a mental image of a troupe of nationalist youth bursting into a Sabbath service and pictures how the congregation's fury would be supressed and masked by obsequious humility, with no one daring to confront the intruders. Wishing to put someone in the shithouse is not the same as having the authority to act on such an impulse.

At the edge of the woods a tumbling outcrop of boulders stretch into the farmland, as if trying to catch the last rays of sunshine. They pause to survey a patchwork of fields dotted with farm buildings and small orchards. Josephine and Emilia approach a weather-beaten cottage, setting off a cacophony of barking from the farm dogs, while the boys linger beside a sprawling apple tree, its branches propped with timber. The girls return with a jug of milk and cauliflowers, partially spoilt by caterpillars, which they were invited to take from the cottage garden. Their lodgings in a hay shed will afford greater comfort than they would have found in the hiking hut and while Karl gets a fire started on the stony ground sloping towards a brook the girls take stock of their provisions. Josephine has brought a bacon-bone for broth and in a flush of embarrassment it occurs to her this will make the meal inedible for Max and Lukas. The problem is solved by setting two separate pots over the embers. One is infused with a smoky bacon flavour and the other is seasoned with sprigs of rosemary and thyme from the cottage garden. Max has brought a loaf of hard black bread used to scoop the broth thickened with potatoes, barley and cauliflower.

Making a point of eating from the unclean pot, Lukas teasingly addresses Max, 'There's nothing more liberating than eating a bacon sandwich on the Day of Atonement, only to find the Almighty Blessed-Be-He, withholds judgement.'

Max ripostes by suggesting Lukas's miserly contribution to the meal proves a secret allegiance to his Jewish ancestors and as the warm camaraderie of shared laughter establishes itself, Lukas, who did not appear to be carrying provisions, theatrically produces a slab of cooking chocolate. After deliberation they decide to melt it into the creamy milk donated by the farmer's wife.

Slumped against the base of the shed Max gazes aimlessly at the delicate tracery of a juniper tree silhouetted against a stony grey sky. Tired limbs, a hearty meal and an idyllic setting have brought a simple contentment, though the memory of their exclusion from the hut still hangs. If left alone it might dissipate like vapour from a shady hollow but Karl cannot resist poking it, unaware his analysis does nothing to lessen the unspoken humiliation. His companions, having made themselves comfortable in the hay, give no indication of interest in what he has to say but Karl proceeds as if he has their rapt attention.

'If we are to counter that sort of bigotry you have to acknowledge hostility towards strangers is natural—it's always been there and in primitive societies suspicion of strangers would have been essential for self-preservation—'

Lukas cuts him off: 'Of course nobody likes strangers. The real question is what makes you a stranger? I was born in Austria and so were my parents and my great-grand-parents. German is my mother tongue and I know more about German literature and music and folklore than any of those oafs, but they get to decide I'm the stranger.'

Max smiles as he notices Karl is unsettled, but the heat of contention only sharpens his resolve. 'That's the point I was coming to, the threat the nationalists feel is an illusion, they've created a bogeyman with no objective basis, but their anxiety is real and it's driven by fear of the unfamiliar.'

'I suppose we should find consolation in knowing we are only bogeymen, but I dare say it won't do us much good when they plant us in the shithouse.'

'That's not the point. What's at issue is making them see their fears are unfounded, and to do that we have to accept the anxiety is reasonable—in their minds we pose a threat to their homeland.'

'So how would you suggest we are to assuage their fears?'

Karl is riled by Lukas's patronising tone. 'We have to face the fact that Jews are guests in Austria—there is no getting around that and there are certain responsibilities that must be accepted to avoid stirring up the native population.'

Max had intended to stay out of the discussion but cannot contain himself. 'We've never done anything but behave like guests—we spend our whole lives apologising and trying not to be noticed. Even our synagogues are hidden behind facades to make them look like ordinary buildings.'

'For the most part that is true, especially in recent years, but in the Jewish quarters people still dress like they are in a ghetto and then you have the Jewish millionaires on the Ringstraße—the nouveau riche with their gaudy displays of wealth when most of the native population are struggling to find enough to eat. I know the demagogues look for scapegoats but people wouldn't respond if their claims didn't match what they can see with their own eyes.'

The indictment leaves a sullen silence and though she cannot fault his logic Josephine wishes he would show some regard for his friends' feelings. Floundering to formulate a response Max is relieved when Lukas rises to the challenge.

'I'm not going to defend the war profiteers, though I think you'll find there are plenty of Austrian and Prussian aristocrats among their number. But where you are most deeply deluded is in believing the problem would vanish if Jews shaved their beards and side curls and threw away their phylacteries. Let's say you put on your best Austrian manners and joined the party up there in the hut—what do you think would happen if one of them knew your family or by a slip of the tongue you gave them a sniff of your Jewish blood? You'd end up in the shithouse with the rest of us.'

'I'm well aware of that, at the gymnasium they never let me forget it. But what I'm talking about is historical reality—when Jews make an effort to fit in, they eventually win acceptance. You just need to look at the government—half of our Cabinet Ministers are Jewish but they have the sense to keep their religion private.'

'You make it sound so easy—but the first Jewish merchants settled on the Danube within a hundred years of the expulsions from Jerusalem. A thousand years later we were being dragged from our homes and burnt at the stake for causing the plague.'

'Well you would have to ask why the Slavs and every other immigrant group blended in and became part of the local population.'

Max wants to say that the Covenant of Sinai can't be put aside like a suit of old clothes, but he knows the futility of presenting religious arguments to unbelievers.

Lukas sighs and replies flatly, 'So the only legitimate response to persecution is to abandon everything that makes us stand out—suicide to avoid being murdered?'

'It's hardly suicide to put aside ancient superstitions or at least show discretion about following worn out traditions—as you yourself showed us by eating pork.'

Lukas' face reddens as Karl continues. 'When people are despised for their race, it's always going to intensify feelings of racial pride, but if you follow that logic it can only end in a racial war. And there's nothing noble about provoking a war you cannot win. That's got nothing to do with being Jewish, it's simply recognising we are a tiny minority among a powerful people who are not afraid to use violence. You see the same thing in the Melian Dialogue. The Athenians offered them a choice—submit and get the benefits of Greek citizenship or resist and be annihilated. And what did they do? They chose to be slaughtered and enslaved because they could not give up their pride in being Melians.'

Bringing Thucydides into the debate eases the tension and with Karl secure in his victory the argument, which no one wishes to prolong, fizzles. Lukas steps outside for a cigarette and Max joins him. They drift from the hay-shed blowing white smoke into the darkness. Erratic patches of moonlight illuminate the forest rising towards Mount Schöpfl and the wind breaks over the tree-tops like waves unravelling on the seashore. Though they were no more than acquaintances at the gymnasium, Max feels a bond with Lukas and imagines for all his blasphemies he is still drawn to the beauty of the Torah. He refuses to believe that having persevered for so many generations, his people would extinguish themselves in the cold logic of assimilation.

Lukas is aware of nothing beyond a profound isolation. He is disgusted by the servility Karl recommends but the exchange exposed the hollowness of his existence. Alienated from his people and unwelcome in the country of his birth he is trapped in a double exile. The alternative of religious observance is a land he cannot enter. He looks on it with faint nostalgia like a brother indulging his little sister as she falls into conversation with her dolls.

They leave early next morning, planning to make the ascent and return to Schöpflgitter before sunset. A crisp frost scrunches underfoot and on the summit of Mount Schöpfl they look down on bleak windswept hilltops dusted with snow. A more promising mood asserts on the eastern slopes where sunlight catches the mingled green and yellow of elm trees caught between seasons. Max withdraws, disappointed his strategy of putting Hanya out of mind has not brought the certainty he hoped for. He has not ruled out any of the pathways before him and in his head, composes a reply to Hanya's letter, determined to speak honestly, even if it means frankly admitting he is incapable of making a decision.

20

The alarm clock Hanya was gifted on her twelfth birthday is a beacon of stability amid the chaos of the boarding house. Late at night the luminous green numerals radiate a calming energy and dispel vague anxieties that would prevent her sleeping. In the morning its thudding metallic clatter rekindles the girlish pride she took in executing her ballet exercises while the household slumbered. The alarm now rings at 9:00am and as her fellow boarders seldom rise before midday, she can use the bathroom at leisure and brew coffee on the paraffin stove. Before leaving she sets the alarm to 1:00pm for Therese. When they first arrived in Berlin they attended the Eurhythmics Institute together, but classes require more musical knowledge than Therese possesses and as soon as they secured positions in a chorus she could see no point continuing. Hanya finds the Eurythmic method easier than Frau Gerty's unpredictable regime, which always left her unclear whether anything she was doing was correct. She's mastered a basic alphabet of 20 expressive actions and is learning to exert independent control over different parts of her body so rhythm can be followed with one set of movements while other gestures respond to the melody. Although most of the exercises interpret classical pieces, the technique is well suited to the syncopated jazz rhythms used for her chorus routines.

After her class she goes to the Ishitar where Therese is usually ensconced in the back room, flirting with the waiters and devouring what she can cadge from the kitchen. Revelling in the city's pulsating energy Therese is immune to the home-sickness that occasionally niggles Hanya. Nothing brings her more joy than an afternoon spent at Wertheim's. Before visiting the store she agonises over what to wear, as if she'd secured an invitation to a society ball. Inside she suppresses her excitement and adopts a languid, elegant poise, gliding up the moving staircases and pretending not to notice the glittering chandeliers. Nonchalantly sampling the most expensive perfumes she draws Hanya into an elaborate charade fashioned from fragments of UFA movies. Inhaling the scent with her eyes closing in a swoon, she urgently consults with Hanya on whether the bouquet is sufficiently refined for the Count's delicate sensibilities. She is adept at deferring actual purchases and the counter staff seem inclined to indulge her fantasy as her enthusiasm inspires other customers to loosen their wallets.

Much as Hanya is amused by her friend's fancies, she regards her as a mentor and appreciates the guidance of her sharp-witted survival instincts. Therese insisted they registered as prostitutes even though they have no intention of competing with the throng of streetwalkers clogging every corner of Friedrichstraße. The precaution makes it possible to walk to their lodgings in the early hours of the morning without unwelcome attention from the police and free medical examinations provide a safeguard for their liaisons with the patrons at the Ishtar, always ready to bundle them into cabs when the club closes. Frau Nolde, in charge of entertainment, was formerly a Ballet Mistress with a company in Brunswick and imposes the most exacting standards. When Hanya and Therese were accepted for a trial she warned they could be replaced at a moment's notice. Lateness is not tolerated and rehearsals begin with a rigorous inspection of fingernails, hair and teeth. The routines are not difficult and the girls' training in improvisation gives them an advantage over the classically trained dancers. The choreography seldom extends beyond establishing positions for tableaux and the dancers are left to find their way between set pieces. When Frau Nolde noticed Hanya's ability to move in time to the music she asked her to prepare a solo piece for the afterhours club in the cellar. Hanya suggested a duet with Therese and they patched together a routine using bits-and-pieces of the choreography they learnt for Frau Gerty's performance at the Konzerthaus.

At closing time the band and most customers descend into the cellar via a spiral staircase behind the bar. The change of location and cool air revitalises the inebriated patrons who throw themselves into the frenetic intimacy of the dance floor. As cigarette smoke fills the room and energy dissipates, the conferencier announces a special performance by a dancer *'direct from Reinhardt's latest sensation.'* The claim has some validity as Hanya's eurythmics class are occasionally recruited for the choruses of Reinhardt's extravaganzas and she once appeared as a Trojan slave before an audience of thousands at the old circus auditorium. Their performance has Hanya dancing as a mechanical automaton while Therese playing the factory worker is mesmerised into mimicking Hanya's jerky involuntary movements. Following Frau Nolde's suggestion her liberation from mechanised tyranny involves discarding every stitch of clothing. They finish with an erotic *pas de deux* accompanied by an oriental melody for which the band leader puts aside the saxophone and takes up his preferred clarinet. The performance brings howls of appreciation and for the rest of the night the girls are inundated with offers of champagne from a throng of admirers.

They seldom return to Behrenstraße before 2:00am and invariably find the living room given to idle conversation. In a cluttered space adjoining the kitchen an oak-leaf dining table, a pair of couches and a haphazard arrangement of chairs provide the setting for an informal congress, which convenes for the sole purpose of deferring sleep. The landlady seldom emerges from her upstairs room, which has its own kitchen annex overlooking the courtyard. She leaves the residents to their own devices and in the face of inflation, collection of the fixed rent has become more a ritual than a requirement. Therese is often beckoned to sit with Ferdinand, highly regarded for his authoritative knowledge of Freud's theories, acquired while studying in Vienna before the war. Her accent reminds him of the city he loves and she is happy to indulge his nostalgia by pretending to be familiar with the cafés and opera houses he frequented as a student. Hanya usually falls in with Hans and Gottfried, unwilling conscripts in the war's final months. Although well-educated, they never have money and would rather attend political meetings than pay for a ticket to the cinema. Their conversation about the latest artistic developments is often fractious and they fall into the most pitiful despair when anyone mentions the triumphs of the Freikorps.

Meandering conversation often continues until sunrise and like an ocean absorbs energy into its incessant ebb and flow. Everyone speaks frankly about sex and all agree an immense spiritual awakening will occur once homosexuality is accepted without shame or censure. Hanya has noticed, and Therese is unafraid to point out, that for all the talk about sex there is little enthusiasm for sexual activity. The only antidote to the lethargy is cocaine and on occasions when someone is prepared to share a screw of the white powder, the gramophone is wound and couples find space to dance around the heavy furniture. Ferdinand may take Therese to his room and Hans and Gottfried hold hands and disappear into the darkness of the hallway. Having observed how the drug whips up a frenzy on the dance floor of the Ishtar, Hanya was reluctant to partake, but when she finally inhaled the powder a surge of vitality flushed away her anxieties. Thoughts and perceptions came with startling clarity and brilliantly spontaneous conversation bubbled out of her unceasingly. The following day she plunged into enervating depression and her only thought was to get hold of more of the elixir. Therese cautioned her to wait a few days. Frau Nolde imposes iron discipline on her dancers and girls who succumb to the turmoil of addiction are summarily expelled from the chorus. Hanya solemnly agrees to limit use of the drug to no more than once a week and they zealously police each other whenever one wavers in her commitment.

With a hectic daily routine Hanya's only moments of reflection are prompted by Mother's letters. She hastily pens replies, filled with nonsense about her eurhythmics classes and chatty comments about operas and exhibitions she has not seen. She sees no harm in reassuring Mother with such things, but writing always leaves her in a sour mood as she glimpses the lies she tells herself. Connections with family are dissolving like a photograph fading through exposure to too much sunlight. Only the image she carries of Max retains its brightness. She's glad he did not come to Berlin. The city would devour him and yet the memory of his eyes bashfully avoiding her gaze stays, more vivid and precious than anything she has found among the city's parade of delights.

By the time Jorg arrives, Hanya has adjusted to her new home and is learning to appreciate the pleasures of carelessness. The inadequacy that prevented her joining artistic conversations vanished as she learnt the trick of flippancy. Whenever serious artistic questions arise she adopts a bored expression and only speaks in earnest about mundane matters or personal obsessions. Jorg is disappointed at Hanya's newfound sophistication. Much as he despises artistic pretention he has a soft spot for the uncorrupted souls naïve enough to believe in art's redemptive power. In Berlin he indulges a taste for extravagance as the modest fees for his journal articles are paid in Swiss francs that multiply into unimaginable abundance when converted to marks. He treats the girls to a magnificent banquet and takes Hanya to a hotel room high above the Unter den Linden where they look down on the surging energy of the street. Though their coitus is perfunctory, Jorg is content and eager to see her dancing at the Ishtar.

When the nigh-club staff get a sniff of his foreign currency, they treat him like royalty. The cigarette boy puts away the Havana cigars he rolls from dried cabbage leaves steeped in nicotine and approaches his table with a gilt case containing the real article. Though he finds the chorus routines pedestrian, Jorg is amused by Hanya and Therese's performance in the afterhours cellar. Ordering the finest champagne he tells them they have brilliantly superseded the work of their teacher. Hanya is mortified and makes him promise not to breathe a word to Frau Gerty about what they have done. Her embarrassment only enhances the mischievous delight he takes in assuring her their dance is vastly superior to the original. Certain she is being ridiculed, Hanya refuses to accept their crude performance could be compared with the artistic genius of her teacher.

Irrepressibly buoyant, Jorg ushers the girls into a cab and whisks them to his lodgings in Grunewald. He makes a beeline for the gramophone and the empty house is filled with the joyous cacophony of a Negro brass band. There is more champagne, a jar of caviar, a tray of cured meats; playing the attentive host, he presents the girls with a silver snuff box filled with cocaine. Therese catches Hanya's eye and a wicked grin makes it clear the occasion demands a relaxation of their rule. Dipping her fingernail into the powder she inhales. Jorg relaxes into an armchair and with subtle suggestions elicits an encore to their performance in the cellar. Therese needs little persuasion. With cocaine coursing through her body she tosses her head and strides towards Hanya who draws a hefty portion of the drug into her nostril. An avalanche of sensation frees her from self-doubt and she slips off her shoes, attuning her body to the lively rhythm tumbling out of the gramophone. Her hips sway with the twang of the bass and her feet kick in response to the trumpets jostling for space within the densely syncopated melody. They throw themselves into a dizzying succession of spins and twirls, releasing shrieks of laughter as the music is abruptly replaced by the crackling of the needle grinding towards the next song. With a sharp awareness of their host's expectations, Therese loosens her shoulder straps and allows her dress to fall. She turns Hanya around and unfastens the hooks at the back of her frock. Her actions are so firm and decisive Hanya has no qualms about surrendering to her purpose. Stockings are unfurled, brassieres unlaced and the two girls stand naked, faintly shuddering in the cool night air. With Therese's arms locked behind her waist, Hanya leans back, arching her torso and raising her arms to the wail of a saxophone. Offering her body to Therese's fluid caress she is unperturbed by Jorg's gaze, his face locked in an implacable stare. With limbs entwined the girls are alert to the shifting dynamics of balance and poise, feeling the weight of each other's bodies pressing and shifting as they merge into a single undulating form.

Unnoticed, Jorg removes his shoes and folds his trousers over the back of his chair. He stands beside them in his shirt sleeves and Therese casually draws him into an embrace. His lips pass from one face to another and an experimental rearrangement of bodies progresses until they arrive at a configuration that allows him to penetrate one while caressing the other. The cocaine has endowed him with enough vitality to switch positions several times and when he withdraws to his armchair, Therese is left hungrily aroused. Latching onto Hanya, she rhythmically grinds her hips until her passion is satisfied and then returns the favour with a caress so delicate Hanya feels her body melt. Trembling she surrenders to a sensation beyond anything she has experienced, until it dawns on her the feeling is not reciprocated. She watches crest-fallen as Therese helps herself to the tray of cured meats before disappearing in search of a bathroom.

Hanya is relieved that Therese never mentions what happened at Grunewald. She's excruciatingly embarrassed about what might have taken place and cannot stop thinking about Jorg's ridiculous insistence that their titillating dance surpassed the artistic brilliance of Frau Gerty. She understands how he loves to *épater la bourgeoisie* but it seems perverse for a man so knowledgeable about art to be elevating crudeness and vulgarity. Hanya knows she does not have the talent of a great dancer but she can hold her own in a chorus and her fondest ambition is to play a small part in the creation of a great work. It maddens her to think that if she were to achieve her dream, Jorg would be there, sneering, letting everybody know he'd seen something better in a cheap cabaret or vaudeville.

Having slipped into a melancholy mood Hanya is jolted from her lethargy by the unexpected appearance of a letter from Max. Fearing she will lose her precious few hours of sleep she keeps the letter unopened beneath her pillow and awakens early, unsettled by a dream suffused with the portentous solemnity of a rabbi drawing aside the ark curtain. Leaving the house, she finds a tranquil corner of the Tiergarten where she can sit undisturbed. She has long since abandoned any hope of seeing Max in Berlin and grimly anticipates having her worst fears confirmed. Unfolding the paper, which looks as though it might have been cut from a notebook, she hears the strange fluting of birdsong she cannot identify; hesitation opens her to the loveliness of the unkempt park. Tilting her head back she gazes through treetops at an opal-grey cloud made luminous in the early morning sun. Her eyes drift across the opening lines and she smiles at the obsequious formality of Max's greeting, wishing to disrupt his seriousness by nudging his ribs or rubbing the sinews at the base of his neck. Hoping for the finality of a tender rejection she is exasperated by the ambiguity of his elaborately qualified declarations. One sentence sticks in her mind and she reads it over and over, lingering on each word.

My feelings for you are such that I could not contemplate entering into a relationship with another woman but as I am unable to act on my feelings I cannot ask you to feel in any way constrained.

She hurries to class, oblivious to the dappled play of light beneath her feet. Working through the familiar warm-up exercises she is gripped by rising fury at how anyone could write such a stupid sentence.

The class have been working intensively with Mendelssohn's Violin Concerto, a piece Hanya knows well, as her inability to master the third movement convinced her to abandon violin lessons and devote herself to ballet. The instructor is impressed at how she anticipates the delicate shifts in rhythm and challenges her to create a *plastique* from the first movement. The sinuous line of the violin intensifies her anguish and she instinctively responds to the reverberation of strings floating in precarious solitude before returning to the resounding fullness of the orchestra. Her interpretation draws spontaneous applause from fellow students and a guarded commendation from the instructor who cannot help pointing to some inaccuracy in the timing of her footwork. She leaves in a fatalistic mood and in a brief tête-à-tête Therese convinces her the best way to deal with Max's unanswerable riddles is to throw herself into the city's abundant distractions.

At home in Vienna she might have withdrawn to her bedroom, but Berlin's restless vitality proscribes the torment of solitary contemplation. When business is slow at the Ishtar, Hanya finds Therese or a companion from among the chorus girls and together they drift through teeming streets to the steam baths on Jägerstraße. In the early hours of the morning the hazy obscurity of the steam room draws housewives driven from their homes by drunken husbands, weary travellers and nightclub staff unable to sleep after twelve hours on their feet. Sitting naked in a room full of strangers, Hanya feels perfectly at ease as an attendant equipped with a gauntlet and long handled brush, moves silently from one person to another scrubbing every section of their pliant bodies. In the enervating heat, the chatter is lethargic and careless. Knowing they are unlikely to meet again, the women have nothing to live-up to and for a brief interlude can be whoever they want.

21

By February all the talk is about the Six Day Race and on the second night Therese gains entrance into the central circle on the arm of a banker who was captivated by her dancing at the Ishtar. Hanya is swept along with a gaggle of students and artists content to enjoy the spectacle from the balcony. Gazing past the action on the track she glimpses Therese in the centre circle carousing with bejewelled ladies in their sable wraps and gentlemen in tails. The balcony erupts with applause as a favoured local rider takes a nasty tumble on a perilously inclined curve and returns with head swathed in bandages to win a prize in a hotly contested set of sprints. By the fourth night Hanya's friends from the boarding house set out to investigate the phenomenon, diligently following Jorg's advice that the only place to experience the event is from the cheap seats in the high balcony. Having failed to find a suitable escort Therese tries to persuade Hanya to accompany her into the centre circle but on learning the cost of mingling with high society, she reluctantly condescends to join the hoi polloi.

Jorg was right about the atmosphere in the high gallery. The view takes in the sweep of the arena and the wooden track acts like a gramophone amplifying the tumultuous applause mixing with the jazz band playing in the central circle. Although Therese cannot stop prattling about the sophisticated companionship she experienced on the second night, she is quickly drawn into the carnival spirit animating the masses peering downwards from their vertiginous perch. With the advantage of elevation, enthusiasts engage in tactical analysis of the race and minor shifts in position trigger vigorous debates that threaten to erupt into violence. A group of workers well supplied with beer and sandwiches insist on sharing provisions with Hanya's party. On discerning the presence of novices, one man offers to initiate the ladies into the intricacies of endurance racing. Introducing himself as a railway man from Dresden, Bruno names each of the thirteen riders and their seconds, offering comprehensive appraisals of their strengths and weaknesses. He pays particular attention to Karl Sadlow and advises the ladies they could do well if they bet on him taking the prize. Hans and Gottfried enthusiastically join the conversation, delighted to commune with the proletariat.

Impressed by Bruno's authoritative tone, Therese rashly empties her purse, entrusting their guide to place a substantial bet on Sadlow. Without showing surprise about the size of the stake, Bruno considers which of the bookmakers are offering the best odds and assures Therese she is making a sound investment. He'd seen Sadlow racing in Dresden before the war and is certain he is deliberately avoiding a show of strength in the sprints to surprise the pack on the final night. As the hours pass Hanya is amused to observe Therese manoeuvring closer to Bruno and hanging on every word as he evaluates the shifting fortunes of the riders. Hans and Gottfried have withdrawn into anxious isolation after they noticed Bruno is sporting a Freikorps pin on the lapel of his leather jacket. By 6:00am the action on the track has lulled into a holding pattern and cleaners are moving among the rows of wooden benches. Therese secures an assurance from Bruno they will meet the following night and he cheerfully departs with his friends, heading into the working day without the slightest sign of tiredness.

On the way back to Behrenstraße, Therese impulsively pulls Hanya from her seat at a tram stop on the corner of Motzstraße, insisting they visit a fortune-teller Frau Nolde recommended. Hanya goes along reluctantly, having invested a considerable sum for an astrological chart that proved useless when applied to Max's ambivalent correspondence. With her usual bluntness Therese negotiates a reasonable fee and they are ushered into a dimly lit booth where Fräulein Meier sits behind a small round table. In a business-like tone she announces she does not answer questions and can only transmit what is given to her. Hanya would have preferred to simply observe proceedings but is told to sit at the table. There is a cursory inspection of the girls' palms and five cards are placed face down in front of Therese. As each card is turned up Fräulein Meier pauses and closes her eyes.

At the second card she proclaims in a flat disembodied voice, 'When the wind blows from the east keep the cellar filled with coal.' The third card reveals: 'There is danger in an unlit street.' The fourth: 'If you wish for peace, avoid the company of women.'

When the last card is turned there is an extended silence and a tremor in the seer's voice. 'Like a crane journeying north in summer your beloved will find you.'

Hanya has had her fill of ambiguity and pays scant attention to the cryptic pronouncements applied to her cards. When her fifth card is turned, there is a pause and the clairvoyant poses a question that makes Hanya gasp: 'Could you die for love?'

She desperately wants to answer yes. Yes!—there was an afternoon in the Prater, gazing at the Danube with her head nestled on Max's shoulder, when she could easily have died for love. Unable to speak or even move, she feels a rising tide of panic, fearing the moment may never be recovered.

Leaving the booth Hanya is close to tears but Therese is in such a buoyant mood she does not notice. The following night she passes up an offer to accompany a gentleman into the central circle to make her rendezvous with Bruno. On the sixth night, as they climb the steep staircase to the high gallery, she squeezes Hanya's arm and breathlessly announces. 'I've figured out the seer's message—you know how cranes always fly at a great height, well I met Bruno on the highest level of the Sportpalast—he even told me he prefers the gallery because you get a bird's eye view. And he's from Dresden—so he travelled north to reach Berlin.'

The workings of Therese's mind are a constant source of fascination to Hanya but the recourse to metaphorical ornithology is so outlandish she tells her to stop being a goose. Therese insists it makes perfect sense. Hanya watches with amusement as Therese suppresses her flirtatious manner and listens with rapt attention to Bruno's tireless exposition on Sadlow's tactical brilliance. As midnight approaches she is not in the least surprised to see Sadlow secure an unassailable lead and the handsome return on her bet is taken as proof of the fortune-teller's veracity.

Much as she admires Therese's toughness, Hanya is touched to see her friend in a state of distracted silliness. She tries to pretend nothing is happening but is clearly enthralled by the hope that she could love and be loved. Even more surprising is the way she brushes off Bruno's constant advances, telling Hanya she would rather put an end to the affair than have it peter out in the predictable routine of cheap hotel rooms rented by the hour. Bruno has seen enough of the world to understand how Therese makes her living, but remains persistent in the face of multiple rebuffs. Therese sustains herself in the nourishment that comes from hope.

Hanya fervently wishes they will find happiness and recognises her vicarious enthusiasm is a way of compensating for the failure of her own lukewarm romance. Taking long walks alone she keeps her gaze low to avoid solicitation from strangers, blocking out the oppressive aura of the rain-streaked stone-work above her. On a particularly dreary morning, meandering on a crowded stretch of the Unter den Linden, she notices a handbill posted outside the State Opera with the name of Max's music tutor prominently displayed. A drift of memories takes her back to the evening at the Café American when Alban Berg appeared at their table, speaking with such charm and offering the most generous affirmation of Max's talent. Hoping to rekindle the intoxicating possibilities of those days, she succeeds in persuading Jorg to accompany her to an afternoon performance.

Since arriving in Berlin she has hardly visited the opera and her excitement makes her immune to Jorg's cynicism. He regards opera as a relic of the old order, soon to be replaced by cinema, and only agreed to come out of amusement at the apoplectic tone of the critics warning against Berg's vulgarity. Having absorbed some of Max's enthusiasm for atonal composition, Hanya is untroubled by the dissonance of the turbulent score but nothing could have prepared her for the violent emotions of the libretto. The action plunges into a nightmarish world where a pathetic young soldier is bullied and humiliated at every turn. Wozzeck's only solace comes from his love for the prostitute who gave birth to his son, and when this is torn from him Hanya gazes at the unfolding desolation through tear-filled eyes, a cry of anguish breaking from her lips as Wozzeck slips a knife into his lover's side beneath a blood-red moon. The unbearable sadness of the concluding scenes leaves her in a kind of stupor, drained of emotion, scarcely breathing. At curtain-call she robotically joins the slowly rising applause that drowns the catcalls and hoots from the gallery, nodding mutely as Jorg delivers his appraisal.

'A very fine piece, though wasted on a bourgeois audience—they won't see their own judgemental moralism is what prevents the poor fellow from having any control over his life.'

Consumed with sympathy for the doomed lovers Hanya is struck by Jorg's suggestion that Wozzeck never had the luxury of choice. She supposes he could have ignored his lover's infidelity and when he was alone with her and their little boy, he seemed capable of forgiving anything, but the way the Drum Major goaded him, what choice did he have? She sees Wozzeck's demise was cruelly inevitable and worries Berg may be saying love is no match for the cold malevolence of our world.

Late at night with these thoughts rampaging through her head she writes to Max, incoherently describing how the opera moved her. She tells him Wozzeck was a victim of circumstance, driven to destroy the only thing of beauty he knew and she fears their love will die as surely as Wozzeck was destined to murder his lover and end his life in a blood-soaked pond beneath a blood red moon with the music evoking such hopelessness she could not stop weeping… She desperately wants him to understand, unless we find the courage to love, we condemn ourselves to emptiness and desolation. If she read it back she knows she would never send it. Resolutely striding through deserted streets she finds a mailbox standing like a tombstone in the lamp-light and thrusts the letter through the slot.

In the morning, tormented by an image of the mail carriage speeding towards Vienna, she cannot distinguish what she wrote from what she intended to write. The letter is addressed to Karl with instruction to pass it on to Max and she considers sending a telegram asking him to destroy it. But then she would have to write another letter and in the cool light of day she knows she would never find the courage to say what she needs to say. Adhering to her daily routine she attends her eurythmics class, wishing she could live with the intensity she felt at the opera or seize the invigorating confidence of inhaling cocaine. Nights at the Ishtar, once so fabulously exotic, have become stale and predictable and the only thing that seems real is the agonising expectation of a reply to her letter.

Also living in a constant state of anxiety, Therese is not in the least constrained by the reticence compelling Hanya to hide her feelings. Every aspect of her relationship with Bruno is thrown open for discussion and the topic seized with gusto by the insomniacs who assemble each night in the boarding house parlour. Dismayed by the Freikorps pin on Bruno's jacket, Hans and Gottfried caution against the affair, recounting scenes they witnessed in the brutal winter of 1919 when Freikorps militia slaughtered workers in the streets outside the Reichstag. Having absorbed some of Bruno's political views, Therese admonishes them as traitors who would have German workers kissing the arses of filthy Russian Bolsheviks.

Ferdinand takes a different tack, ponderously asserting. 'For the patriarchy sexual impulses are a threat to the established order, hence the institution of marriage; specifically designed to control the rebellious energy of female sexuality.'

While the men lose themselves in a fog of contention, flinging words as if skimming stones, Therese rolls her eyes and consults Hanya on the efficacy of a bleaching cream she has recently acquired. The gruff compliments she receives from Bruno always refer to the softness of her skin and she is convinced that by maintaining her silky complexion she will win his heart. Much as she yearns for the luxurious world that reaches out to her from the illuminated window displays at Wertheim's, Bruno has awakened a desire for something more substantial. As a railway man who served in a supply regiment during the war, he is untainted by the hopelessness that consumes so many of his fellows. His work on the freight trains enables him to supply goods to the black-market and inspired by the genius of Stinnes, he speculates in foreign currencies. Against such a man the sages of the boarding-house parlour seem like little children and Therese takes no notice of their sneering disparagement of marriage.

Hanya understands the thrill of living in Berlin, its illicit pleasures and the headlong rush of adventure, has been little more than a means of survival for Therese. She remembers the bleak apartment in the Vorstadt where she met her family and hopes her friend will find happiness in marriage. But she cannot help thinking of the opera. There is a hint of coldness in Bruno's grey eyes and she fears those powerful arms might be capable of the violence Wozzeck unleashed on the only person who loved him. She convinces herself Therese and Bruno are more sensible than Berg's doomed lovers. They are practical people with little use for grand emotions. If Therese does nothing to arouse Bruno's jealousy, they should find happiness and she can easily imagine them ensconced in a railwayman's cottage with a robust brood of blond children.

When Bruno leaves without warning for Dresden there is nothing Hanya can say to dislodge her friend's stoically resigned depression. A few days later Therese purrs like a house-cat, theatrically stretching her arm to a cluster of chorus girls admiring the sapphire set in silver, resplendent on her ring finger. Bruno returned home to acquire his grandmother's engagement ring and the marriage is set down for the first Sunday after Pentecost. While Therese knows Bruno has no illusions about her situation she is determined his family must learn nothing of her current circumstances. Her two sisters are summoned as bride's maids and it is decided Hanya should be introduced as a cousin to allay suspicions about her Jewish features. Therese drills them to memorise an elaborate story about how her father died in the war with a commendation for bravery and she undertook to support her family after she was lucky enough to secure a position as a counter-girl at Wertheim's. Hanya is to say she works as a governess for a distinguished family in Grunewald and under no circumstances is there to be any mention of dancing. On the day the precautions are unnecessary. Bruno's parents are humble folk and opinions about the bride are confined to speculation on her capacity for childbirth. The ceremony at a village church on the outskirts of Dresden is joyous and Therese, glowing with good health in a simple white dress, is regarded as a fine catch.

On the return journey Hanya tries to hold onto the optimism radiating from beneath Therese's veil, but feels her mood edging towards melancholy. Through the carriage window, freshly turned fields show signs of spring growth and a faint reflection of her profile glides over blackberry bushes and hedgerows lining the track. Churches and goose-ponds drift past. A poplar alley leads her eye into the distance, and she sinks into wistful contemplation of the vast network of roadways and villages where people go about their business absorbed by private tribulations. The motion lulls her into a sluggish tranquillity and snatches of dream mingle with the ever-changing scenery. On the outskirts of Berlin she looks out at children running between clotheslines and on a huge billboard the Sarotti Mohr in his red and blue turban, presents a box of sweets on a silver tray. With Therese gone she can think of no good reason for remaining in Berlin. Sighting the platform clock she recalls Frau Nolde will be expecting her. With her night bag hitched over her shoulder she trudges to the tram stop on Anhalter Straße, the evening light glistening on wet asphalt. Approaching the boarding-house she feels oppressed by the heavy stone buildings on Behrenstraße and the starlings swirling over the Tiergarten strike her as an ill-omen.

22

Students filing out of Professor Hahn's class drift from the lecture hall with pursed lips, silently retracing the chain of postulates and axioms that expanded across the blackboard in waves with new layers scrawled on top of the dusty smears left by erasing the previous sequence. Max and Karl stroll to the Volksgarten, soaking up the late afternoon sunshine. Perched on a bench Karl reviews his muddled notes, embarrassed at how easily Max identifies the missing links, restoring the orderly progression that makes numerical logic so appealing.

His friend's mathematical talent has a preternatural quality that arouses Karl's envy and curiosity. Max modestly attributes his gift to his father who introduced him at an early age to the practice of *gematria*. A whole new world opened when his father demonstrated how *YHWH* and Adam have an equivalent value when you assign numbers to the Hebrew letters of each word. Interminable hours spent reading the Tanakh were enlivened as he uncovered hidden patterns and strange correlations encoded in the numerical values of the letters. Karl is certain this is nothing more than meaningless coincidence and demands evidence of the portentous equivalence between the human and divine names. His skepticism is vindicated when it becomes apparent two methods of assigning numerical value are required to attain the same total for the two words. Unperturbed, Max quietly asserts. 'If you use one system for Adam it is only natural that another must be used for the Holy Name.'

It irritates Karl that Max's talent should be squandered on such nonsense. Though he cannot match his friend's facility with numbers, he feels more confident in their tutorial discussions scrutinising the symbolic logic of numerical functions. Professor Hahn rejects the idea mathematics is a purely abstract way of thinking, insisting even the most speculative equations are based on notions of quantity drawn from nature. He finds a mischievous pleasure in presenting paradoxes that undermine the axioms and definitions which make mathematical reasoning possible. Introducing his students to the elegant formulae for space filling curves he challenges them to explain how a one-dimensional line, which by definition has no width, can fill the two-dimensional space of a square.

The paradox confirms Karl's suspicion that mathematics cannot be trusted to provide an accurate description of the world. He understands mathematical logic requires an infinitely divisible progression between any two numbers but argues this should not apply to geometry, which is ultimately based on measurement of things that exist in the real world. With solid objects, he believes it must be possible to count all the atoms and even the quanta that make up the atoms in a defined space and if this is done accurately there would eventually be nothing left to count. For Max the enigma of the infinitesimal reveals the religious dimension of numerical logic. Professor Hahn often speaks of predictability as the essential characteristic of mathematics and Max takes this to mean numbers carry the divine attribute of foresight.

Karl and Max debate such matters on rambling walks through the city, often extending into the early hours of the morning. Walking brings a measure of restraint to the tumultuous flow of Karl's thoughts and for Max the excursions are a welcome release from the claustrophobic atmosphere of his family's apartment. From time to time they are joined by Lukas who enjoys sparring with Karl on philosophical issues. With a comprehensive knowledge of Goethe and Kant, he is a formidable antagonist, deploying heavy doses of irony to counter Karl's relentless badgering. When political issues arise Max falls silent and if pressed for an opinion his oblique comments hint at a deeper reality, beyond the banality of everyday existence. Lukas envies the ease with which Max carries his Jewish identity and recognises his instinctive reverence for the Torah is very different from the rigid conformity imposed by his own religious upbringing.

Anxiety about losing touch with the most vital part of his being prompts Lukas to join a Zionist youth group. They meet in the backroom of a decrepit coffee-house on Dresdner Straße and their aggressively secular manners contradict everything he knows about being Jewish. The group is largely comprised of students from prosperous families, disgusted by their parents' genteel subservience. Their numbers are boosted by Galician refugees fleeing the brutal pogroms that ravaged their homeland. These severe, hollowed-eyed young men latch onto Zionism like a drowning man finding a piece of debris in a storm. The two groups have little in common but are drawn together by the wild romanticism of the Zionist vision and like a band of brigands are unyielding in their loyalty. For some the Dresdner Straße café is the closest thing to a home. They happily spend nights slouched on hard wooden benches, playing chess or cards, sharing jugs of cheap wine. Lukas finds favour among the Galicians as his linguistic studies give him a slender capacity for communicating with the men in their native tongue.

For those attending university, academic study takes second place to *Unitas*—a Zionist duelling fraternity comprising a rag-tag association of foolhardy youth. Their mission, to disprove the myth of Jewish cowardice, is undertaken on Saturday mornings at the Aula where the assembled *Burschenschaften* parade their colours. It is not difficult to provoke conflict as the mere suggestion Jews could participate in such a venerable tradition constitutes an intolerable insult. The pan-German fraternities rigorously enforce a ban on duelling with the sons of Jewish mothers, regarded as devoid of honour. The best the Zionists can hope for is to instigate outbursts of brawling conducted with clubs and fists. Though initially appalled by the ferocity of these melees, Lukas enjoys facing down his fear and releasing the pure aggression sanctioned in the minutes between the outbreak of violence and the moment intervention by authorities makes retreat acceptable. Bruising and occasionally serious head wounds are a small price for the intoxicating sensation of being fully alive and the exhilaration is prolonged as combatants retire to a bierstube to celebrate with singing and toasts.

Unitas is shunned by most Jewish students who resent how a disreputable minority make them all vulnerable to attack. The pious say they reveal the atheistic folly of the Zionist project by shamelessly mimicking the boorish customs of the goyim. For the socialists they are reactionary blockheads mired in a hopelessly immature understanding of their objective condition. Lukas is struck by the irony of Jews asserting their identity by taking on the archaic rituals of European chivalry, but this is a small thing compared with the thrill of seeing fear and outrage in the face of a pan-German *Burschen*, when a blow from a club opens a bleeding gash across his close-cropped Teutonic skull.

After a brief apprenticeship Lukas is initiated as a fully-fledged *Burschen*, joining the drinking sessions at the *Unitas* headquarters in the basement of a fashionable row of apartments in Josefstadt. Their *kneipes* are conducted to strict rules with formal toasts and less than harmonious renditions of songs in Latin, Hebrew and German. As a barrel of new wine is steadily drained the ceremony takes on a course tone and Lukas, who always avoided the back-slapping camaraderie of drinking parties, tastes the bliss that takes hold when aspiration is limited to devising a novel reason for emptying your glass. The wayward reputation of the *burschenschaften* functions like a magnet for a particularly devoted species of das *süsse Weiner mädel*—graceful, flirtatious creatures, as free in granting favours as they are un-demanding in seeking recompense. Reclining on a couch with a fragrant glass of Heuriger and an adorable young shop-girl snuggling against his chest, Lukas feels he has unearthed the meaning of life. The university with its incessant toil and subtle humiliations melts into air along with the finger wagging voice insisting mere hedonism can never satisfy the yearnings of his soul.

The feeling seldom lasts beyond dawn when his sweetheart faces a twelve-hour workday and he lays in bed thinking about the mass of deferred reading for his impending examinations. When they are not drinking or brawling, his *Unitas* colleagues distribute pamphlets, raise funds and convene committees. In Lukas's mind the dry mouth and throbbing headaches that wrack his body after a night of drinking become associated with the political aspects of Zionism. Much as he despises the servile mentality of his parents' generation his commitment to a Jewish homeland wavers whenever he considers the reality of uprooting and travelling to a distant land. Newspaper reports about the Arab riots make it difficult to see Palestine as a haven from the humiliations in Europe. The prospect of facing chauvinistic bigotry in a hot, dusty backwater is considerably less appealing than facing the same attitudes in Vienna, which at least has the advantages of decent coffee houses, fine wines and an abundance of compliant young women.

Strangely, whenever the topic is raised during his nocturnal ramblings with Karl and Max, his reservations vanish and he zealously declares himself for the immediate establishment of a Jewish homeland. Their debates throw up well-trodden arguments without either party shifting their position. Karl is exasperated by supposedly progressive minds refusing to recognise their obsession with a national homeland is reactionary romanticism, no different from the mindless patriotism that sustained the madness of the war years. Lukas is equally frustrated by Karl's obstinate denial of the loss of dignity that comes from cravenly seeking admission to a society that does everything possible to make it clear Jews are unwelcome. Though he fights fire with fire, Lukas has little appetite for the argument. What interests him are Max's opinions. His meagre contributions are calculated to avoid offense, but Lukas imagines Max must be keenly aware of the bitter disputes between Zionists and orthodox Rabbis. The less he says the more Lukas's curiosity is aroused and he looks for an opportunity to hear his views without contending with

Karl's overbearing presence.

He eventually lures Max to the coffee house on Dresdner Straße on the pretext of seeking advice on some Talmudic references he'd come across in Goethe. Max is surprised to learn *Lilith* makes an appearance in Faust and in response to Lukas's enquiries vaguely recalls her story being used to resolve a contradiction in Genesis, which first has man and woman created together and in a later passage describes Eve being made from Adam's rib.

'They say Lilith refused to recognise Adam's authority. She insisted they were both created out of the same earth and when they quarrelled she cursed the name of the Creator and became the Queen of Demons.'

With a series of mischievous questions Lukas coaxes Max into blurting out what he already knew.

'Some of the commentaries say Lilith's companions were created in the twilight of the Sixth Day, but the onset of Sabbath meant they were not given bodies... so they have to make bodies for themselves by inducing young men to spill their seed.'

Though amused by Max's embarrassment, Lukas suppresses the impulse to tease him and abruptly changes tack, asking how his elders viewed the Zionist cause.

Visibly relieved they are done with *Lilith,* Max replies unhesitatingly. 'Most see it as blasphemy—an arrogant attempt to do something that can only be accomplished by God—though there are some who say the Zionists are answering the call of the prophets.'

'And your inclination?'

'It's easy to say *next year Jerusalem* but actually going there is another matter.'

'Stick with what you know,' Lukas tosses his head at the raucous energy of the crowded cafe, 'but isn't that what the grumblers said to Moses in the wilderness— we were better off in Egypt, at least we had our flesh-pots.'

Surprised by Lukas's religious references, Max feels his reticence slipping. 'Rabbi Bauminger says there's no need for a Jewish homeland—wherever we settle we have the bond of circumcision and in the far corners of the earth we fulfil the promise to Abraham—so every nation will bless His Name.'

'But Jews don't even try to be a light to the nations. We set ourselves apart with dietary laws and the Sabbath and the ban on intermarriage. Wherever we go we lock ourselves into our own little homelands and when they're torn down we build another one. What the Zionist want is a real home—one that can be defended and doesn't depend on the generosity of people who despise us.'

Max hesitates, unable to disagree with anything Lukas said. 'But what if we get a homeland? We'd be just like the goyim... we'll need an army to defend our borders and there'll be wars. In exile we are free from all that—instead of fighting for the fatherland, we have the Covenants and wherever we go we take our mother tongue.'

This time Lukas is silenced. He hated the patriotic horse-shit of the war years and the prospect of going back to where it all started and re-enacting the conquest of Canaan seems like an unimaginative solution. Mutual ambivalence makes it easy for the two boys to talk; both are fizzing with half-formed thoughts and their exchanges stir up their own uncertainties. Lukas persuades Max to sample the notorious house-wine and orders plates of fried-fish served with a glutinous parsley sauce. Young women pass their table, lingering flirtatiously while a group of Galicians bawl out Zionist anthems and obscene drinking songs in heavily accented Yiddish. As the wine takes hold Lukas is eager to display his knowledge of the religion he'd abandoned. He mockingly adopts the tone of a rabbinical scholar commenting on the promise to Abraham.

'When Sarah said people would laugh at her for falling pregnant in her old age, she was speaking prophetically—people love to laugh at others' misfortune and to this day the children of Abraham are supplying all the misery needed to keep the nations amused.'

In the morning, shuffling into the lecture hall, Max cannot summon even the most rudimentary concentration. The Professor's voice floats past him and he is drawn back to the café on Dresdner Straße, enviously recalling how Lukas threw back his wine, looking straight into the eyes of the young women hovering around their table. In his chaotic imagining he sees Lukas as a latter-day Moses, calling him from his habit of obedience, daring him to come into the wilderness, a rough place with bitter wine, shameless women and unruly youths singing crude songs in harsh accents. With a shudder he recognises that unless he enters the wilderness he cannot have Hanya. She haunts him like one of Lilith's sprites, wickedly alluring, uninhibited, dancing to the rhythm of negro music. He urgently wants to reply to her letter but has no idea what to say. The wild, barely coherent description of Berg's opera gives him a glimpse of the life he refused. She made it sound easy—just follow your heart—but everything in her world terrifies him. It is all so free and spontaneous. He would always be out of place, trying to keep pace with a score he cannot follow, worrying about petty things like passing exams and honouring his father.

23

To protect himself from the siren call of Lukas's careless hedonism, Max immerses in his studies, avoids distractions and devotes free time to reading. Seated on a bench in the Volksgarten, head buried in Hermann Weyl's *Space, Time, Matter*, he is startled by a pamphlet landing on the pages of his open book. Looking up he sees Lukas smiling provocatively.

'You must read this.'

The pamphlet on the Arab riots is filled with lurid descriptions of Jewish pioneers slaughtered, defenceless women raped, children having their eyes put out. It reminds Max of articles he read at the start of the war, railing against atrocities French soldiers were inflicting on peace-loving German villagers. Sensing his friend's skepticism Lukas admits the writing is rhetorical but assures him the events were all too real. His usual ironic tone is replaced by indignation and he speaks enthusiastically about a meeting Max must attend. His *Unitas* friends are helping to organise a lecture tour for Vladimir Jabotinsky, a hero to the Zionist communities in Palestine after he persuaded the British to create a Jewish regiment to fight the Turks. In Lukas's breathless telling this is the first time in eighteen-hundred years Jews had taken up arms to defend their territory. With an image of the Bar-Kokhba rebels flitting through his mind, Max is tempted to say the last time Jews took up arms it didn't end well. He remains silent, smiling as Lukas recounts chivalrous stories of Zionist heroes coming to the aid of pioneer farmers.

As if seeking an antidote to Lukas's zeal, Max passes the pamphlet to Karl and tells him about the lecture tour. Although he has no interest in attending, Karl has no hesitation denouncing Jabotinsky. He'd read about him in the *Neue Freie Presse* and claims his career shows how nationalism and militarism always go hand in hand.

'By all reports the Arab riots are as bloodthirsty as the Russian pogroms, so the only thing the Zionists have achieved is to transfer violence from one continent to another.'

Max finds Karl's dismissive cynicism even less appealing than Lukas's zealotry and enters the meeting with few expectations. Scanning the crowd of smartly dressed dignitaries scrambling for seats beneath the magnificent chandelier of the Kursalon concert hall he is surprised to see his mentor Dr. Joseph Fleischl sat behind the podium at the official table. On one occasion Dr. Fleischl had sounded him out on his views of Zionism and Max parroted his father's belief that it was improper to rely on the actions of men to hasten redemption. It never occurred that the dignified doctor might be a Zionist. Lukas cajoles Max into sitting at the front of the hall among a rowdy group of *Unitas* members who let loose a barrage of cheering as Jabotinsky is introduced. The audience looks askance at this outburst and the man himself appears embarrassed. Without acknowledging the applause he begins in a conversational tone as if he has no desire to persuade anyone and is simply laying out information for consideration.

'We should not blame the Arabs for opposing our settlements,' he announces, pausing to take in the hall's silence. 'They demonstrate the patriotism every nation feels when their territory is threatened. And they are correct in believing their land is under threat. We do not come to Palestine as tourists and neither do we come as migrant labourers seeking to ingratiate ourselves with the local population. The Zionist Council says we should conceal our true intentions and speak only of the railroads we will build and the countless benefits we will bring to this backward country. This way of thinking assumes the Arabs are either stupid or care nothing for their lands, but the Arabs are no fools—they possess the shrewdness of peasants the world over and immediately understand what is at stake when strangers arrive with designs on their land.'

Glancing at Lukas's colleagues Max notices heads bowed, some fidgeting with the pamphlet they had worked so hard to distribute. They'd anticipated a stirring call to arms and are perplexed to hear approval for Arab patriotism.

'The danger of dissembling,' Jabotinsky continues in the same matter-of-fact tone, 'is not that we might fail to deceive the Arabs but we succeed in deceiving ourselves into believing our intentions are so modest we could not possibly pose a threat to anybody. In this state of deluded innocence we make ourselves vulnerable. We must be honest in our purpose: We aim to establish a Jewish state in Palestine.'

The *Unitas* boys are heartened to hear a more challenging tone and assume the opening remarks were intended to placate the assembled dignitaries listening with wrinkled brows.

'They say we can win the Arabs over by appealing to the solidarity of the working class or the cosmic unity of mankind—but Palestine is no place for dreamers. It is a harsh land, accustomed to conflict and occupation. To achieve our purpose we must do what colonists have always done: Build a secure base before negotiating with the local population. We need an iron wall. And I don't mean a metaphorical wall. In the Jezreel Valley our pioneers were denied access to a well on the land they purchased. In one night, they surrounded the well with roofing iron—two sheets of iron set three feet apart and the space in-between packed with earth. When the Arabs discovered their rifles could not penetrate the wall, they were ready to negotiate. A tap was provided for the local villagers and the settlement is now thriving.'

He continues in this vein for three hours, speaking with the confidence of a man who knows he is telling the unvarnished truth. Each section of the audience falls under his spell. The young men of *Unitas* feel their hearts sing as they hear of the wall impervious to Arab bullets. For the Orthodox he recounts a Talmudic story of two men finding a piece of cloth they both lay claim to. One stubbornly insists he should have the entire cloth while the other shows piety by agreeing to split the cloth between them. When the dispute is taken to court the wise judge notes there is agreement about one half of the cloth and rules the disputed half should be divided. So the obstinate fellow ends up with three quarters and the pious gentleman is sent away with a quarter.

For Max, thoughtfully digesting every word, there comes a point when Jabotinsky turns to numbers to demonstrate the morality of the Zionist cause.

'The land occupied by the Arabs, from Morocco through to Arabia, holds a population of approximately 38 million and when you exclude the deserts, they occupy their lands at a ratio of 16 people to the square mile. In Sicily, which has a similar climate, the ratio is 352 per square mile. By the best estimates there are now 15 million Jews living in exile and wherever we settle we face intolerable persecution. When these facts are considered dispassionately, taking a portion of Palestine as a Jewish state is an act of justice. No one should expect the Arabs will agree but enforced justice is still justice.'

The crowd spill out of the Kursalon oblivious to the biting winds swirling through the Stadtpark and the portico steps are clogged with people engaging in impassioned discussion. Max extricates himself from the *Unitas* faction pressing all and sundry to join them at the Dresdner Straße café. Squirming through the crowd on Johannesgasse he bumps into Dr. Fleischl who firmly shakes his hand. The Doctor is called away by a colleague who'd succeeded in hailing a cab, but as he leaves he calls over his shoulder, 'Come to my study in the morning—I'd very much like to hear what you made of it.'

Max nods, mortified at the prospect of giving the Doctor an account of his opinions.

At home he watches his family prepare for bed and tentatively approaches the table where father reads by the kerosene lamp. Sensing his son's anxiety, the old man sets aside his book and Max gives a brief report of the lecture and Dr. Fleischl's invitation. Though he has never mentioned it, his father is aware of the Doctor's Zionists sympathies. He asks if Max can recall the three oaths of Rabbi Yossi bar Hanina and nods approvingly as his son dutifully repeats what he'd been taught at Sabbath School.

'Israel shall not go up all together to Jerusalem; they shall not rebel against the nations; the idolaters shall not oppress Israel too much.'

Father explains how the *gemara* refers to a passage in the *Song of Songs* when the daughters of Jerusalem are charged three times, not to *arouse nor awaken love until it pleases.* His exposition winds through an ever-expanding web of references and secondary questions, dwelling on the lover of wisdom who stands hopefully outside a wall, believing his beloved will appear at a window to show her face as she in turn is certain her lover will wait outside the gate to catch a glimpse of her.

'The warning against awakening love is conditional and should not be taken as a commandment. Everything depends on what is meant by the words *until it pleases.*'

Max listens with a growing exasperation that he is not gaining anything useful for when he faces Dr. Fleischl.

Exhausted by a fretful night, he stumbles into the armchair when Dr. Fleischl invites him to sit. To put him at ease the Doctor enquires about his studies and even in this matter Max is tongue-tied. Scrutinising his visitor as if considering a diagnosis for an unusual illness, Dr. Fleischl speaks with fatherly concern. 'I was surprised to see you at the lecture and I asked you to come here because I'm most interested to hear your thoughts. I hope you will speak freely.'

Max tentatively expresses agreement on the need for a Jewish homeland but makes his position unclear by applying elaborate conditions and qualifiers to every statement. Listening attentively the Doctor explains he is particularly interested in Max's views because most of the younger Zionists are atheists or fanatical socialists.

'It would be a terrible irony if the Zionists succeeded in creating their homeland only to find they have obliterated everything that makes us Jewish. I understand the orthodox objections, but we must at least entertain the possibility the Almighty-Blessed-Be-He might be using the atheistic Zionists, just as the pagan Cyrus was used to put an end to the Babylonian exile.'

Max recalls his father's words from the *Song of Songs* and as if thinking aloud finds himself saying, 'How can we know when love pleases to be awakened?'

Dr. Fleischl is delighted and repeats the phrase to himself, chuckling warmly.

'Indeed—how can we know? One shouldn't be over cautious in such matters or there would be no fruitfulness.'

In what seems an afterthought, he mentions a dire shortage of mathematics teachers in Palestine. The Zionist Council wisely decided education at all levels would be conducted in Hebrew and though there are numerous mathematicians among the Pioneers, only a tiny fraction have the necessary fluency in Hebrew.

The proposition takes Max by surprise and in the following days he cannot get the idea out of his head. The more he mulls it over the more excited he becomes—he could step into the wilderness and join a great adventure without abandoning the security of a solid career. With his final examinations approaching he's been carefully weighing his options. In spite of commendations he'd received for his doctoral studies he knows it is impossible for Jews to obtain university appointments and has decided to apply for a teaching position at a Jewish Volksschule and eventually a Realgymnasium. With jobs scarce it may be necessary to seek employment in Breslau or Prague so it should not be too greater a stretch to consider Palestine. When he finally summons the courage to raise the matter in hypothetical terms, his Father guesses his purpose and reveals Dr. Fleischl had already approached him about the possibility of a position in Jerusalem. Max is thrilled at his father's solemn pronouncement.

'To live in Jerusalem and await the Messiah cannot be counted as a transgression so long as you reject the wickedness of believing redemption can come through the works of men.'

For the old man Jerusalem is impossibly distant, sometimes forgotten, but always present, imperceptibly drawing him from the meanness of the cramped apartment in Leopoldstadt. He can think of no greater blessing than a handful of Jerusalem soil sprinkled over his grave. He has reservations about using Hebrew to teach mathematics, believing the language of the Torah should be reserved for sacred purposes, though these concerns are allayed by his anxiety that the younger generation are no longer learning enough Hebrew at the synagogue.

As he prepares for his final examinations, Max spends his free time in a remote corner of the university library, studying until a librarian roams the shelves, ringing a bell to signal the library is closing in half an hour. Passing through the arcade on his way home he finds himself following a group of boisterous students and recognises Lukas. His friend looks unsteady on his feet and Max hopes he can remain unnoticed, but as they spill onto the Ringstraße the group halt and spread across the pavement, undecided on their destination. On hearing his name Max feigns surprise and cordially greets Lukas who throws an arm over his shoulder, insisting he joins them for a glass of wine. Recognising the impossibility of declining the invitation Max reluctantly accompanies the group, apologising he will be unable to stay long as his father expects him home. They settle on a bierstube on Schmelzgasse where Lukas guides Max to a small table some distance from the benches where his friends settle. He signals a waiter and ignores Max's request for water. Two glasses of larger are delivered with a bowl of pretzels.

With a mischievous grin Lukas tilts his glass, 'I'm going to Palestine.'

Having observed how Lukas fell under Jabotinsky's spell, Max is not in the least surprised. He smiles warmly and would like to reveal his own plans but remains silent as his position will not be secure until he passes his exams. Lukas is unconstrained by such timidity and with more than a hint of bravado reveals he is leaving within a week for a pioneers' training camp in Crimea.

'What about your exams?'

Lukas laughs. 'I've torn up my Matriculation book so there can be no turning back—never felt so certain about anything.'

Max gazes at the table, shaking his head. Lukas is regarded as one of the most promising students in his field and to abandon his studies weeks before graduation is beyond comprehension. He cannot help noticing Lukas finds a perverse pleasure in the outrage his decision provokes and yet for some reason wants Max's approval.

'Eretz Israel has no use for philologists.' Though he is speaking earnestly, Lukas cannot entirely banish an ironic inflection. 'We need to get our hands dirty, working the soil is the only way to bind the people to our homeland.'

Max listens glumly as Lukas holds forth on *Chavot Hachshara* where he will be taught agricultural skills. He expects to stay at the training farm for 2 or 3 years before one of the coveted immigration certificates for agricultural labourers becomes available. Glancing at his friend's hands, better suited to playing a waltz than wielding a hoe, Max discreetly asks if there might not be some other way his talents could be used.

'To be useful you must know what is needed. Zionist organizations are filled with philosophers, poets, drama critics, but Israel is crying for men who can plant a wheat field or irrigate an orchard. Exile has alienated us from the soil, we've become a nation of parasites relying on the labour of others for our most basic needs.'

'So your university work counts for nothing?'

'So long as we are in exile of course it counts for nothing. I could pass with distinction and even get something published, but when it comes to appointments I have to stand aside and applaud politely while some pompous Teutonic blockhead takes the prize. It reminds me of summer holidays growing up—I used to build magnificent sandcastles on the beach and then watch the incoming tide wash them away.'

Max had never taken a holiday by the sea, nor built a sandcastle. It disturbs him to see the self-confidence he'd always admired, replaced by reckless enthusiasm.

When Lukas runs out of things to say he simply states, 'You know nothing would be lost if you waited a few weeks and sat your exams before going to Crimea.'

Lukas makes no attempt to conceal his disappointment. 'I thought if anyone would understand it would be you.'

24

With the spinning of the Devil's Wheel gaining pace Hanya loses her footing and careens into a group of strangers before catching a railing. When the contraption halts, she leads Werther through the crowd and slips into a contemplative mood watching the metal plates of the tin lake rhythmically rise and fall. Werther's glance turns from the mechanical waves to rest on the side of her face. Sensing she is being watched Hanya feels pleased to have captivated such a sensitive observer. She agreed to come when he waited patiently outside the Ishitar and walked with her to the boarding-house on Behrenstraße. Bashfully declining an invitation to come inside, he asked if he could take her somewhere on Sunday afternoon and on an impulse, she suggested Lunar Park. He's younger than her usual admirers and there was a gentleness in how he asked, as if expecting a rebuff.

She turns to him with a smile but the moment she feels his arm discreetly resting against her lower back she cannot help thinking of Max. Her lingering attachment to an affair that withered before it could blossom makes no sense. Werther's temperament is so much more artistic, his devotion pure and uncomplicated and he seems free from the encumbrance of an overbearing family.

Across the lake they hear a chorus of screams as the Ghost Train disappears into its tunnel. To put Max out of her mind she suggests a ride. As they join the throng inching towards the ticket booth, Werther peppers her with questions about the principles of eurhythmics. Hanya is struck by the incongruity of discussing such things while the boy in front whines about being hungry and the man behind complains loudly about the slowness of the queue. Their frustration vanishes once they board the train, ascending a steep incline which offers a spectacular view of the mishmash of attractions spread below. Plunging down a sharply winding track, Werther smiles knowingly when other passengers scream at a mirror image of their car hurtling towards them. The train enters the gloom of the tunnel where a hunchback drags a mess of chains over a pile of bones and a coffin opens to reveal a jiggling skeleton. There is a momentary jolt of terror as they pass through a cloud of steam and a clammy hand rakes across their faces. Alighting into harsh sunlight they meander down a bustling avenue lined with shooting galleries and caravans. Werther remains oblivious to the crowd and earnestly resumes his enquiries about eurhythmics. At the China Shop a man is hurling hard rubber balls at a rotating display of crockery and Hanya is strangely attracted by the prospect of smashing fine china. When an elegant teapot shatters under the impact of a direct hit, she squeals, vaguely recalling a spanking she received as a little girl when she carelessly broke a china ornament. Werther pays for six balls each. He smashes two tea-cups but fails to make the three hits required for a prize. Hanya sets her sights on the figurines and vases moving rapidly on the most elevated level of the display. After four misses the attendant passes her an extra ball and encourages her to give it her best shot. Summoning the fierce concentration she would apply to a grand jeté she flings the ball with all her might and raises her arms in triumph when a Chinese vase explodes. Turning to the closer targets she makes two more hits, drinking in the onlookers' applause as she chooses a stuffed monkey for her prize.

Returning to Behrenstraße in a cocoon of cheerfulness, she is annoyed she cannot banish Max from her thoughts. The kiss on the step, offered carelessly, is received by Werther as an undreamt honour. As their lips part his hands slide from her shoulders to her hips and an irresistible pressure draws their bodies together. Hanya gives herself to a slow languorous kiss. Without exchanging a word she leads him upstairs, through the parlour where a desultory card-game is proceeding, and into her bedroom. The moment the door closes they pull at each other's clothes and the call of their bodies is answered in frenetic abandon that has the card players smiling wistfully and laying down their cards to listen to the raucous, irrepressible music of love.

He leaves discretely before dawn, pressing his forehead against hers and whispering, 'I'd give anything to be with you.'

Taking a leisurely bath while the other boarders slumber, Hanya feels a slowly rising nausea, as if she'd absorbed a poison her body longs to expel. For all her wantonness she'd always been able to convince herself she was faithful to Max. With Werther it is different. It would be so easy to simply say yes and immerse herself in his unconditional devotion. She contemplates transferring her affection from Max to Werther—could she, or does it just seem impossible because she's never tried? The memory of Max's liquid eyes persists, an itch she cannot soothe. If there was a letter, if Max gave a hint he wanted her, she would drop everything and catch the next train to Vienna. Head resting against the hard enamel of the bath rim her eyes close and somewhere beneath her eyelids she sees the china vase in the moment before she hurled the rubber ball. '*Give it your best shot.*' The bathwater cooling, she summons the dogged persistence she falls into when holding a stretch position, electrified by the conviction that nothing is more pathetic than doing nothing, watching a faint hope fade like flame leaving an ember.

Shaking off the musty dampness of the bathroom she is surprised how easy it is to sever her ties to the great city. At Anhalter Bahnhof she approaches a row of ticket windows where a bored clerk could never guess the momentous promise contained in the scrap of printed cardboard he dispenses without raising his eyes. She will miss the anonymity of Berlin. At the Ishitar she announces she must visit her ill Mother and Frau Nolde assures her she can rejoin the troupe whenever she pleases. To her friends in the chorus she gives the flamboyant hats and dresses she would never dream of wearing in Vienna. Rival theories about her departure provide amusement for late-night gatherings in the boarding house parlour. Hanya smiles inscrutably and avoids mentioning anything about her plans to Werther. On the morning of her departure she leaves a terse, painfully written note entrusted to Hans and Gottfried in case he enquires.

Settling into her compartment she plays the seasoned traveller and as the engine shunts an unexpected calm envelops her. Hours later the train is swallowed by the darkness of a forest and in the cramped space of the pull-down bunk she watches the signal lights flash across the blackness of the windowpane. In the early morning light the outskirts of Vienna are unrecognisable and even when she glimpses St. Stefan's familiar profile she is disoriented. Hovering around the baggage cart it comes as a shock to see Mother scurrying towards her. She'd telegrammed ahead but did not expect to be met at the station. Surrendering to a maternal embrace she melts under the burden of knowing she is loved. Immeasurable seconds pass in silence until her mother's voice unleashes a surge of anxiety. Leaving Berlin with her every thought focussed on Max, she had not considered how to explain her return. She sways under a drift of thought that only becomes manageable when she notices Mother is busily arranging to have her luggage delivered. She has forgotten what it is like to be fussed over and on returning to the Bauernmarkt the stodgy atmosphere of home holds a comforting allure. Mother discreetly prompts her to reveal something of her intentions and Hanya has a premonition of her hard-won independence vanishing. She concocts a plausible account of a plan to open a small studio to introduce Viennese girls to the Eurythmic methods she learnt in Berlin. Mother is taken by the idea and eagerly jots down a list of potential clients. To curb her enthusiasm Hanya insists she must first complete more advanced studies and says she is thinking about enrolling at the new Hellerau school, which has recently moved to the Schloss Laxenburg.

Arriving home after staying late at the university, Karl greets his sister as if the years of separation are a weekend excursion. He questions her about the political situation in Berlin and quickly determines she cannot tell him anything he does not know. Hanya is unsurprised that in manhood her brother is as obnoxious as he was in adolescence. She feigns interest in his academic studies and waits for an opportune moment to enquire about Max. Karl gives a detailed account of his friend's academic accomplishments and oblivious to the impact of his words, casually remarks, 'He often asks about you.'

'What have you told him?'

'Very little I'm afraid—though I did pass on your letter.'

With her heart racing Hanya does her best retain a nonchalant air and Mother fills the silence, 'Such a pity he abandoned his musical studies—his tutor is very highly regarded in some circles.'

The galvanising purpose driving her return evaporates as Hanya contemplates the difficulty of engineering a meeting with Max. After mother retires she finds Karl alone in the library and tentatively sounds out the possibility of visiting Max at the university. Her brother makes it clear it would be terribly inconsiderate to bother him while he prepares for his final exams. The agony of delay is intensified by Mother's relentless cheerfulness. She treats her to coffee and cake at Demel's and the fine grained *sachertorte* dissolving in her mouth awakens Hanya's nostalgia for the indulgent pleasures of yesteryear. Dipping her spoon into the exquisitely contoured mound of whipped cream she hardens against the attraction of bourgeois comforts.

If she had not been so frustrated by the obstacles keeping her from Max she might have noticed Mother's optimism is as fragile as cracked glass. Father is wracked with pains for which his doctor can find no cause and no matter how hard he works it is impossible to mitigate the effects of inflation. His grim persistence is mirrored in Dora's private sorrow, now so dense Mother cannot remember when she answered a question with anything more than yes or no. Despite mother's urging Hanya makes no attempt to converse with her sister. She feels mocked by the blankness in

Dora's eyes; her bedroom door stands like a border-post marking the boundary to the darkness that awaits her if her quest should come to nothing. To keep her spirits up she doggedly recites the refrain that propelled her from Berlin: 'Nothing is worse than doing nothing.'

Preparing for his exams Karl is abnormally cheerful and Hanya can scarcely contain her laughter when Mother reveals he has developed feelings for a young lady he met through the university hiking club. Feeling certain her brother has neither the capacity nor inclination for romance, she is flabbergasted as Mother describes a dinner party Karl organised to introduce the young lady and her parents.

'She's lovely, homely and rather shy, and clearly smitten. Her family are not well educated, but nobody pays attention to such things anymore and frankly we couldn't wish for a better match.'

When Karl suggests Hanya should make an effort to befriend the girl, she spies an opportunity for a *quid pro quo*. 'If I'm to spend time with your belle, you must do me the favour of arranging a meeting with Max.'

She emphasises the need for discretion, but the next day Karl announces he has organised a rendezvous. With characteristic insouciance he fails to allow time for Hanya to prepare. The best she can do is throw on a pleated tunic and matching cloche before being hustled aboard a tram. In a rising panic she worries the sleek green outfit with its low waistline is inappropriate and contemplates abandoning the venture. It is only fear of enduring her brother's ridicule that makes her hold her course.

They alight near the entrance to the Stadtpark and a flicker of memory threatens her composure. She notices the park has regained the manicured elegance entirely absent in that glorious summer after the war, when the lawns were overgrown and pathways strewn with rubbish. The Café Herrenhof looms exactly as she remembers and stepping into the circle of rotating glass she is filled with dread. With no faith in her powers of persuasion all her hopes rest on a brittle conviction that love will triumph.

On the other side of the street, Max watched Karl and Hanya enter the café. He'd arrived early and found a spot behind an advertising kiosk to calm his nerves. His position in Jerusalem assured, it would have been possible to avoid the meeting and quietly slip away, but to leave without explanation would be such miserable cowardice, he could not live with himself. Approaching the café he surrenders to the unanswerable compulsion he knew as a schoolboy summoned before the classroom for punishment. Hanya is so disarmingly sweet he manages a smile as they press cheeks. Showing no interest in their awkward attempts at conversation, Karl orders ice-cream and after devouring his serving feels he has discharged his obligations. He bluntly announces he is going to the library and Hanya and Max exchange nervous smiles as he pays the waiter and departs. She watches Max picking at his mound of ice-cream, eyes fixed on the table.

The heartfelt declarations she has incessantly rehearsed seem hollow and she opts for caution. 'I thought of you a lot in Berlin, all the time.'

Max's spoon stabbing at the ice-cream makes it clear even the most circumspect approach will arouse anxiety and Hanya decides she might as well come out with it.

'I only came back because of you,' she speaks softly, without emotion, hoping his eyes might open towards her.

'You shouldn't have.'

His voice is mangled by ambivalence and even as the words leave his mouth he wants to take them back. Unable to raise his eyes he does not see the shudder pass over Hanya's face, but senses her hurt. In a stammering tangle of apology and explanation he gives a detailed account of his deliberations before accepting a position in Jerusalem.

In none of Hanya's imaginings had she conceived of Max leaving Vienna. She is gripped by the notion the story might be an elaborate fabrication. Max raises his bowed head and catches her eyes, dark and glistening, silvered with a film of moisture. It is more than he can bare and he returns his gaze to the milky pool of melted ice-cream at the bottom of his bowl. As she contemplates the distance between Vienna and Jerusalem, Hanya discerns a faint hope.

'Are you going alone… to Jerusalem?'

Max responds with a nod and Hanya's voice inches into the silence. 'I could go with you.'

'It's not possible.' Max regrets his reply came so fast and again speaks for far too long, enumerating the difficulties of obtaining an entry visa and recounting how his friend Lukas must spend three years at the training camp in Crimea before he can consider applying for an immigration certificate. He explains his own position only came by chance when his patron at the University was charged with finding a suitably qualified mathematician fluent in Hebrew. Hanya's mind drifts as she imagines the devotion that could inspire a boy to submit to three years of study at an agricultural camp. She wonders if her love could withstand such a test. Max's voice expires into a dark silence where her deepest fears find fertile soil.

'So I've made a complete fool of myself for nothing.' She speaks as if the observation is directed at herself and Max's failure to respond deepens her humiliation. 'If you only knew the men I've turned away—a thousand times more eager, more willing—'

'You mustn't.'

'What?'

'Turn them away on my account; I can't give you what you need.'

'What I need?' Hanya is almost shouting. 'What I need is you.'

Enraged by his silence she is ready to upend the table. She pictures herself storming from the café, the ladies at the next table coolly raising their eyebrows and the waiter shrugging as he sweeps the broken crockery Max would be obliged to pay for. It would be a fitting end but a squeaking, barely audible voice draws her back to reality.

'I wish I could…'

The words fade into an impenetrable void, but there is no mistaking the trembling intensity. Even unable to see his eyes she knows there are tears. In perfect stillness she accepts the silence and when she is certain he has nothing more to say, reaches across the table, draws his face towards hers and presses her lips against his forehead.

Leaving him hunched over a bowl of melted ice-cream she passes through the heavy glass doors without a backward glance and merges into the crowd of pedestrians on Lothringerstraße. It is incomprehensible he should be the one reduced to tears while she maintains composure. She had imagined the pain of rejection would be unbearable but the numbness she feels is softened by the perverse pleasure of knowing she has wounded him. The brisk rhythm of her footsteps imparts a vague sense of purpose and she wonders how long he will remain at the table, snivelling, before embarrassment has him scuttling for the door. There is no reason to return home but she cannot think of anywhere else to go and follows a circuitous route, avoiding the Stadtpark which could only raise memories of things that can never be recovered. Drifting through dreary streets a dull yearning arises. She scrutinises the faces of passing couples, trying to decide whether they have attained an inner peace that will always elude her or if the emptiness of their lives has inoculated them against violent passions. Whichever way she looks at it she can see no solution: It is impossible to hate him for his weakness and equally impossible to put him out of her mind.

25

A shiver passes through Hanya's body as she glances at the closed door of Dora's bedroom. She feels grateful to her sister for revealing what it is like to become an object of pity and is determined not to succumb to the grim satisfaction Dora draws from her self-imposed isolation. In the upstairs library she finds Karl hunched over the reading table. Casting an eye over the books stacked in front of him she is amused to see Heine's *Book of Songs* open among an assortment of heavier material. She slumps into one of the comfortable armchairs that affords a view down Jasmirgottstrasse to the western façade of St. Stefan's. Confiding in her brother is an absurd notion, but set against Mother's fretful optimism and Dora's depressing morbidity he seems the best option. There is no danger he will suspect the intensity of her emotions and his pugnacious attitude might be what is needed to overcome her irrational attachment. In a neutral tone she admits she was surprised to learn Max is planning to go to Palestine.

Karl discloses he has done his best to dissuade him. 'He has a mystical streak which makes him vulnerable to romanticism. I told him the Zionists are no different from the nationalist fanatics—they're both infatuated by a utopia that only exists in their imagination.'

Having absorbed a heavy dose of Freudian theory in the boarding-house parlour, Hanya has her own theories on Zionism. She believes the allure Palestine holds for young Jewish men is a neurotic projection of an infantile desire to have intercourse with their mothers. She fears Max will never be cured unless he breaks from the crippling influence of his home environment.

As Karl holds forth on the folly of the Zionist project, she realises he has no inkling of her inner torment and welcomes the distraction when he clumsily reminds her of the promise to meet with Josephine. His voice is tinged with apprehension and she notices he is fidgeting nervously with his fountain pen. Under normal circumstances she would have teased him mercilessly, but is in no mood for mockery. She suspects her precious feelings for Max are no better than her brother's floundering and her only advantage lies in a capacity for concealment. She says she is happy to meet

Josephine and discreetly enquires as to his intentions.

'Mother keeps insisting she's waiting for me to pop the question, but I don't want to propose for the wrong reasons. I have no idea whether she will accept and I don't know if I'm capable of giving her what she needs. After you meet, I'd like to hear your honest opinion.'

Though aware of her inadequacy for the task, Hanya is eager for any diversion. She rises from the armchair and reaches over Karl's shoulder for Heine's poetry, which he has stuffed beneath a pile of books. In her last year of schooling she kept the same well-thumbed volume at her bedside and night after night lost herself in the dream-like verses of *Lyrical Interlude*. Flicking through the familiar pages she finds what she is looking for and reads aloud as if posing a question.

'Many a time in my dreaming
Through that region of rapture I roam
Then the morning sun comes with its beaming
And scatters it all like foam.'

Karl's eyebrows tighten in bewilderment and Hanya is pleased to see her know-all brother recognises she has superior understanding with affairs of the heart. It is flattering to have him seek her counsel, but having made such a mess of her own affairs she doubts she is up to the task. And what if she dislikes the girl? Any off-hand comment might tip the balance on what could be the most momentous decision of his life. As Karl frets over arrangements for the meeting she feels like a maiden aunt summoned to pass judgement on the merits of a prospective daughter-in-law.

They meet Josephine at Nussdorf and after a brisk walk through the woods arrive at a charming little inn with outdoor tables beneath a chestnut tree. Karl takes charge of ordering and Hanya is surprised to see her little brother is not entirely devoid of social graces. Scrutinising the menu card as if it were a philosophical treatise, he engages the waiter in friendly banter and attentively elicits preferences before selecting a fruity dry wine, chicken fried in breadcrumbs for the ladies and Viennese sausage for himself.

A self-conscious formality hovers over the gathering and the unstated purpose of the meeting weighs on Josephine. Though plain and plump her complexion has an aura of wholesomeness and Hanya searches for a way to let the poor girl know she does not need to worry about making a good impression. The idea that two people could be destined for each other appeals to Hanya and though she cannot decide whether they are a good match she fervently believes they should give it their best shot. Her only reservation stems from her inability to discern any spark of poetry in either one of them. Nothing in their manner suggests the wild intoxication she experienced with Max, when she felt her spirit soar into the infinity of the night sky. In a quizzical mood she contemplates the possibility that her lofty conception of love might be nothing more than a childish nonsense. Watching them consider the dessert card Hanya notices they already have the appearance of a middle-aged couple. With a shared passion for sweet pastries she cannot imagine they will ever be troubled by *the morning sun with its beaming*. Raising her glass Hanya toasts to their future happiness.

Supressing a spark of jealousy she resolves to hold onto her *region of rapture*. She can picture herself living without hope of achieving her heart's desire so long as she can clasp a fragment of what she once felt. She will keep it like a memento in a corner of her purse and set it as a seal on her heart. Learning to live without Max will not be easy and she regrets how they parted. She had no right to expect anything from him and is determined there should be no ill-will.

By urging Karl to make discreet enquiries Hanya learns the date of his departure for Constanza and plans to offer him a dignified farewell. Wearing the same outfit she wore at their ill-fated meeting, she moves slyly amid the bustle of the platform. Her hopes for a quiet moment with Max dissolve as she spies him encircled by a knot of family. His father's frail hands cup Max's cheeks and the guttural Hebrew benediction reaches her through the hubbub of the crowd. She watches crestfallen as each member of Max's family holds him in a loving embrace. On hearing the station bell he disengages and scuttles aboard the third-class section. Gripped by an uncontrollable impulse Hanya rushes into the next carriage and jostles past passengers stowing coats and bags until she catches sight of him hesitantly searching for a window seat. Clutching his elbow she drags him into the narrow corridor where the carriages connect. Terror flashes across his face.

'Don't worry I'm not going to cause a scene, I just wanted to say goodbye… properly. I know we cannot be together but I need to know you are all right. You must promise me you will write.'

It takes a super-human effort to restrain herself from forcing a kiss onto his startled mouth, but she smiles benignly and with a gentle tilt of her head pleads for a reply.

'Yes of course,' he stammers.

'Promise me you will write—I can't live without knowing something.'

'I promise.'

With the stationmaster's whistle in her ear and the carriage shuddering,

Hanya steps nimbly from the moving train and joins the waving crowd. She watches Max's mother following the train, wailing a lament and craning her neck to catch sight of her son whose darting eyes settle on a sleek, solitary figure in a pleated chiffon tunic who stands like a statue on the crowded platform.

26

From the high balcony of the Altes Schloss, Hanya glimpses Franzensburg Castle and a trickle of hazy memories mingle with the lush music from the gramophone in the old ballroom. There had been an outing before the war, perhaps a birthday party, she remembers a picnic by the lake with her cousins in pretty summer dresses and a greedy swan pecked a sandwich out of her hand. She looks back with embarrassment at how she'd been awestruck by the fairytale castle with its pointed spires. The staff at the Laxenburg-Hellerau Schule has nothing but disdain for Franzensburg. If it is mentioned at all it's to point to the reckless extravagance of the failed monarchy, the pseudo-gothic castle a fitting symbol for the decadence and dishonesty of the old regime.

Seeking an antidote to the humiliating conclusion of her doomed romance, Hanya embraces the monastic atmosphere of the Eurhythmics Institute. The Habsburg's summer palace is an odd setting for a venture that proudly embraces the spirit of modernism, but when the City of Vienna gained ownership of imperial properties, the socialist councillors were set on sweeping away the depravity of the old order and could not have hoped for an organisation better suited to their purpose. The school sees itself as a social laboratory, revitalising the nation by applying the scientific rigour of Dalcroze's method to a national program of physical education.

Hanya feared living exclusively in the company of women would revive the back-biting nastiness that made her school years miserable, but the demanding schedule of exercise and study engenders an esprit de corps, free from pettiness. The Viennese students are mostly naïve young girls fresh out of school but women from all over Europe are drawn to Laxenburg like pilgrims to a shrine. Hanya shares a room with a Russian trained under Diaghilev, two sisters from Marseille and an 18-year-old girl who travelled alone from Denmark. Conversations are a hilarious mishmash of borrowed phrases but intimate friendships are forged through the language of music and dance. They play for each other, analyse the structure of musical scores and attune their bodies to the most delicate shifts in rhythm and timing. Gramophone recordings are played at mealtime and as they ascend and descend the grand staircases music guides their footsteps. On Sunday afternoons or in the long summer evenings before supper, groups of girls sunbathe in the nude on a large south facing balcony that opens from the Imperial ballroom. It is rumoured the porter leads paying customers from the village up to an attic window where they can furtively gaze on the lithe bodies, but there is such a robust confidence among the girls no one would be in the least perturbed by such prurience.

The woodland park, once a pleasure garden for Franz Joseph and Princess Theresia, is an oasis of tranquillity for Hanya; riotously verdant in summer and breathtakingly romantic in autumn when rust coloured leaves clog reflective ponds and fingers of mist cling to marshes. Whenever a letter from Max is delivered, Hanya keeps it unopened until she has an opportunity to stroll deep into the park. On the eastern border she discovers a meadow of wild-flowers overlooking a patchwork of cultivated fields. The boundary is marked by a ha-ha following the contours of the terrain and Hanya sits, feet dangling, over the sunken stone wall, wistfully absorbing Max's account of life in Palestine.

His first letters are guarded as if to ward off the unspoken fear Hanya might impulsively join him. He gives detailed descriptions of the primitive conditions in Jerusalem, explaining erratic payment of his salary has made it necessary to share a room with a Jewish policeman who arrived years earlier as a refugee from Poland. Their house on the exotic sounding Street of Prophets has neither electricity nor running water and its concrete cistern is filled from a water cart drawn by a donkey. A scorching dry wind called the *khamsin* blows in from the desert and during the summer months it is so unbearably hot he sleeps for two to three hours in the afternoon as soon as school finishes. As one might expect the climate is conducive to mosquitoes, flies and bugs. He says the swarms of cockroaches are so invasive he's been forced to set tin cans with kerosene beneath the legs of his bed. Hanya replies with concern, taking care to steer clear of anything suggesting she entertains notions of reviving their romance. She describes the daily routines at Laxenburg and writes enthusiastically about their musical studies. The newly appointed director of dance, Rosalia Chladek, a devotee of modern music, introduced the girls to Stravinsky and Malipiero and even had them analysing a recording of folk music from Morocco. Hanya proudly tells Max the Schönberg and Berg he used to play in the music room has enabled her to form a special bond with Frau Rosalia.

By scrupulously avoiding personal feelings she lures Max into writing freely about his new homeland. He comments on how Jerusalem differs from the romantic vision which grew in his imagination while living in Leopoldstadt. Each morning he awakens to the muezzin's call to prayer and has breakfast at a street stall where for a few piasters he can have strong black coffee, a disc of unleavened Arab bread and a handful of pressed dates. He writes about the bazaars where woman in black veils mingle with Jewish Pioneers in khaki shorts and Arab merchants wearing dark sunglasses with their Bedouin headgear. Hanya finds herself transported by his vivid descriptions of the street-markets. Visualising the stalls displaying ochre, auburn, and yellow spices she can almost smell the aroma of roasting coffee beans mixing with smoke from lamb charring on charcoal fires. As if to undercut these romantic impressions Max also mentions the stench from the fish-sellers and the pools of urine deposited by camels carrying sacks of flour.

Despite the feelings he stirs, she is calmed by the park's loveliness. The meticulously composed planting imparts an Olympian detachment. Every branch and bush placed according to the most refined aesthetic principals and even the changing seasons built into the design. The gentle curvature of the ha-ha leads the eye into the rural landscape so the splendour of the garden expands into the farmland. And just as the park spreads its uplifting vision to local villagers, Hanya imagines the ideals of the Eurhythmics Institute radiate a therapeutic influence on the nation.

Each summer the Hellerau school performs for the city of Vienna and with Frau Rosalia taking charge of the dance programme Hanya feels she is fulfilling her dream of participating in a truly sublime work of art. The piece is conceived on a grand scale and as soon as the weather is warm enough the spacious lawn in front of the Altes Schloss is marked to replicate the setting for an outdoor spectacle that will spread across the lawns and pathways of the Rathausplatz. Hanya earns a place among a select group of advanced students in the main chorus. They work tirelessly to synchronise their movements with the exquisitely light and vivacious music from Bizet's *L'Arlésienne Suites.* Every bar of the score is analysed and committed to memory with the changing time signatures marking intricate shifts in the direction of the dance. Frau Rosalia works independently with a larger chorus of younger students and a troupe of five male dancers recruited from Vienna. Her choreography establishes finely balanced polarities with elaborately plotted manoeuvres oscillating between circles coiling on themselves centripetally and spreading outwards by centrifugal motion. The men vigorously wield staffs that could be weapons or agricultural implements while the women sway gracefully holding gold metallic discs, both protective shields and symbols of regeneration. For the finale Frau Rosalia's solo draws the three choruses into an ecstatic celebration of unity.

On the last day of rehearsals, the dance troupe assemble at dawn, at a grove in the woods, sitting cross-legged on the ground as if clustered around a camp-fire. Speaking with the rhythmic lilt of a raconteur, Frau Rosalia explains how the dance was inspired by the goddess Harmonia.

'When Cadmus and Harmonia fell in love, the Olympians celebrated their nuptials at the sacred city of Thebes and their magnificent wedding feast was the last time gods and mortals spoke face-to-face. Thebes prospered under Cadmus and Harmonia's benevolent rule, but when their grandson Pentheus was made king, he introduced harsh laws and foolishly tried to assert his dominance over Dionysus. For his arrogance he was torn to shreds by the frenzied maenads and when the great city was laid waste Cadmus and Harmonia went into exile. As they departed, Harmonia gifted the letters of the alphabet to the citizens of Thebes. The gods retreated to their own inaccessible realm but Harmonia's gift allowed humans to compose stories and regain an experience of the celestial presence in the silence of their minds.'

The silence of the listening circle amplifies the dawn chorus and Hanya hears leaves trembling as Frau Rosalia softly pronounces, 'The purpose of the dance is to restore the lost harmony—the sacred thread connecting humans with the divine.'

For the performance a full orchestra assembles before the Rathaus with huge seating scaffolds erected for the audience. The Socialist Council ensure the best seats go to trade unionists and a great throng from all walks jockey for positions at the edges of the park. There is a long speech from the mayor declaring culture belongs to the people and is no longer the preserve of the aristocracy or bourgeoisie. Spontaneous applause punctuates the performance, especially during the adagio section when Hanya's chorus sway rhythmically in a voluptuous formation with sunlight flashing off their golden shields. For the finale the entire audience, which the papers estimate at 15,000, clap in time to the rustic beat of the farandole. The orchestra have not prepared an encore but in response to incessant applause they play a reprise of the farandole and Frau Rosalia is delighted to see female factory workers linking arms in a chain-dance snaking through the park with joyous outbursts of shouting and laughter.

Returning exhausted to the Altes Schloss, the dancers throw themselves into a raucous celebration with champagne corks narrowly missing the chandeliers in the imperial ballroom. Though giddy with excitement Hanya feels compelled to retire to the empty dormitory where she writes a long letter to Max with a rapturous account of the performance.

27

In the harsh environment of Jerusalem, Hanya's letters provide respite from the monotonous routines imposed by Max's duties at the gymnasium. Classes are held six days a week from 8:00am to 3:00pm, except Fridays when students are sent home at noon. His evenings are occupied with marking or preparing lessons and he sets Hanya's letters aside for reading on Saturday afternoons when most take a nap after the Sabbath meal. He is relieved Hanya does not harbour bitterness and enjoys reading her lively accounts of the strange activities at the eurhythmics school. Her unbridled enthusiasm makes him reflect on his habit of avoiding anything that demands wholehearted commitment. The staff at the gymnasium are constantly embroiled in fierce debates about the riots or the latest decree from the British administration. Max feels unmoved by the passions animating these volatile disputes and whenever drawn into political discussions he nods in consent to all positions, so the firebrands of the Labour Movement and the more measured religious Zionist both believe they have won his adherence.

The gymnasium at Rehavia caters to the children of Jerusalem's secular elite and their parents' evenings are attended by professionals from various European cities. Most have fallen on hard times since arriving in Palestine. The local grocer proudly displays a PhD. from the Sorbonne and Max learns the taxi driver with the Fiat Topolino was once a distinguished lawyer in Milan. Hebrew is the only language of instruction but the modern curriculum avoids anything that smacks of mysticism or superstition. In Jewish Studies, the Tanakh is valued as a source of history and literature but obedience to the Law is regarded as terribly old fashioned. The parents look to the teachers to instil a passion for Eretz Israel and there are field-trips to historical sites like the caves at Betar, a refuge during the Bar Kokhba revolt. The tradition of committing Torah to memory is still practiced with the children reciting passages that extol the heroism of Hebrew warriors. Max sometimes feels a little uneasy listening to 12-year-old girls gleefully chanting the *Song of Miriam* with its pitiless exaltation over the annihilation of Pharaoh's army.

As if to compensate for his avoidance of political activities, Max studiously applies himself to his work, which is both demanding and satisfying. Concepts easily understood in German are frustratingly difficult to explain in Hebrew and he attends regular training seminars for mathematics teachers at the University on Mt. Scopus. Their meetings often involve lengthy discussions over the words needed to express modern mathematical concepts. The Hebrew vocabulary, a perfect vehicle for theological disputes, is ill-suited to the precise definitions required by mathematical logic. Borrowing from German or any other language is regarded as an anathema and the Zionists believe Yiddish perpetuates the mentality of exile. To avoid a proliferation of neologisms the textbooks are pieced together with seldom used words pliable enough to accommodate new meanings. It was through a thorny dispute on the terminology for matrix theory that Max was first introduced to Gershon Scholem. He'd heard much about him from the Head of Mathematics at the Gymnasium who regards him as an unparalleled genius. His mastery of ancient Hebrew, Aramaic and Yiddish is widely admired and whenever the mathematics teachers reach an impasse it is universally accepted Scholem should arbitrate. On first impression he appeared pedantic and prickly, but the breadth of his knowledge left Max in no doubt he was in the presence of what his father would have called an *illui*. Without notes Scholem traces the shifting usage of a word through arcane texts, but unlike the rambling discussions Max was used to at Sabbath School, every reference comes with a precise analysis of the authorship and dates of the original manuscripts. Seeing the rigor of modern scholarship being applied to Rabbinical commentaries is thrilling and Max's admiration deepens as Scholem displays an easy familiarity with the most advanced mathematical concepts. The bookshelves lining the walls of his apartment testify to his passion for ancient manuscripts and Max learns he declined a vacant mathematics position at the Teacher's Training College to take the poorly paid job of librarian at the newly formed Jewish National Library.

With encouragement from the head of the gymnasium's maths department, Max joins students and university staff who meet with Scholem for coffee and cakes on Saturday afternoons. He'd hoped he could sit silently and take in the conversation of the assembled luminaries, but Scholem makes a point of engaging with newcomers and is delighted when Max nervously announces, 'My father is a tailor from Leopoldstadt.'

Most of the university crowd are from wealthy assimilated families who seldom set foot inside a synagogue and Scholem relishes the opportunity to converse with someone who has received a traditional Jewish education. Rabbis and sages pop up in his conversation like intimate friends and while Max can usually recognise the names he struggles to recall their teachings. He wishes he'd paid closer attention at Sabbath School though he cannot help feeling the elders in Leopoldstadt would be scandalised by Scholem. Maimonides whom they revere as an infallible authority, is held in low regard and Scholem sets great store on the folk stories Max used to hear from the barely literate Hassidic refugees living in the attic rooms of his apartment block in Leopoldstadt.

Though Scholem is unquestionably the brightest star in the firmament several eminent professors attend the gatherings. There is the renowned physicist Israel Dostrovsky and the mathematician Abraham Fraenkel whose work on axiomatic set theory had been part of the curriculum Max studied in Vienna. The historian, Professor Joseph Klausman, a fiery advocate for secular Zionism, attends regularly along with the mild-mannered Shlomo Goitein, an authority on Arab-Jewish relations in the Middle Ages. He jots down samples of Arabic graffiti in a notebook and amuses the gathering with translations and erudite commentary on the virulent curses routinely called down on various Zionist enterprises.

Although troubled by his unorthodox style, Max is pleased to find Scholem displays a deep respect for Torah, unlike the aggressively secular manner of his colleagues at the gymnasium. Discussion often turns to current events and Max is surprised to learn Scholem declined an invitation to join a British commission investigating the rioting that erupted when a Zionist faction defied municipal regulations by blowing the shofar at the Wailing Wall on the Day of Atonement. Scholem claims he could have cited evidence of Suleiman the Magnificent granting Jews permission to conduct rituals of lamentation at the ruins of their temple, but refuses to do anything to bolster what he calls political mysticism.

He believes the greatest threat to the Zionist project comes from the Revisionists stirring up messianic expectations. His ideas draw sharp criticism from the young students who care little for his academic reputation and have no hesitation advocating for Jabotinsky's aggressive stance. Scholem fights fire with fire and once had the room in an uproar suggesting Herzl, like Freud, only became prominent because his ideas were attuned to the effete neuroses of the assimilated Viennese aristocracy. Tracing the origins of Zionism to the 12th century when Jews from Andalusia took up Saladin's invitation to settle in Palestine, he argues the response to exile developed by Isaac Luria's community at Safed is far more robust than Herzl's bombastic rhetoric.

Max is often exasperated by Scholem's fondness for ambiguity. Whenever he is at the point of revealing the hidden core of his religious beliefs there is a lengthy digression speculating on the location of some obscure book he would like to acquire. He questions Max about the contents of the *Kultusgemeinde* library in Vienna and though Max often accompanied his father to the library on Ferdinandstraße, he paid scant attention to his father's studies and is unable to answer Scholem's enquiries. He undertakes to write to his father about the rare medieval codices Scholem believes may be part of the library's collection.

28

The arrival of Ramadan sees an outbreak of rioting in the Holy City, with a clandestine Zionist faction setting off bombs in retaliation for the killing of a twelve-year-old Jewish boy retrieving a football from a walled garden in Talbiyeh. The gymnasium has been closed for several days and the Polish policeman who shares Max's apartment advises him to remain indoors. Max calculates staying in the unguarded house offers no guarantee of safety and cautiously makes the short walk to Scholem's apartment at 28 Ayaband Street.

Ascending the outdoor staircase he sees smoke rising from the Old City. Some regulars are absent and he senses tension as Scholem's well-known support for cooperation with the Arabs is under attack from an earnest group of young Zionists.

'When they're burning our houses the Arabs don't care about our political distinctions. The Black Hats are just as likely to be attacked as the Revisionists—even your mystical rabbis in Safed have not been spared.'

Scholem wearily recalls Abner's question to Joab: *Shall the sword devour forever?*

'The only time Israel knew anything like peace, was when Solomon took foreign women for his wives and concubines.'

Professor Goitein responds sardonically, 'I can't see that working, nothing enflames the Arabs more than the thought of the Jew eyeing up their women.'

The Zionist students noisily insist the only solution is an immediate and massive increase in migration and Scholem responds sharply, dismissing Jabotinsky's talk of a Jewish majority as a pipedream. Alarmed by the howls of protest Professor Goitein attempts to diffuse the tension.

'The Arabs will never be satisfied unless we take the fez, like Doctor Scholem favourite messiah.'

Glancing at the puzzled expressions of the listening students, the Professor realises his reference has sailed over their heads. He throws and appealing glance to Scholem who remains silent, inscrutable as a sphinx. Feeling obliged to provide an explanation, Professor Goitein adopts an authoritative tone as if addressing an undergraduate seminar.

'In the middle years of the 17th century, the Jewish world was thrown into turmoil by the greatest outbreak of Messiah fever since the Nazarene rode his ass into Jerusalem. The uproar centred on an obscure figure of humble origin, known to us as Sabbatai Zevi. He was a reluctant Messiah but the first inklings of his Messianic identity arose in Smyrna when he publicly pronounced the sacred Tetragrammaton and conducted a marriage ceremony in which his bride was the Torah.'

The faculty members familiar with Scholem's obsessive interest in Sabbatai Zevi have their eyes fixed on their host expecting him to pounce on any inaccuracies in the Professor's account. The younger listeners look bored, disappointed the conversation has swerved from the current situation. Max is fascinated and perplexed. He can recall hearing about Sabbatai Zevi, the false messiah, but his name was only ever mentioned as a warning against the credulity of the unlearned. He cannot imagine why Scholem should be interested in a known charlatan.

'After the college of rabbis placed him under a ban,' Professor Goitein continues, 'the prospective messiah accepted he might have fallen under demonic influences and attempted to rid himself of his delusions through kabbalistic practices. Some years later in Cairo he received patronage from Raphael Joseph—an extremely wealthy leader of the Jewish community who kept a circle of fifty Talmudist and kabbalists at his table. The Messianic calling returned when Zevi heard reports of a mysterious Ashkenazi girl named Sarah who'd been told in a dream she was to be the bride of the Messiah. She'd been orphaned during the Chmielnicki massacres and as a refugee in Amsterdam acquired a reputation as a woman of loose morals. Sabbatai Zevi had her brought to Cairo and they married with great ceremony at Raphael Joseph's house. Her striking beauty made a strong impression and the rabbis noted the marriage echoed that of the prophet Hosea, commanded to marry a harlot.'

The students prick their ears at the mention of harlotry and the Professor gives a lively account of Sabbatai Zevi's fame spreading throughout the Ottoman Empire, inspiring tremendous excitement among the downtrodden communities of the Diaspora.

'The Messiah continued to have doubts about his calling and in a final attempt to exorcise his demons set out to meet Nathan of Gaza, revered for his ability to prescribe the *tikkun* each soul required. Against all expectations, Nathan of Gaza unequivocally announced that Sabbatai Zevi was indeed the Anointed One. He called for a period of repentance to prepare for the Day of Redemption, which was to occur on the 18th of June 1666—a date with apocalyptic significance in the calculations of Christian authorities. With his identity confirmed Sabbatai Zevi attracted an enormous retinue and wherever he went there were reports of miracles. Sombre Jewish observances became occasions for dancing and festivity, commerce was disrupted and the kingdoms of the earth were distributed among his followers. From the far-flung corners of Europe believers travelled to Turkey to witness the great day when the Messiah would seize the royal turban from the supreme ruler of the Ottoman Empire. The uproar came to the attention of Ottoman authorities who were accustomed to dealing with rebellion by the simple expedient of executing rebel leaders. Out of curiosity or perhaps because of bribery, the Grand Vizier Ahmed acted with caution and when Sabbatai arrived in Constantinople he was taken to the castle of Gallipoli where political prisoners were detained.'

Sensing his listeners losing interest, the Professor glosses over the period of confinement and moves to the grand trial.

'The Sultan Mehmed IV, known to be a deeply religious man, observed proceedings from a latticed alcove and when the formalities were over Sabbatai Zevi was presented with a stark choice—convert to Islam or face immediate execution.'

The Professor pauses to heighten the anticipation written in the faces of his listeners. 'The messiah chose apostasy… and you could say there was an ambiguous fulfilment of prophesy when his conversion was publicly affirmed by the placement of a Turkish turban on his head.'

Those familiar with the story watch with amusement as mutterings and contemptuous laughter make it difficult to hear the all-important denouement.

'The Sultan was delighted by the conversion and rewarded Sabbatai Zevi by giving him a royal pension and the honorary title of Keeper of the Palace Gates. However it soon became clear the dramatic conversion was nothing more than an outward display. In his teachings and public actions Sabbatai Zevi led a double life—diligently performing the duties of a Muslim while secretly continuing to practise his Jewish faith.'

These comments only enflame the students, outraged by the unstated implication that the cowardly actions of a false messiah might be a model for Zionist relations with the Arabs. With arguments erupting in all corners Scholem silently observes the chaos. When it becomes apparent no one is attempting to defend Sabbatai Zevi the room quietens and a young journalist, an occasional visitor to the circle, commands attention.

'I've been lucky enough to meet a messiah. One of my first assignments in Jerusalem was to report on a group from the Bukharian quarter who were flocking to the outskirts of the city to hear a self-proclaimed messiah living in the burial shafts at the Tombs of the Judges. A suitably apocalyptic thunderstorm struck just as I reached his cave and I was soaked to the skin. I was told God would soon be appearing in Jerusalem as some sort of hermaphrodite—a man below the waist and a woman above. The messiah assured me I would be among the saved, which is surprising given that I'm an atheist. Then soon after my story was printed a young Bukharian girl who used to take food to his cave, fell pregnant and the Bukharians decided the man was a blasphemer who must be stoned to death. It was only the intervention of a visiting rabbi from Holland that saved his life. I'm not sure how he got out of the country, but I've heard he's found wealthy patrons in California—they're building a temple for him in the St. Lenardo Valley.'

Laughter fills the room and the Zionist students are content to take the case of Sabbatai Zevi as a warning against the foolishness of religious superstition. Amid the merriment Max notices Scholem looks irritated. He speaks softly without directing his remarks at anyone and before long all are craning to hear. 'If you imagine what the appearance of the Messiah would have meant to the oppressed Jewish communities living under Ottoman rule, it's likely many of Sabbatai Zevi's followers felt they were part of a profoundly liberating religious experience. As their Messiah faced the Sultan's judgement, their spiritual deliverance was dramatically put to the test and when the Messiah chose apostasy, they also had a choice. They could conclude they'd been fooled by a charlatan and accept the humiliation of knowing their spiritual transformation was a delusion. This was the path taken by the Rabbis who endured their disillusionment in shocked silence and after a period of repentance did everything to suppress any mention of the failed uprising. But some were convinced their liberation was real, and insisted there must be a spiritual explanation of the messiah's seemingly indefensible actions. Inspired by the Messiah's example, many of his followers converted to Islam and Nathan of Gaza revealed their apostasy was an essential stage on the path to redemption. Drawing on the mythology of the Lurianic Kabbalah he explained that during the process of creation a vast cosmic upheaval caused divine sparks to be scattered throughout the world. The sparks which fell among the gentiles were concentrated in the world of Islam and only the Messiah could gather them up so they could be added to the divine sparks the

Jewish people had already restored through the process of *tikkun*. To carry out this mission it was necessary to submit to the disgrace of apostasy and go down into the realm of the *Kelippah*—like a spy entering an enemy camp or like Judith entering the tent of Holofernes.'

While no one dares challenge Scholem, some roll their eyes as if listening to an eccentric uncle expounding a pet theory. Undeterred, Scholem proceeds with his exposition, glancing at the young journalist in the manner of a schoolmaster dismissing an unnecessary question.

'Modern psychology can best explain the delusions of the messiah complex, but it is possible to assess the impact of certain ideas without passing judgement on whether they are true or false. If the career of Sabbatai Zevi is subject to historical criticism we can see his impact on Judaism is comparable to the revolution Luther initiated within Christianity.'

Though his listeners appear restless, Scholem plunges into a labyrinth of digressions and describes how Sabbatai Zevi's apostasy created an underground movement within Judaism. The Sabbateans outwardly conformed to the Law while secretly engaging in mystical practices that involved sexual transgression and rejection of dietary laws. They were sometimes denounced as hypocrites but in their own minds were practicing a new understanding of redemption that transforms the heart of the believer. Like a benign virus a new spiritual experience spread through the communities of the diaspora and in the late 18th century an extreme form of radical mysticism burst out of the rigidly orthodox ghettoes of Podolia. Their leader Jacob Frank was revered as a reincarnation of the divine spirit that had been with Sabbatai Zevi and his teachings were so profoundly nihilistic the religious authorities denounced him as an agent of the Devil.

Max notices a shift in Scholem's voice. There is a quickening of pace and though the tone of scholarly deliberation remains, it is not difficult to discern his sympathies as he describes how the Sabbateans were ruthlessly harassed by Rabbinical Councils scandalised by reports of sexual licentiousness and ritualistic orgies.

'To escape persecution, Jacob Frank's followers sought protection from Catholic Bishops who viewed the sect as a valuable ally in their campaign to convert Jews to Christianity. With rival ecclesial authorities involved the conflict escalated into a maelstrom of recriminations and violence, culminating in the infamous disputation at Lvov, at which some of Frank's followers publicly testified to the veracity of the Blood Libel.'

Max cannot help letting out an audible gasp, but Scholem proceeds without pause. 'Just as Sabbatai Zevi used Islam to conceal his mission, Jacob Frank instructed his followers to accept baptism and take on the mask of Christianity. His radicle doctrine of *redemption through sin* claimed the Torah must be fulfilled by transgression: Just as a seed must die in the earth in order to live, man had to become rotten and break open to bring forth the fruit of redemption. The ghetto communities, accustomed to humiliating oppression and deadening religious routines, embraced Frank's intoxicating mix of lawlessness and promiscuity. He unleashed a hunger for pure spiritual experience, unfettered by external authority. His followers felt the call of the great Dionysian flood, casting aside the obligations of the mundane world to join an ecstatic celebration of life.'

With his listeners falling into a stunned silence, Scholem pauses to sip water before continuing in a more measured tone. Max detects a melancholy in his voice as he admits the anarchic energy Frank inspired could not be sustained. But he insists the revolution Frank and Sabbatai Zevi initiated had a lasting effect on Judaism. By asserting the primacy of personal spiritual experience the Sabbateans answered the challenges posed by modern science and historical criticism.

'Judaism, like all religions, must choose; it can stand against modernity and demand irrational submission to religious authorities who are beyond criticism—or it can neutralise scientific objections by validating the personal reality of inner spiritual experience.'

He acknowledges the triumph of the Enlightenment makes the choice seem obvious, but asserts that religious experience is not constrained by notions of progress or the laws of history.

'In the 19th century when the ghettoes were opening to the modern world, there was a popular slogan derived from Frank's teachings—"*a Jew at home, a man in the street.*" The maxim encouraged Jews to adopt an outwardly secular lifestyle while maintaining a thriving spiritual life in the privacy of their own homes.'

Though there is nothing conclusive in these remarks, Scholem's demeanour suggests he has nothing more to say. His wife Fania appears with a fresh pot of coffee and cake made with honey and almonds. The refreshments provide cover for whispering among the students, disappointed Scholem's long-winded explanation failed to mention Zionism. A young history student takes it upon himself to vent their frustrations.

'Don't you think enough energy has been wasted waiting for a Messiah?

Zionism means we can finally start building our own future and we don't need a Messiah to tell us what to do.'

Untroubled by the arrogant tone, Scholem responds thoughtfully. 'That may be true, but it depends on what you mean by Zionism.'

'There is no great mystery about what it means—we want a Jewish homeland. We can argue all night about the best way to achieve that, but no one who calls himself a Zionist has any doubt about what we are fighting for.'

Scholem responds with a smile. 'You're avoiding the question—if we accept your definition of Zionism we still have to decide what is meant by a homeland.'

The student shakes his head and Professor Klausman, who has been waiting for an opening, takes up the students' cause. 'Jewish academics are no different from our rabbinical scholars—perfectly happy arguing about definitions and parading our knowledge of arcane references, so long as we don't have to deal with reality.'

Scholem appears stung by the criticism and there is a note of sharpness in his response. 'The one failing academics should be ashamed of is to believe our work has no relevance. When we romanticise the man of action or defer to the wisdom of the man-in-the-street, we admit we have nothing to offer. But when political actions are unexamined the man-in-the-street suffers the most.'

'Why then,' the Professor fires back, 'is it so difficult to plainly tell us what your mystical messiahs can teach us about Zionism?'

'I'd prefer you to draw your own conclusions but if I must speak plainly let me plainly say this—if Zionism aspires to nothing more than numerical superiority and defensible borders it has already failed.'

A ripple of anticipation passes through the room as the listeners sense the master of ambivalence might finally have been goaded into revealing his personal beliefs.

'Zionism has not eliminated our need for a messiah. We are called to be *a kingdom of priests and a holy nation* or else our struggle is no different from the nationalist movements in the British colonies or the Balkans. Self-determination and national sovereignty are reasonable goals but Zionism will fail if it tries to appropriate the promise of redemption. When politicians talk like messiahs they claim an authority that does not belong to them and their utopian visions lead to cynicism and despair. What we need is a dialectical awareness: When the political and the messianic oppose each other the tension is creative, when they merge, both lose their vitality and we are left with empty rhetoric.'

An uneasy silence is broken by a student who speaks as if thinking aloud, 'So what is to be done?'

Scholem raises his eyes, pausing to consider the question. 'I'd say our best hope comes from the agricultural kibbutzim and the encampments for labourers working on the new roads. Hard physical labour keeps them grounded but their daily toil has a higher purpose—they are laying the foundations for communities that might be capable of answering the prophetic call for justice—protection for widows and orphans, hospitality to strangers, compassion for the weak. If they stay the course, we may see a restoration of Jewish ideals, distorted by centuries of exile and alienation. But that kind of back-breaking labour is not easy to sustain, it requires a humble spirit.'

Some students appear on the point of risking a response when Professor Goitein draws attention to the darkening of the sky. Noting the discussion has extended well beyond their usual time, he thanks the Scholems for their hospitality and excuses himself. Others follow suit and the room empties with a hubbub of apologies and parting comments. Max finds himself among the last to leave. As he offers a tongue-tied expression of gratitude, Scholem observes the third star must have already appeared and extends an invitation to stay for Havdalah. Fania hands him a glass of sweet, fragrant wine and with eyes squeezed shut he follows the rhythm of Scholem's voice:

'Blessed art thou Who distinguishes
Holiness from the everyday,
Light from dark and Israel from the nations—'

As the candle is extinguished Fania joins in reciting a psalm Max does not recognise. At the conclusion of the ceremony Max apologises for not knowing the psalm and Scholem says it is one of a handful of poems Isaac Luria composed while in Safed. Turning to his bookshelf he offers Max a Hebrew tome entitled *'Tree of Life.'*

In the ensuing months Max eagerly accepts Scholem's guidance as he explores the treasures of the fledgling National Library. Their conversations are one-sided as Max is intimidated by Scholem's learning and perplexed by his fondness for light-hearted banter.

He delights in mocking the excessive rationalism of Maimonides and jokingly confides how his university colleagues scoff at his enthusiasm for the Kabbalah. 'They say it's improper to undertake a serious study of medieval nonsense, but I tell them there's nothing wrong with studying the *history* of medieval nonsense.'

Beneath the humour Max senses a serious purpose; Scholem earnestly believes the discredited teachings of the Kabbalah will unleash the suppressed energy of Judaism's most vital traditions. He places great value on Isaac Luria's concept of the *Shekinah* as the Bride—a shimmering elusive figure who restlessly walks the earth, yearning to end her exile in an ecstatic *heiros gamos*.

Max carefully reads Scholem's recently published essay on Jacob Frank with its alarming analysis of the doctrine of redemption through sin. He cannot help shuddering at the account of Frank's followers testifying to the truth of the Blood Libel and it is impossible for him to believe anything good could come from such betrayal. But in Isaac Luria he finds a mirror for his uncertainty. His teachings rest on a deep love of Torah and Max feels he is in the presence of something truly ancient and enticingly wild, something that could only have grown in a climate of relentless sunshine and fierce winds.

29

Keeping pace with the orderly, Karl passes a succession of swinging doors, stairwells and corridors. A knot of unfamiliar emotions heighten his senses and he is acutely aware of his shoes squeaking on the linoleum. Disinfectant enters his nostrils and with eyes lowering he falls into dreamy contemplation of the geometric pattern of the tiles. A heavy iron door swings open and he registers the bracing ice-chilled air. With little more than a glance at the rigid face he turns to the orderly, relieved a nod is all that is required before the hospital can arrange transportation for the corpse. He has to consult his pocket-book to confirm the time of the internment ceremony and the fragile equanimity he obtained by focussing on practical tasks unravels. The sharp white bristles on father's usually clean-shaven chin stick in his mind, an unseemly reminder of the spark that had given motion and speech and purpose to substance that can no longer resist decay.

Father had known so much misfortune in recent years, no one would have blamed him if he howled from the roof tops. Perhaps because he had no expectation of happiness he remained resolute. Six months earlier when Mother alternated between convulsive bouts of sobbing and paralytic silence, he'd diligently applied himself to tasks that might alleviate her grief. A roster of relatives was drawn up to provide the comfort he could not supply; Dora's old school friends were notified and her colleagues from the hospital were thoughtfully attended to. With a blunt pronouncement of suicide on the death certificate no one expected the funeral would offer consolation but at the graveside father read a poem Dora had written as a schoolgirl. Delivered in an unemotional voice the verse spoke of a heart that knew its own direction, luminous horizons and the stirring of nameless desires. For a few moments mother could set aside sorrow and recall the brilliant, tender spirited girl who had not hesitated to expose herself to the unmitigated horror of serving in a military hospital. Karl believes suicide was reasonable under the circumstances. Tuberculosis had her in its grip and after the failure of the cure at Merseburg he understood why Dora could not endure becoming one of the helpless patients she'd tended to as a nurse. When he attempted to share these thoughts Hanya flew into a rage, disgusted to have her sister's despair treated as a philosophical problem and furious at herself for failing to offer Dora the love she richly deserved. She was certain she could have supplied a dozen good reasons to go on living if she'd simply found the time to take her sister for a walk through the gardens at Laxenburg.

Father's death at 76 should be easier to accept but for Karl it seems infinitely sadder. He returns to the Bauernmarkt apartment weighed with formless anxieties that disrupt his concentration as Uncle Walter talks about funeral arrangements. They touch on provisions for Mother and Karl undertakes to ascertain what level of support Hanya requires. She is fiercely proud of her hard-won independence and tells Karl she intends to continue her studies at the Eurythmics Institute where board and lodgings are provided and she earns a meagre income from taking foundation courses for physical education teachers during the summer months. When Mother and Hanya retire to their bedrooms Karl instinctively gravitates towards the library. Exhausted, he defers the walk home and settles into father's favourite chair, hoping solitude might calm his mind. It pains him he can't stop thinking about publication. He ought to put his affairs aside and apply himself to comforting mother but since the publication contract arrived in the mail he's had little control over his thoughts.

His wild imaginings alternate between triumphant fantasies of the book being acclaimed and paralysing fear that he'd overlooked an obvious flaw that would see his meticulous reasoning disintegrate under ridicule and derision. Father counselled against writing. He worried it could only lead to journalism and warned publishers see no need to pay writers who will work tirelessly without any remuneration, just to see their name in print. Recalling his father's shrewd assessment of the publishing racket raises a wry smile, but he has no expectation of financial reward, wishing for nothing more than an opportunity to test the merits of ideas he regards as vitally important.

He believes the rigorous logic of scientific thinking is threatened by a new dogmatism, more insidious and dangerous than the old religious adversary. By laying claim to an infallible system for ascertaining truth, the new creed turns science into a substitute for God and fatally distorts its method. He is confident his insights will provide an antidote, but stepping into the role of science's shining knight is a presumptuous conceit and he knows the smug self-satisfied circle at Vienna University view him as a meddlesome crank. Publication will deliver the vindication he craves, but first he must bury his father and compress the unwieldy manuscript into 240 pages. An impossible task but the publisher will not countenance anything beyond eight sheets.

Comforted by the firm upholstery of father's armchair, Karl feels the allure of sleep and tries to calm the riot of thoughts racing through his mind. He wonders if he did the right thing baulking at the suggestion he should deliver the eulogy. There are things he would like to say but he could not speak with confidence about the best period in father's life when he rose out of lowly circumstances to build one of the city's most respected legal partnerships. Uncle Walter is better placed to speak of those years and will be more discrete in alluding to the family's ugly behaviour when he converted to Lutheranism. If he were to speak Karl would mention the library. He sees a kind of heroism in father's allocation of what must have been a significant portion of his income, to acquire the thousands of volumes now resting in their cabinets like sentinels watching over a vanished city. His university colleagues would dismiss the leather-bound collection as a typically haute bourgeois indulgence, but there was nothing acquisitive or ostentatious about father's love of books. He felt a duty to make himself familiar with the ideas that shape the world and possessed a robust confidence in his ability to draw his own conclusions on competing points of view. His respectful curiosity extended to writers whose views he abhorred and Karl worries this way of thinking is vanishing, displaced by dismissive cynicism and relentless questioning of motives.

The concept of honouring your father holds little meaning for Karl but somewhere within the drowsy churning of half-formed thoughts he is aware of something hardening into a conviction. He will stand against the sneering arrogance of those who would consign the Enlightenment to the dustbin of history without thought for what might be worth keeping. He thinks of Mach, intoxicated by his facile system of inductive reasoning, refusing to give credence to Kant's insights into the conditions that make logic possible. Or Neurath with his half-baked understanding of indeterminacy and absurd belief in the predictive quality of social sciences. It seems incomprehensible they should visit him at this hour, and when they jauntily step into the library his first impulse is to grab his manuscript and stuff it inside his jacket. He's long suspected that as soon as they recognise the superiority of his theories they will steal his ideas. When he sees there is to be no exchange of pleasantries he understands they have come to torment him. Mach plucks volumes from the shelves, tossing them to Neurath who stacks them in precarious columns on the floor.

They've devised a game that involves snatching a book from a stack without causing the column to collapse. And directing the sport is Wittgenstein, the ringmaster, cross-legged on father's writing desk squealing with delight whenever a column tumbles. Karl is surprised he's deigned to appear. He'd refused to meet with the logical positivists, even when they held seminars where every sentence of *Tractatus* was read aloud like Holy Scripture. Wittgenstein interrupts the merriment to rescue a volume of Schopenhauer and returns to his perch muttering in gibberish. When Mach enquires as to the content of the incantation Neurath responds in a hushed whisper, 'He's using a Sanskrit dialect reserved for sacred philosophical treatise.'

Karl trudges doggedly towards Hietzing, the regularity of his footsteps settling the turbulence inside his head, the crisp night air lending a bracing clarity to his senses. The song of an unseen blackbird sounds like it is coming through a loudspeaker and the new concrete apartment blocks on Fleschgasse loom like monoliths silhouetted against the grey of the approaching dawn. An image of Josephine sleeping alone plays in his mind, giving rise to an overwhelming sense of gratitude for his underserved good fortune. He feels a sharp pang of embarrassment recalling numerous occasions when he's arrived home beside himself with rage after an all-night debate. Josephine would listen patiently to a blow-by-blow account of his rhetorical gallantry and make sure he had breakfast and coffee before heading into work. Her cool-headed appraisal of his intellectual grievances made him realise no one ever changes their mind as a result of being defeated in argument. The more thoroughly they are vanquished the more their opinions harden into dogma. He supposes she encourages his writing for its therapeutic value. It softens his indignation and occasionally bestows the lucidity needed to anticipate his opponents' objections.

Karl wistfully imagines how life might change if the book receives half the praise it deserves. Frustrated by the drudgery of eking a living as a school-teacher he yearns to put an end to the humiliation of seeking approval from condescending academics who refuse to take his ideas seriously. He knows he will be attacked by fashionable thinkers who have appropriated the prestige of scientific method to bolster their mystical speculations on the laws of history and other such nonsense. On rare occasions when he gets a hearing there is a grudging acknowledgment he may be onto something. Professor Hahn encouraged him to structure his arguments into a more coherent form and warned that theories challenging an established order must be presented with the utmost clarity.

But achieving such clarity requires fastidious concentration, almost impossible to obtain while teaching at the Hauptschule.

The task of imparting knowledge to boys with no desire to learn is a Sisyphean torment and with his nights devoted to the manuscript he's become adept at functioning in perpetual exhaustion. Despite their surliness, his students understand he wants the best for them and the exam results his classes achieve arouse the envy of colleagues. There is a faction among the staff who view modern educational methods as a Jewish plot to sap the manliness of Austrian youth and they make sure Karl overhears them singing the praises of the National Socialists. With his mind absorbed by other things he can ignore these taunts and in the classroom is untroubled by casual displays of insubordination that drive other teachers to dish out brutal punishments for minor infringements. He's more concerned by his failure to combat the despondency in the faces of his working-class students. Many show signs of intelligence and their natural curiosity has not been entirely extinguished, but there is an obstinate refusal to engage in a disciplined approach to learning. The one thing that might offer an escape from the misery of unemployment remains closed to them. From time-to-time he raises a flicker of enthusiasm with a provocative question or humorous aside, but more often the boys retreat into an impenetrable cocoon of boredom and he watches his brightest students succumb to the fatal combination of ignorance and resentment that makes them receptive to the fiery rhetoric of the Nationalists.

30

In the weeks after his father's funeral, pressure to produce an abridged version of the book becomes all-consuming and Karl resorts to carrying the manuscript with him in the classroom. In the brief interludes when his students work quietly or subside into lethargic day-dreaming, he hacks at sentences that have already endured multiple revisions. With the publisher's deadline looming he is relieved to find a passive mood in his Friday afternoon class. A persistent downpour has dampened the restless anticipation with which his students await their dismissal. The prospect of walking through the rain to their dreary apartments can hold little appeal and most of the students are staring blankly at the windows or resting heads on their desktops.

When one notices Karl scribbling in the margins of a typed manuscript, he sees a chance to relieve the boredom. 'What are you writing Professor?'

Karl suppresses his irritation and with a hint of pride admits he is writing a book. The students are not altogether surprised their Professor should do such a thing. There is something different about Doctor Popper and they welcome the opportunity to find out what makes him tick. A volley of questions leaves Karl daunted, but he's amused his delinquent pupils are more interested in his work than his esteemed colleagues at the university. Their curiosity flags once they learn the book has something to do with science, but Karl is intrigued by the notion his theories could be understood by a disgruntled mob of wayward youth. He asks if any of them have thought about how scientific discoveries are made. Blank stares prompt him to reframe the question.

'How do you think scientists discovered the laws of gravity or learnt how to generate electricity?'

Newton's falling apple gets a mention and there is talk about telescopes and experiments before the chatter is cut by a sneering comment from a student who must have picked up on the rising hostility towards Einstein.

'It's just the Jews peddling their crazy ideas.'

Ignoring the racial slur, Karl tells the class scientific theories often sound crazy and claims he has a method for deciding whether ideas are crazy or useful. Suggesting they think of science as a tool for solving problems he asks the class how they would decide the best solution to any problem. The ensuing silence reminds him of the folly of putting abstract problems to minds that think concretely. Noticing their attention drift towards the rain pounding the window-panes he tries again.

'What about the problem of rain?'

His students are already thinking about walking home through the downpour and he invites them to consider there must be several ways of solving the problem of rain.

'Don't come to school,' is called out from the back of the room, while more diligent students offer the alternatives of carrying an umbrella or a hat and coat. A dreamy boy who seldom has anything to say suggests a glass roof could be built over the entire city. Writing their proposals on the blackboard Karl suggests criticism and testing of competing theories makes it possible to find the best solution—though he emphasises there may be an even better solution as yet undiscovered. Having captured their attention he asks the boys to think more carefully about how they might avoid getting drenched on the way home. With a little prompting they agree there are several effective ways of staying dry so long as you know when it will rain. 'For a scientist,' he explains, 'the real problem is how to accurately predict a downpour.'

Thrilled by the prospect of having his ideas understood, his delivery takes on a manic tone the students find highly entertaining.

'Anyone can offer a solution. Someone might say, experience tells me storms never come on Mondays. Someone else might believe storms can be avoided if animals are sacrificed to the gods as the Greeks believed. And someone else who knew a bit about air pressure, might speculate that storms are caused by changes in the weight of the air and if there was a way of measuring these changes it would be possible to accurately predict the onset of storms. Nothing should be ruled out as unscientific and there is no reason why theories should be based on empirical observations.'

Although his students fail to grasp the significance of this point he reiterates that solving the problem of rain does not depend on the experience of getting rained upon. Raising his hands above his head in a theatrical gesture he exclaims, 'I could experience a thousand storms or tear off my clothes like the mad King Lear so I'd feel the full force of the tempest—but this will not help me solve the problem of rain.'

As the laughter subsides he contemplates explaining how the logical positivists stubbornly refuse to concede on this matter. It would require a lengthy digression and he suspects his brood of delinquents will have little interest in the arguments that kept him awake through so many sleepless nights. He senses they'd be untroubled by Mach's claim that scientific thinking can only include statements derived from sensory experience and can't imagine they'd be even mildly perturbed by Wittgenstein's solemn decree that propositions are meaningless unless they can be logically reduced to statements that model reality. Though he can see his exposition is little more than a source of amusement, it's intoxicating to imagine his students might understand the importance of his book and recognise what is at stake if opposing theories prevail.

'There is no need to exclude anything from science. Gut-feelings, intuitions, wild guesses or unfounded speculations can always be put forward—but anyone who wants to have their proposal considered scientifically must offer statements that can be tested. This is what makes science so effective and surprising. It doesn't matter how weird or outlandish a theory may seem, so long as it can be tested—and the testing must involve things that can be measured or recorded by many different observers.'

Mindful the dismissal bell will soon ring he returns to the three proposed solutions to the problem of rain. The idea that storms never arrive on Mondays can be tested and might be verified if there happened to be a string of fair-weather Mondays. But a single instance of a storm falling on a Monday would show the theory false and it would have to be discarded. Expecting prayer and sacrifices to provide a safeguard against storms is different because there is no way of testing such a theory. The minds of the gods are beyond the reach of human knowledge and if a storm were to appear in spite of appropriate prayer and sacrifice it could always be argued the gods had their own reasons for being displeased. Wrinkled brows remind Karl many of his students are from devout Catholic families and anticipating their objections he maintains science cannot pass judgement on whether untestable theories are true or false. He points to the Greek philosophers who came up with surprisingly accurate theories on atoms using nothing more than intuition and logical reasoning. For the best part of two thousand years it was impossible to say whether their atomic theories were true or false and it would be ridiculous to say their ideas suddenly became true once technology allowed us to observe and measure atoms.

'Science is a method for solving problems,' he declares. 'It does not claim to know the truth. If testing does not prove a theory is false it may be accepted as the best available solution to a problem—but this does not mean it is the truth.'

Turning to the third hypothesis Karl wants to demonstrate the practical benefits of scientific thinking. With his students counting minutes before school ends, he rattles off a potted history of the strange idea that shifts in the weight of the atmosphere offer a means to predict storms. His students have a vague awareness of how a barometer works and are surprised to learn Goethe invented a simple but effective version of the device after studying techniques for siphoning water. He admits the predictions made with barometers are far from perfect, but each time a prediction is found inaccurate the theory can be refined or replaced. Noticing the clock is closing in on bell-time he concludes with a triumphal flourish.

'This is how science progresses—you put forward a theory then do everything you can to prove it's wrong. Sounds odd, but it works. Every time a barometer prediction proves to be false, the techniques of weather forecasting can be improved. This method has made it possible for ships to avoid storms and countless lives have been saved.'

His students depart in high spirits, wishing him good luck with the book. Fingering the manuscript Karl is quietly elated. The boys might have absorbed something and he imagines, as they make their way home through the downpour, one or two might see miserable weather is not an unavoidable fate to be stoically endured, but a problem that can diminish under the persistent application of a rigorous and open-ended method of thinking.

31

The impossible task of reducing the book to the prescribed length is solved by asking Uncle Walter to make the cuts and Karl only accepts the abridged version after succumbing to chronic exhaustion. With the typing complete, the pristine stack of unmarked pages presents an irresistible temptation. Josephine conceals every pen or pencil and monitors his movements whenever he approaches the desk where the manuscript is stowed in a locked drawer. When the package is delivered to an exasperated publisher Karl is consumed by dread. Although they can scarcely afford it, they take a long-promised holiday in Semmering where two days of skiing pass like an hallucination. Josephine ensures they utilise every moment of light and though Karl cannot match her dexterity on the slopes he is content to follow cautiously, turning continuously to slow his descents. With his concentration directed at avoiding a fall, he frees his mind from the anticipation and at night slips into dreamless sleep.

On returning to work the fretting resumes and seeking a distraction he makes a concerted effort to help mother put her affairs in order. She readily agrees to reduce the number of rooms on the lease and has no trouble accepting the library must be sold. Her only stipulation is to hold onto the music room. Freed from the demands of nursing father she has returned to her musical interests, a consuming passion in the years before she married. As Karl contemplates how to arrange the sale of the library he is drawn downstairs by Mother's voice, sombre and melodious, rising from the music room. He is impressed by the ease with which she handles the intricate phrasing of the lieder and recalls hearing she was once considered a promising soprano. Mother brushes aside his clumsy compliment and tells him the piece was composed for her by Alexander Zemlinsky, who recently returned to Vienna after the Nazis hounded him out of his position at the Kroll Opera. When she learnt he was being shunned by the Viennese orchestras, who once regarded him as a prodigy, she organised small gatherings for him in the music room.

'I'm afraid some of my invitation cards were returned with ugly notes scrawled across them—I've been accused of polluting Viennese culture with degenerate Jewish music.'

The uncharacteristic indignation in Mother's voice loosens dark thoughts and Karl releases a sigh like the groan of a wounded animal. He knows the humiliation of being assigned to a racial category and imagines it must be worse for Zemlinsky whose conversion involved a sincere decision to reject his Jewish identity. When asked about his origins, Karl always calls himself a citizen of Vienna and it pains him such categories have simply ceased to exist. He is a Jew whether he likes it or not and the baptismal certificate that made it possible for Father to work at the highest levels of the Municipal Council is worthless. Being defined by his blood terrifies him. It's beyond the scope of criticism and the best he can do is to view it as a brute fact to avoid, like the hunger of a tiger or the viciousness of wild dogs.

Disquiet about the worsening political situation is suspended by the arrival of a small package, fretfully torn open on the kitchen table. Cradling a freshly printed copy of *Logik der Forschung*, his eyes linger on his name embedded in the cloth cover and he enjoys a moment of elation. The euphoria is short-lived, the familiar dread returning even before he finishes inscribing the front pages with messages of gratitude to Uncle Walter and some university colleagues. Anticipation of the reviews drives him into paroxysms of anxiety and when they arrive he obsessively pours through the polite, laudatory phrases, enraged by a wilful refusal to recognise the revolutionary impact of his ideas. The oft repeated judgement that the book *'makes a significant contribution to our understanding of science'* leaves him cold and he's exasperated that none of the so-called experts understand how he has systematically obliterated the theories of inductive reasoning. He finds more satisfaction in the rabid ad hominins from the likes of Neurath, who clearly recognises the book poses a mortal threat to the edifice of fallacious reasoning thrown up by the luminaries of the Positivist Circle. The arrival of a warmly appreciative letter from Einstein brings pride which quickly evaporates as the great man discreetly points out Karl's rebuttal of Heisenberg's indeterminacy principle relies on a misunderstanding of how probability calculations apply to quantum theory. Sleepless nights spent in meticulous analysis of the offending section inexorably leads to the conclusion that Einstein is right and Karl is mortified by the error.

The only thing keeping him from despair is Josephine's patience and good sense. 'You should be delighted Einstein thought the book important enough to comment on—besides no one else will even notice the error, let alone understand it.'

Her down-to-earth perspective restores a measure of calm and her comments about the value of the controversy prove prescient. There is an invitation to deliver a lecture at Bedford College in London and requests to read papers at Oxford and Cambridge. None of the prestigious engagements come with fees or even an offer to cover travel expenses and any leave of absence from his Hauptschule will be without pay. In spite of the financial hardship Josephine declares it would be madness to pass the opportunity and insists she is happy to remain at her teaching job so he can take up the offers.

Karl is painfully aware the book would not have made it into print without Josephine's tireless support and while fêted in London he cannot stop thinking about her alone in Vienna. His guilt deepens on reading her letters: A teacher at her Hauptschule came across a review that spoke of Jewish influences within the Vienna Circle and she now faces vicious denunciations for marrying a Jew.

After the unrelenting hostility he received in Vienna, Karl is delighted by the warmth of his reception in London and dares to imagine an academic career could be attainable. The British sense of fair-play recoils at the notion of excluding an entire race from the universities though Karl soon learns his chances of securing a position are slim. Many of the Continent's most distinguished professors have been dismissed from German universities under the Aryanization policy and minor positions at provincial English colleges attract desperate pleas from a throng of absurdly overqualified applicants. The situation in Vienna is regarded as relatively benign and Karl finds he is ineligible for attractive positions reserved for German refugees.

Sensing it is a matter of time before Vienna's socialist council is forced to adopt the anti-Semitic policies sweeping Europe, he seeks advice from the Academic Assistance Council and fires off a cable expressing interest in a lectureship in New Zealand. The location is ridiculously distant and on a visit to the famous reading room of the British Museum he's amused to discover that if any place were to be described as the ends of the earth, it would be New Zealand. Its islands, in the southernmost corner of the Pacific Ocean, lay claim to being the last significant land mass inhabited by humans. The British took possession the country less than a hundred years ago and he learns the native Māori population only settled the islands sometime in the fourteenth century. Mammalian evolution never reached its shores and while civilisations rose and fell, New Zealand enjoyed supreme isolation with its primordial forests populated by large flightless birds and small reptiles. The prospect of a fresh start in these pristine isles fires his imagination and he conjures a picture of a remote sanctuary where he can immerse in sustained philosophical thought. He knows Josephine is unlikely to share his enthusiasm and worries he is taking advantage of her compliant nature. His letters emphasise the position should be viewed as a temporary refuge, a stepping-stone to more suitable appointments.

Before returning to Vienna he attends a scientific congress in Copenhagen and is honoured to meet Niels Bohr, who expresses guarded approval of his work. The long train journey home takes him through Germany and impressions of the new regime harden his resolve to leave Europe. Waiting to switch trains at Frankfurt Hauptbahnhof he settles into a quiet corner with a copy of the *Frankfurter Zeitung*. Although he has done little more than gaze at the countryside passing the train window, he notices a mood of buoyancy evident in the simplest things. The ticket inspector, baggage handlers and even lavatory attendants go about their business with a robust purpose as if playing an important role in a grand experiment. With the country still basking in the prestige of the Berlin Olympiad every article in the *Zeitung* exudes confidence and statesmen from all corners of the globe heap praise on Hitler's achievements.

He's mystified by the ease with which people accept the brutality of the Brownshirts and regards the socialist opposition as hopelessly deluded. In the distant isles of New Zealand he hopes he may be able to discern why so many have succumbed to the dark mysticism of the Nazis or the irrational utopianism of the socialists. He believes philosophers bear some responsibility for the turn to extremism. By treating philosophy as a game they have sown seeds of chaos. The fashionable academic dogma elevating will-power and spirit over rational thinking strikes him as appallingly irresponsible. Devaluing the rigor of scientific method has given rise to a netherworld of irrational impulses while confidence in democracy has been undermined by incessant attacks on Enlightenment ideals. If he is to make any contribution he must find a way to show that epistemology matters, that errors in the way we think give birth to monsters.

Speaking with Josephine Karl keeps such grandiose thoughts to himself and paints a picture of the tranquillity they will find in the islands of the South Seas. It is frustratingly difficult to get hold of information about their destination. Stieler's Atlas shows high mountain peaks near the town where Karl will teach and he feels certain there will be ski fields and hiking tracks. He learns the country's socialist government effectively combatted unemployment with public works schemes and finds something in *Neue Freie Presse* about the athlete Lovelock who was a gold medallist in Berlin. Leading the New Zealand team at the opening ceremony he refused to acknowledge Hitler's Nazi salute as they marched past the official dais. The article points out the New Zealanders' snub was in stark contrast to the French who enthusiastically returned the Nazi salute, and even the British did an eyes-right for Hitler. Josephine shows little interest in the snippets Karl assiduously collects. Her position at the Hauptschule has become untenable due to relentless bullying from her Nationalist colleagues and she is resigned to leaving the country she loves. She's learnt if there is one crime worse than being born to a Jewish mother it is the scandal of an Aryan maiden marrying a Jew. The antipathy against race-mixers arouses atavistic passions and her students have picked-up on the vile, often obscene taunts thrown at her by fellow teachers.

When confirmation of his appointment arrives Karl tries to persuade Mother to join them, but her health is frail and she is daunted by a long ocean voyage. She is delighted Karl has secured an academic appointment and assures him she is content to see out her years in the city that holds such fond memories. Hanya is bemused by the thought of Karl travelling to the ends of the earth. The Hellerau-Laxenburg school supplies everything she desires and she is proud to be working with the Dance Director Rosalia Chladek whose reputation spread far and wide after the success of the outdoor performances at the Rathausplatz. She brushes off his concerns about how unpleasant things could become if the Nazis get the upper-hand.

'There's been mutterings about the number of Jewish teachers at the institute, but everyone says Hitler was delighted by the Eurythmics displays at the Olympiad so I can't imagine anyone objecting to what we do. And if there's trouble the local villagers will look after us—the Institute has been a great boon for Laxenburg.'

In the weeks before departure Karl and Josephine are consumed by small tasks. The enormity of their undertaking only sinks in when they reach London and absorb the bustling energy of the docks with vessels arriving and departing to all points of the globe. Their ship is a modern diesel-powered liner built to carry a large amount of cargo and Karl watches with interest as huge crates of what he guesses must be agricultural machinery are eased into the hold by stevedores. His boyish enthusiasm cannot dislodge the sadness in Josephine's eyes. When they cast off she remains in their cabin and Karl finds a spot on the boat-deck to observe the ship gliding smoothly into the Thames. The regularity of shipboard life appeals to him, but Josephine only ventures from the cabin for meals and occasional visits to the ship's library. The *Rangitata* is a top-heavy vessel and she rolls easily in the broad swells of the Atlantic. It takes time for Karl to learn the sailor's trick of matching his gait to the swing of the sea, but once he gets the hang of it he roams incessantly around the decks and through the network of white painted companionways. He is determined to use the five-week voyage to improve his English, though most of the passengers are put off by his heavy Viennese accent and he finds it easier to converse with crewmen. One of the New Zealand deck stewards is an avid reader of George Bernard Shaw and he is eager to talk once he discovers Karl is taking up a university position in Christchurch. On his night-watch he brings Karl into the crew's messroom where they drink tea made with condensed milk. He presents lively retellings of plays he's read and speaks admiringly on Shaw's sympathetic understanding of the working man. To reciprocate Karl talks about the worker's education programmes in Vienna and does his best to explain Bertrand Russell's theories on mathematics.

His buoyancy wanes as the ship grinds through the Panama Canal where they face oppressive humidity and unrelenting attacks from mosquito swarms. In thc Pacific Josephine spends more time on deck, scanning the ocean, taking pleasure in sightings of porpoises and petrels. Karl is unsettled by the featureless horizons and late at night, when sleep eludes him, seeks the cool air on the winch deck at the ship's stern. Rising and falling on the ocean swell he gazes out at the reeling stars and feels certain the venture is a mistake. He regrets how he'd always been so critical of Vienna and is overwhelmed by a tender nostalgia for the city. Vivid memories wash over him. He recalls arguing through the night on long looping walks through city streets and pictures the sun rising over the Volksgarten, the paper boys spilling into the streets with the morning edition and elegant young men stumbling out of late-night cafés. Vienna, for all its faults and pretensions, made him feel he was at the heart of everything. He fears he'll never again experience the exhilaration of debating issues that could shape the future of Western civilisation. Perhaps it was all an illusion, the triumph of overblown egos and fraught emotions, or perhaps the world where ideas matter has already vanished. With his body absorbing the throbbing vibration of the ship's engines he opens to the restless infinity of the ocean and feels lost. It is inconceivable that a port will emerge from the emptiness and he will be expected to find a place and purpose in an unknown land.

32

On days when the morning papers are filled with momentous developments in Europe, the teachers at Gymnasia Rehavia huddle around a short-wave radio receiver in the staff dining room. British broadcasts are regarded as the most authoritative, but each staff member craves news from his own country. Max still feels a twinge of homesickness when he hears German voices, though news from Berlin is unrelentingly ghastly. Surprisingly the letters he receives from Vienna give little cause for concern. Father writes at length on religious matters and has nothing to say about politics. Hanya mentioned a nationalist youth group is using the gardens at Laxenburg for marching drills, but feels certain the Viennese are too cultured to succumb to the barbarism of the Nazis. Her equanimity provides a welcome buffer to the gloom and anxiety pervading the staff-room. Max tries to steer clear of political discussions, but like everyone devours any fragment of news to dispel the uncertainty. The well informed maintain Hitler is too shrewd to risk everything in a war he cannot win. Others insist war is inevitable and their predictions seem more plausible after the League of Nations was unable to stop Mussolini taking Addis Ababa.

There is agreement that if it came to war Hitler could quickly seize Cairo or Beirut and anyone following accounts of the Abyssinian campaign understands how easily the Zionist dream could be snuffed out by a squadron of bombers spraying poisonous gas. This sobering thought enflames already heated disputes between Zionist factions. The prospect of Arabs throwing in their lot with the Nazis, as the Grand Mufti of Jerusalem advocates, brings grudging acknowledgement the British must keep the Arabs onside to have any chance of standing up to Hitler. Max watches events unfolding like moves in a chess game, unable to discern whether new developments are fatal errors or clever strategies.

Beyond the fractious atmosphere of the staff-room he has reason to be optimistic. With his salary paid regularly he moved from the primitive room shared with the Polish policeman and found more agreeable accommodation at a new worker's housing development on Arlosoroff

Street. The austere cement building has modern facilities and many residents speak German. Coffee houses and bakeries have sprung up in his neighbourhood and though he avoids spending on luxuries in order to send money home, he appreciates the touches of European culture creeping into the city. On occasions he watches German and American movies shown in an open-air cinema behind the markets. By chance he re-established contact with Lukas after spotting him among a gang of labourers repairing pot-holes on the Jaffa Road. He almost failed to recognise his old friend as the stylishly attired student he knew in Vienna has transformed into a proletarian pioneer with swarthy complexion, calloused hands and an open-necked blue shirt hanging loosely over his threadbare khaki shorts. On exchanging stories Max learns Lukas endured years of abject poverty in a remote *kvutza* on the slopes of Mount Gilboa before finding a home among one of the most radical and idealistic Labour Legions.

Whenever possible Max visits him at their encampment on the outskirts of Tel Aviv, a ramshackle establishment with furniture hammered out of old packing crates. A corrugated-iron shed serves as a communal dining room and residents, mostly young and single, have devised their own secular rituals for observing the Sabbath. On Friday evenings when Max visits, Lukas presses him to join folk-dancing circles and as night falls the workers gather around an open fire to sing Zionist anthems. Their camaraderie is forged out of hardship with twelve hour shifts under the scorching sun, leaving little time for anything besides working, eating and sleeping. Max cannot understand why Lukas would choose the drudgery of manual labour over the stimulation of an intellectual career. He tries to persuade him to attend the gatherings at Scholem's apartment but Lukas shows little interest and Max senses his reluctance is driven by fear he might be seduced by the pleasures of his former life. The rudimentary conditions at the encampment are a far cry from the coffee-houses Lukas frequented in Vienna. Max is pleased his friend has found a place to call home and admires how the Labour Legions protect themselves from the increasingly regular outbursts of rioting. At the university, well-intentioned efforts to cooperate with the Arab leadership have come to nothing and when violence erupts the university staff are at the mercy of the mob while the roadbuilders of Tel Aviv swing into well practiced drills that provide some security as riots run their course.

With gloom spreading over the university, meetings in Scholem's living room are increasingly fractious and Max finds more satisfaction immersing in the rapidly expanding collection of the National Library. As his guide and mentor, Scholem never directs his reading but by following hints and vague suggestions he's become familiar with the eccentric mystics from Martin Buber's *Tales of the Hasidim* and delved into the vibrant intellectual life of Cordoba in the early medieval period. On warm evenings, after the library closes, Scholem invites Max to stroll with him through the tree lined boulevards of Rehavia. Under the shade of an ancient olive tree they buy drinks from the Arab boys in striped tunics who ply streets with copper gourds filled with ice and brightly coloured bottles holding the juice of lemons, oranges and tamarinds. Their conversation inevitably drifts to the increasingly dire political situation. Scholem is well informed on the situation in Europe and voices his disquiet at recent developments.

'Anti-Semitism is always in the air but whenever it gets concentrated in the personality of a powerful leader we face a far more potent menace. Rameses II, Nebuchadnezzar, Haman, Antiochus Aristophanes, the Emperor Titus, Martin Luther—the list goes on. We must expect the worst.'

When Max asks if demonic forces could be driving Hitler's rise, Scholem sips his iced drink and looks to be choosing his words carefully. 'The news-reels of his night rallies are troubling, there seems to be a kind of magnetism that defies rational explanation, and if that is the case it would be reasonable to speak of diabolical forces.'

'If he is not demonically inspired…' Max hesitates before posing the question; 'would you say he's been sent as judgment upon us?'

'That would be an elementary error of interpretation—of course *HaShem hardened Pharaoh's heart* and the Babylonians were sent against us like a devouring wind. The Rabbis like to call this divine judgement, but there are deeper levels of interpretation.'

With Max looking chastened, he continues in a more conciliatory tone, 'For the pagans military victory proved the superiority of their gods and if defeated they could always find new gods. But for Jews there is only One. Those who defeat us are instruments *HaShem* has raised against us; we can only repent and look to the time when our oppressors will also face judgement. This is why monotheism was such a great spiritual innovation. In victory or defeat we face the same choice; remain faithful to the Covenants, or devise our own schemes. Hence Moses's warning before Israel entered the Land of Promise—*I set before you a blessing and a curse.*'

When news of the Anschluss reaches Jerusalem, Max plunges into despair. Listening to the radio broadcast of cheering crowds welcoming Hitler into Vienna, he feels a rising dread and as colleagues debate the significance of events his only thought is to join his family. Everyone counsels against it, warning rash action could jeopardise his own freedom without helping his family. He is told to be patient, but with ever more alarming news spewing out of the radio, the need to be with his family becomes unbearable. The only glimmer of hope comes from Lukas who calmly tells Max his family could be smuggled into Palestine with help from clandestine networks operating out of Constanza. He speaks with reassuring confidence about Jabotinsky's paramilitary brigades who operate beyond the sanction of the Jewish Council. When he is certain Max is serious, Lukas introduces him to a member of *Haganah* who supplies a contact in Bucharest. He's told if he can get his family to Romania, a fishing vessel will deliver them to a safe location outside Jaffa.

The plan strikes Max as akin to a modern-day miracle, as unlikely as the parting of the Red Sea, but Lukas assures him several men in the Labour Legion entered Palestine by this method and it is not only possible but a good deal less hazardous than working through official channels. Plagued by inadequacy Max focusses on practical tasks and his hazy intentions solidify. Colleagues who counselled against the idea are eager to help once it becomes clear he will not be dissuaded. The gymnasium grants him a leave of absence and he is able to save money when a fellow teacher arranges for him to sleep in the living-room of his house. To ensure he will be able to re-enter the country he obtains a Palestinian passport, issued by the Mandatory Authority.

Although Scholem is sympathetic he believes once you have left Europe there should be no looking back, least you end up like Lot's wife. He warns Max the greatest obstacles may come from his own family and recounts how many of his closest friends in Europe choose to accept abject humiliation rather than uprooting from the country of their birth. 'We have a genius for perseverance—every Jewish child knows we always outlast our persecutors but it boils down to a kind of stubbornness.'

For Scholem the tragedy of the Anschluss is intensified by the loss of the *Kultusgemeinde* library in Vienna, which he regards as one of the world's most significant depositories of Jewish learning. He is intimately familiar with the library's contents and in an elegiac tone laments the loss of irreplaceable manuscripts and incunabula from the Halberstamm collection. Choked with emotion he describes how Rabbi Nahum Beer Friedmann gifted his collection to the Vienna *Kultusgemeinde* to safeguard the precious legacy of Rabbi Beer whose manuscripts are the only surviving commentaries on the revelations of the founding Hassidim, Baal Shem

Tov.

Max asks what the Nazis will do with the books. Scholem responds with an anguished sigh. 'In Hamburg and in Munich, the community libraries were crated and sent to Berlin. They've assembled a group of scholars called the *Ahnenerbe* to examine the loot. Some priceless manuscripts have appeared in auctions for American collectors, but most will be pulped.'

He confides that a delegation of Rabbis recently consulted with him over fears Hitler would use the magical properties of stolen Kabbalistic books to subjugate human souls. 'I told them they shouldn't worry—if the *Ahnenerbe* experts diligently follow the ancient recipes for creating golems and such like, they'll eventually discover the thaumaturgical practices are spiritual exercises aimed at entering into communion with the Great Name.'

As Max's departure approaches, staff and students at the gymnasium take up a collection and present him with a substantial sum, which he converts into German marks. The cheapest route is to travel by rail to Alexandria and embark on a Rumanian steamer for Constanza. A school delegation accompanies him to the station, singing *Hatikva*h as his train departs. He is moved by the gesture but feels like an imposter and as the train rattles through the desert he can't help dwelling on his inadequacy. In his pocket he carries pebbles for his family from the rocky terrain on the edge of Gaza Street. He decided on stones in preference to the devotional objects from the street stalls in Mea She'arim, as he knows his father will treasure anything from the soil of Jerusalem. Fingering the pebbles, he is struck by an image of the five smooth stones David put in his *keli haro'im* before confronting Goliath. With a wry smile he recognises his prospects are as daunting as those of his illustrious ancestor. At sea his hopes dissipate into fatalism, and he tells himself even if he fails miserably it is preferable to sitting in Jerusalem doing nothing.

33

In the self-contained world of the Eurythmics Institute the demanding routine of musical study and physical exercise leaves little room for politics. Whenever she visits Mother, Hanya notices more Nazi lapel badges on the streets of Vienna, but always feels reassured on seeing the solid and imposing *Vaterländische Front* building on the Kohlmarkt, an unassailable bulwark against German barbarism. She believes Schuschnigg's old-fashioned patriotism will prove more resilient than the fanaticism of the Nazis. Having steadfastly refused to give any credence to the doom mongers, she listens in stunned disbelief when the Chancellor interrupts a broadcast of a Mozart symphony to announce he has tended his resignation. In the faded opulence of the old ballroom the residents of the Altes Schloss stir in their armchairs as Schuschnigg's disembodied voice croaks through the static. He signs off with a dismal plea for God's protection over Austria and with an unnerving silence filling the room Hanya contemplates a future in which her oasis of tranquillity might cease to exist.

The Director puts a brave face on it. 'We must stay calm. Hitler has a keen interest in health and physical fitness—I'm sure the new regime will value our work.'

Jewish staff members take a different view and once Hitler addresses the adoring multitude at the Heldenplatz the atmosphere in Altes Schloss is bitterly pessimistic. In less than a week an official accompanied by two SS Officers delivers a terse decree requiring the Institute to vacate the premises.

Frau Rosalia calls everyone into the Grand Ballroom and calmly addresses the mournful gathering. 'There must be no tears or despondency. For the Greeks a crisis was an opportunity for decisive action, it revealed the true nature of things. We depart with our heads held high and like wind-blown seeds, we will proudly carry the lessons of the Hellerau-Laxenburg School to wherever we find fertile soil.'

In the emotional farewells, Hanya feels the truth of these words. Her roommates chat excitedly about plans to open dance studios in their hometowns, inspired by Frau Rosalia's call to form a Republic of Dance without regard for national boundaries—like the old Republic of Letters. Hanya is pressed to join ventures in Zurich, Toulouse and Copenhagen and her address book is crammed with invitations to all the capitals of Europe.

The excitement rapidly fades when she receives a telegram from Mother saying she's fled from her rooms on the Bauernmarkt and moved in with Aunt Zipporah. Having accepted an invitation to stay with her friend Trudi until things settle down, Hanya delivers her luggage to Trudi's apartment on the Kohlmarkt and rushes to her aunt's tenement in Tempelgasse. The shock of eviction has shattered Mother's wilful optimism and she shows no interest when Hanya urges her to move in with her at Trudi's apartment. As she gets a better grasp of the situation Hanya sees the working-class area provides a small measure of protection. With the cool-headed menace of a criminal gang the Nazis focus their attention where money can be made. Jews are being tossed out of the fancy mansions on the Ringstraße and in the middle-class areas residents face ruthless harassment and appropriation of property. Stories circulate of men answering a late night knock on the door and being dragged away to a concentration camp at Dachau. The tenements in Leopoldstadt are seen as little more than a source of amusement for the Nazis. Smoke bombs are lobed into synagogues and red painted slogans daubed over Jewish shop-fronts, but the impoverished residents are ignored, so long as there is money to be made tormenting wealthy Jews.

At her friend's chic Kohlmarkt apartment, Hanya passes unnoticed in a world where there is grudging admiration for Hitler. The family are respectable Aryan stock with no reason to fear the Nazis, though Trudi's father is a well-known supporter of the Social Democrats and on the night of the Anschluss he'd been arrested and briefly detained. Travelling between Kohlmarkt and her aunt's tenement Hanya feels like a spy and carries off her disguise with aplomb, returning the Nazi salute with a flirtatious smile appreciated by patrolling SS officers. Weeks pass uneventfully as she alternates between sitting at mother's bedside and helping Trudi set up a dance studio offering Eurythmics and *Ausdruckstanz* classes to a select group of private pupils. Mother urges Hanya to flee but stubbornly insists she is content to see out her days so she can be buried with Father in the plot he purchased in the Central Cemetery. Much as she longs to leave Hanya cannot contemplate abandoning her mother. She is disgusted at how easily the proud Viennese spirit has given way to fawning adoration for all things German. To see Mother's life of quiet devotion ending in such misery is heartbreaking and when she passes peacefully in her sleep Hanya views death as a release and a blessing.

Aunt Zipporah wants a Jewish funeral but cannot go against her sister's stated wishes. Hanya watches numbly as her Aunt lovingly washes the body and mutters Hebrew prayers over the sister who abandoned the faith of her ancestors. Uncle Martin worries there might be unpleasantness about an officially designated Jew being laid to rest in the Protestant section of the cemetery, but Reverend Mueller, the Lutheran priest who prepared Hanya for confirmation, is old-fashioned enough to believe the sacrament of baptism supersedes the authority of the state. A small group of Mother's friends, including the composer Zemlinsky, gather for the burial service and everyone is moved to tears when he sings his own setting of the 13th Psalm as the casket is lowered.

How long, O Lord? Will you forget me for ever?
How long will you hide your face from me?
How long must I bear pain in my soul,
and have sorrow in my heart all day long?
How long shall my enemy be exalted over me?

After what she hopes is an appropriately respectful period, Hanya thanks her Aunt for her kindness and announces she is leaving for Zurich to visit a friend from her dance school. Zipporah presses her to eat some *schnecke* with her coffee, pausing thoughtfully before she speaks.

'That would be best, there is nothing to keep you here.'

There is a coolness between Hanya and her Aunt as neither has made mention of the failed romance with Max or Zipporah's efforts to promote the match. Gazing at her niece unblinkingly, Zipporah flatly announces, 'We saw Max at the synagogue last week, he's returned from Palestine and is staying with his family.'

Hanya stiffens, her head filling with wild speculations as to why there is no reference to such plans in his last letter. Trying to remain nonchalant, she squirms under her Aunt's scrutiny and realises how ridiculous it is to pretend. With her voice betraying a tangle of emotion, she asks if it is possible to see him.

Visiting Max at his family's apartment is out of the question so Zipporah dispatches her son Ezra to make arrangements. With her cousin as chaperone, Hanya is taken to a coffee-house near the *Kultusgemeinde* building on Ferdinandstraße. Peering through the narrow glass door panels she sees Max perched on a stool, head resting in his hands. Ezra ushers her in and Max springs to his feet like a startled cat. He mutters a greeting and introduces his younger brother Moshe. The two escorts discreetly move to a long bench in the centre of the room while Hanya and Max sit at the only window table. Hanya gazes mutely at Max's downcast eyes. Memories of happier times flicker across her mind and she searches for a way to dispel the grimace dragging Max down into the floorboards. Summoning a theatrical sigh she adopts the accusatory tone of a jilted lover.

'You might have told me you were returning to Vienna.'

Max's timidly raised eyes are met with an ironic grin and when she releases a peal of laughter he chuckles nervously.

'It happened so suddenly, I had to be with my family and I didn't want to cause any alarm.'

'Thoughtful of you,' Hanya responds with a giggle. With the tension dissipating, she tells him about the closure of the Eurythmics Institute and her Mother's funeral. A mysterious chemistry re-establishes the easygoing intimacy they enjoyed in their youth and Max explains how a grand plan to smuggle his family into Palestine has come to nothing.

'Papa is unwell and has religious objections to entering Jerusalem by illegal means. The elders are urging him to flee but he will not abandon his people and his synagogue.'

'It was the same for my mother—she became fixated on being buried alongside Daddy.'

Gesturing towards his brother, Max tells her Moshe has joined a Zionist Youth organisation and desperately wants to take the family to Palestine.

'We've decided I should return to Jerusalem—I want to stay but nothing will change Father's mind and there are no jobs here. At least in Palestine I can earn money and we hope when the time is right the family will join me.'

'You've obviously given the matter a great deal of thought,' Hanya responds coolly. 'Returning to Palestine sounds like the most sensible thing.'

Her feelings for him are undiminished and she silently accommodates the sadness of knowing they will never be together. She longs to rest her cheek on his shoulder as she used to when they sat together in the Prater watching the sunshine sparkle on the surface of the grey Danube. By municipal order Jews are now forbidden from using the benches in Vienna's parks. When she learns Max must attend to family matters before returning to Jerusalem, she decides to delay her departure and writes the phone number of Trudi's apartment on a serviette. Captivated by the way his darting eyes never alight on hers Hanya surrenders to a sense of recklessness. Pressing her ankle against his calf, she rubs gently to indicate contact is not accidental. He acknowledges the gesture by returning her gaze and Hanya catches a glimpse of her face reflected in the watery darkness of his eyes. On the adjoining table Moshe discreetly clears his throat and Hanya senses it is time to leave. They press cheeks and he shuffles out of the coffee house with his brother in tow. Feeling she's been given more than she dared hope, Hanya stares blankly at the closed door, cradling an image of what might have been.

Walking from the café Max drifts through familiar streets with his face locked in an idiotic smile. A mess of half-formed thoughts collide with jolts of raw emotion and his brother's sideways glances go unnoticed. As they approach their apartment Moshe's curiosity gets the better of him. 'Do you have feelings for her?'

Max's mumbled reply is barely audible. 'I suppose so.'

In the moment when their eyes met a wave of emotion swept away the numbness of the years he'd wasted. He sways under a deluge of remorse, bewildered by his inability to do the one thing he most wants to do. It seems inconceivable Hanya has remained devoted to him but he dares to imagine she would join him in Palestine, if he could just find the courage to ask. He could not expect her to risk the dangers of illegal immigration but the PE teachers at his gymnasium are well informed about the Eurythmic method and Hanya's expertise would be highly valued, especially at the new, progressive schools in Tel Aviv.

Vivid imagining opens a tantalising world of possibility, until an inner voice insinuates, he could have misinterpreted her gesture in the café. He feels his mind slipping, succumbing to his debilitating habit of vacillation. In the fetid atmosphere of the crowded apartment exasperation grips him. Mother has got it into her head he must return to Palestine with a wife and she's pursued the idea with such zeal he's been forced to acknowledge it is not without merit. There are countless young Jewish women who will do anything to secure an immigration certificate and he'd convinced himself he should go along with the arrangements, if only to provide an escape route for someone desperate to leave Vienna. If he were honest he'd admit he was attracted by the idea of obtaining a wife without the agony of courtship but the memory of Hanya's gaze sets his mind ablaze. He grits his teeth and contemplates the terrifying prospect of forging his own future.

34

With his family preparing for Shabbat, Max jumps at the opportunity to accompany his sister when she is sent to buy fish at the Karmelitermarkt. Walking briskly through bustling streets he's unsettled by the normality of life under the swastika. People go about their business, shopping for food, finding entertainment in the cafés and cinemas as if nothing had changed. At the Karmelitermarkt he watches his little sister confidently exchange banter with the fish-sellers. He treats her to coffee and encourages her to continue her studies even though she is now barred from attending university. When they return to the apartment with a package of herrings Father is huddled in conversation with a guest and gestures for Max to join him. Scrutinising the hunched figure seated at Father's work bench Max gasps as he recognises his mentor Dr. Fleischel. Barely hearing the Doctor's muttered greeting he gazes dumbstruck at a spectre of the man he knew. The robust beard has been replaced with spikey white stubble and the working-man's jacket hanging loosely over his shoulders jolts Max's memory of the immaculately tailored gentleman who exuded sophistication and refinement. Dispensing with pleasantries the Doctor questions him about the situation in Palestine and when the subject of immigration is raised Max adopts a reassuring tone that is bluntly dismissed.

'No need to sugar-coat it. I hear the British have naval patrols turning back boats.'

Recognising Dr. Fleischel would be well informed through his contacts with the Zionist leadership Max has no idea how to respond. The best he can offer is an account of the fiery debates consuming his colleagues at the gymnasium. He describes how the Zionist faction are reluctant to oppose British policies out of fear for what could happen if the British were forced to leave.

The Doctor responds with bleak laughter. 'We also have learnt to deal with the lesser evil. We threw our weight behind Schuschnigg and never said a word about his anti-Semitic policies.'

The bitterness in his voice hints at what he must have endured and with the conversation trailing into silence Moshe supplies a discreet account of the indignities the Doctor suffered. On the night of the Anschluss the leadership of the *Kultusgemeinde* was arrested and Doctor Fleischel was among a group of elders forced to scrub painted slogans from the streets while a jeering mob gleefully vented their malice. They were taken to Dachau and the Gestapo used their detention to extort a huge ransom as a penalty for the *Kultusgemeinde's* support of the plebiscite. At this point Dr. Fleischel appears agitated and takes-up his own story.

'When I was released my only thought was to flee to Palestine but much as the Nazis long to see the city *judenfrei,* no one is permitted to leave until the SS is certain we have surrendered every last shekel.'

He explains he has been unable to obtain an exit visa on account of his brother who had the foresight to leave before the Anschluss and is now running the family's textile business from Lyon. By preventing him from leaving, the Gestapo believe they can extort ownership of the firm's lucrative trading interests. The Doctor is refusing to cooperate and at one point made an illegal crossing of the Hungarian border. Without the necessary documents he was detained and spent four weeks in a Hungarian prison before being returned to Austria. Max tentatively makes mention of the contact address he has from Constanza, but it is clear Dr. Fleischel has decided against leaving. He's reached the same grim conclusion as Max's father and is set on remaining in Vienna to serve the community. The *Kultusgemeinde*, with its Nazi appointed leaders, is reduced to running soup kitchens and schools for Jewish children now excluded from public education. Dr. Fleischel's medical expertise is urgently needed and he is resigned to playing his part while encouraging the younger generation to flee by whatever means available.

Embarrassed that his story has engendered a sombre mood the Doctor peppers Max with questions about the University at Mount Scopus. He shows a lively interest in Gershom Scholem's work at the National Library and on hearing how deeply Scholem was affected by the loss of the *Kultusgemeinde* library, the Doctor adopts a more serious tone. Lowering his voice to a conspiratorial whisper he reveals a small number of books have been smuggled out of the library at enormous risk. A well-educated *Untersturmführer,* Eichmann, is charged with disposing of the library's collection and has taken a personal interest in acquiring rare and valuable manuscripts. The Nazis are fighting amongst themselves over which entity should take possession of the library and the conflict has created an opportunity to rescue a few books deemed of crucial significance for rabbinical scholars. The action is dangerous as Eichmann has made it clear the head librarian, Dr. Moses, will be held personally responsible if items from the catalogue go missing. Before books can be saved, facsimiles are prepared and the smuggled works replaced with fakes cobbled from the pages of less important works. With enormous pride the Doctor discloses some of the most precious books are now securely hidden within basement walls or beneath the concrete foundations of Jewish buildings.

It occurs to Max that for all their crudity, the Nazis instinctively understand that to destroy the Jews they must destroy their books. He assures Dr. Fleischel that Scholem will be thrilled to hear about the rescued books.

'He'll be hoping some of the manuscripts might one day find a safe haven at the library on Mount Scopus.'

On hearing these words the Doctor pauses and his eyes rest on Max's face. 'There is a book that would be of particular interest to Dr. Scholem.'

Max feels his heart pounding as Dr. Fleischel describes the library's fourteenth century manuscript of the *Sepher Yetzirah*, which includes a handwritten commentary by the great Spanish kabbalist Nachmanides. The book is revered as one of the earliest, most significant works on cosmology and though Scholem could access other manuscript copies, the commentary by Nachmanides would be invaluable for his work on the origins of the Kabbalah. The possibility of transporting the book to Jerusalem is raised hypothetically and the Doctor calmly outlines the hazards. 'There are arbitrary searches of Jews leaving the country and the border guards are always on the lookout for Jews carrying anything of value.'

Despite the danger Max makes it clear he would be honoured to be entrusted with the mission. Returning to the safety of Jerusalem while his family are at the mercy of a malicious and unpredictable regime has tormented him and in this small gesture he sees a chance to assuage his guilt. After a lengthy discussion on the most effective method of concealing the manuscript it is agreed Max is well placed to undertake the task. His Palestinian passport makes it easier for him to avoid scrutiny and the pages of the manuscript can be concealed within a plain cover which should not attract attention. Father gives his blessing and with his mind reeling Max contemplates the enormity of his mission.

Dr. Fleischel has warned the greatest threat comes from informants who supply intelligence to the Gestapo to gain favourable treatment or secure the release of detained relatives. To minimise the risk Max will not collect the manuscript until the day of his departure. He decides to write to Hanya rather than facing the complications of another meeting. In a carefully worded letter, which she will receive after he has left the country, he plainly expresses the hope she might consider living in Palestine and suggests he could help in obtaining an immigration certificate if she is prepared to work at one of the progressive schools in Jerusalem or Tel Aviv.

When the family assembles to pray for his safe passage Max knows he will never see his father again and struggles to keep his emotions in check. In a sombre mood he walks with Moshe to the book-binder's workshop carrying nothing more than a satchel for the journey. With the sun sinking in a clear sky, the heavy stone buildings on Czerninplatz cast deep shadows on the narrow footpaths and Max can't shake a feeling he is being watched. Arriving at Bernhard Landau's workshop he longs for the open vistas and stark white buildings of Jerusalem. His brother raps lightly on the glass panelled door and Max raises his eyes to a narrow strip of blue sky. They are ushered into the workshop by Herr Landau's wife who serves coffee as her husband engages in small talk. The old man asks about the library in Jerusalem and is pleased to hear about Professor Scholem's passion for ancient manuscripts. Turning to a pile of old books on his workbench, he hands over a well-thumbed edition of *Gesenius' Hebrew Grammar* and guides Max towards the middle section. Tentatively turning pages he is astounded to discover handwritten lines of ancient Hebrew letters inscribed on surprisingly bright pages. Enormous skill has been applied to concealing the precious text and Herr Landau talks about how hard it was to find a paper to match the texture of the velum manuscript.

Gazing at the ancient writing Max does not notice the rumbling of a powerful automobile engine from the street. Moshe leaps to his feet and peers cautiously through the workshop window. Seeing SS officers climbing out of a sleek black Mercedes he freezes. The instinct to flee only takes hold as the uniforms approach the door. Yanking his brother by the collar and grabbing his satchel he scrambles into the living quarters adjoining the studio. Bernhard's wife silently directs them to a corridor leading to the back of the building and once they find the courtyard entrance they can hear barking voices and fists thumping on the workshop door. Max hesitates, torn by an impulse to turn back. His brother drags him across the courtyard and into an atrium opening onto Ferdinandstraße. Peering left and right Moshe is relieved to see a tram approaching and the pavements filled with workers and shop-girls making their way home. Guessing they will only have minutes before the SS are searching for them, he tells Max to stow the book in his satchel and they merge with pedestrians walking towards Fruchtgasse.

Moshe nudges his brother into an apartment building and they climb four flights of stairs to an attic landing where they are admitted to a small room shared by Zionist students. Facing the quizzical stares of his friends, Moshe gives a terse account of their predicament, explaining Max is scheduled to catch the 8:30 train departing for Budapest and onto Constanza. It is agreed they cannot risk being seen in the streets and two of the students leave to ascertain the danger. Max is embarrassed to find he is trembling and as they wait he fretfully imagines what will happen to the book-binder and his wife. Hours later a report from returning students enflames his worst fears. The workshop was searched and though nothing incriminating found, Herr Landau was taken for questioning. It must be assumed he will be interrogated under torture and the immediate concern is to warn those involved in smuggling books from the *Kultusgemeinde* library. The second student confirms extra patrols are watching the trains departing Franz-Josefs-Bahnhof and it is decided Max and Moshe should remain in the attic while they assess the situation.

By the second day they learn the Gestapo visited Father's apartment and left dissatisfied after being told Max and Moshe had departed for Palestine. When he hears the authorities have circulated their names and descriptions, Max is gripped by a vivid premonition of being caught. His paranoia is intensified by confinement in the tiny attic room where he must sleep on the floor and only use the bathroom late at night to avoid arousing suspicion from the building's occupants. Paralysed with fear and pessimistic about his fate he fixates on the need to apologise to Hanya. When they met at the café she gave him the number for her friend's apartment, but Moshe insists it is too dangerous to use a telephone booth as the Gestapo will be monitoring the lines. Max will not let the matter go and to prevent him falling into despair one of the students offers to visit Hanya's apartment.

He returns within an hour accompanied by Hanya who casts aside decorum and wraps her arms around Max. The students exchange glances and depart to a nearby coffee-house, leaving Max and Hanya alone with Moshe, who tactfully withdraws to a bunk and feigns sleep. Max blurts a barely coherent apology and Hanya responds calmly, 'You can't be expected to express feelings you don't have, that would be terribly unfair.'

'But that's not the case,' Max replies in a tortured squeak. 'I've always loved you, I've just been too scared to admit it.'

With the words sinking into her consciousness, Hanya's emotions jerk between anger, disbelief and anticipation. She fixes her eyes on Max who is shuffling nervously, head bowed, gaze set on the floorboards. He cautiously raises his eyes and she inclines her body towards him. An imperceptible force draws them together and his arms clumsily encircle her waist. Hanya wraps her arms around his shoulders and a rocking motion tightens their embrace. The evening sun throws an eerie light into the sparsely furnished room where they cling, aware of nothing beyond the gentle pressure of their foreheads touching.

With sniffles blurring his voice Max apologises over and over. Above all he wants to let Hanya know how much he regrets the way he has acted, but cannot find the words.

'And now it's too late,' he mutters.

The finality in his voice jolts Hanya out of her reverie. She fires questions, urgently trying to make sense of the cryptic story she heard from the student who brought her to the room. Drawing his brother into the conversation she is relieved to find Moshe does not share Max's pessimism. He believes if they remain out of sight for a few weeks the Gestapo will conclude they have left the country and shift their attention to other matters, at which point Max should be able to make an illegal crossing into Hungary or Czechoslovakia and travel to Jerusalem using his Palestinian passport. Hanya observes that with the Gestapo hunting for two brothers it makes sense for them to separate and when Moshe concurs she suggests Max could easily be hidden in her apartment on the Kohlmarkt. Anticipating how she could help brings a rush of excitement which is deflated when Max insists he will not do anything to put her in danger. Breathing deeply to mask her disappointment Hanya asks if she could speak with Max alone. Moshe withdraws to a corner where there is a makeshift kitchen and lights a small paraffin stove.

Pausing until their eyes meet, Hanya addresses him with compelling sincerity. 'You must let me do this, the danger is nothing compared with how I would suffer if you do not let me help you.'

The objections rising inside Max's head are silenced by the need to atone. The only thing he has to give is obedience and he nods his consent, silently resolving to submit unquestioningly to whatever she asks of him.

Moshe places a mug of watery coffee before Hanya and listens with skepticism as she lays out her plan to conceal Max in the Kohlmarkt apartment. As she speaks Moshe can see the advantages of removing his brother from Leopoldstadt where gossip is rife and everybody knows everybody else's business. He reiterates that the greatest danger comes from anonymous informants and is pleased that Hanya takes the warning seriously.

'I know my friend will be happy to help, her family were strong supporters of the Social Democrats, they are Catholics, highly respected and the apartment has private rooms where he will be undisturbed.'

She turns to Max who affirms his agreement by rhythmically nodding. Noticing his shabby clothes and scuff-marked boots, Hanya suggests she will bring new clothes so he will not look out of place when they enter the apartment building. She senses any hesitation could lead to second thoughts and briskly takes her leave, promising to return as soon as possible.

As anticipated, Trudi is more than willing to help. She takes Hanya to her brother's wardrobe and pulls out a stylishly tailored jacket with wide lapels.

'Do you think this will fit?'

'It will be perfect,' Hanya replies with a smile. 'He's the same height as Wilhelm, though rather more slender.'

Giggling like a schoolgirl she selects a shirt, tie and a fashionable pair of brogues to complete the disguise. Fearing Max will change his mind she quickly returns to the attic room in Leopoldstadt. He offers no resistance to the change of clothes and with his hair oiled and combed, a white silk shirt, dark flannel suit and matching tie, he appears unrecognisable. His scuff-marked travel satchel is incompatible with the new outfit and it is decided a student will deliver the bag, along with the precious manuscript, once he is safely installed in the Kohlmarkt apartment. Two of Moshe's friends escort them out of Leopoldstadt and as they cross the canal at Franzensbrücke, Hanya takes hold of Max's elbow. Although he walks stiffly in the ill-fitting brogues they look like any bourgeois couple and merge into the theatre crowd spilling out of the Ronacher. Hanya feels so confident she considers popping in to one of the coffee houses where groups of SS Officers loudly hold court at the best tables. Noticing Max is petrified she opts for caution and guides him to the taxis waiting outside the Ronacher. At the apartment building on the Kohlmarkt the doorman sees nothing untoward as Hanya leads her companion to the elevator. When they arrive Trudi has chilled champagne and supper waiting. Out of politeness Max gulps a glass and Trudi does her best to make him welcome.

'We've told the staff you're a distant cousin from Innsbruck, I'd trust them all with my life, so please don't hesitate to ask for anything you need.'

Max's mumbled thanks alerts Hanya to how uncomfortable he must be. Explaining he has hardly slept for the last few days she ushers him to the prepared room.

Alone in the tastefully appointed bedroom, Max carefully hangs his borrowed clothes and pulls on the silk pyjamas laid out for him. He is too exhausted to reflect on his situation and as his limbs subside into the luxurious softness of the mattress, the tension that prevented him sleeping is replaced by welcome blankness. In the drawing room, Hanya adds sugar to her coffee, noisily stirring the dark liquid as she tries to still her thoughts. Though she's said nothing about her feelings for Max, she suspects Trudi has guessed at her romantic yearnings and worries it might look like she's manipulating the situation.

'It's such a relief to have him here. I don't know how we can ever thank-you enough.'

Trudi responds nonchalantly, 'It's nothing, he's a sweet boy and we're glad we can be of use.'

Her aristocratic charm heightens Hanya's uneasiness. She feels guilty about the advantages she enjoys on account of the bonds formed at the Altes Schloss. While Max and his family are trapped in a closed world where everyone shares the same misfortune, she can reach out to loyal friends untouched by the menace of the Nazi regime. With so much on her mind she cannot engage in conversation and though she has little expectation of sleep, retires early.

In her bedroom she tries to take stock, her concentration disrupted by the image of Max asleep on a bed in the adjacent room. After Mother's funeral she had been making preparations to visit Charlotte in Zurich and planned to go on to Toulouse where she'd been offered a teaching position at a Montessori school. She naively assumed the Nazis would do everything to hasten her departure and was ill-prepared for the bureaucratic obstacles. Swiss visas are almost impossible to obtain and Jewish emigrants require a tax clearance certificate, a declaration of assets and payment of special departure taxes. With Austria officially incorporated into the German Reich her passport is no longer valid and a new passport would be stamped with a J, in accordance with Nuremburg laws. When she visited the *Zentralstelle* for Jewish Emigration, housed in the former palace of Lord Rothschild, despair hovered over the queue outside the building. Rising indignation made her recoil from entering into the entanglements of the Nazis' bureaucratic machine. She remembered a family holiday at Lake Constance where she and Dora made a game of jumping backwards and forward across the Swiss border and felt certain she could leave Austria without seeking permission from a regime bent on causing as much misery and humiliation as possible.

Rising early, Hanya pauses, wistfully contemplating the sunlight slanting across the parquet floor of Trudi's exquisitely decorated apartment. She asks a housemaid to prepare a breakfast tray and takes it to Max's room where she finds him perched awkwardly on the edge of the neatly made bed.

'I hope you slept well.'

'Very well, thank you,' Max replies with forced cheerfulness. As Hanya places the tray on a writing desk he bolts for the wardrobe and reaches into the pocket of the jacket he wore last night. Turning to face her he holds out a stamped envelope and thrusts it into her hands.

'I was going to post this before I left…'

Recognising his handwriting on the envelope, Hanya opens the letter with trepidation while Max fidgets, gazing at the breakfast tray as if it were the last meal of a condemned man.

She scans the contents then rereads the letter slowly, absorbing the carefully chosen words. There is none of the ambivalence that made his letters so infuriating and though the offer is couched in ridiculously formal language, it is clear he is inviting her to join him in Palestine.

'I've always been ready to follow you anywhere,' she says, wiping moisture from her eyes. 'You only had to ask.'

Max launches into another outpouring of apology and self-recrimination but she cuts him off, insisting they forget the past. She explains she'd been planning to leave for Switzerland and suggests they travel together, crossing the border at Lake Constance and moving on to Marseilles where they could take a steamer to Cairo and on to Palestine.

'Switzerland will be much safer than going east, I have friends in Zurich and Toulouse, so we'll be able to travel without attracting attention.'

Having decided the only way he can make amends is to comply with her every wish, Max consents. His only reservation is the danger Moshe faces from the SS if he remains in Vienna. Even if he successfully crosses into Hungary, Max fears that without a passport or visa his brother will suffer the same fate as Dr. Fleischel and be returned to Austria. He decides he should give his Palestinian passport to Moshe. The family likeness means the photograph is unlikely to be challenged and the passport will allow his brother to travel through Hungary and join them in Palestine. Hanya points out that as refugees they should be able to obtain Nansen Passports when they reach Zurich and as they consider the obstacles she is surprised at how easily she has taken on the role of fugitive.

With their options so limited, she's pleased to see Max is clear about what needs to be done.

She offers to take his passport to Moshe in Leopoldstadt as it would be dangerous for the brothers to be seen together. On arriving in the attic room she joins with Moshe and his Zionist friends in a conspiratorial huddle around a pot of fresh coffee. She presents Max's letter offering Moshe the use of his Palestinian passport and urging him to do whatever he can to convince their family to join him. Hanya explains they will make their own way to Jerusalem, travelling through Switzerland and France where she can rely on support from friends she made at the Eurythmics Institute. The threat from the Gestapo leaves them with few alternatives and Moshe acknowledges the plan is the most sensible use of their meagre resources. The Zionist students have plenty of advice on illegal border crossings and their stories confirm Hanya's intuition that success depends on assuming a convincing disguise. Those who look or act like fugitives are certain to be caught as everyone, from hotel staff to local postal workers, are on the look-out for strangers lingering near the border. They part in a spirit of cautious optimism and Hanya supplies Moshe with the address in Toulouse where they can receive his letters.

35

Pouring over maps of Lake Constance Hanya searches for the most favourable location for a border crossing. The warm autumn weather should see the region filled with families and young couples on hiking holidays and she knows Max will need to be carefully tutored to look like a middle-class holiday-maker. Their disguise will be more convincing if they travel as a couple and she agonises over how to put forward such a proposal. When she summons the courage, she assures him marriage would be a useful pretence that will not alter their relationship. Though acutely embarrassed Max recognises the advantages of the arrangement. The possibility of actually becoming husband and wife hovers between them like a spectre neither is prepared to acknowledge. Hanya dispels the tension by focussing on practical issues: She supplies her parents' rings as their wedding bands, suggests Max grows a small moustache and cuts his hair in the close-cropped style favoured by the Nazis. Moshe's Zionist friends introduce her to a passport doctor who provides a Marriage Certificate and changes the name in Max's old Austrian passport from Elstein to Eckhardt. Hanya supresses a fit of giggling as Max is told to practice introducing her as *'my wife, Frau Eckhardt.'*

On her frequent trips from the Kohlmarkt to Leopoldstadt, Hanya learnt the best way to pass unnoticed among SS Officers is to make a show of enthusiasm in giving the Nazi salute. She raises the matter with some trepidation and unspoken emotions well up as Max contemplates feigning support for the persecutors of his people. Recalling Gershon Scholem's story about Sabbatai Zevi's followers taking on the religious observances of the goyim, he gingerly submits to Hanya's tutelage and learns to return the Nazi salute without a hint of his inner revulsion. Hanya purchases a guide to hiking trails around Lake Constance and with everything in place Trudi announces she and her brother Wilhelm will join them for a few days holiday. They travel to Salzburg in Wilhelm's Opel, taking inexpensive rooms at the Hotel Sacher where Max tests his assumed identity. With nothing to set them apart from other guests they enjoy a leisurely evening in the hotel dining room and Max's uneasiness slips away as he sees the efficacy of their disguise. When they retire he prepares to sleep on the floor, but Hanya insists they share the double bed to avoid raising suspicions from chamber-maids. Unnerved by the request he says he'll wait until she is asleep before getting in and bashfully withdraws to the bathroom. Awakening in the early hours of the morning, Hanya adjusts her eyes to the darkness. She studies the profile of Max's head resting on the pillow next to her and wonders how long she can maintain the charade.

The next morning they drive to Innsbruck and on to Bregenz where they find rooms at an inn overlooking Lake Constance. For two days they take to the hiking trails and enjoy the picturesque beauty of the region Hanya recalls so fondly from family holidays before the war. On their third day, the weather favourable, she sends a telegram to her friend in Zurich and they drive across the Rhine to the village of Höchst, little changed from the way Hanya remembers it. After a hearty meal at an old-fashioned restaurant they drive to the lakeshore and take photographs in the late afternoon light. When they are certain they are alone, Trudi and Wilhelm depart, promising to forward their luggage by rail to Zurich. With well-stocked knapsacks Hanya and Max find a secluded hideaway among the reeds and willows bordering the lakeshore. Huddled beneath a tarpaulin they observe a strict silence and before long even the birds are oblivious to their presence. Hanya feels strangely placid observing the night herons noisily flitting out of their roosts in surrounding trees. Max keeps his eyes shut and tries to overcome raging fears by silently reciting the psalms he memorised as a child.

A half-moon shining intermittently through a thin veil of cloud allows them to follow the shore-line of Lake Constance until they are well inside Switzerland. Max doggedly follows in Hanya's footsteps, his nerves on edge. The moonlight brightens spectacularly whenever it finds a gap in the cloud, lending a serenity to the rustic landscape, the only hint of danger coming from the occasional barking of farm dogs. Striding boldly through wetlands and lakeside paddocks, Hanya expertly discerns the best places to cross numerous streams feeding into the lake. When they sight a country lane she consults her guidebook and finds a hiking trail into Rorschach. As dawn approaches they withdraw to a hiding place in the forest. Exhausted but in high spirits they change their wet stockings and Hanya produces a bar of chocolate from her knapsack. Waiting until they are warmed by the mid-morning sunshine they hike into Rorschach looking like tourists enjoying the leisurely delights of a walking tour. Hanya engages in friendly banter with the café waiter who serves them coffee and deliciously fresh pastries. They take a train to St. Gallen where Hanya telephones Charlotte and arranges for her friend to meet them at the railway station in Zurich.

Although enormously relieved standing on the platform at St. Gallen, they are both sharply aware their position is far from secure. Without visas or valid passports it is impossible to stay at hotels and any encounter with police or local officials would result in an ignominious return to Austria. Max's nervousness is blunted by a growing realization he does not look out of place so long as he is with Hanya. Gratitude is coloured by an uncomfortable awareness of his indebtedness. It would have been inconceivable to make the journey without her and he has done nothing to deserve such kindness. It never occurs to him Hanya is basking in the pleasure of providing valuable assistance to the man she loves. Their disguise has erected an unseen barrier between them and their private conversations are blighted by the strain of maintaining a public display of intimacy.

Hanya has not told Charlotte anything about their circumstances. With growing alarm in Switzerland over the influx of Jewish refugees, she felt it would be prudent to maintain the pretence of their recent marriage. Greeting them at Zurich Hauptbahnhof, Charlotte aches to talk about what she assumes is a whirlwind romance. Hanya falls easily into the role of love-struck bride and the girls strike a vivacious conversation spiced with peals of laughter. Max remains aloof and Hanya excuses his taciturn demeanour, explaining he is unfamiliar with the Swiss dialect. They are warmly received as guests in Charlotte's home and the next day, visit a dance studio where Max is coaxed into providing piano accompaniment at a Eurythmics class for a charmingly studious group of Swiss school girls. When Charlotte discovers Hanya and Max have not had a proper honeymoon she insists they spend time at her family's cottage on Lake Maggiore. Caught offguard by her friend's generosity, Hanya feels ashamed. Her subterfuge has been so convincing she cannot see a way of undoing the deception and gratefully agrees to a few days at the cottage before moving on to Toulouse.

In the backseat of Charlotte's Lancia Aprilia, Max looks out at the charming scenery of the Ticino valley as if in a dream. Chatting distractedly in the front seat, Hanya is relieved Charlotte has not noticed how badly she is playing the part of an excited bride anticipating her honeymoon. She fears her relationship with Max is sullied by deceit and worries it will be impossible to recover genuine feelings once they cast off their disguise. The rustic stone cottage overlooking Lake Maggiore is as beautiful as Hanya imagined. Charlotte stays the first night and just as they did in Zurich, the newly-weds fall asleep silent and motionless on opposite sides of their double-bed. In the morning they try to appear cheerful as Charlotte treats them to a grand breakfast at a nearby hotel. She introduces them to shopkeepers in the local village, before departing with fond farewells and a flurry of suggestive glances.

Despite the idyllic setting, the honeymooners cannot face each other. Hanya clings to the forlorn hope that if she is patient, Max might rise to the occasion, but he withdraws into a listless torpor, immobilised by the belief that he should wait for Hanya to initiate any discussion about their relationship. Hanya finds a diversion in the Victrola, which has an automatic record changer allowing the music to play for hours. Nestled in comfortable armchairs, they let the music wash over them as each tries to figure out what the other is thinking.

As the Victrola grind through a Grammophon recording of the *Magic Flute,* Hanya notices the afternoon sun casting a shadow on an oriental rug and suggests a walk in the woods. Ever compliant, Max remains inscrutable as their fingers intertwine. His senses are quickened by the bracing scent of resin from pine trees, but fear of the unknown locks him in a cocoon of passivity. They pause to gaze at the evening light awakening ripples on the surface of the lake. Neither is prepared to risk the first step and with the fading light seeping through branches of ancient conifers, they trudge back to their hideaway in silence.

In the solitude of the cottage, driven mad with anticipation Hanya decides anything is preferable to the endless deferment. She pulls him into an impulsive embrace and with a shocked expression contorting his face, he inclines towards her. Prizing his mouth open with her lips she tastes his saliva on her tongue. Lost in a torrent of unfamiliar sensations Max gives himself to Hanya's firm guidance. He dimly perceives clothes being discarded and their bodies tumbling awkwardly beneath cool bed-sheets. The warm pressure of her body dissolves the boundary between them and convulsions of his hips subside as quickly as they arose. Suddenly aware of the weight of his body laying on her stomach he eases onto a pillow without daring to open his eyes. With an arm lacing behind his neck and her head resting lightly on his chest the tension that kept his muscles knotted gives way to a serenity, unlike anything he has known. Air flows silently from his lungs and he subsides into a deep sleep. Noticing the rhythm of his breathing, Hanya disentangles her arm and resigns to the frustration of being aroused and unfulfilled. Lying close enough to feel his body's heat she is determined to show nothing but gratitude. She's achieved her heart's desire and it would be childish to complain the reality does not match the perfection of dreams. A swirl of emotions stir unanswerable questions until exhaustion ushers in a fitful sleep.

Max is awakened by the crowing of a distant rooster and the bliss of oblivion is replaced by a surge of fretful imaginings. Feeling Hanya's sleeping body at his side, he edges out of bed, stumbling on clothes scattered on the bedroom floor. Grabbing his trousers he creeps towards a pool of moonlight spilling onto the kitchen table. As he pulls on his clothes the cacophony in his head builds to a riotous crescendo and he slumps onto a chair, face cupped in his hands. He makes a concerted effort to recall the moment before sleep and though his memory holds nothing more than a remnant of the tranquillity he felt, it is enough to still his mind. Feeling the chill night air on his neck he senses a sinister force lurking in the darkness of the stone cottage. Goose pimples rise on his arm and in a whisper he recites the *Song of Miriam*, which the children at the gymnasium in Rehavia sang with such gusto when they assembled in the dining hall. With mounting dread his head fills with jumbled recollections of the strange ideas he encountered during his time in Jerusalem. For the kabbalists of Safed everything holy is under constant threat from demonic powers and in his fevered state Max imagines malevolent spirits are attacking the communion he experienced with Hanya. The crowing of a cock pierces the silence and he remembers reading that when the mystics of Safed heard the midnight call of the rooster they would rise to engage in ritual Torah study. A hazy recollection of their liturgy floats through his mind and a strange compulsion drives him to imitate whatever he can recall of their midnight devotions.

Veiling his head with a scarf Hanya left on the kitchen table he kneels before the stove and reaches into the grate for ashes, which he applies to his forehead. He steps outside, pausing to absorb the opulent tranquillity of the night. The ritual calls for the dust of the earth, plentiful in the streets of Safed, but the ground is carpeted with pine needles and moistened with dew. Returning to the stove he pulls out a piece of burnt charcoal, crushing it with his fingers until his palm is filled with fine black dust. On the dew-softened ground outside the cottage, he lays down on his back and looks up at the slender crescent of a waning moon poised above the pine trees. He sprinkles the black dust over his eyes. Fierce stinging unleashes a rush of moisture beneath his frantically blinking eyelids. With tears streaming over his cheeks he recites Psalm 137. Bleak images of abandonment sink into his consciousness and his throbbing, tear-filled eyes slowly regain the ability to focus on distant stars. He rises stiffly and returning to the cottage finds his Tanakh. Standing beneath the lintel of the open door he reads the bitter words from the *Book of Lamentations*.

let tears stream down like a river;
day and night,
do not give yourself relief,
do not give your eyes rest.
"Arise, cry out in the night,
You have made us filth and rubbish
among the peoples …
panic and pitfall have come upon us,
My eyes flow with rivers of tears
because of the destruction of my people.

With the pain of exile infused into every cell and fibre of his being, he is ready to attempt the second phase of the ritual, turning towards the promise of redemption. Carefully wiping ash from his face he splashes cold water over his swollen eyes and returns to the doorpost, trying to recall a hymn the Kabbalists of Aleppo used during this part of the ritual. Though the words elude him he remembers the *Shekinah's* lament about the misery of exile is set in counterpoint against uplifting images of divine mercy. As a substitute he reads *Hosea* and his desolation eases as Gomer's whoring is forgiven and the stern judgement poured on the faithless tribes of Israel gives way to the joy of reconciliation:

I will be like the dew to Israel;
he shall blossom like the lily,
he shall strike root like the forests of Lebanon.
His shoots shall spread out;
his beauty shall be like the olive tree,
and his fragrance like that of Lebanon.
They shall again live beneath my shadow,
they shall flourish as a garden;
they shall blossom like the vine,
their fragrance shall be like the wine of Lebanon..,

The final stage of the ritual involves a strange form of meditation, with the mystics making their bodies into chariots for the *Shekinah*, imagining each organ as a vehicle for communion with the Ineffable Name. Though he feels unworthy to attempt such a practice, the first parts of the ritual have brought such peace of mind he is determined to continue his clumsy efforts. Drawing capriciously on images from the *Song of Songs,* his ears catch the footsteps of the Bride as she roams like a vagabond beside the Bridegroom's flock. His nostrils fill with fragrances of myrrh and frankincense and his lungs draw in the essence of saffron, cinnamon and all the incense bearing trees. His neck bends under the weight of golden necklaces and beads of silver. He tastes the sweetness of honeycomb and raisin cakes and in his skin feels the heat of the desert sun burning the swarthiness of the Bride's complexion.

Each image draws him closer to the bedroom where he glimpses the shape of Hanya's body beneath a rippled quilt. The stillness he'd struggled to obtain vanishes and as if a veil were lifting he sees the union of the Bride and Groom as a radiant spiral connecting heaven with earth; *HaShem* with Israel and the Sabbath with the profane world of the working week. His mind expands to embrace the mystery of the *Shekinah* and the Groom becoming one flesh, igniting the spark that brings forth new life. The only thing holding him back is anxiety about being unmarried and it takes considerable effort to overcome this stumbling block. He convinces himself that even though it was nothing more than a disguise, by wearing rings and taking on the outward signs of matrimony they have fulfilled some of their obligations under the Law. He supposes it must be counted as a transgression but feels certain their union is redeemed and sanctified by love—just as it was for Hosea when he took the harlot Gomer as his bride.

His awareness of Hanya sleeping, brings quivering intensity to his meditations and with the wild poetry of the *Song of Songs* surging through his head he no longer distinguishes his feelings and those he attributes to the Bride. In the beating of his heart he feels her palpitations as she awaits the lifting of the veil. He longs to taste kisses more delightful than wine. He is sick with love stronger than death, its flash, the flash of fire. Standing at the edge of the bed in perfect stillness, he gazes at Hanya, his mind empty, hair moistened with dew from the ground where he lay. In the softening darkness of the approaching dawn he notices her stirring almost imperceptibly in her sleep. Trembling from the core of his being, he removes his clothes and slips beneath the covers. Inching towards her he hears the words from the *Song of Songs.*

I adjure you, O daughters of Jerusalem,
by the gazelles or the wild does:
do not arouse or awaken love
until it pleases!

Pausing, the coldness of his body absorbs heat from hers. She turns to him blindly and receives caresses, given with such tender attentiveness she is unsure whether she is awake or dreaming. Their coitus is slow, purposeful and ecstatic and afterwards, when the dizzying sweetness of memory washes over them, Max believes they have tasted the holy joy of redemption.

The day breaks and shadows flee. Hanya sates her hunger with a breakfast assembled from a larder well stocked with cured meats, cheeses, black-bread, pickles, sauerkraut and smoked sausages. Although she knows she is temperamentally unsuited for the role, she yearns for an old-fashioned marriage and tries to imagine attending to housework and raising children. Charlotte urged them to stay at the cottage as long as they wish and the days slip by filled with long walks on the lakeshore, gramophone records, log-fires, idle conversation, and loving embraces. At times when they draw apart, Hanya listens to the Victrola or runs through her eurythmics exercises while Max applies himself to deciphering the dense, enigmatic phrases from the smuggled copy of the *Sepher Yetzirah.* Hanya's curiosity is aroused as she notices how he is absorbed by the manuscript. She coaxes him into translating some of the archaic Hebrew and though he lacks the confidence to describe the book's weird cosmology he explains the Kabbalists belief that ritual actions can restore the connection between the earthly and the divine. Hanya excitedly recalls Frau Rosalia's words about Cadmus and Harmonia, how her dance aimed to reestablish harmony between mortals and the gods. Embarrassment prevents Max from speaking plainly about the ecstatic union of the *Shekinah* and the Groom and Hanya bluntly paraphrases his tongue-tied explanations.

'So you are saying our connection with God was lost when the Bride went into exile—and to bring them back together we must copulate lovingly?'

Her flippant tone adds weight to the pronouncement and as he chuckles in agreement, Max believes with all his heart, the long, sorrowful exile of the *shekinah* would end, if the world could hold fast to the love they have known.

The sensation of tasting something beyond anything they could dare to hope for has a strangely unsettling effect and there is a creeping recognition that the seclusion of the cottage offers a poor defence against the enmity of the world. On an excursion to the village shop Hanya picks up a copy of Basel's *National Zeitung* and at the kitchen table they read a harrowing account of a vast pogrom launched in retaliation for the assassination of a German diplomat in Paris. An almost paralytic chill envelops them as they absorb the stark descriptions of organised mobs systematically ransacking synagogues and smashing the windows of Jewish businesses. In Vienna it is reported every synagogue in the city was burnt to the ground and hundreds were rounded up and sent to Dachau. The news is made more unbearable by knowing any attempt to contact Max's family could only increase the dangers they face. Hanya prepares to leave, aware that any slip-up, will have them sent straight back to Austria. She expects crossing into France should be a good deal less hazardous than their escape from Vienna, but is determined to leave nothing to chance. She telegrams her friend in Toulouse, asking her to meet them in Basel where they will make arrangements for crossing the border. As they prepare to abandon their sanctuary a melancholy grips them. It is unconscionable to have experienced such bliss while men are dragged from their homes and dispatched to concentration camps where they must endure without mercy whatever cruelties await.

36

At sunrise, with dew-drops still thickly clustered on the foliage, Josephine visits her vegetable garden to surprise the slugs attacking her lettuces. The slime trails made silvery in the morning light reveal their hiding places, and with gloved hand she drops the squirming creatures into a jar of water before scattering them on the lawn for the thrushes and blackbirds. Aphids on the tomatoes and caterpillars embedded within her cabbages and cauliflowers are more intractable foes, but she prevails with regular applications of derris dust. Tomatoes, beans and peas are firmly staked against the southerly wind and with a staggered planting scheme she supplies home-grown produce for most of their meals during summer months. Their sloping section on the Port Hills has a charming view of the township and a patchwork of fields spreading across the Canterbury plains. While turning the soil or uprooting weeds Josephine sometimes pauses; her gaze, rising to the bluish profile of the alps low on the horizon, awakens an aching for her homeland, only partially dispelled by the satisfaction of tending her garden.

At the start of summer students return to family farms or find work on the wharves, but instead of taking much needed rest, Karl has succumbed to chronic anxiety, fretting over the situation in Europe. With his eyes hopping restlessly over the morning paper he is infuriated to find the fortunes of the local cricket team are regarded as far more significant than the Sudetenland crisis. His earnest attempts to explain the significance of the Anschluss are met with bemused indifference from university colleagues and the breakfast table is the only arena where he can voice his frustrations. Spreading marmalade on toast, he holds forth as if addressing an assembly of international statesmen.

'It's no wonder people are turning to primitive hero worship. They're fed-up with pretentious intellectuals sneering at anything decent and reasonable. They're longing for something solid, sanity and common sense but all we get is adolescent resentment and this hysterical nonsense about the spirit of the nation asserting itself on the stage of history.'

'Write it down,' Josephine urges as she replenishes the toast rack. 'It's no good warning me about the collapse of civilisation, I've got my hands full dealing with those little white butterflies laying eggs in my cauliflowers.'

Karl falls silent, embarrassed. He knows he's ill-suited for politics and has concluded the only thing of value he can do is write. His scattered thoughts have coalesced into a resolution to publish a challenge to the recklessly irresponsible intellectuals giving credence to totalitarian ideologies by constantly undermining public confidence in democracy.

The thought of a philosophy professor standing against a mob of uniformed fanatics raises a smile, but Josephine understands he is deadly earnest and she is willing to play Sancho Panza to his knight-errant. On some days she spends ten or twelve hours at the typewriter keeping pace with a deluge of hand-written pages and an unending stream of scribbled revisions. Keeping busy helps to ward off the overwhelming sadness that grips her as she absorbs news of Austria's incorporation into the German Reich. The Law for the Protection of German Blood and Honour now applies to Austria and if she set foot in her homeland she would be imprisoned for the despicable crime of marrying a Jew. It's easy to rail against it, but shaking off the insidious shame is another matter. She knows her neighbours and even members of her family would not hesitate to denounce her as a race traitor. Typing keeps her from falling into despair and if further motivation is needed it comes almost every day when she opens the mail. The letters never fail to congratulate Karl on his foresight in fleeing Europe and there is an unmistakable desperation as friends describe the nightmare of trying to obtain an immigration visa when no one is willing to accept refugees.

Karl is embarrassed by praise for foresight he did not possess. Like everybody else he believed the Nazis would moderate their programme once their authority was secure and he only looked to New Zealand when it became impossible to secure an academic appointment in Vienna. With friends and family members facing intolerable circumstances it is difficult to enjoy their good fortune. The unspoken guilt heightens the urgency with which he throws himself into his self-appointed task. He is under no illusions about the Nazis or any other political party taking the slightest notice of his ideas and his endeavour rests on the slender conviction that the conditions of political debate can be influenced by philosophical ideas. His investigations take him into areas where he doubts his expertise and he misses the opportunity to test his ideas against the towering intellectual antagonists of Vienna. He maintains a stimulating correspondence with Carnap in Chicago and exchanges ideas with professors who were kind to him in London, but the remoteness that made New Zealand so attractive is a constant source of frustration. The airmail service running from Sydney is ruinously expensive and ordinary mail requires an agonising three-month delay before he can expect a reply.

There are distinguished scholars at Canterbury College, though most give Karl a wide berth as they are unaccustomed to the ferocity with which he throws himself into debate. He latches onto anyone prepared to engage in intellectual conversation and has established a bond with Henry Broadhead, an authority on Aeschylus. The classics Professor is bemused to be subjected to belligerent interrogation as Karl works through an obsessive engagement with Plato's political philosophy. Preparing material for his ethics lectures Karl hastily revisited the *Republic* and was shocked to find Plato's prescription for the ideal state is almost indistinguishable from the utopian collectivism peddled in much cruder terms by Hitler and Stalin.

It worries him no one else has noticed the glaring equivalence between Hitler and Plato and he harasses Professor Broadhead to provide criticism. The amiable Professor is used to being ignored as a respected but irrelevant relic and he learns to welcome the unheralded door-knocking that frequently disrupts the tranquillity of his office. Before he has a chance to answer, Popper will burst into the room, an open volume of Plato in hand, and commence his inquisition without greeting or small talk.

'You realise he advocates for eugenics—selective breeding for the Guardians, not to mention children taken from their mothers at the earliest opportunity.'

'Quite so,' the Professor responds with genial curiosity, 'though the term might have had different connotations at the time—if we were to look more closely at usage I suspect you'll find "good breeding" would have been the natural aspiration of any prospective parents, possibly still is.'

'It's a lot more than good breeding—he claims the state must be the sole authority for the allocation of mates.'

'When you put it like that, it's rather disturbing, but one must be wary of anachronism. Free choice in marriage would have been virtually unheard of in Plato's day. Besides which I wouldn't assume Plato was proposing a political system, the ideal state could easily be a state of mind.'

'It's the plain meaning of his words that concern me. I have no interest in deciphering the intricacies of his hidden intentions.'

'Try to bear in mind that by any reckoning, you are dealing with one of the world's most subtle and complex thinkers, perhaps of all time.'

Karl bristles. 'We have to put an end to the veneration of great names. I've always regarded the *Apology* as the finest, most moving defence of critical rationalism ever made, but with the *Republic* the primacy of the individual conscience goes out the window and we get this abhorrent nonsense about Guardians and Philosopher Kings who are born to rule.'

Though alarmed by Karl's antipathy towards the Father of Philosophy, Professor Broadhead sheds light on the matter by pointing out that Plato's formative years coincided with the most harrowing episodes of the Peloponnesian Wars and his aristocratic family favoured the Spartan system of absolute monarchy over the Athenian passion for democracy.

'I suppose you are aware that when Lysander destroyed the Athenian fleet at Aegospotami, Plato's family supported the call for surrender. Two of his maternal uncles were prominent among the Thirty Tyrants who relied on a Spartan garrison to support their reign of terror—and of course they were dealt with very harshly when the Democratic faction won back control of the city.'

Karl sheepishly admits he's never examined the historical context of Plato's philosophy and the professor's comment sparks a ferocious bout of reading that rapidly exhausts the meagre ancient history collection at the university library. On gaining some familiarity with the political situation in Athens he can see why Plato would have despised the democratic regime that slaughtered his uncles and he imagines his bitterness intensified as he witnessed the trial and execution of Socrates at the hands of a democratic mob. He learns the popular antagonism towards Socrates may have had nothing to do with philosophy and was probably driven by a desire to expunge the memory of the treacherous oligarchs who colluded with the Spartans in suppressing Athenian democracy. Though suspicious of such psychological speculation, he confronts Professor Broadhead with an assertion that in his later writings, Plato knowingly distorts Socrates' teaching and turns him into a mouthpiece for his own rabidly anti-democratic obsessions. The Professor responds with an exhaustive digression on disputes about the chronology of Plato's works.

'Dating of the texts is far from definitive, though it would be fair to say the Socrates of the *Apology* or *Protagoras* is a very different beast from the one we find in the *Republic* or *Crito*.'

Karl considers this a significant concession. It is clear that at some point Plato turned against the radical doctrine of individual freedom Socrates was prepared to die for and he believes the change of heart is most clearly marked in the *Republic's* enticing vision of an ideal state, where everyone knows his place and accepts without question the wisdom of the Philosopher Kings. A similar nostalgia for the certainties of the old patriarchal order can be seen in the doctrine of the Forms with its mystical appeals to an eternal, unchanging perfection beyond the sordid, ever-changing world of everyday experience.

Plato's betrayal of Socrates' democratic vision looms in his mind as a crucially important moment, but Professor Broadhead's reservations make him anxious. Any suggestion that the Father of Philosophy could be implicated in the barbarism of the Nazis will enrage Plato's legions of devoted admirers and Karl recognises he must make his case in meticulous detail. As he throws himself into the task the manuscript pages pile up at an alarming rate and Josephine worries he may be losing sight of his topic.

'Nobody cares what Greek philosophers were arguing about in the 4th century BC. I thought you wanted to say something about Hitler and Stalin, the threat to democracy.'

'But I need to show how it began—when Plato proposed worship of the state as an alternative to Socrates call for individual responsibility, he made totalitarianism look respectable.'

Josephine inhales through her nose and returns to her typing. 'Your readers might have better things to do than raking over a dispute between ancient Greek philosophers.'

Picking up a sheath of the most recently typed pages Karl worries the complaint has merit. 'I want people to see the enemies of democracy were there right from the start. It's what drove the dispute between Sparta and Athens. When the old empires collapsed, they faced the same kind of chaos and uncertainty we're facing today. The Spartans thought they had the answer by shutting out foreign influences and reinforcing their old tribal allegiances. They banned intermarriage, imposed a militaristic code of honour, and their entire economy was based on conquering and enslaving their neighbours. The Athenians did the exact opposite—they open the gates of the city, promoted trade and commerce and became a naval power; they made alliances with rivals and established colonies to spread their influence.'

'That makes a lot more sense—people will see the parallels. Spare us the philosophising.'

'But the philosophers started it—the Athenians were constantly arguing about the best constitution for their city. That's how we got critical discourse, democracy, individual freedom, equality before the law—it was a great spiritual revolution and Plato was the most eloquent voice for the counter-revolution.'

'Well you need to show how it is relevant—and brevity, there's nothing wrong with brevity.'

Karl gathers his handwritten pages and returns to his office. Hours of fretful pacing only conclude when he recognises Josephine is right—the conflict between Sparta and Athens is far more compelling than Plato's disagreement with Socrates. Though naturally suspicious of all-encompassing explanations he's struck by the image of human history oscillating between the two poles represented by Sparta and Athens. He regards Marx's laws of history as the worst kind of mystical thinking and the last thing he wants is to propose an alternative set. He must demonstrate there is nothing inevitable about human progress. At every moment we can opt for the security the Spartans found in their authoritarian regime or choose the Athenian alternative, the risk and adventure of rational, open-ended debate on the best solutions to our problems.

Ideas flow with the pulsating energy of an electrical current and he sees the appeal of totalitarianism is driven by fear and uncertainty; the threat of losing what little control we have over our lives triggers our most primitive impulses, rational thinking vanishes and we retreat to an ancestral valley, standing with kith and kin to defend the sacred homeland. We look for a hero to resurrect a glorious past or lead us into a utopian future. Modern life with its complications and stresses generates a powerful nostalgia for the simplicity and innocence of childhood, a place where we can rest secure under the watchful eye of a revered patriarch. People yearn to be part of something bigger than themselves and in the absence of anything reasonable they cling to an ancient memory—the tribe, the enchanted circle, the paradise we enjoyed before tasting the fruit of knowledge.

Despite Josephine's objections Karl cannot entirely rid himself of his obsession with Plato. He recognises it is ridiculous to blame a Greek philosopher for the enduring appeal of totalitarian politics, but remains convinced Plato cast a malignant spell over European thought and those who have never read his works are most susceptible to his influence. He regards Josephine as an accurate gauge of his likely readership and uses her as a sounding board for an everchanging torrent of half-formed ideas.

'The trouble with Plato is his ideas are so subtle they seem benign—he's made it natural to assume altruism is all about sacrificing yourself for the good of the collective—so any demands for individual freedom can be condemned as selfishness. He doesn't mention how collectivism dehumanises anyone who does not belong to the chosen race or class.'

'You can't blame people for showing loyalty to their own kind.'

'That's the crux of the problem—we naturally define ourselves by allegiance to a larger clan, our ancestral affiliation, but when real tribal bonds are lost we use politics and ideology to create artificial tribes. Collective identity becomes all-consuming and irrational, like the promise of salvation. Anyone outside the collective is an enemy, you're either Roman or barbarian, Jew or Gentile, Christian or heretic; nowadays it's proletarian or bourgeoisie, Aryan or *untermensch*, party-member or enemy-of-the-people.'

'So what is your solution?'

'I don't know—I'm still trying to define the problem. But when we only think in terms of what is good for my tribe or my class or my party we lose our common humanity. Rational scientific thinking vanishes because the only acceptable facts are those that benefit the collective.'

As his theory solidifies Karl surrenders to the intoxication of believing he has stumbled onto something important. Like the Ancient Mariner accosting the hapless wedding guest, he seizes on anyone who shows the slightest interest and with glittering eye, holds forth as if the future of civilisation depends on winning acceptance of his ideas. Although he craves the stimulation of robust criticism, few risk the perils of a one-sided debate in which mild reservations or tentative suggestions meet with a belligerence beyond all bounds of propriety. Josephine urges him to show restraint and reminds him they are guests in a country where people have good reason to be suspicious of impassioned rhetoric delivered in a German sounding accent. It is sensible advice Karl would follow if he were not gripped by an exhilarating compulsion. In a ham-fisted attempt to uphold the decorum of academic discourse he takes to prefacing his rebuttals by politely asking; '*Would you like me to criticise that?*' The question draws audible groans and even when his interlocutors retreat into sullen silence or are goaded into responding with vituperative insults, he remains fixated on demonstrating the unassailable logic of his cause. He excuses his behaviour by appealing to Socrates' claim that vigorous criticism is the greatest service a man can render to his fellows and vehemently proclaims we cannot afford to mince words when the world is descending into a maelstrom of fanatical violence.

In his dealings with the Head of the Philosophy Department Karl makes a concerted effort to follow Josephine's advice and does his best to avoid offense. Though he has scant regard for Professor Sutherland's intellectual acumen he appreciates his kindness. They are often invited to meals at his home and Ivan's wife Nancy is the only New Zealander to break through Josephine's shyness and establish a friendship. The two wives share a love of the outdoors and Nancy, a vivacious and intelligent young woman, takes Josephine on long walks over the hills near their home and for picnics at the wild ocean beaches on the outskirts of Christchurch. Having travelled to London and Paris as a student Nancy finds Josephine's sophisticated conversation welcome relief from the gossip of faculty wives whose interests seldom extend beyond cooking, sewing and child-rearing.

Karl and Ivan maintain a cordial relationship, though Karl struggles to conceal his irritation at being subordinate to a man he regards as poorly equipped to lead a philosophy department. With a doctorate in psychology from a provincial British University, Professor Sutherland is an enthusiast for the social sciences and keenly involved in the issues of the day. He sees little value in Karl's epistemological speculations and from time-to-time insists that personal research must not interfere with teaching duties. These mild reprimands are difficult to swallow given the world-changing significance Karl attributes to his insights on the origins of totalitarianism. It is only Josephine's calming influence that enables him to retain some perspective. She points to the debt of gratitude they owe the Professor for how he has devoted himself to the plight of Jewish refugees. Within weeks of arriving in New Zealand, Karl was inundated with letters from friends and colleagues desperately seeking the visas needed to escape persecution in Europe. After the Anschluss the volume of requests grew exponentially and Professor Sutherland was the first to offer assistance, holding a series of public meetings and convening a committee to coordinate the efforts of voluntary organisations. His network of contacts and political knowledge proves invaluable as they establish a process for handling the stream of applications.

Karl quickly learns the New Zealand government, which he regards as the best in the world, is in no mood to open their doors to Jewish refugees. When mass unemployment threatened, the country elected a socialist government led by trade unionists. They introduced employment schemes and provided healthcare and education, but unlike European counterparts showed little interest in smashing capitalism. The Prime Minister calls his policies 'applied Christianity' and Karl cannot help wondering how different the European situation might be if the German socialists had adopted a similar programme of piecemeal reform. He is disappointed that a government with a proven capacity for rational problem solving should fall into hysterical paranoia at the thought of accepting a handful of Jewish refugees. Embarrassed by his countrymen's xenophobia Professor Sutherland scathingly points to the hypocrisy of the trade union leaders.

'A few years ago they were asking workers who could barely feed their families, to contribute to the International Brigades and now that we have some prosperity, they won't lift a finger to help the victims of fascism.'

Karl sees the irrational obsession with protecting New Zealanders' jobs as disturbing evidence of the way collectivist thinking corrupts the best intentions. There is some reassurance in finding ordinary New Zealanders often at odds with their government on the issue. The committee is inundated with offers from families prepared to open their homes to Jewish refugees and with pressing shortages in skilled labour there are many employers willing to act as guarantors for immigration applications.

Every fortnight the committee sends the immigration minister a list of supported refugees. Only a fraction have hope of securing approval and as the volume of applications increases the government's intransigence only hardens. Karl tries to treat each case objectively but it is impossible to remain detached as he learns of the horrendous circumstances faced by friends and family. He's particularly distressed by a letter from a distinguished Viennese doctor who had acquired his address from a mutual acquaintance. He wrote in desperation from the concentration camp at Dachau and though he had never met the doctor, Karl knew of his reputation and could vouch for his credentials. While the application was processed the wretched man was taken to the even more notorious camp at Buchenwald and the bureaucrats handling the case were un-moved by heartrending letters from the Doctor's family. The New Zealand Medical Council vigorously opposed allowing a refugee doctor to practise in New Zealand and when all avenues seemed exhausted, Professor Sutherland used his political connections to secure a personal interview with the immigration minister. To appease the Medical Council, Karl resubmitted the application with the guarantee of a job as a printer's assistant and at the last hour a visa was approved.

37

Fretting about news from Europe, Karl often leaves the house before dawn for rambling excursions over the Port Hills. He used to find solace gazing at the long channel of Lyttleton harbour opening to the immensity of the Pacific Ocean. But hours wasted in fruitless scrutiny of newspaper columns have obliterated the comfort bestowed by distance and he longs to taste the urgency proximity imparts. All the earnest prescriptions on how to deal with Hitler strike him as hopelessly inadequate and his pessimism deepens on seeing a newspaper photograph of Chamberlain clasping an umbrella as he approaches Hitler on the steps of the Berghof. With the world clutching at straws, he tells himself his philosophical weapons cannot be any less effective than Chamberlain's umbrella.

He believes he has something important to say but cannot imagine how he might get a hearing. The socialists will not tolerate any deviation from the Party line and the Nazis have no hesitation in saying *'if you disagree I will kill you.'* Dialogue is futile when proposals can be dismissed simply by pointing to class or racial origins and tribal loyalties have eliminated any desire to consider ideas on their merits. The threat of violence makes it easy for collectives to demand absolute conformity and in the absence of common ground there is only one option; disputes will be settled on the basis that might is right.

Challenging this way of thinking seems a hopeless task and Karl fears the struggle may last for generations. He recognises the problem won't be solved by high minded appeals to reason and doubts philosophy has much to offer. In an atmosphere of unbridled belligerence Socrates insistence on the primacy of individual conscience or Kant's assertion that a person must never be used as the means to an end, count for nothing. Searching for alternatives he senses the old religious certainties are more potent than the cherished ideals of the Enlightenment. Without the fatherhood of God, the brotherhood of man is just another abstract concept. There is no compelling reason to believe all citizens, regardless of class or racial origins, should have their voices heard. Though it offends his secular instincts he recognises democracy may ultimately depend on the old worn-out notion that every human being is a child of God. The most effective challenge to collectivism may come from the simple, steadfast faith that once made it possible to look into the face of an adversary and see a fellow human being made in the image of our Creator.

Turning to religion to combat irrationalism seems an absurd paradox, but Karl's interest is stimulated when the Workers' Education Association invites him to speak at a series of public lectures on the theme of Science & Religion. Most participants are devotees of the American theologian Reinhold Niebuhr and as Karl reads *Moral Man, Immoral Society* he is surprised to discover Niebuhr's critique of collectivism offers a striking affirmation of his own analysis. While he makes no attempt to conceal his scepticism about an unseen God, he endorses Niebuhr's condemnation of the idolatry that grants the State absolute authority over ethical issues. He praises the courage of Christian martyrs who refused to bend to the demands of Roman law and points out that Socrates died for the same cause when he insisted the inner call of his conscience was stronger than the external authority of the state.

The Christian speakers have a more realistic understanding of the Nazi threat than the Socialists who maintain, against all evidence, that fascism is the last gasp of a capitalist system that will collapse under the weight of its own contradictions. Karl uses the seminar to test his proposal that once scientific method is properly understood, there is no meaningful distinction between religious belief and atheism. Humanist ideologies claiming the mantle of science all require a leap of faith as science itself rests on an irrational belief in the lawfulness of the universe. He acknowledges that religious devotion can have dangerous consequences, but placing your faith in Marx's laws of history is no less irrational than believing the Gospels. Rather than erecting boundaries to separate religion from science, he urges his listeners to carefully distinguish between ideas that are useful, and those which are harmful. Belief in racial superiority or the moral imperatives of socialism will always lead to violence and if society is to move beyond the belligerence of rival collectives, it is essential all ideas, religious or secular, be judged by their fruits.

His lectures are well received and in discussions that follow he develops a warm friendship with Dr. Merlin Findhorn who lectures in Divinity at a neighbouring theological college. He is intrigued to find Dr. Findhorn has a thorough understanding of Hegel and eagerly takes up an invitation to visit him at his home. None of the staff at the university have more than a passing familiarity with Hegel's work and Karl is grateful for the opportunity to discuss the philosopher who has become the primary target in his analysis of totalitarian ideology. He opens the conversation provocatively, 'I've come to regard Hegel as the most dishonest, corrupt and pompous writer in the history of philosophy.'

This draws a wry smile from the Divinity Professor. 'So you would concur with Schopenhauer's assessment—I believe he once called him *a monument to German stupidity.*'

'That's putting it mildly, I'd say one of the reasons fascism hasn't flourished in England or America is that the English-speaking world never granted Hegel the uncritical adulation he commands in Europe.'

The Doctor listens with interest as Karl holds forth on the insidious influence exerted by Hegel's notion that dialectical contradictions are resolved by the World Spirit asserting itself on the stage of history. 'It is a monumentally stupid idea, pure mysticism—but it appeals to both the Marxist and the fascists because it encourages them to believe their actions are sanctified by the Spirit of the People. I've often suspected it is a secular appropriation of the Christian belief that Divine Providence rewards the righteous and punishes the wicked.'

'If that were the case,' Dr. Findhorn replies, 'you would have to say Hegel based his theory on a heresy. Using historical circumstances to bolster your own righteousness is a neo-Protestant blasphemy that denies the essential meaning of the crucifixion—Christ did not triumph in this world, He suffered.'

'But surely Christians take the historical success of the church as an expression of Divine Providence?'

'I suppose Christians might say such things,' the Professor concedes, 'but they shouldn't—if you take the worldly success of the church as a sign of God's favour you would have to elevate the church of the Inquisition above the church of the martyrs.'

Although Karl feels out of his depth discussing theology, he is reluctant to abandon the idea that Hegel's World Spirit has a religious foundation.

'I understand the will of God must ultimately remain inscrutable but wasn't Moses's triumph over Pharaoh a vindication of the Hebrew God and all those victories over the Philistines—surely they show God as the final arbiter of history?'

'What you are proposing is a theological error which comes from a failure to interpret the Old Testament in the light of Christ. The love of God is not revealed through force or coercion and Israel's tragic cycle of triumph and oppression teaches us God always desires faithfulness and justice—love of neighbour, kindness to strangers and so forth.'

Although not entirely convinced, Karl is pleased to learn that when Christianity is properly understood it does not involve the mystical appeals to historical destiny that inspire the Nazis and Bolsheviks. The encounter with Dr. Findhorn leaves Karl energised and he throws himself into his writing with renewed vigour until his fragile equilibrium is shattered by a letter from Hanya. He's maintained a steady correspondence with his sister since Mother's passing and felt enormous relief on hearing she had somehow made her way to France. Reports that she was planning to travel to Palestine with Max made him uneasy but he is painfully aware refugees must accept whatever haven is available. It appears she entered France illegally and she writes about living at a chateau outside of Toulouse where she is the physical education instructor at a Montessori school run by one of her friends from the Eurythmics Institute. She says nothing about the nature of their relationship but mentions Max is also living at the chateau where he works as a gardener and provides musical accompaniment for her eurythmics classes. It appears they have made numerous attempts to travel to Palestine together, but it is impossible to leave France without the necessary exit visas. Her description of the conditions in Marseilles confirms what Karl has learnt from other sources. The port city is awash with hordes of undocumented refugees who are subject to constant harassment and arbitrary detention by the gendarmerie.

Hanya's desperation is unmistakable and her pleas for assistance come with the familiar assurance that any employment will be gratefully accepted. Tormented by the prospect of having to tell her there is no possibility of obtaining immigration approval, he makes urgent enquiries at the Education Department, but in a country where everyone is mad about sport it is considered the height of absurdity to grant an immigration visa to a P.E. teacher. By personally visiting local schools he obtains a job offer for his sister, but files the immigration application knowing it will be declined. His letter to Hanya is sombre and he includes contact addresses in Australia where her application is more likely to be successful. He mentions he has considered living in Australia himself and some months ago applied unsuccessfully for a position at Sydney university. He is attracted by the direct airmail service between London and Sydney and in a light-hearted tone confesses to an irrational impulse: *'I regard the Australian koala-bear as the most marvellous animal in the world and there are times when the thought of living in close proximity to such a creature pushes aside all other considerations.'*

The prospects for Max look more promising and Karl quickly discovers a pressing shortage of qualified mathematicians in the country. Max's doctorate from the University of Vienna makes it easy to secure an appointment with the Department of Statistics and as the job is deemed to be a position of national importance there is every reason to believe he will obtain an approval.

The agony of waiting for replies to letters is exacerbated by newspapers filled with hysterical commentaries on Chamberlain's dismal efforts to reach an accommodation with Hitler. For the most part New Zealanders are mystified by the violent passions enflaming Europe and there is absurd confidence that if war cannot be avoided, the Kiwi boys will give Hitler a bloody good hiding. The communist students are better informed and Karl often engages in debate with a small group he suspects are Party members. When news comes through of the Molotov–Ribbentrop pact he takes three of the boys to one of the town's milk-bars, the New Zealand equivalent of the Viennese coffee-houses. The country has been built on butter-fat and the abundant dairy products are ridiculously cheap. Karl buys American style milkshakes thickened with ice-cream and listens with sympathy as the boys contemplate the betrayal of everything they believe in. One tries to make the case for Stalin's strategic genius, claiming the pact is a tactical move to allow the Party to choose the right moment to strike a decisive blow against Hitler. The others remain unconvinced and cannot conceal their bitterness. As Karl listens, he thinks of Ruth and Gebhardt and all the other decent, well-meaning believers, risking their lives and enduring all kinds of hardships as they threw themselves into the brutal battle against fascism. It can't be easy to accept they were conned. There will be no glorious revolution, no liberation of mankind, no end to exploitation. As gently as he can, Karl explains they have simply been swept up in the rivalry between two hostile tribes.

'If the Party has decided class interests are best served by an alliance with Hitler there is nothing in Marx or Lenin to refute the claim. The iron laws of history and dialectical analysis mean whatever Stalin wants them to mean. But the trick only works so long as you are prepared to surrender your own critical abilities and bow to the wisdom of the collective.'

The expectation that war is imminent creates a strange dislocation. While the grind of marking essays and preparing lectures continues, Karl is haunted by the prospect of once again living in a world at war, with every endeavour oriented towards a single imperative: kill or be killed. He writes to Hanya with news that Max's immigration visa has been approved and a few weeks later receives a terse telegram from Lisbon confirming Max has secured a berth on the *Rangitata.*

The Prime Minister delivers a radio address to the nation affirming New Zealand will stand alongside Great Britain to defeat what he calls '*the militant and insatiable paganism*' of the Nazis. Karl decides that as a New Zealand citizen it is his duty to volunteer. Although he has no trouble passing the medical examination he feels misplaced among the robust young men cramming into the church hall, hastily transformed into a recruitment centre. The officer handling his application is disconcerted by his German sounding accent and pays scant attention to Karl's attempt to explain that Austria used to be an independent nation. The man scribbles a note on the application form before disappearing into a back room. After a lengthy wait Karl is ushered into an office where an elderly Sergeant-Major invites him to take a seat.

An orderly places a tea tray on the desk and the Sergeant-Major leans back in his chair, scrutinising Karl's face. He gestures towards the tea. 'Help yourself to sugar. I understand you are a Professor of Philosophy—not something we see a lot of in the infantry.'

'I'm willing to serve in any capacity,' Karl replies firmly. 'Whatever is deemed most useful.'

'Glad to hear it. We made a terrible mistake in the last war signing up teachers and university professors, all kinds of intellectuals and poets—hopeless soldiers, they'd have been more use staying at home. You should stick to your job and do your best to educate the young men who'll be running the farms and factories. The war will be won by the side which is most efficient in managing their resources.'

It is humbling advice. Making his way past the line of young men stripped to the waist for physicals, Karl sees there is no shortage of volunteers better suited to handling a rifle. The experience leaves him vaguely humiliated and returning to his office at the university he doggedly tells himself his writing will be his war effort.

38

On the quay at Lyttleton harbour, Karl recalls his anticipation at his own arrival two years earlier. The port's haphazard arrangement of corrugated iron sheds, cranes and railway tracks is like a forgotten outpost of a distant empire and watching the stream of disembarking passengers, he marvels at how the efficiency of commerce has diminished the vast oceans separating Europe from New Zealand. Max barely raises his eyes as he joins passengers trudging across the gangway as if disembarking at a provincial railway station. He emerges from the customs shed bewildered and forlorn. Karl greets him with a handshake and Max struggles to respond to his enquiries about the voyage. Recognising he must be intensely disoriented, Karl takes charge of his friend's suitcase and fills the silence with small talk. He speaks in English as a few weeks earlier the newspaper ran a story about a Croatian gentlemen who was knocked out at a railway station when an outraged New Zealander overheard him speaking to his son in his native tongue.

Driving over the hills surrounding the harbour, Max hesitantly voices thoughts that have burdened him throughout the long sea voyage. 'I didn't want to leave, but Hanya was insistent and I owe her so much... I can't tell you how kind she has been to me.'

Hearing anguish in his voice Karl tries to sound cheerful. 'We had a telegram from her, a few weeks after you departed. She's arrived safely in London and promises to write—there are terrible delays with the mail, but we should hear something soon.'

Max hardly touches the meal Josephine has prepared and the long silences make it clear he is not ready to talk. They have arranged for him to stay with a neighbour who has an empty farm-labourers cottage on his property. He will only be in Christchurch for a week before travelling to Wellington to work in the government offices. As Karl must attend to his teaching duties they ask him to join them for dinner on Friday night. Max thanks them for their kindness and asks if he could prepare the meal. 'I have little to do for the next few days. It will keep me occupied.'

They arrive at the humble cottage with a salad produced from

Josephine's garden. She notices the rough-sawn timber table has been beautifully laid with candles and sprigs of greenery around a freshly baked loaf.

'I thought we might take a walk before dinner,' Max suggests. 'I've been strolling the hills—the farmland is very beautiful.'

They follow a gravel road which leads over a ridge and into a gently sloping valley. It is obvious Max has a lot on his mind and after walking in silence for some time he blurts, 'I am very much hoping to marry your sister and we'd like to receive your blessing.'

'I have no idea how one might bestow such a thing,' Karl replies with a broad grin, 'but I'm delighted, I'd suspected Hanya was hinting something was afoot in her letters.'

Josephine offers her congratulations and Max explains that as soon as he can, he intends to join Hanya in London where he hopes it may be possible to enlist in the British army.

Karl suggests Max's mathematical talents could be utilised in the code-breaking section of Army Intelligence. He undertakes to write a letter of reference to the New Zealand High Commissioner in London who has been extremely helpful processing refugee applications. They descend into the valley with Karl chatting amiably about his writing. Josephine watches a harrier hawk wheeling high above the paddocks in search of rabbits and Max's attention drifts towards a strip of vegetation running between the gravel road and the wire fence which marks off the farmland. There is a profusion of plants growing in this narrow margin: blackberry, thistle, bracken, sprigs of gorse, clumps of honey-scented lupins, paspalum and dandelions, competing for space before abruptly giving to the regular texture of pasture where sheep are grazing.

Noticing Max humming a tune, Josephine bends her ear towards him catching the guttural sound of a chant in a strange language. She guesses it must be Hebrew and when he pauses, she politely asks what he was singing. Max looks embarrassed but does his best to satisfy her curiosity.

'It's something I picked up in Palestine—very old. It was written in the 16th century for a group of rabbis who'd been expelled from Spain—they established a community in a small village in the northern part of Palestine, near Lake Galilee.'

Karl's interest is aroused and with a barrage of questions he demands an explanation of the song's significance.

'It's difficult to say what it means,' Max replies cautiously. 'It was sung on the eve of the Sabbath when the community set out on a procession into the countryside. They'd make their way through the orchards and fields searching for the *Shekinah*, a sort of symbolic bride figure, living in exile. The local villagers supported the ritual by having a girl dressed in white who'd be left alone in one of the fields. When the rabbis found her, they'd carry her back to their dining room with great ceremony and she was seated on a throne of honour at the Sabbath feast.'

With more than a hint of belligerence Karl throws out a series of questions and sarcastically summarises what Max has to say.

'So the *shekinah* symbolises the exile of the Jewish people as well as the efforts of individuals seeking union with God—and it could also represent the female aspect of God. It seems this bride can be whatever you want it to be?'

Max shrugs in agreement, searching for words. 'The community believed if these sort of rituals were performed often enough and with the right intentions, they'd eventually bring about the reconciliation of heaven and earth.'

Unable to contain a snort, Karl throws out his favoured question, 'Would you like me to criticise that?'

'By all means.' Max chuckles recalling the intensity with which his friend would enter debate on their hikes through the Vienna Woods. He's surprised to find Karl adopting a restrained tone.

'There may be some psychological benefits or social value in such superstitions, but when belief systems claim certain knowledge of things that are inherently unknowable, they become dangerous.'

Josephine rolls her eyes and tries to deflect by pointing to the swooping of the harrier hawk but entranced by his own logic, Karl will not be diverted.

'Of course I agree with Socrates—wisdom depends on acknowledging what we don't know—but it's quite another matter to turn the unknown into a system of positive knowledge.'

His unanswered arguments are interrupted when they reach the base of the valley and come across an apple orchard where a Māori woman is sitting cross-legged at the gate. She calls out to Max. 'Can you spare a few coins?'

Max apologises that he is not carrying money and invites the woman home with them for a meal. When she demurs, he assures her there is plenty of food prepared and says he has coins in the house he is happy to give her.

She rises and with a provocative wiggle of her hips, cries, 'If you want some of this, it'll cost more than a few coins.' Taking in the mortified expressions on the faces of the three strangers she releases a peal of throaty laughter.

As they trudge uphill a smudge of pink spreads across the cool blue of the evening sky. Max is relieved to find Karl has no difficulty engaging in conversation with the Māori woman who gruffly introduces herself as Rangimarie. He questions her intently and ascertains she has travelled some distance from a small town on the East Coast to take up work as an apple-picker. Her wages, due at the end of the month, seem appallingly low and she is staying with other seasonal workers at an encampment on the farmer's land.

When they reach the cottage the first stars have appeared and Max ushers Rangimarie to a seat at the head of the table. Josephine notices an extra place has already been laid and looking at the fried-fish and bread understands they are partaking in a Sabbath meal. Pouring from a flagon of home-made fruit wine he acquired from the owner of the cottage, Max asks their guest if she would like to bless the food. She rises to her feet and with eyes squeezed shut and head bowed, intones a lengthy prayer in her native tongue. A lively conviviality is established as their guest has no hesitation knocking back the wine. Each time her glass is filled she empties it in a gulp and at one-point Max excuses himself and returns with another flagon of the sweet acidic wine.

With darkness closing on the candle-lit table, Karl announces he must return home to work on his book and Josephine expresses gratitude for the meal. Max sees them to the gate and on returning to the cottage finds Rangimarie slumped in her chair, snoring loudly. He inserts a cushion behind her head and drapes a blanket over her knees. The call of a morepork coming from the conifers on the border of the property turns his thoughts outward and standing beneath the lintel of the open door, he gazes at a row of poplar tree silhouetted against the night sky.

In the distance a drift of stars rises above darkened hills. Sitting at the window of her room in south London, Hanya looks on the entrance to a tube station encased by a wall of sandbags. She thinks of Max and feels a sharp kick against the edge of her belly.

ACKNOWLEDGEMENT OF SOURCES

The fictionalised account of Popper's experiences between the two World Wars follows the established biographical record, relying predominantly on Malachi Haim Hacohen *Karl Popper - The Formative Years, 1902-1945: Politics and Philosophy in Interwar Vienna (*2010); William Warren Bartley III's unfinished biography *Karl Popper: A Life* (presented at Pacific Regional Meeting of Mt Perelin Society Christchurch NZ Nov 1989) and Popper's *Unended Quest: An Intellectual Autobiography* (1982).

In Chapter 1, the portrayal of Ivan & Nancy Sutherland draws from Oliver Sutherland *Paikea: The life of I.L.G. Sutherland* (2013). Some descriptions and colloquial expressions in this chapter draw from Robyn Hyde *The Godwits Fly* (1938).

In Chapter 2, page 15 the Friedrich Schiller quotation is from *The Artists,* Fidelio Volume 4, Number 1, Spring 1995 The Schiller Institute (archive.schillerinstitute.com). Author's translation.

In Chapters 2-6 impressions of Vienna and the events Popper witnessed in the aftermath of WW1 closely follow William Warren Bartley III's *Karl Popper: A Life.*

In Chapters 2, 7 & 12 Dora's recollections of her war service in field hospitals draws from John Reed *The War in Eastern Europe* (1916).

The account of political activities at the Grinzing barracks in Chapters 8, 10&11 draws from Fritz Werfel *The Pure of Heart* (1929) and the portrayal of Ruth & Gebhart Eisler draws from Ruth Fischer's memoir *Stalin & German Communism* (1948). Much of the political rhetoric in these chapters and Chapter 6 draws from the writing of Rosa Luxemburg, Karl Liebknecht & Karl Kautsky sourced from the Marxist Internet Archive.

In Chapter 4, page 21 the Thucydides quotation is a paraphrase which draws from *Thucydides History of the Peloponnesian War* Translated by Rex Warner, Penguin Books. (1954).

In Chapters 5,9,13 & 15 impressions of Jewish community life draw from Israel Zangwill *Children of the Ghetto* (1892) particularly the account of family life in Chapter 13 and the synagogue scene in Chapter 15. The accounts of antisemitism and Viennese politics draw from Harriet Pass Freidenreich *Jewish Politics in Vienna, 1918-1938* (2011).

The rabbinical discussion in Chapter 9 draws from Lieve M Teugels *Bible & Midrash: The Story of the Wooing of Rebekah* (2004).

The portrayal of Gertrud Bodenwieser in Chapter's 7,15 & 16 draws from Shona MacTavish *An Ecstasy of Purpose—Life & Art of Getrude Bodenwiesser* (1987).

The discussion of Einstein's theories and Eddington's proof in Chapters 13 & 14 draws from Bertrand Russell *The ABC of Relativity* (1925).

In Chapter 12 & 16 impressions of the Prater amusement park draw from Erich Remarque *Flotsam* (1939) and Jorg's seduction of Hanya draws from *The Seducer's Diary* in Soren Kierkegaard *Either / Or* (1843).

The café & restaurant scenes in Chapters 14 & 16 draw from Fritz Werfel *The Pure of Heart* and Trudi Kanter *Some Girls, Some Hats and Hitler* (1984)

For the hiking scenes in Chapter 18 & 19, descriptions of the flora and fauna draw from Rosa Luxemburg's *Prison Letters* and Robert Louis Stevenson *Travels with a Donkey* (1879).

In Chapters 20, 21 & 24 impressions of Berlin in the Weimar period draw from Otto Freidrich *Before the Deluge—Portrait of Berlin in the 1920's* (1955) and Christopher Isherwood *Berlin Stories* (1945).

Descriptions of the Steam Baths, the Six Day Race and Lunar Park closely follow Joseph Roth's reportage published in *What I Saw - Berlin 1920- 1933.* (Ed. Michael Hofmann 1996) The fortune teller's pronouncements in Chapter 21 draw from Alan Brunton's poem *For the Asking* from *Slow Passes* (1991).

In Chapters 22 & 23 the accounts of the Zionist duelling fraternity Unitas and Vladimir Jabotinsky's visit to Vienna closely follow Arthur Koestler's memoir *Arrow in the Blue* (1952). The account of Jabotinsky's Vienna lecture closely follows Ze'ev Jabotinsky's 1923 essay *The Iron Wall.* The incident where Jakob speaks of tearing up his Matriculation book is also drawn from Koestler's memoir.

In Chapter 25, page 137 the Heinrich Heine quotation is from *Heinrich Heine, Book of Songs Compiled from the Translations by Sir Theodore Martin, K.C.B. and Edgar A Bowring, C.B.* New York Edward A. Stokes & Brother (1888).

In Chapter 26 impressions of the Laxenburg-Hellerau Eurythmics School are drawn from Toepfer, Karl. *Empire of Ecstasy: Nudity and*

Movement in German Body Culture, 1910-1935. (1997) and Samuel Beckett *Dream of a Fair to Middling Woman* (1932).

The portrayal of Rosalia Chladek and descriptions of her performance at the Rathausplatz closely follows Karl Toepfer's *Empire of Ecstasy.* The references to Cadmus and Harmonia draw from Roberto Calasso *The Marriage of Cadmus and Harmony* (1988).

Impressions of Jerusalem under the British Mandate in Chapters 27,28 & 32 draw from Walter Laquer *Dying for Jerusalem: The Past, Present and Future of the Holiest City* (2006); Anita Shapira *Israel a History* (2012) and *Land & Power—The Zionist Resort to Force 1881-1948* (1992); Simon Sebag Montefiore *Jerusalem a Biography* (2011); Arthur Koestler *Arrow in the Blue.*

The portrayal of Gershom Scholem draws from his memoir *From Berlin to Jerusalem: memories of my youth* (1980). Description of the seminars at Gershon Scholem apartment and the list of attendees draw from Walter Laquer's *Dying for Jerusalem.* The story of the messiah living at the Tomb of the Judges closely follows Arthur Koestler's *Arrow in the Blue.*

The account of Sabbatai Zevi and the dialogue in Chapters 27 & 28 closely follows Gershon Scholem's writing in: *On the Kabbalah And its Symbolism* (1960); *Sabbatai Sevi: The Mystical Messiah* (1973) *Redemption Through Sin* (1937).

Scholem's discussion of the political situation in Jerusalem draws from D Biale *Gershom Scholem: Kabballah & Counter History* (1979) and Gabriel Piterberg *The Returns of Zionism—Myth, Politics & Scholarship in Israel* (2008)

In Chapter 29 the account of Popper's relations with members of the Vienna Circle draw from Popper's *Unended Quest: An Intellectual Autobiography* and Allan Janik, Stephen Toulmin *Wittgenstein's Vienna* (1996). The account of Popper's work on scientific method draws from Karl Popper *The Logic of Scientific Discovery* (1934) and *Unended Quest.*

In Chapter 31 impressions of Nazi Germany draw from Julia Boyd *Travellers in the Third Reich* (2017). The account of the opening ceremony at the Berlin Olympics draws from James McNeish *Lovelock* (1986). Descriptions of the sea voyage to New Zealand draw from Malcolm Lowry *Ultramarine* (1933).

In Chapters 33 & 34 impressions of Vienna during the Anschluss draw from Harriet Pass Freidenreich *Jewish Politics in Vienna, 1918-1938* (2011); Trudi Kanter *Some Girls, Some Hats and Hitler* (1984); Edmund de

Waal *The Hare With Amber Eyes* (2010).

In Chapters 32 & 34 accounts of the Nazi regime seizing control of the Kultusgemeinde library in Leopoldstadt draws from Richard Hacken *The Jewish Community Library in Vienna: From Dispersion and Destruction to Partial Restoration* (2002).

In Chapters 33 & 34 the plight of Jewish refugees and descriptions of border crossings draw from Erich Remarque *Arch of Triumph* (1945) and *The Night in Lisbon* (1962); Arthur Koestler *Scum of the Earth* (1941)

In Chapter 36 the description of Josephine gardening draws from Mary Ursula Bethell's poem, *Pause* (1929).

Accounts of Kabbalistic rituals and beliefs in Chapter 35 & 38 draw from Gershom Scholem *On the Kabbalah And its Symbolism.*

Accounts of Popper's philosophical work in Chapter 36 & 37 closely follows Karl Popper *The Open Society and Its Enemies* (1945).

Descriptions of Popper and Ivan Sutherland's work assisting Jewish refugees draws from Oliver Sutherland's *Paikea: The life of I.L.G. Sutherland.* In Chapter 37 the discussion of the Molotov–Ribbentrop pact draws from Arthur Koestler *Scum of the Earth.*

The account of Popper's public lectures on Science & Religion for the Christchurch Workers Education Association draws from the text of the lectures published in Karl Popper, Piers Norris Turner, Jeremy Shearmur, *After The Open Society - Selected Social and Political Writings* (2008).

ACKNOWLEDGEMENTS

Thanks to Jan Fortune and Cinnamon Press for their expert guidance and encouragement, especially the sensitive mentoring and editing provided by Rowan Fortune.

Thanks for the encouragement and suggestions from those who read early versions of the manuscript: David Greeney, Jenny Stevenson, Chris Barton, Diana Wichtel, Stephen Stratford, Rangihīroa Panoho, Karl Goddard.

Special thanks to Paddy Richardson for her valuable appraisal provided under the NZSA CompleteMS programme of the New Zealand Society of Authors Te Puni Kaituhi o Aotearoa (PEN NZ) Inc supported by Creative New Zealand.

Heartfelt thanks to my family for their constant love and support.

www.ingramcontent.com/pod-product-compliance
Ingram Content Group UK Ltd.
Pitfield, Milton Keynes, MK11 3LW, UK
UKHW012316150625
459610UK00017B/138

9 781788 648707